IN THE TIME

OF THE

AMERICANS

BY

OSWALD RIVERA

In the Time of the Americans

Copyright © 2019 by Oswald Rivera

This book is a work of fiction based on historical facts. Most of the names, characters, organizations, and incidents are factual; the remainder being the product of the author's imagination.

Editors: Earl Tillinghast, Regina Cornell

Cover Design: 3Sixty Marketing Studio - 3sixtymktg.com

Interior Design: 3Sixty Marketing Studio - 3sixtymktg.com

Photographer - Jay Kennedy

Indigo River Publishing

3 West Garden Street Ste. 352

Pensacola, FL 32502

www.indigoriverpublishing.com

Ordering Information:

Quantity sales: Special discounts are available on quantity purchases by corporations, associations, and others. For details, contact the publisher at the address above.

Orders by U.S. trade bookstores and wholesalers: Please contact the publisher at the address above.

Printed in the United States of America

Library of Congress Control Number: 2019935005

ISBN: 978-1-948080-81-1

First Edition

With Indigo River Publishing, you can always expect great books, strong voices, and meaningful messages. Most importantly, you'll always find . . . words worth reading.

This terrifies me: To think that the present, which we are living this very day, will become the mirror in which we shall later recognize ourselves; and that by what we have been we shall know what we are.

—André Gide, journal entry, 1891

PROLOGUE

1898

IN THE TIME of the Spaniards, the ship was first sighted from doña Lourdes's house, about half a mile up the street from the *cafetín* owned by Rafael the undertaker and leased to Andres, the son of Dámaso Piquito. Doña Lourdes was not the first to see them. Her cat, Figaro, was the first to see them. The cat lounged lazily across the veranda facing the sea, licking itself in the shade and having just awakened from feline slumber, while doña Lourdes snored slightly in the back room with the curtains drawn.

The boat was painted the color of gray ash, oversized yet sleek, with armament that peered out toward doña Lourdes's veranda, and showing phallic tubes blackened by sulfur and gunpowder from the recent engagement in Manila. There, in three hours' time, the empire of Spain had been supplanted by the empire of free markets, free trade and ten-cent cigars. The Americans called the boat a cruiser. To *ponceños* it looked like a massive tin can floating two leagues out in the ocean.

From the bridge of the floating tin can, Captain Whitehall scanned the shoreline through his bulky black binoculars. All he saw was a sandy beach peopled by long, tubular coconut palm trees, and behind them, a house of white-washed wood now peeling and stripped in places from the effects of the salty air. His vision danced inside the binoculars, taking in every particular of the beachfront house: the flat stumps of the stilts on which the house rested, the roof tiled with sections of tin, a hammock on the left side next to a wooden veranda on which, yes, a cat glowered back at him.

Captain Whitehall turned to his aide, Lieutenant Walker, and demanded to know, "Where is our contact?"

Pinched-faced, freckled Lieutenant Walker sneaked a peek through his own bulky black binoculars, replying, "I don't know, sir. They were supposed to meet us at the landing site."

"They?" The Captain speared Walker with one imperious, questioning glance. "I thought it was only one contact that was meeting us."

"It's only one, sir," Walker amended quickly. "But he was supposed to meet us with another representative. The town doctor, I believe."

"The town doctor?"

"Yes," Walker said. "The man, I believe, had his training in Boston."

"A spic training in Boston?" Captain Whitehall sounded incredulous.

"They come from a well-to-do family, so my contact informed. Name is Ferrer, I believe."

The Captain was still spearing Walker. "You seem to believe a lot of things, Lieutenant. But my belief is that we have no contact on this part of the island. Not even a representative. How are we to proceed if we don't know the lay of the land?"

"I'm sure we'll be able to find some representatives on this side of the island, sir," Walker said, trying to sound positive in the midst of a slowly crumbling strategy.

What had happened to Walker's contact was simple. The man, one Ignacio Romero, a product of San Juan schooling, who considered ponceños no better than dirt, had decided to stop by Rafael's tavern, where Andres plied him with drink until our San Juan don passed out on a table in the middle of a game of dominoes after having peed in his pants since he was too inebriated to navigate the four steps it took to reach the outhouse in back of the tavern.

So, while the American cruiser sailed up and down the coast, trying to get a fix on a debarkation point, the fifth-columnist-educated spy was out like a light in Rafael's cafetín. The other customers had left him there since, really, they didn't like him that much. A man with his nose in the air who acted like his shit didn't stink. The peasants always got their revenge by simply getting the señor drunk on rum, and if no rum was available, on the moonshine brew always abundant when the good stuff ran out.

The man, who, by a strange twist of fate, would years later gain fame as one of the island's first *independentistas*, slept peacefully in his drunken stupor, while his American sponsors couldn't figure how the hell to get the invasion going. In later years their ineptitude at colonizing would infuriate Ignacio Romero and turn him into a Nationalist. There was more. To his dying day he couldn't stomach the hubris of a people who would take solely onto themselves the name of two continents.

Now, this invasion was a singular event in the history of the town. Mainly because, like most invasions, no one knew it was coming, and for years townspeople would wonder why anyone would want to invade Ponce. As my great-grandfather described it, the town was a backwater then, far from the prime commercial metropolis it is today as the island's second-largest city. In those days, San Juan was where the action was. There, all the grandees and madams pranced about in starched-collared splendor, basking in their *danzas*, conversing in English or French or Castilian Spanish, the women always staying out of the sun—not for reasons of health but because the palest of skin was a sign of regal birth, and besides, only common laborers could endure its suffocating rays. The ladies whirled in long hourglass skirts, while their swains suffered the heat in frocks and waistcoats. Their only concessions to the tropical clime were white linen suits and wide-brimmed straw hats. But that's as far as they acknowledged their roots. No one but no one in San Juan society would be caught dead in *jíbaro* dress or dancing the plena or reciting bawdy verse, which were so popular in the hills. They lived just like their forebears, those who had come from Spain or other parts of the Carib-

7

bean. Even their talk affected this, and they rolled their tongues when speaking as if they were in Sevilla or Andalucía.

It would take a generation of Americanization before they got over this nonsense.

But I digress. In point of fact the invasion had come; its main contingent via the northeast coast. Eventually, San Juan was occupied and the damsels of capital society found themselves entertaining ignorant sailors from such places as Biloxi and Minnesota.

On the deck of his ship, the representative of this new order, Captain Whitehall, decided to take action. His military training had instilled in him one unassailable concept: to wait spelled caution. But not to act spelled doom. Besides, his backside hurt like the dickens. Four months before, the flotilla had stormed into Subic Bay. The ensuing naval battle would set the tone of the war. The Spanish fleet, motley as it was, had been completely routed, but not before shrapnel from a Spanish shell had embedded itself in the left cheek of his buttocks. Ever since Captain Whitehall had walked with a stiff gait, sometimes having to drag his left leg over cowlings and bulkheads. And the hot, humid weather had made a barometer of his rear end. He could tell if it was going to rain by the soreness in his ass.

He told Walker to inform the gunnery officer that two warning shots would be fired, by the left bow, high overhead. Resistance wasn't expected this far up in the Antilles. This was not the Philippines, but you never knew. To have one great, glorious battle under his belt was all he had wished for since his youth at the Virginia Military Institute. Except for the Plains wars against the Indians, not much had happened in a long time.

All these thoughts coalesced in Whitehall's psyche as his gunners estimated distances and trajectories. Soon the shells thundered, and the vessel shook with the blast as plumes of smoke belched upward. The shells overshot their mark and whizzed above the beach. Townspeople roused from their siestas or labors, gazing at the sky. None had ever heard such crushing noise.

The shells landed two miles out, behind the sugar cane fields on the edge of town, creating large craters next to a muddy stream where two jíbaros were washing their shirts. The peasants' first instinct when they heard the noise coming their way was to run, which they did, the earth spewing up behind them and falling on top of a couple not far away and in the clutches of passion. She screamed, he screamed, and then they ran, leaving their clothes behind.

Those shells roaring overhead did much the same to doña Lourdes, wrenching her from a deeply felt dream about her late and lamented husband, Gustavo, who had died ten years earlier when he choked on the pit of an avocado during a town festival. Unfortunately, after his departure, Gustavo would roam throughout the house after midnight, looking for the avocado. This phenomenon had unnerved her cat to no end.

Gustavo slipped back into the reams of memory, and she bolted upright on the bed. "What was that?" she asked in the silence of the room. It wasn't thunder; it was something ripping the sky. Her first thought was not about Gustavo, bless his soul, but of Figaro, her cat. She jumped from the bed, fully clothed except for her shoes, rushing to the veranda and finding Figaro mewing at the big boat out in the ocean.

More thunder spewed from the cruiser. Three crazed dogs ran past the house, howling in their unique tongue; and, in the middle of the day, a rooster slammed down from one of the coconut palms, flapping its wings and scattering feathers.

Doña Lourdes, a righteous and superstitious woman, feel to her knees in fervent prayer, for the Coming was at hand, just like Gustavo had predicted before he choked on the avocado pit. Near her house, some locals had gathered at the beach, among them my great-grandfather, a mere boy then, so he told us. Ponceños all, but from a part of town known as "La Playa" (the beach)—then, as now, the forgotten stepchild of the more prosperous, more elegant part of the "Pueblo" (the town).

The beachfront people, some young, some old and all male since the women had enough sense to remain indoors, pointed and gestured at the strange vessel looming over their part of the island. They ogled and waved at the large cruiser hanging limply out in the ocean. From its sides were lowered wooden boats, which soon filled with men in khaki uniforms, white leggings, and funny round hats.

The boats waded toward the beach, and Lieutenant Walker, resplendent in white naval uniform, led his party ashore. Walker, foisting a revolver, issued orders left and right. All he saw was a deputation of people, if it could be called that. Sugar cane cutters and farm workers, some naked to the waist and still holding their machetes from the day's labor.

Walker ordered that all machetes and whatever weapons the natives had be confiscated. No one thought of bringing along an interpreter. And Walker's contact was nowhere in sight. Walker gesticulated first with his gun, then with the other arm, trying to explain to the group that he needed to be taken to their leader. The beach people looked at him and smiled.

Someone in the back said, "¿Quien son esta gente?"

Someone else said something else. Soon they were all chattering among themselves. Now the marines looked at them dumbfounded.

Using primitive sign language, Walker announced, "I am Lieutenant Walker, US Navy." Motioning to the group: "Who are you?"

"Yo no se," someone answered.

"We need to see your . . . *jefe*."

"Jefe?" A sign of recognition from one of the locals. "Si, mi jefe." He pointed to somewhere.

Walker strained to look beyond the native. "Jefe? There?" he asked, raising a hand to somewhere beyond the beach.

"Si," the man said. "Alla vive mi jefe."

"Good," Walker nodded. "Uh, very good, bueno."

"De nada. Un placer."

Not knowing what else to do, Walker acknowledged the man by bringing his hand to his cap in an informal salute. He waved the pistol over his head and told his men, "Follow me."

He led the party inland away from the beach. The strange thing was that the paisanos and sugar cane cutters who had come out to greet the invading party followed them. The marines, for their part, tried to ignore the escorting procession. They were set on their mission to route the last of the Spanish garrison from this part of the island. If only they had known that the Spanish garrison has ceased to exist in these parts over twenty years ago. After decades of waiting, the conscripts from such places as Bilbao, Pamplona, and Saragossa had deserted into the nearby hills to marry and propagate mixed-blood children of all shades and types.

Walker and his twenty-four marines could only dream of the possibility of resistance to come. The locals around them jabbered incessantly in their incomprehensible dialect. The Americans remained with eyes straight ahead, rifles at port arms, marching in lockstep on the road bordered by palm trees. Barefoot youngsters aped the invaders, marching alongside the column in a parody of the practiced cadence of the leathernecks. They had never witnessed such a sight: ruddy-faced young men sweltering in the heat but grimly forging ahead, keeping cadence like human machines. And if anyone deigned to sneak a peek at the locals, the platoon sergeant, on cue from Lieutenant Walker, would growl for the men to keep focused on the objective, whatever the objective was.

The first obstacle was doña Lourdes's house, with its wide veranda facing the sea. Walker followed the manual, instructing his marine counterpart to send out two-man teams on either side of the house. The men approached the veranda cautiously. Who knew if this house itself was a stronghold of old Spain? Walker wasn't taking any chances. The locals gawked at the antics of these foreigners, who seemed to be putting on a show exclusively for ponceños. Walker instructed his men to keep the throng back, lest noncombatants be hurt. The marines formed a ring around the house, containing the crowd as best they could.

Out into the veranda came doña Lourdes, dressed in corseted white and holding the gray-and-brown cat to her bosom.

Before his men could blow away the lady, Walker hollered, "Halt!"

Upon seeing twenty-four rifle barrels aimed her way, doña Lourdes shrieked and scurried back into the house, the cat leaping from her arms, bolting over the veranda and into the chest of one of the marines. The cat clawed; the marine yelped, his Springfield rifle dropping to the ground and going off in an accidental discharge.

Two marines approaching the veranda dropped to the ground, flattening themselves to the earth, since they thought they were under attack.

The accidental discharge unhinged the already unhinged marines, who began firing volley after volley into the back of the house. Lucky for her that doña Lourdes had already scampered out the front door, screaming at the top of her lungs that the Day of Judgment had come. She equated the soldiers surrounding her house with ghosts from the underworld.

Walker's order to cease fire was lost on the trigger-happy marines. Their fear was compounded when one leatherneck lowered his rifle long enough to spy a group of disheveled locals rushing toward them. These were the regulars from Rafael's cafetín, who stopped in their tracks when they saw the strangely uniformed men in a cordon around doña Lourdes's house.

The marine who first saw them bellowed, "Spaniards!"

Andres the innkeeper was at the head of the group who had rushed out of his place. Into his head came long-ago tales his father had told about Spanish troops who had once occupied this part of the island. By his father's account they had been a lowly and bestial lot who delighted in torturing the populace. Dios mio, he thought. They're back!

"¡Españoles!" he screamed. "¡ESPAÑOLES!"

At this rallying cry, the six or so men from the tavern turned tail and ran back from whence they came. Nobody wanted anything to do with the Spaniards.

Across the path, the marines also turned tail and ran for some cover, even while Walker and his marine counterpart exhorted them to stand and fight. The marines were prepared to fight, but not in the open, and not against what they perceived to be the first echelon of the Spanish garrison.

Only the sugar cane cutters and jíbaro men and children remained where they were, watching the drama with curious intent.

One of the marines, not looking where he was going, ran straight into a palm tree and was dazed somewhat when his head hit the bark. This wasn't the source of the injury. A coconut, hanging from a tiny sliver, snapped and bopped the marine on the head. The marine fell unconscious. Another man near him shouted, "They're attacking!" and shrank back, firing his rifle at the phantom Spanish garrison.

A round whizzed by Walker's head, missing him by inches, but knocking his naval officer's cap off his head.

Walker touched his head to make sure it was still there. Then it dawned on him: My God, I'm being shot at!

He dropped to the ground and squeezed off shot after shot from his revolver with his eyes rammed shut.

Most of the marines had found cover behind palm trees or else lay flat on the dirt, still shooting at everything that moved. And hitting nothing.

By now the crowd of onlookers had taken off in all directions, trying to outrun haphazard bullets zinging far and wide.

* * *

The second wave of marines met no resistance, and key installations were commandeered immediately, or so it was noted in Captain Whitehall's log. The phantom garrison that had, ostensibly, attacked Walker's reconnaissance party fled into the hills. This was also duly noted in Whitehall's log.

Within two days a provisional military governor had set up residence in the mayoralty house in the middle of town. And it soon became clear that the new conquerors were far different from their Spanish predecessors, who had shown scant interest in the welfare of the townsfolk. Their main concern had been to get the sugar cane harvest in on time. These *yanquis* were different. They brought with them the zeal of a new nation with a new mission. The natives had to be taught about democracy and good old Protestant ethics, such as abstinence and industry and going about dignified and wearing heavy woolens even in the middle of summer.

A committee of prominent townspeople was appointed to assist the new overseers in their task. They were the intermediaries, as it were, between the newly arrived liberators and the populace. By no surprise, Walker's inebriated contact, don Ignacio Romero, was placed in charge of this committee since his previous contacts with the Americans gave him a leg up on everyone else. Also, he spoke English. It was he who also got his friend Vicente Arrias-Ferrer, the town doctor, appointed to the committee as well. They were now, under the new regime, the most prominent citizens in town.

Thus it came to pass that more of the more humdrum tasks required to manage the region were delegated to Ignacio Romero and his crony, the good doctor. And they made the most of it. Within five years they owned most of the sugar cane fields, had gained majority interest in the local iron and foundry works, and had complete ownership of the leather-making factory in the area of La Playa. Their descendants would be among the most prominent and well-known families on the island.

It helped that the military governors didn't last long. They considered the duty to be a necessary steppingstone toward some command in the States. Keeping account books and mediating peasant grievances was not their style. As long as Romero and Arrias-Ferrer kept the locals pacified, that was good enough for their overlords. The best of these military men got out of the duty as fast as they could, and the worst, languishing in the indolent heat, trotted out their horses for leisurely morning rides in the countryside and got drunk on bourbon in the afternoons. And when there was no bourbon, they'd switch to the local rum.

The plan to capture Ponce had gone as well as expected. There were no serious casualties, and the goal had been accomplished. But it wasn't a glorious encounter either. A nice, dirty, little war doesn't usually garner the accolades accorded larger engagements, and this war in no way matched the war to preserve the Union, or even the romance of the Indian wars. Anyway, recognition was scant, and promotions were few. Captain Whitehall got his admiralship and was transferred to a cushy post in Washington. Unfortunately, Lieutenant Walker remained behind as a junior officer, consigned to a posting far from a tropical paradise, where the sun seared his freckled skin and the mosquitoes feasted on his limbs. No cushy assignment for him. He became part of what was called a liaison group. What kind of liaison no one knew. He wasn't even consigned to San Juan, the capital, where at least he could converse in his native tongue with educated ladies and gentlemen. No, he was exiled to Ponce, indefinitely, under the command of superiors who hated the place as much as he did.

A slide was inevitable given Walker's propensities and low self-esteem. And like a badly written Latin romance, it invariably involved a woman.

Walker met Maria Benítez Izquierdo at a function given at the mayoralty. She was the daughter of don Pablo Benítez Calderon and doña Isabela Izquierdo de Rosado. If Ponce was said to have any society folk, they were it. Their forebears had made their fortune in (what else?) sugar cane, which was quickly converted to rum that since even before the founding of the American Republic had been sold to colonists, British merchants, and Spaniards. Maria, as befitted her status, was educated overseas in the precincts of Spain, then considered the mother country. Her Castilian was flawless. Alas, she knew not one word of English. When US troops occupied the town, she regarded them with the bemused look of someone at a large fair who wasn't sure what to purchase.

When Walker first saw her, he was astounded by her beauty and somewhat haughty bearing. He was totally engulfed by black-onyx eyes, light skin, and full cherry lips. If anything could mar her beauty it was the conspicuous, though smallish, mole on the left side just above her mouth. Walker found the mole both fascinating and repulsive. The fascination won out.

Upon introduction by his new superior, Captain Andrews, Walker, after uncomfortable seconds, managed to utter something incomprehensible, which set the lady in question to burst out in unaffected laughter right there in the middle of the great hall in the mayoralty building, with its wrought-iron gates and crucifixes worthy of the Spanish Inquisition. Her parents, also present, and not knowing what else to do, smiled benignly at their daughter's faux pas. Captain Andrews was stuck with a perpetual grin on his face and didn't say anything, either in English or Spanish, least he offend the native gentry. Poor Walker stuttered some more, the woman laughed some more, and the atmosphere was saved when don Ignacio, the same one who had served as spy for the new overseers, took Lieutenant Walker away on the pretext that he was needed elsewhere. Walker kept looking back, entranced by the laughing temptress, as Ignacio Romero hustled him into another room in the mayoralty building.

"Who is that woman?" Walker inquired, almost out of breath and swallowing his words.

"Someone you do not want to know," Romero warned him. "Believe me, when one meets a scorpion one tramples carefully on the sand."

"What?"

"Never you mind, Lieutenant," Romero said in his Boston-lectured but heavily accented English. "You would be better off on the other side of the earth than consorting with the Benítez spawn."

Poor Walker was hooked, Benítez spawn or not. He just couldn't get that face or mole out of his mind. The next few days he walked as in a trance, as a sleepwalker might when living in a perpetual dream. He had to see the woman again, no two ways about it. In the heat and mosquito-infested province, she was the only sight that had brought pleasure to a shriveled heart. He was head over heels, and had no defenses against it.

At the next mayoralty function he was there, standing with his back to the wall, eyes never deviating from the Benítez family and their precious issue. He was like a lovesick puppy yearning from afar. The Benítez parents paid no attention to him, but the daughter occasionally looked his way and smiled, and his heart both leapt and sank.

In the outside air, even the mosquitoes buzzing about his head failed to attract his notice. They dive-bombed on his skin at will, but he was impervious to it. The image of Maria Benítez Izquierdo was imprinted somewhere between his gut and loins.

How to see her again? How to meet her? He knew enough Spanish protocol to know you just didn't go calling on a lady. There were certain rules to be followed. A formal request must be made. And if nothing else, Lieutenant Walker was a stickler for rules, his or anyone else's.

Yet love inspires derring-do, even in introverts such as Lieutenant Walker. He took to loitering, in his spare time, in the central plaza where the big church cathedral stood, ostensibly to admire its sculptured architecture; but in reality, a subterfuge to view Maria Benítez as she was escorted from the church, chaperone in tow, back to her house after noon mass.

In his white naval officer's uniform he was an incongruous sight. Tall, gangly, face blotched by the sun, and sweating endlessly even under the shade of a flamboyan tree on a stone bench in the plaza. Those melancholy blue-gray goo-goo eyes riveted on Maria Benítez as she entered and exited the church.

Her chaperone, an aged widow aunt and upholder of family tradition and respectability, upon sighting the lovesick American, would tilt her nose upward in a highly visible sign of disapproval and shoo Maria away as fast as possible into a waiting horse-drawn coach that would spir-it them back to the spacious white-columned house on Victoria Street, not far from the town square. There, Maria Benítez would be consigned to practice the piano, the lute, and embroidery. In the evening she would keep company, under the eagle eye of her aunt, with the son of Alexan-dro Vargas, the town's chief merchant. Young Clemente Ordoñez Var-gas would sit out on the balcony and read poetry to Maria Benítez. She would listen with stolid disinterest as the *coquis*, the crickets native to the island, chirped in the evening air. Poetry bored her, classical or otherwise. But it was that or having to suffer long passages from Cervantes, which she found even more boring. If young señor Vargas tried to initiate some other topic of conversation, whatever its nature, her aunt would loudly clear her throat; and if the young suitor persisted, she would order tartly, "Get back to poetry; that's why you're here."

Clemente Vargas would get back to poetry.

Meanwhile Lieutenant Walker would be pining away in the large residence that served as both quarters and guesthouse for military offi-cers and visiting dignitaries. Walker would ensconce himself in his room, away from his colleagues, weaving fantasies about Maria Benítez, only coming down to dinner call and not eating or drinking much. His com-rades, all young ensigns mainly, would while away the hours drinking the local rum since they couldn't afford to have bourbon shipped in like their captain. But not Walker. He always went back to the plaza, where he maintained a late-night vigil hoping for a glance of the woman who had trapped his soul.

It was through the intercession of her parents that Walker was finally able to approach his beloved. They couldn't help but notice the lovesick officer who was always turning up at whatever function they happened to attend, and besides, the aunt had already told doña Benítez about the white-uniformed shadow trailing them daily from church.

Don Pablo was shrewd, and not only as a businessman. He rea-soned that it might not be so bad for his prospects to cultivate an American presence in his home. If all conventions were strictly observed, it wouldn't hurt, and if nothing else, it might ingratiate him with the new regime. So he sent a request to Romero stating that as a goodwill gesture the Benítez household would be honored to entertain a representative of the new American government, specifically Lieutenant Walker, if he was available. Ignacio Romero smelled a rat, but he couldn't keep Walker in the dark about the invitation, though again he warned Walker about the Benítez spawn.

Walker was undaunted. At last he would meet that which had consumed him. The fact that he spoke no Spanish and she spoke no English didn't enter into the equation. Nearness to his heart's desire was all that mattered. Ignacio Romero came along as a sort of go-between where the language barrier was concerned. Lest any unwanted gossip stain the family name, Mario's aunt and chaperone was ever by her side, shooting stern glances at the young American upstart.

Dinner was in the main dining hall, and then the men retired to cigars and rum on the veranda and listened to the coquis, while the women finished cleaning up the table. Finally, Maria Benítez was allowed onto the balcony in the company of Walker plus, of course, Romero and the chaperone. It began with the usual pleasantries: Romero inquiring as to the young lady's (and her chaperone's) health and commenting on what a lovely evening it was, albeit a bit hot for this time of year. To which the chaperone answered that it was always hot in Ponce. Some people on the northern coast called it the cauldron of the devil, the chaperone commented, all the while staring at Walker.

The nervous lieutenant remained quiet. When Romero translated for him, he gave a self-conscious laugh, but clammed up immediately when he saw Maria Benítez giving him a rather odd look.

Then Romero prompted the lieutenant by asking if he wanted to say anything to the young lady, some worthy comment perhaps. Walker swallowed with a loud gulp and in hesitant sentences stated that the young lady was beautiful beyond . . . beyond . . .

His mind drew a blank. And the minute he opened his mouth again, Maria Benítez broke into squeals of high-pitched laughter. She laughed so hard her cheeks flushed and it seemed tears rolled from her eyes. She was in stitches, beside herself. The lieutenant drew back, clamped shut again, not knowing what to say or do; and every time he tried to speak, the greater the merriment enveloping Maria Benítez.

Romero and the aunt-chaperone exchanged confused glances. It was as if the young señorita had been possessed, but by a demon of mirth. So much so that she jumped up from the settee on the veranda and ran back indoors, her convulsive laughter leaving a stark trail.

Now it was the aged chaperone of an aunt who stuttered in bewilderment: "She . . . she . . . is not feeling well." And she jumped up from her chair, rushing after her charge.

Walker was left dumbfounded.

"It . . . it must be the shock of . . . of joy," Romero offered feebly. "That's it, señor, she is so shy that it is a shock to her to finally meet such a fine specimen of a man such as yourself."

There was a dazed look on Walker's face. He didn't move, almost mummified. Romero became concerned, then alarmed. Walker had the look of someone who had witnessed his greatest tragedy, or his greatest miracle. Like Lot watching his wife be turned into a pillar of salt. Or was it Walker who was turning into the pillar of salt?

"Lieutenant?" Romero's hand was gently tugging at the pillar of salt. "Lieutenant? Are you well, Lieutenant?"

Walker's head turned as a slow wind to face Romero. The blue-gray eyes seemed blank, lifeless.

"Lieutenant?" Romero shook Walker's elbow. "Perhaps it is best if we leave. We can always return tomorrow. Lieutenant? Do you hear me?"

The pillar of salt finally mouthed some words: "Yes, we can always come back tomorrow." But it was said in such a low, plaintive voice Romero could barely hear him.

"What?"

"Tomorrow," Walker repeated forlornly.

"Yes, tomorrow," said Romero, placing a hand under the lieutenant's elbow and assisting him to his feet. Walker had the worst ailment of all, Romero thought. He was irrepressibly and completely in love. And love of the worst kind, the kind that gives all and asks nothing in return. He had fallen for someone whose heart was as vacant as her mind. Heaven help the poor fool.

As for the elder Benítez, he would think twice about again inviting the foreigner to their home. They knew their daughter to be pampered and flighty, but this strange reaction to the young naval officer left them bewildered. When her mother tried to coax some explanation from her daughter, Maria Benítez's response was to again burst into bouts of laughter at the mere mention of Walker's name. He had struck a funny bone in her. Whereas other men coveted her heart, Walker's sole passion was her funny bone. For some odd reason, he brought on these bouts of uncontrollable mirth. It was no fault of his. Maria Benítez was sure he was an honorable man, but an honorable man who made her funny bone itch.

Her parents threw up their hands, knowing it was a hopeless quest. No one could ever figure out the convoluted workings of their daughter's moods.

Walker remained as before, completely enthralled and possessed by the laughing señorita. Like a dog mooning at a distant star, he was ever faithful to his vigil, again spying on her from the safety of the town plaza, waiting patiently and anxiously while she was at mass. It began to dawn on her parents that this was proving to be an embarrassment. Having a prospective American son-in-law, and a naval officer at that, was one thing; having a foolish, lovesick puppy follow their daughter around was another.

The daughter, for her part, began to feel sorry for him. Twice she stopped her carriage and asked the aunt-chaperone to beckon him over.

The minute he opened his mouth, the funny bone was struck and out came the laughter. Maria Benítez could not contain herself, hooting in racking convulsions and eyes watering, a reaction so strong it was akin to an epileptic fit.

The aunt-chaperone yelled for the driver to go, a whip fell on the horse's back, and away they went, leaving Walker astounded and helpless as before. Another man would probably have taken it as a sign of rejection. Not Walker, possibly because he couldn't help it. This laugh-racked creature was the only thing that kept him going in the desolation of a heart wasting away in a swamp-infested, mosquito-ridden town.

As for Maria Benítez, she continued, unconcerned, with her piano lessons, her evening chats with Clemente Ordoñez Vargas, and her chaperone's constant watch.

This went on for weeks, with Walker's admiration from afar striking the chaperone more as stalking than as romantic fever. She complained to don Pablo, who in turn complained to Captain Andrews, who brought it to the attention of his subordinate. But whereas Captain Whitehall would most likely have demoted the smitten officer, Andrews had more of a paternal streak. He actually felt bad for the young man. So he counseled him in the manner of an elder rather than a superior. It was a lost quest, he told the lieutenant. Not only that, Walker was making a fool of himself.

Walker didn't see it that way.

"I love her, sir," he said solemnly to his commanding officer. "I love her with every fiber of my being."

"You've never even spent five minutes alone with her," Andrews countered. "How can you love somebody you hardly know?"

"Oh, I know, sir. I know."

That's when Andrews laid down the law. "Lieutenant, this behavior is unseemly. Her parents do not want you to harass their daughter, and that's what they call it: harassment. It's an embarrassment to everyone.

You're an officer of the US Navy. As such, you're a representative of the fleet in this part of the world. You shall conduct yourself accordingly at all times. Otherwise, I'll have no choice but to relieve you of duty. You will not make any attempt to see this young woman again. Is that clear?"

A straight stare in the void of space told Andrews he wasn't getting anywhere.

"Lieutenant, is that clear?"

Walker just stared and said nothing.

The Benítez family were not the only ones preoccupied with Walker's strange behavior. Clemente Ordoñez Vargas had a jealous streak. He knew about Walker. Town gossip could not prevent him from knowing. When he quizzed Maria Benítez on why this *americano* was always shadowing her, Maria just shrugged.

"Doesn't it bother you that this man constantly follows you around?" asked Clemente Vargas with no small amount of irritation.

"No," she replied in all honesty. "It matters to me none at all."

"Maria, we are betrothed," Clemente Vargas reminded her. "It's not right for this man to be following you. It's . . . it's an insult, to your family and mine. It must stop."

Maria seemed unconcerned. "It may stop. My father has complained to his superior officer. My parents are as put off by his behavior as you are right now."

Maria's neutral tone set off red flags in Clemente Vargas. "And you are not?" he asked warily.

"Not what?"

"Not put off by his behavior?"

Another shrug. "Why should I be? He is a man who finds me attractive. I can't help that."

"You can at least make it plain to him that you reject his advances."

"He hasn't made any advances."

Clemente Vargas showed alarm. "You don't consider what he did making advances?"

"No," Maria said calmly.

Clemente Vargas turned to the aunt-chaperone, who had listened to their exchange without comment. "Señora, don't you agree that this man's actions are improper?"

The chaperone gave Maria Benítez a brief, cool glance, then said to the young suitor, "Of course I consider it most improper. But it's a matter which Maria must resolve. I have told her constantly to just tell this, this *extranjero* to cease and desist in his actions. But what can I say, señor? Maria has a mind of her own, as you well know. She can be disconcertingly stubborn sometimes."

Maria Benítez took her aunt's remark in stride, not once diverting her attention from her knitting. It was as if the conversation whirled around her and above her. Nothing affected her directly. It was true, she didn't care either way.

Clemente Vargas did care. "It has to stop," he said, his voice rising.

"And how do you intend to do that?" asked the chaperone.

"I will find a way," swore Clemente Vargas.

Aunt-chaperone wasn't convinced. "It will take much more than entreaties to stop that crazy americano."

"There will be no entreaties," Clemente Vargas said with haughty arrogance.

"Remember, my son," Aunt-Chaperone counseled, "they are the government now. And this American is part of the government. We do not want to make things difficult for the Benítez family, now do we?"

"I will never grovel before any foreign aggressor," Clemente Vargas ground out. "And besides, the honor of this family is at stake. My honor is at stake."

Maria lifted her eyes from her knitting. "What honor? What are you talking about? He hasn't done anything to my honor. That crazy American hasn't done anything at all, except look. I haven't had two words with him. I find him funny."

Clemente Vargas sniffed loudly. "I do not find him funny."

"Clemente," Aunt-Chaperone said, "don't do anything rash. You mentioned family honor. Well, remember, we have that honor to uphold."

"Do not fear, señora. I won't do anything to embarrass the family nor Maria. But I promise you, this affair will be dealt with."

By now, not only the Benítez family but the whole town knew of Walker's obsession. Andrews's talk with him had had some effect—for two days. And when, unexpectedly, Maria Benítez alighted from the coach and did not see the lieutenant, she felt a twinge of regret. She had come to expect his presence, something she hadn't confided to anyone, and definitely not her aunt. She scanned the street, hoping to see him, and felt a hand on her elbow. It was her aunt prompting her to step up into the coach.

Though he was nowhere in sight, it didn't mean he had given up on his quest. He just did it more furtively. No longer the lonesome sight perched upon a stone plaza bench, instead he took to strolling on Victoria Street at odd hours, mainly just after and before her attendance at church mass. Maria Benítez and her chaperone would alight from the coach and there he'd be, seemingly taking his constitutional. Maria would offer a rare smile, and he would lower his eyes, maintaining his diffident manner, while the chaperone glared at him.

Now, there was no law that stated Lieutenant Walker couldn't stroll on such a lovely street when it struck his fancy. What complaints could the Benítez family make? Besides, Maria Benítez, far from being put off by his attention, was becoming receptive to it. Oh, she didn't exhibit such in public. After her single, solitary smile she would prance back into the house as fast as her feet would take her, but always regarding the sailor with one lingering look.

At least she didn't burst out laughing anymore, which her parents considered an improvement.

In the safe confines of her home, Maria would confide, ever so discreetly, to her parents and the chaperone that the young naval officer was probably lonely, being away from home and family. One could not help but take pity on him. And he was rather dashing in his uniform.

Whenever such comments escaped her mouth, her parents would cringe and the aunt-chaperone would fix Maria Benítez with a hard stare, her mouth set in acute disapproval.

Emile Edward Walker wasn't the only one with a plan. While he was spying on Maria Benítez, the watcher was himself being watched by Clemente Vargas and his cronies. These consisted of three young stalwarts whose dislike for the new overseers mirrored his own. They considered themselves heirs to Spanish culture, and this new regime was a canker sore on their pride. To have one of its representatives, and a naval officer at that, get his comeuppance was an idea wildly hilarious to them. Besides, aping Clemente's clarion call, it was a matter of honor. This impudent yanqui needed a lesson in etiquette.

Though etiquette wasn't exactly what Vargas and his compadres had in mind. The plan started off well. They hid themselves behind a tall wooden gate in a house a block up from the quarters Walker shared with his fellow officers. The house belonged to the parents of one of the conspirators. And the conspirators were full of sass. They would show the americano.

Clemente Vargas was in the lookout spot, straining to see from behind the wooden slats on the gate, and not getting any help from the flickering candle of a street lamp some feet away. The burlap hoods they wore impaired their vision even more. Clemente Vargas was beginning to think it was a dumb idea to wear hoods in the first place. The material scratched the skin, and it made them sweat like pigs. He was beginning to consider it would have been better if they hadn't masked their identity. Better to have the upstart American know who his attackers were.

No, not attackers, but men of honor bent on retribution, on proclaiming their zeal to one of their own. The fact that Maria Benítez had not asked for anyone to defend her honor was something he never even considered.

It got dark pretty soon, and their impatience simmered. His three partners badgered Clemente Vargas: "Where is he? Do you see anything? What's taking him so long?"

"Quiet!" Clemente Vargas hissed.

"When is he coming?"

"I don't know. Keep quiet!" With effort, Clemente Vargas kept his eye on the peephole formed by the wooden gate.

"He's coming!"

His companions drew closer, trying to catch a glimpse through the flimsy wooden slats.

"He's coming right around the corner," Clemente Vargas informed. "Get ready."

They heard plodding footsteps on the outside path. When the officer passed by the gate his white uniform showed a dull-gray in the evening dark. The men flung open the gate and pounced on their prey.

The attack so was sudden the man was wrestled to the ground before he could react. One of the attackers pulled a burlap sack over his head, while the others turned him over on the ground and began tying his hands behind his back with sturdy rope. Muffled screeches issued from inside the burlap sack. The men lifted up the officer and rushed into an alley formed by two rows of houses.

"He's heavy!" one of the men gasped. "Damn!"

"¡Coño, este es un gordo!"

Clemente Vargas, who held tight to one leg, stopped in his tracks. The others bumped into him and almost dropped the load. He is fat! Clemente Vargas looked down at the corpulent mass they strained to lift up. The white naval uniform was the same, but this guy was not thin.

Lieutenant Walker was thin.

Clemente Vargas let go of the leg, its foot dragging on the ground even while his companions held on to the other three limbs. He grabbed at the burlap and whisked it off the man's head.

"It's not him!" he cried. "This is not the man!"

They dropped their captive right then and there. Poor Captain Andrews, mistaken for Lieutenant Walker, landed on his behind. His captors jabbered in Spanish, and he couldn't understand a thing. They were just strange forms in the dark. "¡Vámonos! ¡Vámonos!"

The good captain was left in the alley, shouting for help, with no one coming to his aid.

The would-be kidnappers vanished.

The ensuing uproar did not. From San Juan came a proclamation of martial law to be imposed on the town of Ponce. A United States naval officer had been attacked by ruffians, hooligans, and it was an outrage. Undoubtedly, agent provocateurs from Spain still roamed abroad in the land. The American garrison was reinforced, and for the first time since the invasion, armed US Marines patrolled the streets of Ponce. From La Playa to the mayoralty, sweating leathernecks with rifles and stony faces stood wilting in the heat. A few houses were searched, the leather tanning warehouses in La Playa were closed temporarily, and contraband rum was confiscated on the docks. Nothing was found, certainly not bombs or arms or any kind of munitions.

Extra guards were posted at the railroad depot that connected Ponce to San Juan, also at the post office and other government buildings. For a week all military personnel were confined to barracks, and when they traveled into town they had to travel in pairs and with sidearms. This made it somewhat more difficult for Lieutenant Walker to see his beloved Maria Benítez.

He got around this by convincing one of his fellows to take over his watch duty in the evenings. Thus he would sneak out of barracks and pine from behind a tree and under a full moon on Victoria Street, keeping his protracted vigil toward Maria Benítez's balcony.

She would always be there, dutifully knitting under the ever-constant eye of her chaperone. And every evening Clemente Vargas would visit and sit by her side, keeping a respectful distance as they discussed this and that and saying nothing of import. A few times Maria would break from her knitting, rising from the cane chair and fanning herself with an ornate feathered fan, then dabbing at her forehead with a handkerchief but arching her back just enough so that the high-collared dress would stretch taut across her young and full breasts, and she would exhale a hot, humid sigh; and Walker's legs would turn to jelly, for he could hear her heartfelt murmur even from the distance.

Clemente Vargas would watch as she turned left then right, as if showing off her corseted but voluptuous form. He would beg for her to sit down lest she tax herself, for she was a delicate flower and all delicate flowers need care.

Except that this delicate flower had a mind of her own, and twice more during the night she would stretch and pose, and drive Walker insane behind his hiding place in the tree.

This went on for another week, by which time martial law was rescinded. But the curfew that had been policy since the Americans' arrival was kept in place.

While Walker pined, plans were announced for the upcoming nuptials of Maria Benítez and her suitor. The couple's parents thought it prudent, under the circumstances, that the young lady be wed as soon as possible. She was just past her eighteenth birthday, which was just right. Twenty-year-old Clemente Vargas was beside himself with joy. He walked in the clouds. To think, he would marry the most beauteous woman in all of Ponce, not to mention from one of its wealthiest families.

Ignacio Romero was the one to inform Walker, in passing, of the upcoming wedding. Walker remained impassive, just staring past Romero to some spot beyond. He mouthed a low "thank you," and Romero

29

watched him disappear inside the house that served as the officers' barracks. The older man shook his head, thinking it was best that the young man be told about the wedding. He couldn't be kept in the dark, and such news must come from a friend. Yet Romero knew that in matters of love nothing is certain, and this left him with a feeling of unease. Walker had not shown any reaction at the news. For some reason, this bothered Romero more than if the young officer had howled in anger.

For Ponceños it was the event of the season. Its two most prominent families would unit biologically as well as commercially, a good match all around. Throughout the preparations Maria Benítez remained, as always, unaffected. If she was at all excited about the marriage, she didn't show it. Not like Clemente Vargas, who preened and swaggered hither and dither, basking in his good fortune, buying rum for everyone in the cafetines, and even going as far as to cease frequenting the storied brothel on the outskirts of town.

Maria's family attributed her lack of ardor to pre-wedding jitters. At least that's what her chaperone surmised, and they all fervently wished to believe it.

Lieutenant Walker continued his surveillance from the tree on Vitoria Street, while Clemente Vargas, for the moment, nixed any idea of retaliation. Why should he? In a week's time Maria Benítez would finally and forever be his. Not even a pathetic yanqui could deny fate.

Mysteriously, Walker's venue changed. He disappeared. Well, not exactly disappeared. He didn't spy on her anymore. Suddenly, he kept his distance. No longer could Maria Benítez stretch and flutter her fan on the veranda knowing that the lieutenant was eyeing her from behind a tree.

Everyone was relieved. It was taken as one more positive sign. This was indeed a marriage made in heaven, or somewhere in between.

September 22—a day that would be enshrined in memory. It would rate up there with other tales harking back to the time of Spain; to tales of headless viceroys galloping at night through the Ponce streets in doomed carriages; levitating apparitions raising from the cemetery tombs at night; Spanish noblemen, attired in costumes of the previous century and always in black, seen strolling around the plaza cathedral on a wet dawn and then disappearing into thin air with the advent of daylight. To this was added the tale of the love-crazed americano and his hopeless quest. Songs would be written about it. Grandparents would regale their grandchildren for years to come of a saga so improbable few would believe it yet would come to be fascinated by its outcome.

September 22. Maria Benítez arose, bathed in the ornate ceramic tub her parents had imported from Spain. Pails of cold water had been laboriously hefted from the outside well to fill the giant tub. Thus Maria Benítez bathed ritually as any virgin being prepared for sacrifice; said her morning prayers and breakfasted on coffee and *pan de agua* with butter. This was followed by the painstaking ritual of dressing the bride. Her mother, her aunts, and the chaperone all gathered around her and began piling on garments as if she were an idol being dressed for deification. From slip to corset to camisole to pannier, layer upon layer until she felt her ribs constrict with every breath. At last, assured that all was in order, her guardians led her outside to the waiting carriage.

At the plaza cathedral Clemente Ordoñez Vargas waited with nervous anticipation.

And waited.

And waited.

The church door stayed open for every passerby and well-wisher seeking to fete this princely couple on their voyage of marital wellbeing. The ceremony was set for 2 p.m., when the tropic sun would be at its apex and pure rays of daylight would echo on every stained-glass crevice of that venerable cathedral in the Ponce square. This would be followed by a reception promptly at 4 p.m., and it was assumed with great certainty that the merrymaking would last well into the night. Ponce at last had something to celebrate.

Lieutenant Walker had other ideas. Not far from the cathedral and just across from La Perla Theater, where a group of traveling actors from Spain were performing in a musical comedy known as the zarzuela, Walker ran from the theatre with a pistol in hand. He waylaid the coach, ordering the terrified driver to jump out. Then he hauled out the screeching chaperone and jumped atop the carriage, grasping the reins and steering the horses at a fast clip. He was last seen galloping toward the hill beyond the cemetery, a not-so-terrified Maria Benítez sitting calmly in the back of the carriage.

Walker's action not only scandalized the town, it threatened to provoke mass disorder. It was expected that Clemente Vargas would be incensed; same for family and friends. But more, this was the height of insult. What insolence from these barbarian yanquis! There was talk of local youths arming themselves, of revolt against the *norteamericanos*. The Spanish had been harsh in their rule, yes, but they had never flouted their authority nor acted in such a high-handed manner. Captain Andrews had to use all of his meditative powers to calm down Maria Benítez's father and future in-laws. He issued a decree for Walker's arrest and, fearing uprising, increased the nightly patrols and reinstated the 8 p.m. curfew, which had been briefly rescinded in honor of the wedding festivities.

Walker's caper became the talk of the region, not only in Ponce but in neighboring Cuamo, Salinas, and Santa Isabel. Even to the capital of San Juan it spread, the abduction, the passion, the adventure. In present day, no doubt, it would have been featured in one of those insipid Spanish TV *novelas*.

Truth is more subjective; as it was in this case. There was no great romance, simply because Maria Benítez could feel nothing for anyone save herself. She cared for her parents and family, but to commit herself to the kind of passion felt by both Walker and Clemente Vargas—never. She liked the attention foisted upon her by these men and the world in general, but she accepted it with equanimity. Had the men and the world ignored her, she would have been just as happy and noncommitted. Her thought patterns could not conceive of need. Or want, or love. She was a creature of whim. And a creature of whim she would remain all her days.

To the south of Ponce lay the central mountain range, La Cordillera. Here Walker hid his captive in a small hut owned by a jíbaro who gladly gave up ownership for the five American dollars Walker offered. The country peasant took the money and ran off, which suited Walker just fine. He had no clear idea of what was to come; indeed, had not planned for it. He acted on the spur of the moment, content just to have Maria Benítez by his side. He did not impose himself upon her, nor did he entreat her for favors. He devoted all his time to looking after her. For her part, Maria Benítez offered no reaction either way. She didn't complain or make a fuss. She didn't do a damn thing except sit in the hut while Walker took pains to discard her wedding dress and train. Then she put on a gingham sack-like costume and went about barefoot. Walker threw off his naval tunic and likewise walked barefoot. They were like two children on an outing. It was new and exciting, bathing in a creek close by, eating mangoes and coconuts that Walker sliced with a machete the jíbaro had left behind. They fed on bananas and root plants, and spent nights in silence, counting the stars forming around the Big and Little Dipper.

The novelty wore off soon enough: a hut in the middle of nowhere, no amenities, and mosquitoes eating them alive. Maria Benítez, who had never been communicative, sank further into her lassitude. It was more of a consuming depression. She never made a sound, while he expounded on everything from Cajun cooking to modern naval military theory. She riveted her eyes on the door of the hut, not hearing nor listening, lost inside the gingham dress. In time she made no effort to bathe in the creek, nor sampled any more coconuts or bananas. She huddled in her corner of the hut, not even bothering to flap at the mosquitoes swarming around her. She became a solid lump inside the hut, a silent presence devouring him and his irrational love.

She was languishing. Walker did all he could to coax her out of it. He even went into town, broke into one of the stores, and brought back candies and sweets for her to eat. But the licorice sticks and fudge candy he spirited in a paper bag couldn't snap her out of her funk. He would coo to her, speaking to her in baby talk, trying to get her to laugh, to weep, to do something. Afterward he would rant and rail, blaming all his failings on her. No response either way. She wouldn't sleep and was drawn into some secretive place inside herself to which no one, especially Walker, was privy.

It began to rain, and as the rain increased so did Walker's apprehension. Maria Benítez simply slumped to her side and closed her eyes. Walker became frantic, rushing to her side. He implored God to please not take her away from him. When he placed his ear to her breast, he could hear her heartbeat, feel the breathing, even and rhythmic.

She remained like that for two days, sleeping without interruption.

To be honest about it, Walker wasn't in such great shape himself. Never a stocky man, he had lost weight drastically. He couldn't eat unless Maria Benítez ate, and she didn't eat anything. He felt Maria Benítez giving way, losing her will to live, and he could not help but identify with her pain. Her listlessness, her depression became his listlessness and his depression. Her ache became his ache, but in him it multiplied twofold, threefold. He believed she was dying; just as something in him was dying.

In the middle of the rainstorm he set out for town, intent on finding a doctor, or someone he could bring back to save his world.

From the mountains to Ponce is a long trek, especially in those days when there were no paved roads and all avenues were swamped with ravines and ditches. In that cascade of a storm Walker trudged toward Ponce, wet and shivering.

He made it to the wooden bridge that in that time served as the boundary between the town and the mountains. Walker managed to cross the bridge, and in doing so was spotted by the two sentries huddled

inside a box-like sentry post at the foot of the bridge. These local consta-
bles, not military police from the occupying force, at first thought Walker
might be some country peasant coming in from the interior. He looked
incongruous: barefoot and bare-chested in the rainstorm and walking
haphazardly like a drunken man would.

Walker wasn't drunk. The two sentries thought him insane. No man
in his right mind would be out in such inclement weather. It was worse
than any storm, this rainfall. And it wasn't the hurricane season, even. It
was the gods battling for the sky.

The sentries yelled for Walker to get inside the sentry post. Light-
ning was rampant. They hollered some more. The man didn't hear or
didn't listen. He staggered forward, then fell on the dirt road. Even on
the ground the man still clawed his way forward. That's when the guards
left the safety of their sentry box and ventured out into the deluge. Soon
they dragged the poor man back to their shelter.

They recognized him immediately, scraggly beard, gaunt cheeks and
all. The one the whole town had been searching for. He was in a bad way,
the americano; that was obvious. His breathing was raspy and labored,
and he spoke incoherently in English, which was lost on them.

After much argument and protestations back and forth, the junior
man agreed to go into town and inform the mayoralty office. The americano had been found.

But what of señorita Maria Benítez? After they dumped Walker in
the mayoralty infirmary, the grilling began. By then Maria Benítez's father
and fiancée had arrived; so had Dr. Arrias-Ferrer and Captain Andrews.
The doctor cautioned that Walker was in no condition to talk. But don
Pablo and Clemente Vargas insisted on interrogating him anyway, and
got nowhere. He mumbled this and that, calling out Maria's name. All
the while Maria's father and fiancée shouted and shook him on the cot,
demanding to know, where was Maria Benítez? Finally, Dr. Arrias-Ferrer
and Captain Andrews interceded, asking that the two men leave. Walker
was just too weak to answer anything. They could continue questioning

tomorrow. Don Pablo and Clemente Vargas balked at the suggestion. But firm and decisive argument from both the doctor and the captain convinced them that it was the better course.

When they returned in the morning, Walker wasn't there. Somehow he had given the slip to his marine guard and escaped.

The frantic search was on again. They didn't have far to look this time.

By some stroke of luck, on the bridge outside of town, they ran into the same jíbaro who had sold his hut to Walker. The country peasant was lugging a wheelbarrow full of root plants, which he intended to sell in the town market. The two bridge sentries became suspicious when the peasant tried to bribe them with American money. It was customary to pay off the sentries before one's produce was allowed across the bridge. Not many jíbaros paid with American greenbacks. The hapless peon was detained until the doctor, Captain Andrews, don Pablo, and his future son-in-law arrived.

They quizzed the peasant and found out Walker's hiding place. The captain was able to procure four horses, and they set off at a gallop for the Cordillera. Part of the way, they rode. The rest they trod on foot since the path leading to the hill was too rocky and uneven for the animals.

Walker was found outside the peasant hut, still barefoot and bare-chested. He was just about gone. Maria Benítez was inside, sleeping peacefully. She was a bit skinnier and more drawn, but she wasn't dying. Walker was dying.

While don Pablo and Clemente Vargas cursed his name, Captain Andrews cradled his head. Walker made one last effort to speak. Dr. Arrias-Ferrer looked at the Captain and shook his head, indicating nothing could be done.

Walker uttered one word: "Beaners." And died.

Maria Benítez was carried back to the horse path in Clemente's arms, and taken home. Her recuperation was marvelously quick. But something had happened during her ordeal. She was the same and she wasn't the same. Still distant and flighty, but now she didn't want to marry Clemente Vargas. She decided he wasn't for her. When Clemente Vargas and her parents begged for some reason as to why the change of heart, she replied, "Yo no se" (I don't know).

Her parents knew better than to contradict their stubborn and hardheaded daughter. The marriage was called off, and don Pablo's dream of uniting Ponce's two most prominent families, for the time being, seemed dashed.

Pablo Benítez was resourceful. He managed to pawn off a niece on Clemente Vargas. Clemente took the offer on the rebound, and thus he was wed to Carmelita Lucia Benítez, daughter of Guillermo Enrique Benítez, brother to don Pablo. The union was finally realized.

Conventions were stronger back then, and Maria Benítez still had to pay for the embarrassment she caused the family by refusing to wed Clemente Vargas in the first place. Her perceived punishment was not bad when you think about it. She was sent abroad to study in Spain. What she would study no one knew, and her parents never mentioned it.

In the former mother country she met Mauricio Joaquin de Rodrigo, some bigwig connected with the ambassadorial service. She married the gentleman and thus obtained the title duquesa de Rodrigo since her husband's family traced its royal lineage to before the time of Philip II. La duquesa de Rodrigo enjoyed a leisured existence shuffling back and forth between the court in Madrid and the ancestral home in Aragon. It is said that she bore don Rodrigo three children, a daughter and two sons. The sons were the spitting image of their father, with prominent cheekbones and regal Latin looks. The firstborn, the daughter, was somewhat different from her siblings. She was very fair for a Spaniard, with a lanky face, blue-gray eyes, and freckles. When friends and acquaintances judiciously remarked as to her daughter's extraordinary looks, the duquesa would reply, "Yo no se."

BOOK ONE

LA PLAYA
(1926–1944)

CHAPTER ONE

WITHIN A GENERATION, the saga of Lieutenant Walker and his obsession became Ponce folklore. It receded into the dim mists of memory, and with the passage of the seasons it was spoken of no more. The town settled into its humdrum existence, as it had for centuries, with the new American overseers proclaiming their rule from the distant precincts of the old capital in San Juan. To the townspeople they became a distant presence, like specters from a foreign realm, there and not there, seen and not seen. The politicians saw it differently. They wanted to keep the benefits and perks of their positions, so they had to keep the American overseers happy. This, as it will be revealed, sometimes put them at odds with the rest of the Puerto Rican people.

The townsfolk went back to their existence of heat-induced inactivity during the day and torpid movement during the night; of daily gossip, and Sunday mass in the cathedral in the central plaza; domino games in the cafetines; siestas in the noon hour; horse-drawn carriages tapping on the cobblestones of the mayoralty; and the town elite still attending the weekly plays at the Teatro La Perla in the center of town.

Into this never-changing orbit there appeared one fine day Antonio Boglione. No one actually knew where he came from. His heavily accented Spanish led most to deduce that he was not a paisano. There was talk that he came from a world away beyond the sea, from a place called Napoli somewhere in the Italian peninsula.

Somehow this gangly youth with a shock of black hair and brown perceptive eyes had landed in San Juan and then had made his way to La

Playa with nothing more than the shirt on his back and some monetary notes with the likenesses of royal personages in fancy uniforms and the word lira inscribed on them. The notes were worthless in Ponce since greenback dollar bills, the currency of the americanos, had long replaced the old Spanish silver coins.

Antonio Boglione traveled all over La Playa from the decrepit wooden bridge built over the river named Portugues that crisscrossed the village, and which was the official entry point into the slum. From there he went back to the far-flung sugar cane fields on the other side of town, desperately trying to get someone to exchange his foreign currency for nominal notes, but no takers. No one knew nor trusted this skinny young man with the odd accent and orange-green paper with the funny people painted on it.

Antonio would have ended up in the street had it not been for the old widow, doña Saro, who sold homemade liquor to all and sundry from her house on Lorenza Bizo Street. Doña Saro had built a functioning apparatus in the back of her place that produced pretty-good homemade rum. The apparatus, a still, if you will, consisted of metal basins and tubing all hooked together in some slapdash manner, which somehow managed to ferment the local sugar cane with various other fruits to produce a heady drink enjoyed by all, and her price for the booze was far cheaper than the labeled and bonded stuff you could get elsewhere. In fact, locals would bring in their empty old pints and liter bottles, even their milk and soda pop bottles, to have them refilled with doña Saro's concoction.

Doña Saro was an astute business woman, as her illegal enterprise had shown. She also had a good heart, and she took pity on this disheveled, emaciated bumpkin with the earnest look of a vagabond.

She told him, "I will not exchange money for your pretty paper with the faces on it. But I will instead offer you a deal: I need someone to help me with my business. My old bones are getting creaky from handling basins and carrying sacks of cane sugar and fruit. I will show you how to handle the equipment and prepare my beverage. In turn, you'll get lodg-

41

ing in the back next to the rum basins." She frowned knowingly. "There's been more than one attempt to steal my beverage. You'll be my guarantee that it will be there from day to day." She added, "Oh yes, you will get three meals a day; I am a very good cook."

Antonio accepted the offer.

The next day, townsfolk lining up for their measure of homemade rum were surprised to find this stranger lugging out the large cast-iron containers of booze, and then ladling out the prescribed amounts to Saro's customers. As befitted her new status as an employer, doña Saro stood alongside collecting the money and giving back appropriate change when required.

As was bound to happen, soon tongues were wagging up and down the barrio as to the relationship between this older woman and the skinny youth. Exactly what was going on between her and this guy? Was it possible that old doña Saro had taken a lover? Was there more to this business arrangement? And who was getting the better of this deal?

To her credit, Saro ignored the local wags, who soon grew accustomed to seeing Antonio Boglione regularly carrying sacks of sugar cane, bags of breadfruit, and jars of rubbing alcohol from the local stores back to the doña's modest home.

Antonio Boglione became a common sight in La Playa, although he would never be seen inside one of the cafetines. He didn't have to. As part of the deal, he would get a pint of homemade rum each week for his work. He didn't drink the rum. Instead he would hoard his pint bottles and sell them for whatever amount he could get, to merchant seamen and laborers in the nearby Ponce pier at the outskirts of La Playa.

Doña Saro didn't mind this. After all, she didn't pay him a wage. And in a town where everyone was given a nickname, whether deservedly so or not, complimentary or not, Saro started calling him Toño, the diminutive of Antonio.

Soon, he was Toño to everyone.

Part of doña Saro's dealings were with Juan-Carlos Quiles. Juan-Carlos was another popular person in La Playa. He was not a merchant or employer or property owner, but he did provide one great essential service to the *playeros*: he was the numbers dealer. Out of his home, at the other end of Lorenza Bizo Street, he carried on a numbers racket. This was not the national lottery that had been instituted by the Spaniards and remained in place under the American overseers. No, this was a local numbers setup, which had proved very profitable for Juan-Carlos.

For those who, for whatever reason, could not come to Juan-Carlos's joint to place bets, he would go to their homes and collect the numbers. Doña Saro was one of those beneficiaries. Juan-Carlos would dutifully bring a sheet with names on it, doña Saro would give him a folded slip of paper with her number written inside, and the numbers dealer would write down her number on the sheet.

After taking the five cents doña Saro had paid for her bet, what struck Antonio Boglione was the wad of bills Juan-Carlos brought out of his pocket. As usual, he had also purchased a liter bottle of moonshine. He had tied the bills with string (rubber bands were still unknown in La Playa). He took out one dollar from the roll and handed it to the lady, who immediately gave him his change.

Antonio Boglione had never seen such a roll of money before. It left an impression. Yes, someday he too would have a big wad of bills in his pocket.

CHAPTER TWO

ON A CERTAIN day, after the last of doña Saro's customers had gotten their refills and all the rinsing and cleaning of the bottles and basins had been done in the back, Antonio made his way toward the home of Juan-Carlos Quiles, at the other end of the street.

Juan-Carlos, as always, was in the back of his house, counting out the daily numbers receipts. He was somewhat surprised when his eldest daughter, Estrella, announced that Toño Boglione requested an audience with him.

Looking up from his bifocals perched at the end of his nose, he inquired as to what service he could provide the young man.

Antonio answered quickly. He had a proposition for señor Juan-Carlos.

"Proposition?" Juan-Carlos asked warily.

"Yes," Antonio replied, trying to sound self-assured, though fidgeting with his hands joined in front of his body.

"What do you mean by a 'proposition'?" Juan-Carlos asked again.

"You're a man well known in these parts," Antonio began. "You have created a profitable and viable business. I admire such resolve, and I would like to assist you in your endeavors and—"

"Endeavors?" Juan-Carlos interrupted. "What do you mean?"

"You provide a service to all in La Playa," Antonio stated. "I believe I can be of assistance, and even increase your profits as well if you would give me the chance."

Juan-Carlos eyed Antonio from beneath his bifocals. "Increase my profits?" He paused reflectively. "And what do you mean by 'provide assistance'?"

"Just that," Antonio said plainly. "I've seen you work hard each day when you come to doña Saro's. You have no assistant, no one to tend to your books. I know you're a busy man, and I could relieve you of some of your burdens. Not only that, I may be able to increase your profits substantially. I have ideas as to how your business could be improved."

"Improved? How?"

"Right now your business is confined to La Playa. What if you could expand to include the town? There are many there who would consider your services if they had the opportunity."

"I'm aware of that," Juan-Carlos argued. "But in town you have the police station and the bureaucrats who would want their share of my 'business.'" He let that sink in. "How would you, someone who knows nothing about my operation, handle that?"

Antonio gave his response. "I learned in my homeland that any obstacle can be surmounted if one has enough funds. And as to your business, I have watched you conduct your affairs. You have a knack for putting people at ease. Not only are you well respected, you are well liked. That goes a long ways."

Juan-Carlos clasped both hands on his desk and asked directly, "What is it that you want from me, Toño?"

"I want to become a partner in your business," Antonio spoke distinctly. "I want to assist you and make your business grow. And I believe I can."

"How?"

"By buying a share into your business, helping you gather proceeds. You can keep all the profit. In return, all I ask is that you teach me all you know. I will work diligently for you, and I will be loyal."

"Speaking of loyalty," Juan-Carlos referenced, "does Saro know about this?"

"I've already spoken to her about it, and she agrees that I should better myself. I will still tend to her equipment and assist her in making the rum. That will not change."

Juan-Carlos thought for a moment. "I agree to your request." Raising a finger for emphasis, he added, "But on one condition. And that is that if you want to become my assistant and partner, you provide me with some initial collateral for this proposed business venture." He leaned back in his straight-backed chair, resting his hands on the armrests. "Scrape up fifty American dollars as a down payment, and you have a deal."

Standing there in front of La Playa's premier numbers dealer, Antonio shifted nervously. He swallowed and said, "Agreed. I will get you the fifty dollars."

"Good," Juan-Carlos said cordially. "That will be your initiation into my business world."

CHAPTER THREE

IN THOSE DAYS, fifty bucks was a fortune. Most laborers in Ponce were fortunate if they made a dollar a day. Antonio calculated that even if he robbed someone, and that included the well-to-do, he'd have to spend a year robbing people just to get the amount needed. Too much work for not enough return.

And it was at Carmelo's cafetín that, providentially, the idea came to him. The minute he entered, heads turned since he was not one to frequent the watering hole. This was indeed a unique occasion. But Antonio was there to get ideas, to find out what made La Playa tick and how he could use it to his advantage. He ordered an India beer and sat at a table in a far corner, sipping quietly and thumbing his bottle of brew.

By chance, three locals were recounting the daily gossip. "It's true," one of the locals was saying. "She went blind when she saw the ghost."

"Are you sure?" another man with a scraggly beard inquired.

"Yes, I swear. She's at the Hospital de Damas right now, having her eyes checked. They figure she's now as blind as a bat."

A third man shook his head solemnly. "That woman was crazy. She should've known better. There's a reason why the plaza is deserted after midnight and no one goes out. I heard that a man from beyond the hills dropped dead when the headless count touched him in the plaza, and the man was there after midnight." He nodded gloomily. "Really shitty. People should know better than to tempt the fates."

In the midst of the conversation, the first local noted Antonio sitting alone in the corner. "Hey, Toño," he called, "you here to sell Saro's rum?"

Antonio shook his head. "No, I'm just here to relax. It's been a long day."

"Did you hear about that lady in La Playa last night?" The scraggly bearded one asked.

"No, what lady?"

"The one that went blind after seeing the Headless Count drive in his carriage through the plaza."

"The Headless Count?"

"Yeah, you know, the one who has cursed this town since the time of the Spaniards." Scraggly Beard snorted indignantly. "And it's happened more than once."

Antonio picked up his drink and approached the men at the other table. "What curse?"

"The curse of the headless guy," one of the locals told him.

"You haven't heard about the Headless Count?" Scraggly Beard asked, dismayed.

"Yes," Antonio said, "but I thought it was just rumor, old wives' tales."

"This is no old wives' tale. This is fact. You mess with the Headless Count, and you pay." At the last remark, the three men nodded in unison.

Antonio wasn't convinced. "You believe that?"

All three men looked up at Antonio in disbelief. "You don't?" one of them asked.

"No, I don't believe in ghosts," Antonio said with conviction. "My father used to say that you have more to fear from a live ghost than from a dead one."

From the table: "Do you know what you're saying? Are you crazy?"

"He's not crazy!" came a roar from the other end of the room. "He's a man with balls who doesn't believe this bullshit about ghosts and witches and what have you." The voice was high, but slurred, and it came from Manolo, considered the town drunk. He slouched back on the chair, with his shirt unbuttoned and showing tufts of gray hair on his chest.

"Shut up, Manolo," someone else chimed in. "You don't know what the fuck you're talking about."

"Screw you!" Manolo shouted back. He waved a hand vigorously. "You're all idiots—believing this crap!"

At this moment, an old, wizened individual at a center table stood up from his chair and declared, "I have seen the Headless Count in his carriage, and I say he lives!"

"If you've seen the fucker," Manolo jibed, "how come you're not blind?"

The old man clutched the rosary around his chest. "I was a boy at the time, and I was wearing my mother's rosary."

"So you were a young boy out at the plaza at midnight?"

The old, wizened man could not be shaken from his memory. "It was at sundown when I saw him. The medals on his uniform glittered in the waning light as he sat, without a head, in his black carriage driven by two black horses with blazing red eyes. And his driver . . ." The aged ancient paused, gripped by fear. "Oh, that driver. A more frightening sight I have not seen in my days."

"You actually believe this?" Antonio said incredulously.

"Yes, I do. Whoever dares to look upon the Headless Count goes blind or worse."

"I won't go blind or worse," Antonio said to all.

"WHAT?" It was a collective chorus from everyone in the room except for Manolo the drunkard.

51

Antonio sounded complacent. "I won't go blind. I don't believe any of this."

Carmelo, the owner of the cafetín, had been standing quietly behind the bar, taking everything in with growing interest. And he spoke up: "Do you know what you're saying, boy?"

"Yes, I do. I don't believe any of it."

"Are you willing to put your life on the line for this?" the ancient challenged.

"Yes," Antonio answered unequivocally.

"Be careful of what you're saying, boy," Carmelo cautioned.

"You're a young fool," the aged man accused.

One of the men at the table in front of Antonio came out with a suggestion: "If you don't believe that the Headless Count exists, then I dare you to spend a night at the plaza alone."

A hush gripped the room. The hot, humid air hung in the silence.

Antonio knew he couldn't let this pass. "I will spend a night at the plaza."

"Wait a minute!" roared the drunken Manolo. "This is isn't right. The young man, to his credit, agrees to spend a night in the plaza and confront the Headless Count. He could be stupid or brave. At this point I don't know. But it's not fair that he should do this without some . . . some compensation!"

Carmelo idly scratched his nose. "Compensation?"

"Yes, compensation. I say we bet on it. Whoever thinks he can do it, or not, put your money where your mouth is."

"I accept your wager," Antonio declared.

"It's not my wager," said Manolo. "It's all these guys' here. Let's see how brave they are."

"I accept," the ancient announced, his voice strong.

The chorus went around the room, "And so do I!"

"And me."

"And me too."

"Count me in."

Carmelo held up a palm for silence. "Wait a minute. We have to do this right. I say we do it proper. Whoever wants to bet can do it. But, to be fair, we have to give odds." He motioned toward Antonio. "After all, this young man is putting his life on the line."

Nods all around, everyone in agreement.

"Since it's his neck on the line," Carmelo explained, "I say we give odds of two to one."

"Two to one?" snarled Manolo tipsily. "That's bullshit. If this kid goes blind or worse, that's a tragedy. I say we put the odds at eight to one." Manolo clenched his fist for emphasis. "And I'm putting my money, what little I've got, on the kid. Any takers?"

The chorus again: "I'll take that."

"I'll bite."

"I'll put two dollars on the Headless Count."

"Make that three!"

"Kid, it was nice knowing you."

Looking at a surprised Antonio, the old wizened man intoned gravely, "You have sealed your doom."

CHAPTER
FOUR

THE OLD MAN'S words rang in Antonio's head. Had he sealed his doom? Bravado had induced him to take on the challenge, and the money won would go a long way toward his plan to buy into the lottery business. Yet in the back recesses of his mind, he wondered, "What if after all the tales of those who had suffered trying to disprove the Headless Count were legion in the barrio . . . What if . . ."

He spoke to doña Saro about it, and she was nonplussed. He had committed himself, and he had to go through with this plan whatever the consequence. "Yes," he replied, "but what if . . . ?"

"What if?" Saro sniffed. "If you die, you die."

"Do you actually believe I can't survive the night at the plaza?" Now Antonio sounded nervous.

"You need counsel on this," Saro said. "The only one who can help you in this matter is the Scholarly Jew. He's the only one I can think of who can advise you in this."

"The Scholarly Jew?"

"Yes, Jacobo. He lives on Dead-End Street. Go to him. He's smart. He reads a lot. He'll advise you."

The Scholarly Jew lived in the area next to the river known as the Dead End. It was a narrow strip, bounded by the river on one side and a grassy pasture on the other. The strip was the unofficial dividing line between La Playa and the area farther up bordering the hills. That's why it was called Dead-End Street. A series of houses formed a small triangle next to Dead-End Street. In one of these houses, on the second level, lived Jacobo Levy. The first level was the residence of Domingo Madera the carpenter, and Jacobo's landlord.

Jacobo Levy's tale was similar to that of Antonio Boglione. No one really knew much about him. He had arrived in Ponce years before, and he was a Spaniard; his Castilian accent could not hide that. And he was a Jew, most likely a Marrano who had been driven from his home. He had the honor of being the only Jew in Ponce. He was also a man of learning; that was obvious to all. He maintained himself by working during the day at the only store in town that prescribed eye glasses to the well-to-do. He was a lens grinder, and his talent was in great demand. Even so, he preferred to live at the modest house on the Dead End. If he had ever had a wife or children, no one knew. And when anyone inquired, he would decline to answer.

Doña Saro had asked Juan-Carlos Quiles to bring Antonio to the home of Jacobo Levy. Juan-Carlos would be the intermediary, as it were. It was evening, and the first thing Antonio noticed was that, even though Jacobo had a balcony-veranda overlooking the outside street and a large living room at the front of the structure, Jacobo welcomed them in a small, cramped room in the back of the house. The room was filled with stacks of books on every corner. Jacobo sat hunched over a small desk, reading from some arcane volume, his eyes peering through eyeglasses in the dark illumined by one solitary wick lantern. Jacobo was a stocky man with a gray beard. Despite the heat of the evening, he wore a white shirt buttoned up to his neck. He also wore a black skullcap on the crown of his head.

"Jacobo?" Juan-Carlos addressed the figure hunched over the books. "Jacobo?"

The figure stirred. Eyes flitted up to survey the two men in the room. "Ah, Juan-Carlos. So this is the young man you told me about." The voice was deep and resonant. "So good to see you."

"Yes," Juan-Carlos affirmed. "This is indeed the young man. His name is Antonio Boglione, known as Toño to one and all."

"And one who has challenged the prevailing norms of this community," Jacobo remarked.

"He only seeks to advance himself," Juan-Carlos said.

"By risking his own demise?" Jacobo questioned.

Juan-Carlos looked levelly at Jacobo in the light of the lantern, and ventured to say, "So you believe in ghosts and goblins, Jacobo? I would not expect that from a man of learning."

"What I believe is irrelevant," Jacobo said. He gestured toward Antonio. "It's what this young man believes that is important."

"He needs your counsel," Juan-Carlos responded. "That's all we ask."

"Let the young man speak for himself." Jacobo spoke to Antonio directly, "What do you want from me?"

"I need advice and I'm told you're smart," Antonio answered.

"Then you've been misinformed," Jacobo said dryly.

"Don't be so modest, Jacobo," Juan Carlos mocked. "Toño is here because he needs your counsel and, as we know, in a most important matter."

Jacobo joined his hands atop his desk. In the dim light they seemed like gray, disembodied appendages sprouting out of his shirt sleeves. "Yes, I've heard of this stupid betting that has been going on. It's a topic of gossip even in town."

"It may be stupid, but the young man can make some money out if it and—"

"If he survives," Jacobo interjected. He looked up at Antonio and asked, "Why did you make the wager?"

"Because I need the money," Antonio answered simply.

"But there are other ways of making money."

Antonio looked at Juan-Carlos, then back to Jacobo Levy. "I need it fast for a business venture."

"Hmmm." Jacobo stroked his beard. "A business venture. A most worthy aspiration." Through his eyeglasses, Jacobo watched Antonio with a detached gaze. "Do you think you can spend a night in the plaza under the circumstances?"

"I've slept in the plaza before. No big deal."

Jacobo cocked an eyebrow. "Oh, you have?"

Juan-Carlos turned to glance at Antonio, who said to Jacobo, "Yes. When I first got to La Playa and didn't have a place to stay."

Jacobo showed his palms. "Then it's settled, you have no problem. You slept in the plaza before, and the Headless Count didn't come to take you away in his ghostly carriage."

"Yes, but I didn't know about the Headless Count then."

Jacobo looked puzzled. "Does it make any difference that you know about him now?"

"I didn't expect him when I was in the plaza before."

"And you do now?"

"I don't know," Antonio said faintly.

Jacobo looked thoughtful. "Before you heard of the Headless Count, you slept in the plaza. And now that you know about him, you're afraid to sleep there again." He shook his head. "You suffer from what is known as the power of suggestion."

"What?" Juan-Carlos asked, peering from one man to the other.

Jacobo waved his hand dismissively. "Never mind. Go back to the plaza and have a good sleep."

"But others in the plaza who have dared to sleep there have come to harm and worse by the Headless Count," Juan-Carlos objected. "It's not prudent to tempt the fates."

"It's not prudent to make stupid wagers," Jacobo reminded.

"What should he do?" Juan Carlos asked anxiously. "What if the headless demon shows up and . . ." He stopped, going no further.

"Do you think the headless demon will show up?" Jacobo asked Antonio.

Antonio seemed perplexed. "I don't know."

"Simple," Jacobo said to him. "If the Headless Count shows up and you don't see him, nothing will happen."

Both Antonio and Juan-Carlos said, "What?"

"What can't be seen cannot harm you," Jacobo said.

"How can he not see him?" Juan-Carlos asked. "What if he wakes?"

"What if he doesn't?"

"You mean, die?"

"No, stays asleep so that he doesn't bother the Headless Count and the headless demon won't bother him."

"How can he do that?" Juan-Carlos said, truly confused.

"You still make rum for doña Saro?" Jacobo asked Antonio.

"Yes," Antonio said.

"Have you ever tried some of her rum?"

"Yes."

"It's a potent beverage, I'm told."

Another yes from Antonio.

Jacobo sat back in his high-backed chair, showing approval. "Then the problem is solved."

Juan-Carlos scratched his head. "Solved? What are you talking about?"

"I think Toño knows what I'm talking about," Jacobo said, looking squarely at the young man.

CHAPTER
FIVE

ANTONIO PICKED THE following Saturday as the day of reckoning. There would be a good crowd in the morning to see if Toño had survived his ordeal or not. It would also give Domingo Madera enough time to fashion a coffin for the local undertaker when Antonio's lifeless body was lifted from the plaza bench. This is, if he didn't go blind like the last woman who had dared to look upon the Headless Count. And what if there was no body? What if the headless demon took poor Toño away to the depths of hell? In that case, a mass would be said for him in the local church.

No one came to see him off at the plaza. Most playeros were too scared to risk the wrath of the Headless Count. At sundown, everyone made it to their homes; even the cafetines were emptied. Those who dared looked out through crevices and small openings in their shuttered windows as Antonio made his way up Calamar Street to the plaza square. No one was seen even in the outhouses in the backyards. They all held it in until the trial by fire was over, or kept their chamber pots close by.

Antonio, for his part, seemed unconcerned. He strode to his favorite spot on the plaza, a stone bench not far from Sabatino's bakery across the street, where this evening no one was buying Sabatino's flavorful pan de agua for next day's breakfast.

Antonio sat on the bench, furtively looked around, then took out of his pocket a pint bottle of Saro's potent rum, and took one good snort. After the burning in his throat had eased, he had another shot, and another gulp, and then another.

* * *

A hand tugging at his shoulder shook him awake. He opened one bleary eye. Juan-Carlos's jowled, mustached face came into view. "You're alive!" he rejoiced. "You've done it! You won the bet!"

Antonio managed to raise himself up and sat upright on the bench. Juan-Carlos had not come alone. Manolo, the village drunkard, was there, plus three other paisanos, with their mouths agape, and almost in shock that, yes, Toño had defied the Headless Count and survived! This would be something they would tell their children and their children's children.

For Antonio, it wasn't over yet. Although he had defied the Headless Count and won his bet, he was still short of the needed funds to buy a share in Juan-Carlos's enterprise. And he decided he could ride the wave of superstition even further.

At the far edge of La Playa, just beyond the tree line from the beach, was the municipal cemetery. And Octavio Mendosa, a regular at Carmelo's cafetín and known to all as Papo, had held everyone spellbound one evening after work with his tale of what had transpired just a week before at the hallowed cemetery. As Octavio told it, he had been drinking with some friends at the cafetín, which Carmelo corroborated, and had left quite inebriated at closing time. It was Saturday and the cafetín had closed promptly at midnight. Octavio staggered home. But in the dark of night, he had spied a lovely young woman holding a saucer with a solitary candle and walking down the deserted street.

Octavio thought it odd that anyone, especially a woman, would be out at this time. He approached her and, in all courtesy, asked why she was out at this hour. It wasn't safe to be abroad at this time. He managed to get a good look at the woman in the gloom of night. She was strikingly beautiful.

The woman had lifted the candleholder to show her face: round, dark eyes, fair skin, and tressed hair that fell over her shoulders and down her back. He had never seen her before and asked where she lived.

The woman replied that she was on her way home.

"At this hour?" Octavio inquired. "In this dark?"

And she said yes, but she needed to get home right away.

Being a complete gentleman, Octavio volunteered to walk her home for her own safety, of course.

This beautiful lady thanked him and began walking, holding out the candleholder in front of her.

Now, Octavio had lived in La Playa all his life, so he knew every street and every corner. Except it was dark and hard to see where she was going. They continued walking, beyond the wooden bridge on the river, past rows of houses, now dark and silent with their owners safe and in bed under mosquito netting.

Onward they went. Finally, Octavio asked again, "Where do you live? Is it far?"

"Oh, it's not far," she said in a melodious voice.

Melodious voice or not, Octavio began to feel a shiver of uncertainty. They were now far beyond the confines of La Playa proper. That he knew. He could feel the breeze coming from the beach beyond the tree line. What the hell is this? he asked himself.

They came upon a well-trod path that, in the dim light, seemed familiar to Octavio.

Then he looked up and saw it: the large iron gate to the cemetery, locked at this time of night.

The woman stopped and raised the candle to show her lovely face again. "We are here," she said. She stepped up to the gate and raised her hand, beckoning Octavio to follow her. "Come," she urged. "Come. I am home."

His drunkenness suddenly vanished. Octavio murmured, "What?"

"Come," the woman said in a loud, defining voice. "Come with me to my home."

Octavio peered in the dark, and before he knew it, she was behind the gate, inside the cemetery.

"Come," she entreated. "Come."

Beads of sweat coursed down Octavio's back. He looked closer and then he saw it: the woman again raised the candle to show her face, but it had transformed into the face of a skeleton!

And she beckoned him forward.

Right then and there Octavio took off running for his life, back to La Playa, his blood racing, his heart pounding, until he made it back to his parents' house on Belén Street, where he hid all night under the covers of his bed, with his mother praying to the spirits at large that they would not take her son.

When Octavio finished, not a word was spoken. Everyone shuddered; some men made the sign of the cross. Some gulped down their rum as if it were their last drink. Only Antonio Boglione, sitting in a far corner, listened intently but quietly, surveying a new opportunity.

The next day, Antonio made another challenge to all who would take him on. He would, after midnight, spend a night in the cemetery, not to corroborate Octavio Mendosa's tale but to show his courage for those who would gamble on it.

Yes, not only would he spend the night in the cemetery, he would sleep on the tomb of the suspected ghost, a young woman who had died of malaria years before and who was thought to be the beautiful temptress seeking live beings in her travels throughout Ponce after dark.

Many advised Antonio against this scheme. Even doña Saro thought it foolish. He was tempting the fates again. One did not deny nor defy the spirits that course about in the darkness.

"I beat the Headless Count," Antonio would retort. "Childish fears will not deter me."

"Childish fears can sometimes come to pass," Saro advised.

As before, the bets were taken at Carmelo's cafetín. But this time the odds were not as generous: it was six to one instead of eight to one. It should be noted that Jacobo Levy, the Scholarly Jew, who had never been known to gamble before, ever, placed a sizeable bet on Antonio.

Dutifully, on the prescribed date, a weekend again, Antonio made his way to the cemetery after dark, accompanied by three stalwarts, including Octavio Mendosa, who, before Antonio lay himself prone on the tomb, implored him to reconsider and not go through with this craziness.

Antonio thanked him for his concern and lay down on the tomb, closing his eyes as if going to sleep.

When his companions had left, he rummaged in the dark for the pint of rum in his pocket. If it had worked before, it could again, he reasoned. He downed the rum in a few long gulps. Then he lay back and awaited his fate.

CHAPTER
SIX

ANTONIO WOKE UP the next morning at daybreak, none the worse for wear. Soon as he opened his eyes, he saw his three companions from the previous night running up to him.

"Antonio, you're alive!" they said.

"And why shouldn't I be?" he responded.

He had beaten the superstitious odds again, and this time he had enough funds to buy into Juan-Carlos's business. Nothing could stand in his way now, not dead spirits nor earthly ones.

He celebrated his good fortune with everyone at the cafetín, for now they were, all of them, remarkably, his friends since he was buying everyone drinks.

For the first time in his life he got raucously drunk. And he and Octavio Mendosa were the last ones to leave the bar. Octavio offered to see him home since Antonio was a little wobbly.

Antonio said no, he would make it back on his own, and besides, Octavio's parents would worry about him, and it was not right to worry your parents.

Octavio marveled at what a good friend Antonio was, embraced him in a strong *abrazo*, and staggered down the street to his parents' home.

For the first time Antonio knew what it was to be uncoordinated. He put one foot in front of the other, hesitantly, gently. Any minute he felt he would keel over. He was new to the drunken state, and it was as if his brain told him one thing and his body told him another.

Still, he managed to make it to Lorenza Bizo Street, albeit slowly and rocking from side to side. It was compounded by the dark. Street lights would not appear in La Playa for a while yet, and after dark one had to guide one's self by instinct, trying to make out familiar sights with hampered vision, made more difficult in Antonio's case by being smashed.

He heard it: a low hum; a long, slow groaning sound, like prayers in the dark.

He widened one blurry eye, trying to focus ahead of him. And in the non-light he saw them: gray-black figures drifting out of the night. Soon he made the outlines of what appeared to be men, maybe five or six of them; he couldn't tell in the darkness. They wore long hooded robes so that their faces were hidden from view.

More, he noted that they seemed to be carrying something, and then it materialized as they came closer. They were carrying a huge silver crucifix, about five feet high above their shoulders, and it seemed heavy. Yet the hooded figures carried it as if it were light as paper.

They came closer, this procession slowly striding in the middle of the street, in the dim of night. He saw that the robed figures held rosaries in their hands. Yet he couldn't see their hands; only the rosaries sticking out of the robes where the hands should have been.

"What the . . . ?" He didn't finish. They were almost upon him. He heard the hum again: a slow, low drone, like the voices you would hear of penitents in church.

"What the f—?"

His voice was lost in the hum. They now were so close. They passed by him as if he weren't there. They ignored him completely.

He had to find out what was going on, drunk or not. One of the robed figures was passing right alongside him. Antonio marshaled his courage and took a step toward the man. He was soon walking alongside

68

this man, hearing those murmurs, those prayers, with the procession carrying the large crucifix.

Instinct took hold. He turned to look at the man beside him, whose face was shielded by the hood. Then, slowly, in what seemed like an eternity of time, the hooded figure turned his head to look at Antonio. Staring back at him was the face of a skeleton!

Antonio took off running for his life, his blood racing, his heart pounding, until he made it to Saro's house, where he jumped into bed, not undressing but pulling the sheets over his head and sweating, his body trembling until he saw the rays of the morning light.

He never told anyone about his experience with the apparitions. And he never again challenged the spirits, whether of this world or not.

CHAPTER
SEVEN

WITHIN THREE YEARS, Toño Boglione had become a person of note in La Playa. Not only that but also in town. His proposition to Juan-Carlos that they expand their business to the town proper had paid off. The people from town were just as addicted to the lottery as the peons from the slums.

Juan-Carlos took on an apprentice, and Antonio learned all he could about the business. The one problem they encountered were the authorities in town. La Playa did not have any police force, no magistrate, not even a sheriff, and Juan-Carlos could conduct his business with impunity. Not so in town. The local police, all eight of them, were always on the lookout for crime and all wicked dealings since now the orders came from the americanos in San Juan, who, unlike their Spanish predecessors, put great stock in law and order.

The minute Juan-Carlos went to town to indiscreetly sound out the locals as to his lottery scheme, he was taken in for questioning by the local gendarmerie. Not only that, even worse, doña Saro's place was raided by the authorities. Her homemade rum confiscated, and her still apparatus destroyed.

In this moment of crisis, Antonio took a page from his experiences back home in Napoli. There, the local mafia had simply bought off the police. If it could work there, it could work in Ponce as well.

And it worked as planned. A greased palm here, a greased palm there, and, presto, Juan-Carlos could sell his tickets in Ponce proper, even in the main plaza if he so desired.

Doña Saro was a mite more difficult. Here, Antonio and Juan-Carlos had to buy out the local judge, one Eduardo Benítez, from the prominent Benítez family in town. The donation was made, and Saro was free to continue her service to La Playa.

By now, like most men in town, Antonio had grown a mustache. This was not the full growth handles that had been favored for generations. He opted for a pencil-thin mustache, just like those he had seen sported by John Gilbert and John Barrymore in silent movies back in Napoli. Again, he was ahead of the trend. By the decade's end almost every young man in Ponce would be wearing a pencil-thin mustache.

It was during the annual fiestas *patronales*, the patron saint festival, that Antonio, wearing his newly acquired mustache, first laid eyes on Leticia Benítez Izquierdo. He could tell she was a modern girl, unlike the older woman chaperoning her. Leticia Benítez wore a short-sleeved cotton dress with the hem just below the knee. Not like her chaperone with a full-length skirt that went down to her feet. Also, the chaperone wore a mantilla. Leticia Benítez did not. In fact, she wore no hat at all, unlike most women at the festival.

The patron saint festival was one of the social high points in Ponce. It was held on a grassy field not far from the center of town and included dances, parades, religious processions, and, of course, food and drink. The food included meat pies called *pasteles*, and deep-fried savories known as *chuchifritos*. In deep platters you had *tostones*, or fried plantains, beloved by all; not to mention *pernil*, roasted pork shoulder, and the green bananas and cassava stuffed with sautéed pork and called *alcapurrias*; also, *pollo frito*, or simple fried chicken. There was steamed conch meat, or *carrucho*, and sautéed island crabs, and yellow rice. All these delicacies combined in a deep, redolent fragrance that wafted over the whole festival. And to quench your thirst, there was not only the traditional beer and rum but also coquito, the powerful rum-based drink made with coconut. And for the teetotalers, there was fresh coconut water from green coconuts on ice with their tops sliced off with a machete.

Antonio was oblivious to it all. And this included the guitar-strumming troubadours roaming the grounds and singing "Las Mañanitas," the traditional birthday song in honor of the patron saint, Our Lady of Guadalupe.

His eyes were fixed on the Benítez girl, standing a few yards away and licking a stick of cotton candy, a new treat to Ponce.

Standing alongside him, Juan-Carlos knew something was going on. "Toño?" he nudged. "Toño?"

Antonio, snapping back to reality, turned to his friend and asked, "Who's that girl?"

"Which one?"

Antonio motioned with his head in the direction of the Benítez girl. "The one with the print dress."

Through his eyeglasses, Juan-Carlos scanned closer. "Oh. Funny you should ask. That's the daughter of Eduardo Benítez. You know him, the local judge. We had recent dealings with him."

Antonio had quick recall. "Oh yes. He granted us permission to work the town."

"Yes, he did." Juan-Carlos had a hint of caution of his voice. "And we want to keep it that way."

"What do you mean?"

"It would behoove us to stay in his good graces."

"I don't understand."

"I know what you're thinking, Toño," Juan-Carlos surmised. "I would advise, proceed with caution. We don't want to antagonize the good judge."

"I would never consider anything like that," Antonio said. "You know what a cautious fellow I am." He tapped Juan-Carlos on the arm, adding, "I'll see you later," and was about to depart.

Juan Carlos clutched Antonio's arm. "Where do you think you're going?"

"I'm going to say hello to that young lady."

"Let me warn you," Juan-Carlos said carefully, "that young lady is the daughter of the town magistrate. And she is new to our society. She has just returned from Spain, where she was raised and educated. She's not used to our ways."

"I'm not going to accost her," Antonio maintained. "I simply want to welcome her to Ponce."

"Toño . . . ," but before Juan-Carlos could stop his apprentice, Antonio was gone.

Leticia Benítez was trying to wipe off some cotton candy from her chin and laughing at her efforts. Then she noted the presence of the young man with a silly little mustache who was staring at her, but in a funny way. Her chaperone immediately turned and glared at the intruder.

"Yes?" Leticia inquired.

What Antonio noticed immediately was that, though she had dark hair, her eyes were blue-gray. No one in Ponce had such eyes. They mesmerized him. After an embarrassing silence, he managed to say, "My name is Antonio Boglione, and I wish to . . . to greet you on behalf of Ponce." Then, aping what he had seen in those silent movies of by-gone days, he bowed slightly.

"Greet me?"

"Yes, I would like to."

"Who are you?" the chaperone demanded to know. And turning to Leticia: "Who is this impudent young man?"

Leticia raised a hand. "No, let him speak."

Haltingly at first, Antonio Boglione, on his best behavior, told the young lady that he too came from overseas, and wished her happiness in her new life in Ponce, and that he was a humble servant who had done business with her father and, as such, hoped that if he could assist her or her family in any way, he was at her disposal.

The young lady had no idea what he was talking about. But she did like his smile and earnestness, whether her chaperone approved or not.

After he had finished and an uncomfortable, long moment of silence, she handed her half-eaten cotton candy stick to Antonio, said, "Thank you," and departed with her chaperone in tow.

Antonio stood moonstruck where he was, holding the stick of half-eaten cotton candy. "Toño? Toño?" He barely heard Juan-Carlos calling his name.

"I'm going to marry that girl," he said then and there.

"What?"

"I'm going to marry that girl," he repeated.

"You're out of your mind," Juan-Carlos told him.

CHAPTER EIGHT

INDEED HE WAS crazy, doña Saro echoed. The Benítezes were one of the most prominent families in Ponce. And the Benítez patriarch was the town judge. How could they allow their daughter to consort with a nobody from La Playa?

"I have prospects," Antonio told doña Saro.

"They damn better be good prospects," Saro replied.

After some reflection, Antonio went to visit the Benítez family at their spacious home on Victoria Street. He went unannounced and was denied entry by a snooty, elderly maid who mistook him for some laborer or, worse, some farmhand.

How to get to see the Benítez daughter? It was a confounding problem and a challenge. He had beaten the Headless Count and the spirit of the cemetery. He could lick this problem as well, though he would never tell anyone about his encounter with the robed apparitions carrying a crucifix in the middle of the night.

He sought counsel with the only person wise enough to advise him, the Scholarly Jew, who told him, unless he made a quick fortune or upped his status quickly, he had no chance of bridging the gap between himself and the Benítez clan, let alone of wooing their daughter. "You need to do something impressive," Jacobo advised him.

Chance intervened once more. At the time, La Playa had no movie theatre. In fact, there was no movie house in all of Ponce. On special occasions, a blackboard from the local school would be set up in the plaza, a white bed sheet placed over the blackboard, and some silent cartoon or old movie would be shown from a 35mm movie projector someone had brought in from town. On these evenings almost everyone in town crowded into the plaza to see this miracle of cinema.

One night, watching an American cartoon called *Steamboat Willie,* one of the first of its kind and with primitive sound effects, Antonio turned to Octavio Mendoza and declared, "We need a movie theatre."

Sitting on the stone plaza bench, his eyes fixed on the happenings on the movie screen, Octavio said, "What?"

"We need a movie theatre, a movie house."

Octavio turned his head to Antonio. "You're right. We do need a movie house." Then he thought on it. "How're we going to get one?"

"I'll build one," Antonio said.

The next day he approached the Benítez residence in town, this time dressed in a dark suit with a white starched collar and appropriate tie. He also wore a stylish straw boater hat, what in those days was known as a "pra-pra." Again facing the snooty maid, he stated that he, Antonio Boglione, had a business proposition for don Eduardo Benítez, and handed the maid a business card with his name typed on it.

The maid went indoors, and Antonio waited.

She returned and opened the front gate to let Antonio enter.

Don Benítez met him in his study, a room full of books, mostly law journals in Spanish. Antonio, with his boater hat held deferentially in his hands, was struck to see that a big black metal typewriter nestled on a stand next to don Benítez's desk. The only other typewriter Antonio knew about in Ponce was the one owned by the local printer, where Antonio had had his one business card made.

After perusing the card in his hand, don Eduardo looked up and asked formally, "What can I do for you?"

"It's not what you can do for me, don Eduardo," Antonio answered in the same formal tone. "It's what I can do for you."

Two months later, La Playa had its first movie theatre, right across from the plaza, the first genuine cinema in Ponce. How had it come about? Simple: Antonio had proposed to Eduardo Benítez a business endeavor. The town and La Playa were growing. There was new leadership in San Juan. The mantra coming from the American overseers was one of industry, entrepreneurship. New technologies were evolving; among them, movies. And there were talking pictures now. Amazing! Who wouldn't pay to see such a thing, no matter what their standing in society? The movie house was an investment that would pay many dividends in the long run. Antonio had seen movie houses in his native Napoli, and they were packed every night. He was sure the good don Eduardo had noticed the same in San Juan. Why not take advantage of it?

Antonio stated that he and his partner, the esteemed Juan-Carlos Quiles, would fund the project out of their own pockets. They would be honored if the esteemed don Eduardo Benítez would become a part of such a progressive and profitable project. Don Eduardo, in his capacity as magistrate, would ensure they got all the proper warrants and forms needed for the construction of the theatre. In return, don Eduardo would share in the profits from such a venture, say ten percent?

Eduardo Benítez agreed. Even so, he stipulated that his share be fifteen percent of the profits, never missing an opportunity to increase his wealth. They shook hands, and Ponce had its first movie house.

And it became a big deal, both in La Playa and in Ponce proper. The date for the inauguration of the Ponce Theatre was on a Saturday night. And a talking picture would be shown, a movie from Latin American starring the Argentine actress Libertad Lamarque. The citizens of Ponce could hear her talk and sing!

As befitting a special event, everyone came in their best attire. No *guayaberas* or work shirts. Instead, suits, hats, and ties for the men; and for the women, elegant dresses and, despite the heat, the appropriate hats and gloves. Antonio and Juan-Carlos came attired in white dinner jackets, which they had rented from a garment house in Ponce. Don Eduardo, as befitted his station, came attired in tails, white gloves, and top hat, as if he were Fred Astaire. Leticia came in a strapless formal gown, which had the tongues wagging in La Playa: the tops of her tits were almost visible!

Antonio was enraptured anew by this lovely young thing with the blue-gray eyes. She, for her part, barely acknowledged him, which bothered him no end.

"She barely looked at me the whole time!" he complained to Juan-Carlos after the evening was over. "I spent the whole night making small talk with don Eduardo."

"That is her part in all of this," Juan-Carlos explained. "She knows you're interested, but for her to show similar interest would be unbecoming, given her status. Go slow, Toño. She'll come around. You'll see."

There was no way Leticia could deny this ardent suitor who, after his business success in Ponce, visited the home almost daily, always bringing flowers or candy, a suggestion from Jacobo Levy who thought it might help matters.

Her father seemed to have developed a liking for this industrious young man. He knew where he was going, and he wanted to get ahead. This impressed Eduardo Benítez no end. They would sit in the parlor, smoking cigars, and talk about this and that, and how Ponce could be put on the map so that someday it would rival San Juan as a depository for commerce, learning, the arts, and, yes, tourism. Why not? There were always Americans with good money looking for warm, exotic climes. So why not Ponce?

He had gained the old man's favor, but the daughter still maintained her cold demeanor. And this riled him even more.

So back to the Scholarly Jew he went for advice. And Jacobo told him that there was more to life than lottery numbers and commerce.

Young women sought to be enchanted, pampered, and swept off their feet. There had to be some romance somewhere.

"What can I do?" Antonio asked helplessly.

"Do you know about the week of *la danza?* About the ball?"

Antonio had no idea what Jacobo was talking about. "What?"

"The week of *la danza.*"

"What's that?"

"It's a cultural and festive event in these parts. All members of society from the highest to the low, but mainly the highest, attend the annual dance at the La Perla Theatre. And they all have a dance where they sway to the waltzes of Juan Morel Campos."

"Who's he?"

Jacobo was shocked. "You've never heard of Juan Morel Campos?"

"No."

"He's one of the great exponents of *la danza,* a form of waltz native to this island."

"What has that got to do with me and Leticia Benítez?"

"Toño," Jacobo counseled, "invite her to the dance. She probably knows about it and is dying to go."

"But," Antonio spluttered, "I don't dance."

"Well, you better learn. The danza as a waltz is considered sacred in these parts."

"What's a waltz?" Antonio wanted to know.

Jacobo Levy rolled his eyes.

CHAPTER
NINE

JACOBO KNEW HE had his work cut out for him. How to instruct a local yokel in the fine points of the danza? He himself had never danced a waltz, though he knew about its social standing. Antonio needed a tutor, and it had to be done quickly since the ball was in a week's time.

Among his possessions, Jacobo had an old gramophone, which you had to play by cranking a lever on the side of the record player. He also had some old records, among them some danzas. Doña Saro had been a partisan of the waltz in her youth, and she was recruited as Antonio's dance tutor. Dutifully, every evening after the chores were done, Saro would show him in her cramped living room how to master the danza.

It wasn't easy. Antonio had two proverbial left feet. Yet he was determined.

Doña Saro was just as determined, and motivated as well. The scratchy needle on an ancient disk brought back memories of long-ago nights with music and young dandies twirling and whirling with her to the strains of piano, violin, and trombone. She actually enjoyed instructing Antonio, even though her poor toes had to bear the brunt of more than one misstep. "One-two-three, one-two-three, left foot forward, right foot back, turn, one-two-three, one-two-three . . . Let the music guide you, loosen your hand, don't press so much on the waist . . . Relax, relax."

A week later, Antonio escorted Leticia to the ball at the Teatro La Perla. He was in his best suit, and she was ravishing in a long red gown, with her hair up in a formal cut and those luscious blue-gray eyes.

Everyone remarked as to how beautiful she was. Just like Ponce itself, which was called the Pearl of the South. Eduardo Benítez, standing among his friends and other notaries, beamed as she and Antonio took to the floor.

Doing their first turn at the waltz, Leticia remarked, "I didn't know you could dance this well."

Antonio smiled. "I had a good teacher."

"Indeed, you did."

When the orchestra of local musicians stopped playing and the dance was over, Antonio escorted Leticia back to her place alongside her father. "That was very good, Toño," don Eduardo complimented.

"Thank you," Antonio said. The advice of Jacobo Levy had not left him. Be solicitous, be attentive, impress her . . . "Would you care for a refreshment, Leticia?"

Leticia flapped at her face with a small handmade fan. "Yes, I would. It is rather hot in here."

Antonio bowed formally. "I shall be back with refreshment."

When he had left for the long side table laden with punch bowls and snacks, don Eduardo asked his daughter, "What do you think of this young man tonight?"

"Well, he has changed," she replied. "He comports himself well and does know how to dance." She eyed him at the table with the punch bowl. "I never suspected he knew so much about our culture."

Eduardo cast a side glance at his daughter. "What do you mean, 'our culture'?"

"You must know that he's not from here. I'm told he comes from overseas."

"Yes, I've heard," Eduardo said. "And it's to his credit that he has accommodated so well to our island."

Antonio returned with a glass of rum punch in his hand, which he handed to Leticia. "Thank you," Leticia responded.

Eduardo turned to acknowledge some new arrivals. "Excuse me, my dear, but I must greet some guests from the mayoralty. I shall return shortly. You and Toño enjoy yourselves with some more danzas."

When Eduardo had left, Antonio said to Leticia, "You must be very proud of your father. He's very well regarded in this town."

"Yes, I am very proud of him, and so is my mother."

"Where's your mother tonight?" Antonio asked. "Why isn't she here to enjoy this festive occasion?"

"Alas, my mother doesn't feel well tonight. I think it's the heat. She can never get used to it. When we were in Spain it never got this hot. I think she misses a more moderate climate."

"And do you miss Spain?" Antonio asked.

"Yes, and no," Leticia said. "Believe it or not, they're stricter there than they are here. People in Ponce seem to be more convivial. Not as educated or cultured, but more convivial."

Antonio gave a questioning look. "So you think Ponce is less cultured?"

"I was raised in Spain. My parents sent me there to obtain the best of all educations, and besides, we have relatives in Spain."

"I imagined as such," Antonio ventured to say. "Is your family originally from Spain?"

"Not exactly. My grandmother lived in Spain. She was a duchess. My mother was born in Spain. My father met her there, and after they married they came back to the island, where he had his business."

"I imagined you were not from the island. Your blue eyes give you away and—"

85

"They're not exactly blue," Leticia broached. "I'm told they're more greenish-gray than blue. But to your original question, I was born in Ponce. I got my eyes from my mother, who got the same coloring from her grandmother. What's odd is that my mother's brothers all had dark eyes. The females seem to be fairer."

"That is unique," Antonio had to admit. "But whatever the reason, your eyes are truly lovely."

Leticia blushed. "Well, thank you, Antonio. What a nice compliment."

"Please call me Toño. I would like to think that we're friends."

"We are friends, Antonio—I mean, Toño."

CHAPTER
TEN

THEY WERE MARRIED a year later. True, Leticia did not love him, and Antonio suspected as much. No matter. He assured himself that in time she would come to love him. It was just another obstacle to be overcome. She accepted his formal proposal, and Eduardo Benítez gave his blessing unequivocally to the union.

The only one not too enthused at the outcome was his partner, Juan-Carlos, who had always harbored a wish that someday Antonio would marry his eldest daughter, Estrella. But he acquiesced and wished Antonio well in his nuptials. Not only that, he gave Antonio a loan with which to build a new home on a vacant lot on Alfonso XII Street in La Playa. This and the money Antonio had saved was enough for him to contract Domingo Madera to build a large house made to Antonio's specifications. It would have a concrete veranda, not a wooden one as was the custom, three spacious bedrooms with windows facing north to get as much evening air as possible, and large cotton curtains to mitigate the heat of the day. Each room would have standing candelabras and candleholders to illume the house at night, and not just wick lanterns. In the backyard there would be two *letrinas*, not just one, and of the best construction. And the best furnishings and tableware would be brought in from retailers in San Juan and parts beyond. He intended it to be a grand house, with opulence and renown.

At Antonio's insistence, and to don Eduardo's chagrin, the wedding was held at the local church in La Playa, not at the cathedral in the Ponce square. Reluctantly, Eduardo agreed, though he could not understand why Antonio would prefer the poor parish of La Playa instead of the grand church. Though the local priest, Father Ignacio, was overwhelmed with joy to preside at what would be not only a mere wedding but the social event of the season. Little did he know that it was all due to doña Saro, who confided to Antonio that she would be immensely happy if he, whom she considered as a son, would wed in the same church that she and her beloved, departed husband, Ramon, had wed forty years before. And how could Antonio deny her that wish?

And so it was that for the first time in its history the street adjoining the church was crammed with carriages and automobiles from the town proper, with proper ladies and gentlemen from Ponce and beyond who came to witness the event. Even the mayor sent a representative to witness the wedding. Those who could not get in or didn't have the clout to be inside the church stood outside in a throng to see Toño, the local boy made good, marry into the prominent Benítez family.

Inside the church, don Eduardo and his immediate and extended family sat like royalty in the front pew. On the other side, representing Antonio's kin, were Juan-Carlos and doña Saro, looking nothing like the bootlegger she was, but regal and proud, for the first time dressed to the nines in an ermine dress and wearing a huge white hat with flower patterns on it.

Antonio's drinking buddies from Carmelo's cafetín sat in the back pews, and they hollered and whistled when the bride appeared at the hand of her father as she walked down the aisle. A stern glance from Father Ignacio, standing in front of the altar, quieted them down immediately.

Almost everyone in La Playa was present at the church since everyone was invited. The only conspicuous absence was Jacoby Levy, who, for reasons only known to him, never attended town functions, social or divine.

The ceremony went like clockwork; then the carriages and automobiles departed for the reception at La Perla Theatre, which had been decked out with bunting, tables and chairs, musicians, and all manner of food and drink. Antonio had insisted that there be plenty of rum and beer for everyone, and this included some of doña Saro's product.

As was the custom, the bride and groom left in the early evening, while the revelers stayed behind dancing and partying until the wee hours of the morning.

Antonio and Leticia were driven to the Melia Hotel, not far from the plaza. A special suite had been reserved for them on the top floor, with their bed decorated with flower petals and perfumed branches.

The wedding may have been grand, but the wedding night was not. Antonio, like his new bride, was a virgin. He had never consorted with a woman in a carnal way, not even in his native Napoli. He was woefully deficient and did not know what to do. The equipment was there, but not the skill. And Leticia, who harbored romantic dreams of a special day and special night, was left disappointed and unfulfilled. And Antonio could not understand why the next day she was crying. "Aren't you happy?" he asked.

Her response was to turn her head and sob into the pillow.

What now? Antonio was left bewildered. And when they went to their new home, her mood had not changed. She barely spoke and was glum.

Antonio realized he might know something about life but he knew nothing about women.

So back it was for another counseling session with Jacobo Levy, who, after listening quietly to Antonio's tale of woe, said simply, "In this matter I cannot help. You need the advice of someone who can counsel you in matters pertaining to women. What you need is a primer on what to do."

After a somber pause, Jacobo added, "Papo Mendosa may be of more assistance in this than I."

"Papo?"

"Just do as I say."

Antonio went to Octavio Mendosa, who realized what was up immediately. "You've never been with a woman before, have you?"

"Not until my wedding night," Antonio admitted.

Octavio drew a breath. "The Scholarly Jew was right. You need a primer."

"He said that too. What do you mean?"

"Come by tomorrow and bring money," Octavio said hastily.

"Bring money?"

"That's right, bring money."

They met at Carmelo's the next evening, had two drinks, and then Octavio called upon Rumaldo Garcia, a local who had a carriage that he used to ferry people to town. Except this time they were not going to town. They went to the outskirts of Ponce and the fabled Red House, which was so called because it had a massive red door in front. Inside was a different story.

They were greeted by the madam, doña Fela, an obese woman with garish red lipstick and permed hair. "Papo!" She spread her arms wide, and Octavio was deep into the folds of an embrace, his head nestling on massive breasts constrained within an all-too-tight dress.

"Papo, it's been ages. Where have you been?"

"I've been rather busy," Octavio said, "but even at my busiest I make time for your glorious establishment."

"And you're always welcomed." She turned to gaze at Antonio. "And who is this handsome man?"

"This is Toño, my friend. He seeks companionship and comfort. But more, he seeks knowledge in the ways of . . ." Octavio paused, seeking to explain.

90

Fela fondly sought to touch Antonio's cheek. He drew back. She lowered her hand and, smiling, said, "Have you been with a woman before?"

"I am a married man," Antonio said with conviction.

The madam gave Octavio a puzzled look.

"Fela," he explained, "my friend Toño is recently married, and he needs a primer in such matters, if you know what I mean."

Recognition flooded Fela's face. "Ahhh. Yes. I understand now. In fact, I have more than one married gentleman here who needed, as we say, 'coaxing.'"

"Yes, that's precisely it," Octavio agreed at once.

Doña Fela snaked her hand through Antonio's arm. "Don't worry, Toño. When you leave tonight, you'll be a tiger in bed. Not only that, you'll know how to please your woman."

Antonio turned to Octavio, looking concerned.

"Don't worry," Octavio reassured. "Just follow Fela and do as she says."

Fela took him upstairs, where scantily clad women varying in ages and sizes were parading about. Fela ignored them and instead guided him toward one of the bedrooms. "What you need is my best girl. You need a true expert. Wait here."

She opened the door to let him into a room painted totally yellow, with two wick lanterns on each side of a massive dresser, also painted yellow. The room had one window with red curtains, which showed dim outlines of the surrounding hills in the encroaching dark. There were no chairs. He sat on a bed festooned with cushions and frilly pillows, and waited.

The woman finally came in. She was not the beauty he had expected. She had cropped black hair, and her face was angular, with high cheekbones. She had a fine nose and small mouth, and her skin was tawny colored, almost cinnamon. She wasn't beautiful, but she was striking.

"My name is Milagros," she said in a throaty whisper, "and I have come to show you things."

Antonio put to good use the things Milagros showed him. It did make a difference in his marriage. And a year later Antonio was blessed with a son, who was named Camilo in honor of Camillo di Cavour, one of the founding fathers of Italy. For a while, Leticia was put off by this decision. She had wanted to name the boy Eduardo, after her father. They compromised a year later when a girl was born and named Maria, after her grandmother.

Yet despite increasing family happiness and obligations, Antonio could not forget nor put out of his mind the tawny-skinned woman with the cropped black hair.

CHAPTER
ELEVEN

ANTONIO WAS NOW totally accepted within the community. Indeed, he had proved his worth. After Americo Pichón's house, in the center of Lorenza Bizo Street, had burned down, he was there with all the others, hauling buckets of water from the local well, trying to stem the flames.

It was in vain. Americo Pichón's house all but disappeared in the inferno. Fortunate for him and Dionisia, the woman who looked after him since Pichón was an invalid, both got out alive from the burning house, with Dionisia cradling her beloved cat, Romeo, in her arms. Then and there Antonio decided that La Playa needed a firehouse. Not like the one in Ponce proper, which was being refurbished so that it looked like a candy-colored fire station; no, La Playa required a genuine local fire department since it could not be dependent on Ponce for fire safety.

Antonio set to work, sounding out Juan-Carlos, don Eduardo, and even getting to sell his proposal to the Ponce mayor. He had become that well known, and besides, he was paying off everyone in the mayoralty in order to maintain his numbers racket and Saro's moonshine.

Up to now his business dealings had been profitable, much more so than he had imagined. He would pay to restore Americo Pichón's house out of his own pocket. More, he would put up the initial investment in a firehouse. Not only that, he would equip the firefighters with the equipment and clothing needed. As to the fire wagons, horse-drawn vehicles were a thing of the past, although everybody loved them. Even the main

Ponce firehouse had transferred over to automotive fire trucks. He and the mayoralty came to an agreement: since he would supply the firemen with their needs, the mayoralty would donate one of their fire trucks to La Playa, provided Antonio would pay for the upkeep. It was a good deal all around. La Playa would get its firehouse and fire truck, the Ponce mayor would get credit for his innovation and goodwill toward the playeros, and Antonio would enhance his standing with everyone.

At the inauguration of the firehouse, the mayor insisted that Antonio be honored as an honorary fireman and that he, like the other firefighters, wear their formal blue-and-white uniform with appropriate cap and epaulettes. Antonio readily agreed, standing proud with the others in his formal uniform. And henceforth, on every anniversary honoring the firehouse, he would wear the full regalia.

Among those witnessing this majestic event was a tawny-skinned young woman with closely cropped hair. Milagros Pagan took note of the young man being feted by everyone, and whom she had tutored. He was unlike her other customers. He had been so vulnerable and naïve, yet determined in his performance. It had left an impression.

Neither had Antonio forgotten his experience. He went back to doña Fela's place, and this time without Octavio to accompany him. Milagros was not surprised to see him again. Somehow, she knew he would come back. In the back of her mind, she heard Fela's constant admonition: don't get involved with the customers. Somehow, she felt, this time it was different. And after his third visit to her, he asked if he could see her unofficially on the outside, beyond the confines of her place of work. It was an unusual request, one that no one had ever offered to Milagros. At first, she said no. By this third visit, she revealed that she did her shopping every Wednesday morning at El Mercado, the marketplace in the center of town.

Not far from the main plaza, and bordering the streets of Guadalupe and Leon, was the old marketplace. Actually, it was two markets in one: a main marketplace with stalls full of local produce and retail items and the smaller market stalls to one side known as the Plaza of the Dogs since stray dogs congregated in this area at night.

The main marketplace carried everything from root plants to coconuts, live chickens for sale, blood sausage, and every condiment and herb imaginable. The first thing that hit you when you entered the *mercado* was the smell, a congruence of ripe fruit, stale vegetation, live poultry, and caged rabbits—all mingling in one enclosed area a block long and teeming with buyers and sellers, with beggars on the sidewalk, hands outstretched for a coin; old women haggling with the vendors over the price of a yam or plantain; men playing dominoes on an empty chicken coop that served as a stand; fishmongers unloading the day's catch from the Ponce docks; buyers poking at a ripe avocado or sniffing at some octopus or ink-stained squid fresh from the sea; and everywhere the sound of voices: high cackles, low groans, exultant yelps, men and women gesturing at this or that item, whether fresh or dried, day old or week old; trying to decipher whether the eggs on sale were freshly laid, *del paiz* or the country, or from neighboring Mayaguez or points beyond.

Among the many stalls, Milagros frequented one that was known as a botanica. This stall sold potions, tarot cards, powders and oils, and esoteric manuals based on the Santeria religious cult that had been fostered by African slaves since the time of the Spaniards. Here, Antonio found Milagros purchasing red glass candles and a small bottle with water colored green from a root plant stuffed inside.

"You came!" Milagros was surprised to see Antonio. Honestly, she had not expected him to show.

"Of course, I came," Antonio said. "When I make a promise, I keep it." He noted the items she held in her hands. "Do you practice Santeria?"

"Not really," Milagros said. "But my mother does believe in certain things." She held up the items she carried. "These are for her. She believes that Obatala looks over her."

"Obatala?"

"One of the spiritual saints."

"A spiritual saint?"

"One who watches over people."

"Do you believe it?" Antonio asked.

Milagros thought for a minute. "It makes no difference whether I believe it or not. She does, and it's important to her."

"You're a good daughter to look after your parents," Antonio said. "It's an obligation and a duty. I believe the same."

"Are your parents here, in Ponce?" Milagros asked.

"No," said Antonio. "My parents came from Napoli, where I was born. I have no one there now. But I do believe that family is important."

Milagros studied him for moment and said, "You believe in family. That's good; so do I. Family is all we have in this world, whether they approve of you or not."

"Does your family approve of you?" Antonio asked guardedly.

"Some do and some don't. But my mother and I are still close."

"I admire that! Your loyalty. That's one of the reasons I wanted to see you again. And I hope I can."

"So do I," she said.

Antonio asked suddenly, "Would it be proper to ask if we could perhaps have dinner sometime. I'm told that in Los Meros, along the seacoast, they have fine seafood restaurants and . . ."

Milagros was wary. "I don't know if that would be good. You see—"

"Please," Antonio said, looking right into her eyes, "I really would like to see you again. I know it may be strange, but I believe we have so much in common. We both honor our families, and"—he fumbled for the right words—"I can tell you're a good person."

Milagros smiled. "It's nice to know, to think that I'm a good person. I think you are one also, and—"

Antonio didn't let her finish. "So it's settled! We'll have dinner at Los Meros."

She was still hesitant. "I . . ."

Antonio reached out and touched her hand. "Please. I really would like to see you again, on a social occasion."

His eyes seemed so truthful. Her reservations vanished. "Yes," she said.

CHAPTER TWELVE

HE SAT CROSS-LEGGED behind the podium, this olive-complexioned man with the hollow cheeks and well-groomed mustache. He was dressed in a formal dark suit and black bow tie. Anybody present would have taken him for a school teacher or an academic, which he was. This was the first time he would speak before a crowd at La Perla Theatre. The anticipation had been great.

He sat in the middle of a row of notables from the Ponce elite. But all attention was centered on him, and only him. When he was introduced by the first speaker, he rose, bowed formally to the man who had introduced him, and proceeded to the podium, holding a sheaf of papers in his hand.

Behind him was a large banner hanging from the ceiling and, in bold black letters, proclaiming: "THE MOTHERLAND IS VALOR AND SACRIFICE."

At first he spoke quietly, slowly, almost in a conversational tone. And, measure by measure, his voice rose, like a wave building upon the ocean, drop atop drop, until it was roaring, gushing. He spoke about how he believed in "numbers," and how these numbers would grow and multiply until independence would be achieved by those numbers and those who believed in the "Nationalist Ideal." He decried the "yanqui war against the Puerto Rican nation" and how that nation had been subjugated, humiliated, enslaved, and colonized; how "our national territory" had been invaded and occupied by a foreign power; and how the yanqui government had been at war against the Puerto Rican nation since that invasion.

"But ours is a party of struggle!" he thundered. "A party whose only sacred mission is for the independence and liberty of our people." And he spoke of how he was dedicated to that cause and genuine social justice.

"We demand Puerto Rican independence!" he shouted. "We demand our rightful place in the sun!"

His voice grew stronger, bigger; his body shook with every word as he raised a fist denouncing an invader whose policy of hunger and slavery had emasculated the Puerto Rican heart. And he spoke of how the people could no longer allow the destruction of their history and culture, how they could no longer allow their sons to be killed and their women to be raped. "Just as the Irish patriots in Ireland have struggled for their freedom, so must we," he exhorted. "When tyranny is law, revolution is order! The Nationalist Party will not remain quiet in the face of such travesty! We will not allow this tyranny! We must remove the yoke of oppression in our land!"

He ended his fiery oration by declaring, "We are not yanqui citizens. We are Puerto Ricans!"

The audience surged with every utterance and every denunciation. Sitting in the back row, Octavio Mendosa hung on every word, visibly moved and elated at the majestic, scathing pronouncements of El Maestro, don Pedro Albizu Campos.

Sitting next to him, Antonio Boglione remained quiet and rather pensive, given the tumult around him. Octavio rose to his feet, clapping enthusiastically along with the rest in the cavernous hall of La Perla. "Isn't he great?" Octavio gushed. "He speaks from the heart of every Puerto Rican!"

Antonio forced himself to stand with the adoring crowd, politely clapping and genuinely wondering what it was all about.

When the event was over, Octavio was among the first to rush to the front of the theater to shake don Albizu's hand, while Antonio waited for him in the back row.

Outside in the street facing the theatre was a group of young men handing out pamphlets advocating the Nationalist cause. They were all similarly dressed in black shirts, black ties, and white pants. Antonio saw that at one end of the line a black-shirted young man carried a banner, more like a flag, with a white cross on a black background. At that moment, Antonio had a feeling of unease.

Octavio grabbed a pamphlet and showed it to him. "It's all there—what we need to know," said Octavio. "The Maestro speaks the truth."

Antonio asked, "Why do they call him the Maestro?"

Octavio was dismayed. "Didn't you hear him speak? The man is a genius. He was the first paisano to graduate from Harvard! He speaks six languages. He's our finest orator."

"He does speak well," Antonio mused.

"Speak well? The man tells the truth! We are the colonial subjects of a colonial power. And the sooner we realize that, the sooner we can fight for our freedom."

"But aren't you free?" Antonio said.

"How can one be free when you are under the colonial yoke of the yanquis?"

"So, you want Puerto Rico to be a free nation?"

"Yes!"

"Aren't you free in what you do now?"

Octavio shook his heads doggedly. "No! We're not free. We are slaves!"

"Slaves?" Antonio wondered. "How can you say you're a slave? You work, you get paid. You go to Carmelo's cafetín and get drunk, and once in a while you get laid at doña Fela's."

"It's not the same," Octavio disagreed. "We're not free men!"

"How are we not free men?"

"We don't rule our own country. Don't you understand that? Being a Puerto Rican and all?"

"I'm not a Puerto Rican," Antonio let know. "I come from Napoli. Still, from what I see, things are better here than they ever were in Italy. And Italy is an independent country, so I'm told, and it's run by Fascists."

Octavio looked bewildered. "What are Fascists?"

"People who run the government in Italy. And there, if you speak out against the government, you get in trouble." Antonio looked around. "Here that doesn't seem to be the problem."

Octavio drew back, casting a long, measured gaze at Antonio. "You're right, you wouldn't understand. You're not a *boricua*."

That same evening at dinner, Antonio poked at his food, his brow furrowed, and nursing a glum silence. Leticia noticed it, as she noticed something else. "We're serving wine tonight," she observed. "When did this happen?"

Lifting his silence, Antonio replied, "I thought you might like it. I'm told they serve wine at dinner in Spain, as they do in my homeland." He shrugged. "So I told Elena to get us some wine."

Leticia showed pleasant surprise. "Elena is our cook. Where would she know to get wine?"

"She knows where to get it," Antonio said. "She knows all the purveyors in town. We're not the only ones here who enjoy wine from time to time."

"Well, in that case, I'm glad you asked her." Leticia reached for her wine glass, holding it up appreciatively. "Thank you."

Antonio gave a wan smile, holding up his glass as well. "My pleasure." Without tasting it, he placed the glass back on the table.

Leticia scanned her husband's face. "Toño, what's wrong?"

"I'm sorry," Antonio said. "Please forgive me. I'm just not feeling all that good tonight."

"Are you unwell?"

"No, I'm well. Just that today was an unusual day."

Leticia showed concern. "In what way?"

Antonio stopped playing with his food, put down his fork. "I went with Papo Mendosa today to one of those meetings they have in town. You know, one of those political meetings. This one was held at La Perla Theater, and this guy gave a speech. His name is Campos, Albizu Campos."

Leticia's eyes went wide. "You mean, don Pedro?"

"I don't know about any Pedro. Everybody called him Albizu."

"Yes," Leticia said. "I heard that Albizu Campos would be in town today. He's a famous man in this island. In fact, he was born in Ponce. He's the head of the Nationalist Party."

"Yeah, that's what it was," Antonio revealed. "This Nationalist Party thing. Well, he spoke, and everybody went delirious. Like he was a god or something."

"To some people he is a god," Leticia explained. "He espouses Puerto Rican independence."

"Independence from what?"

"From the Americans. We are a colony."

"Are we?" Antonio wasn't so sure. "From what I see, Puerto Ricans run everything here, from the mayoralty to the police. I should know, I pay them off. What's the complaint?"

Leticia sought to explain further. "To the Nationalists, they see us as being totally dependent on the Americans. We don't have our own army or navy; the Americans call all the shots from San Juan. They, the Nationalists, want a free country."

"A free country from what? People would starve if it wasn't for the Americans."

"Look," Leticia said reasonably, "I have no problems with the Americans. Supposedly, my family had dealings with them when they first came, and it was profitable to all. I'm just telling you what the Nationalists stand for." She paused, gazing at her husband keenly. "But that's not it, is it, Toño? There's more. I've never heard of you involved in anything political. So what's this all about?"

"Oh . . ." Antonio grasped for words. "It's just that . . . what I saw today gave me cause for concern. Papo Mendosa is really infatuated with these people and—"

"What's wrong with that?" Leticia broke in.

"Nothing's wrong with that. It's just that . . ." How could he explain it? "They worry me."

Leticia's eyebrows shot up. "Worry you? Why?"

"When we left the meeting today," Antonio remembered, "there were these young guys outside handing out pamphlets and stuff. Papo said they were the Cadets of the Republic. They're part of this Nationalist movement, and they were all dressed in black shirts, and that bothers me."

"Why?" Leticia asked.

"Back in my country we had people with black shirts. They weren't good guys. They went around giving funny salutes. They were Mussolini's thugs. You've heard of Mussolini, right?"

Leticia said yes.

"Well," Antonio continued, "they were Il Duce's bully boys. Before you knew it, they were running the whole damn country, and it wasn't good."

CHAPTER
THIRTEEN

DOÑA SARO WAS in crisis. Every so often the letrina in the back had to be cleaned out. That was just a normal part of living in La Playa. Every house or establishment had to have its outhouse flushed out once in a while. Normally, this job was done by Manolo, the town drunkard. This is how he supported himself and had enough cash to get drunk.

Except that now he had competition. One Lorenzo Santiago, who at one time had worked in the Ponce pier but lost his job over some altercation with the pier foreman, had started up his own letrina cleaning detail. When he heard that doña Saro needed her outhouse done, he hightailed it to her place. Except that Manolo had been contracted first, but he had been delayed with a prior job in another residence. When he got to Saro's place, there was Lorenzo Santiago already getting set to shovel the shit into buckets and cart it away in his wheelbarrow.

Manolo and Lorenzo got into a shouting match as to who had legal access to the letrina. Manolo claimed that he had been contracted first, and even though he was late for the job, it was because he had to finish his prior assignment. Lorenzo countered that he had as much right as Manolo to the work, and he had been the first on the premises, ready to do his duty. Poor doña Saro was beyond herself with worry.

Manolo accused Lorenzo of being a blackheart, a pirate, a man with no moral scruples. Lorenzo argued that this was his job and this shit in this letrina—overflowing, by the way—was what was going to feed his three children once he got paid and went home for dinner.

The two men screamed at each other, ready to do battle. Doña Saro feared that they might come to blows right there in back of her house.

Providentially for all concerned, Toño Boglione showed up at the right moment.

He intervened and wedged himself between the men, who continued shouting vehemently, spittle sprouting from their mouths. Antonio told each one to shut up and stop this nonsense. It was no way to act in front of a lady. Hadn't their mothers instructed them in good manners? Had they no shame?

Both men drew back and stared at the ground, shamed-faced, their hands stuffed into their pockets, not daring to antagonize one of La Playa's leading providers.

"What's this all about?" Antonio needed to know.

They both spoke up, seeking an advantage.

Antonio put up a restraining hand. "Enough!"

Both men quieted down.

He then proceeded to have each man give his side of the story. Manolo was first and said he had been duped, cheated out of a job. Was that right?

Lorenzo said he was first on the scene, according doña Saro the benefit of a job well done and in a timely manner.

"That's a lie!" Manolo yelled, whereupon Lorenzo took umbrage, taking a threatening step toward Manolo, his fists raised, and Manolo put up his dukes as well.

Antonio came between them again, telling each to step back or he would get mad. Once more both men backed down.

"Listen," he said, "Manolo, you're right in that you were contracted first for the job, but through no fault of your own, you were late. And Saro was in crisis. Her letrina had to be attended to immediately. She couldn't wait." He then addressed Lorenzo. "And you were right in attending to the job." He held out both hands in a conciliatory gesture. "You both have an argument here. There's no need for insults. This is just a misunderstanding." He then offered a compromise: "Tell you what I'll do: Lorenzo, you began the job, so you can finish the job."

"Wait a minute!" Manolo protested.

"Manolo," Antonio said, holding out a palm, "you were contracted first, so you should get paid for the job. I will pay you for the work since it was a contract, and a contract should be honored."

Before Lorenzo could object, Antonio said to him, "Lorenzo, I will also pay you for the finished work." He smiled knowingly. "So, you see, you'll both get paid for the job. All I ask is that in the future you, Manolo, inform doña Saro if you'll be late for the work. And you, Lorenzo, check with Manolo to make sure you have no conflicts in scheduling." He swiveled his head from one man to the other. "Is that okay with you both?"

Both men approved.

"How much do you think this job is worth? Seeing as the letrina is overflowing?" he asked.

Manolo rubbed his jaw. "Well, I would say, two dollars?" He looked at Lorenzo for approval.

"Yeah," Lorenzo eagerly agreed. "Two dollars is okay."

Antonio took some bills out of his pocket. He counted out the appropriate amount and gave each man his two dollars. "There, that's settled. Now shake on it like true gentlemen do when they reach an agreement."

Hesitantly, both men shook hands.

Antonio said, "What I suggest you both do is go home and get some lunch and forget about this misunderstanding."

"I can't go home for lunch," Manolo complained. "There's nobody there, and it's too early for siesta time."

"I live too far away to get lunch," Lorenzo said.

"Well, can't you guys go to Carmelo's cafetín and get something to eat?" Antonio suggested.

"Carmelo's place doesn't serve food," Lorenzo said. "They just have drinks, which is okay. But if you're hungry, there ain't much."

Antonio looked baffled. "Isn't there some place you can go to get some food?"

"Nope." Manolo was just as grim. "If your woman is home, it's okay. Otherwise, there's no place around here at all to get something to eat in the middle of the day."

"That is true," Lorenzo concurred sadly. "We'll just have to stay hungry until it's dinner time, unless somebody invites us to share their lunch."

"That's too bad," Antonio sympathized. "Just try to make good use of the rest of the day." He made a departing gesture. "Lorenzo, you have work to do. Manolo, I'll see you later at Carmelo's. I'll buy you a drink."

Manolo bobbed his head and waved goodbye, and Lorenzo went back to shoveling waste out of the outhouse.

Saro came up to Antonio. "Thank you, Toño, I was really worried they would kill each other"—she motioned toward the latrine—"and all over shit."

"It's a job like any other," Antonio said. "Somebody has to do it."

Saro rested a hand on her cheek. "Just as long as my latrine gets cleaned."

"Oh, it will." Antonio flicked his head toward Lorenzo, busily shoveling the feces into his wheelbarrow. "Lorenzo is two dollars richer. That's a great incentive."

"Thank you again, Toño. You showed up at the right time." Saro glanced at her backyard, taking stock of the metal basins and tubing scattered about. "You haven't been around lately, and I'm running behind. I know you're very busy with your new projects and all, but I—"

Before she could go further, Antonio broke in: "Saro, I know I haven't been around that much, and for that I'm sorry. It's just that I'm so busy these days, I just can't—"

Saro cut him short: "I know, I know. Toño, you're a busy man, I realize that, and you have your own life to lead. I understand. It's just—"

"Look," Antonio continued, "if you want, I can send someone to help you with the stuff."

"That's not necessary," Saro said.

"You sure?"

"Yes." Saro sighed wistfully. "But there is something I need to speak to you about, and it's—"

Antonio didn't let her finish, taking hold of her hands and looking concerned. "Is everything alright? Are you okay?"

Saro cast a dismissive hand. "Oh, I'm fine, everything's alright. It's not about me." She gave a worried look. "It's about your friend Papo Mendosa."

Antonio gave a sidelong glance. "What about Papo?"

"Well, maybe you don't know, but he's been going around lately handing out pamphlets and newsletters advocating the Nationalist cause. Now, that in itself is worrisome to some people, especially those who work in the mayoralty, but he's now wearing the black shirt of the Nationalists. He's had more than one argument with the people around here about it. I know you're his friend, and that's why I'm telling you this." She showed a pained expression "Toño, you've become a man of influence and means in this town. And you have a bright future ahead of you, everyone says so. You're one of us now; you have a family here. I would advise you to keep your distance from your friend, especially if he's gone over to the Nationalists. It's caused great divisions in Ponce, and a lot of people are worried. I wouldn't want to see you or your family hurt by all this."

Antonio absorbed everything that Saro said, chewing at his lower lip, his eyes fixed on the ground.

CHAPTER FOURTEEN

WHEN HE ARRIVED home, Leticia was getting ready to nurse their daughter, whose hungry cries let everyone know she was ready for her dinner. As to Camilo, his son, he toddled forward held by the guiding hand of Elena, their housekeeper. Antonio's heart leapt every time he saw his children after a hard day in the confines of La Playa. He held his arms out wide for Camilo to toddle up to him. He scooped up his son, nuzzling his face. "How is my little man today?"

The baby wrapped his arms around his father's neck and nestled his face into Antonio's shoulder. Antonio grabbed one of his little hands. "How is my little man doing?" he cooed.

Elena looked on approvingly and said, "He was a handful today, cruising from one place to the other, exploring the whole house. At this rate, he'll not only be walking but running everywhere."

"Has my little man been running?"

"Pa-pa! Pa-pa!"

"Yes, Papa is here." He lifted the little hand and kissed it. Then he puckered his lips and uttered, "Whaaa."

Like a prize mimic, Camilo did the same, uttering, "Whaa."

Antonio laughed at his son's babble, and the baby laughed along with him.

Sitting at the table and holding their daughter, Leticia marveled, "I swear, you two are the same. Sometimes I wonder: Who's the baby and who's the parent?"

"He's my little man and he'll always be." Antonio ambled to the table and, holding his son, beamed down at his daughter, snuggling in Leticia's arms. "Just like she's my little princess. Look at those beautiful blue eyes of hers. Just like her mother."

"I don't have true blue eyes," Leticia reminded him again. "Mine are more grayish than blue. And hers will be the same."

"No way," Antonio objected. "Her eyes are blue. She's my blue-eyed princess—the only one in Ponce."

Leticia hefted her daughter higher on her breast. "I have no doubt she's the only one in Ponce, and she has the temper to prove it." Then she said to her housekeeper, "I think it's time for Camilo's bath, Elena. We don't want to keep him up too late."

"You're right, señora." Elena took hold of the baby from Antonio. "I'll make sure he's in bed after his bath." She departed with the baby to the other room, with Antonio holding on to his son's little hand for as long as possible.

When they had gone, Antonio said to Leticia, "And how was your day?"

"Up to now, strenuous," Leticia said. "Elena is right: your son is a handful." She laughed coyly. "He takes after his father."

Antonio gave a broad smile. "That's good. He'll be able to hold his own." He pulled back a chair and sat down facing Leticia across the table.

"I don't think that will be a problem with our son," Leticia said. The baby in her arms started yelping again. "And this one knows what she wants." She held the swaddled child in one arm, calmly unbuttoned the two top buttons of her blouse, and bared a breast for the child's lips. While she nursed her baby, she demurely covered her breast with a handkerchief.

Antonio looked approvingly. "You're beautiful."

"Even with my big breasts?" Leticia frowned.

"Especially with your big breasts. I always dreamed of a big-breasted wife."

"Now you have one," Leticia said, sounding none too pleased.

"Yes, that's good." Antonio stared at the floor, silent for a moment.

"You seem worried," Leticia deduced. "What's wrong?"

Antonio drew a heavy sigh. "It's Papo Mendosa again. It seems he's really gotten infatuated with this independence thing. People have noticed, so I've been told."

"Papo has to find his own path," Leticia stated. "And it seems he's chosen one."

"Yes, but is it the right one if it's going to bring problems?"

"Bring problems to whom?"

"To Ponce, to the people he knows here. I mean, you know, this independence thing—the government considers it a problem."

"Are you worried?" Leticia asked.

"I'm worried for Papo," Antonio said. "He's a good friend. I don't want him to get in trouble."

Leticia pulled the handkerchief higher on her breast. "It seems to me that it's for Papo Mendosa to decide his own course. He's an adult. He's responsible for his own actions. Now, if he decides to join the Nationalists and their cause, that's his choice as long as it doesn't endanger anyone else. If his actions affected us and our family, then I would definitely not approve."

She let her words hang in the air. After a small silence, Antonio said, "I tell you what, let's not talk about this. I don't want to upset you or—"

"It doesn't upset me," Leticia cut him short. "It seems to me you're the one that's upset. And if you are, you should talk to Papo about it."

"Look, let's not talk about it, okay?" Antonio objected. I'll . . . I'll see Papo about it." He changed the subject. "Anyway, Saro finally had her latrine cleaned today, and because of it she almost had a fight on her hands."

"I heard," Leticia recalled. "Manolo and Lorenzo Santiago had a row over it. But I'm told you were the hero in the whole thing and a fight was avoided."

Antonio downplayed it. "I wasn't any hero. It just seemed ridiculous to me that men should be fighting over a shit hole."

"These are hard times," Leticia commented. "Men will do anything to make some spare cash since there's none of it around. It's a bad time we're going through right now. They call it a depression. I call it a catastrophe, from what I've seen. And how long it'll last, no one knows."

"That was another thing about today," Antonio said. "Not only are there no jobs or no money but, for those who have some work, there's no place they can get something to eat even if they wanted to." He seemed genuinely surprised. "I'm amazed. There's not one restaurant or food shop in La Playa. And these are men who need sustenance during the day." He shook his head sadly. "Truly amazing."

"What the people need here is a *fonda*," Leticia said abruptly.

"A what?"

"A fonda. A *bodegón*. Like a cheap restaurant." Leticia explained further: "Back in Spain almost every town had one. In Madrid a fonda was a boarding house, but in the countryside a fonda was a place where workers came to eat during the day. It was like a restaurant that offered nourishing food at cheap prices, so almost anybody could afford it. I remember that in Valencia we had one called 'La Fonda del Sol.' In Zaragoza there was one called 'La Fonda de la Tierra.' And they were very popular places with the workmen."

"Hmmm, a fonda." Antonio scratched his chin. "Yes. Why didn't I think of it?" He rose up from his chair, went over to Leticia, and kissed her on the forehead. "Thank you, darling, you've just given me a great idea."

And so it came to pass that La Playa had its very first eatery. It was simply called "La Fonda," and situated next to doña Saro's place. You could have a quick, inexpensive meal of rice and beans, but you could also stock up on your daily dose of Saro's homemade rum.

Soon, Manolo, Lorenzo Santiago, and every other workman were congregating in the lower section of the vacant house that Antonio had purchased for his newest project. The house had two stories. The lower section had been hollowed out for the eatery, with two big kitchens in the rear where massive cast-iron stoves heated huge pots of rice, root plants, and ground meat. No seafood as of yet; it was too perishable. But there were large wooden coolers filled with iced beer to quench the thirst.

And they came, before and after the siesta hour: stevedores from the Ponce docks, sugar cane cutters from the local fields, and workmen and machinists from the Porto Rico Ironworks, the big iron foundry built by the Americans and located a few blocks from the Ponce pier. Among the first customers was Juan-Carlos Quiles, who thereafter made it a habit to eat his lunch at La Fonda.

It became a family affair, with Leticia putting up her hair, rolling up her sleeves, and helping prepare meals in the back kitchens. Elena, the housekeeper, was put in charge of the three other women who had been hired as cooks. And when one of the girls needed a day off, doña Saro would fill in as a replacement.

Benches were provided by Domingo the carpenter, and the men would sit before long communal tables, eating their meal and airing the local gossip. "Did you hear about how Americo Pichón peed in his pants last night while watching a musical at the movie house?"

"Did you know that Jorge Gutierrez hit the numbers again? Is he lucky or is he paying off somebody?"

"Carmelo's wife left him again!"

"Who was that woman with Luis Suarez last night? They sure seemed chummy."

"Did you hear about the fight in town last night? Papo Mendosa was at it again. That asshole is gonna get in trouble if he keeps up this independence shit. The police are beginning to notice this stuff."

CHAPTER
FIFTEEN

ON PALM SUNDAY, March 21, 1937, Antonio and Leticia went to the local church in La Playa, where Father Ignacio gave a homily about the Lord's triumphal entry into Jerusalem, lo, those many centuries ago; how it affirmed that He was Messiah and King sent to cleanse mankind of its sins.

After the sermon, as was customary, palm branches were distributed to the worshippers and a procession of palm bearers proceeded from the church to the plaza. After the services and procession, Antonio went home to look in on his progeny and enjoy a Sunday lunch.

Across town, in Ponce proper, at the intersection of Marina and Aurora Streets, a different procession was taking place. The march had been organized by the Puerto Rican Nationalist Party, and it was held, in part, to commemorate the abolition of slavery in the island by the Spanish government way back in 1873. There was another reason. The march also was a protest against the US government's imprisonment of Pedro Albizu Campos on sedition charges.

Upon hearing of the proposed march, the US-appointed governor-general of Puerto Rico, Blanton Winship, ordered an increase of the police forces in Ponce. He also ordered that any demonstration conducted by the Nationalist Party was to be stopped "by all means necessary." When he was appointed, Governor Winship had been given a mandate by the authorities in Washington. His primary mission was to stamp out the Nationalist Party, decimate its leadership, and quell any rebellion on the island. Within this framework, it was also ordered that any demonstrations conducted by the rank and file of the Nationalist Party be stopped quickly and decisively.

When the Nationalist cadre reached the intersection, they found themselves face to face with fourteen policemen, dressed in khaki, carrying wooden batons and clubs, and barring their way. Immediately behind the procession were nine policemen armed with Thompson submachine guns. An additional eleven policemen, also armed with machine guns, stood to the east of the parade group, and another group of twelve policemen armed with Springfield rifles stood to the west of the marchers.

The marchers themselves were spearheaded by a unit of black-shirted Cadets of the Republic, among them Octavio Mendosa, who stood behind the flag bearer, a young man who resolutely held on to the Puerto Rican banner with hands taut and mouth tight. Behind the Cadets were scores of marchers: men, women, and children who had come to voice their opposition to Albizu's imprisonment.

Octavio would remember that it was a hot, sultry day, more so than usual for mid to late March. He stood in the second rank, behind the flag bearer, holding on to a sheaf of pamphlets that he was to distribute to onlookers and passersby after the march. He was sweating profusely beneath his black shirt and tie, and his armpits were damp. Next to him, a fellow cadet, Bolivar Marquez, was also armed with the flyers to be distributed, and he sweated as well.

A typical humid Ponce morning, but Octavio felt a cold chill run down his spine when he spied the police forces arrayed before them. This was not expected. "What are they doing here?" he voiced out loud.

Standing next to him, his friend Bolivar Marquez answered, "I don't know. We have a permit to march." Like the others, he viewed the armed police standing before them with some alarm. This was not the way it was supposed to be. "We have a permit," he repeated.

"Permit or not," Octavio said, "these guys look serious." He craned his neck to look forward, waiting for some signal from the commander

118

of the cadets in the front rank. Directly behind them, and in front of the other marchers, was a cadet corps of musicians with a horn section and drums. As had been agreed beforehand, they began to play "La Borinqueña," which later became Puerto Rico's national anthem.

The commander of the cadets gave the signal, and the marchers began moving forward.

No one knows who gave the signal on the other side, but as previously ordered by Gov. Winship, grim-faced policemen began firing their weapons.

Octavio remembered the noise as deafening; men, women, and children screaming, scattering in whatever direction they could, and meeting an onslaught of bullets since they were hemmed in on all sides by police. The first row of cadets fell like sprouts of wheat being cut by some huge, horrendous scythe. Octavio saw people falling all around him, bullets slamming into chests, arms, necks, faces, with streams of blood gushing from veins, sinew, and muscle. The flag bearer in front of him went down. For a second, Octavio stood still, rooted in place; then his legs moved as if of their own accord. He dropped his leaflets and ran. As he was fleeing with the rest, he felt a hot, piercing pain in his right leg, just beside the hamstring muscle, but he kept moving until he ran smack into a young girl, perhaps no older than ten or twelve. The young girl pushed him aside, and he fell on the pavement, feeling a rush of pain from his leg. He was bleeding! He rolled over onto his back, hearing the pop-pop of rifle fire, the rat-tat-tat of machine guns. Instinctively, he snapped up his head, trying to make out something, anything, through the smoke of gunpowder and the screams around him. The policemen were firing into the crowd of civilians. The cadets were no longer the important target.

And then he saw the young girl who had rushed by him, scrambling to the front row, where cadets lay bleeding and dying, and she scooped up the flag from the flag bearer who was no longer among the living. She hoisted the flag, turned, and held up the banner. She too was shot. A plume of blood sprouted from the side of her scalp, and she fell.

He felt something moving along his legs. He looked down and saw his friend Bolivar Marquez dragging himself along the ground, crawling with one hand while pressing the other to the splotch of blood on his chest. The bullets whizzed above their heads now; the police were aiming for targets of opportunity elsewhere in the crowd. They were aiming at those seeking escape. And many who were wounded were now being clubbed to death by the group of policemen who had taken a position in front of the marchers.

Bolivar Marquez kept dragging himself toward a nearby wall in one of the residences, and he clawed at it, as if seeking something behind the wall. Octavio's vision went hazy; the smoke and smell of sulfur clogged every pore, with the screams rending all around him.

CHAPTER SIXTEEN

ANTONIO PUFFED ON a cigarette and pored over the receipts in a back room of the house. This had become his unofficial office. Just like Juan-Carlos's inner sanctum, his was filled with piles of record books and lists, all tied with string. Even his desk was covered with receipts, tickets, and numbered slips.

He took a deep drag on the cigarette and continued plowing away, adding and compiling numbers, trying to accommodate as much waning daylight as he could before the house went dark and the candles and lanterns were lit.

In the midst of his drudgery, Leticia burst into the room with Manolo, the drunkard. "Toño, we need you, now!"

He looked up. "What?"

"There's been some trouble in town. Please stop what you're doing. I need you as of this minute," implored Manolo.

"Whatever it is, can't it wait?"

Leticia asked, "What kind of trouble?"

"What the hell is going on?" Antonio asked. He jammed the cigarette butt into a nearby ashtray, put down the receipts in his hand, rose, and followed Leticia into the main living room, where he saw Octavio, whose right leg had been bandaged with some linen. Manolo gestured to Octavio's leg and said, "As you can see, bad trouble."

Antonio saw the red flecks of blood oozing from the bandaged wound. "What happened to his leg?"

Manolo turned his perpetually bloodshot eyes and leathery cheeks to Antonio. "He got shot," he said.

"Shot?" Antonio was incredulous. "Papo, you got shot?"

Octavio managed to nod his head feebly. "Yes, I got shot."

"By whom? Why?"

"He was at that parade in town," Manolo disclosed. "You know, the Nationalist protest, and there was trouble. The police started shooting everyone in the parade. It was a massacre. It was awful."

Antonio took it all in. "I see."

Standing beside her husband, looking doubtful, Leticia said to Antonio, "Whatever happened, I don't like this. I don't like this at all."

Antonio ignored her and came up to Octavio. "We need to get you some medical attention. Come into the guest room."

"Thank you," Octavio wheezed.

Propping him up, one on each side, both men guided Octavio toward a room next to Antonio's office. Antonio placed a pillow beneath Octavio's bandaged leg and peered close. "You're still bleeding. We need to stop that. And we need to clean the wound; otherwise you'll get an infection." He told Leticia over his shoulder, "Get me some sheets, some hot water, and the rubbing alcohol."

Leticia stood in place, ogling Octavio's wound.

"Letty!" he bellowed.

She snapped to and rushed to get the items.

Antonio addressed Manolo: "You say he got shot. I assume the bullet is still lodged in his leg."

"Yes," Manolo affirmed.

"That bullet has to be removed. We need to get Dr. Rincón here." Antonio looked pensive, suddenly remembering: "But he's in town, and the longer we wait, the greater the chance of infection."

"I didn't know of any other place to come," Manolo sought to explain. "He showed up at my place, and I could see he was in a bad way. How he got there from town, I don't know."

"That's not important," Antonio said. "He needs a doctor, and quick!"

Manolo wiped a drop of sweat from his forehead. "Problem is, I hear the police are looking for Nationalists everywhere and arresting anyone connected with them." His rheumy eyes became gloomy. "I'm truly sorry I got you involved in this, but I couldn't leave him to die."

"Don't worry. We'll get him a doctor." Antonio dropped a hand on Octavio's arm. "Papo, how are you feeling?"

"I'm okay," Octavio said through clenched teeth. "I'll survive."

"I'm sure you will," Antonio remarked quietly. "But first, we gotta get you a doctor, and then we'll need to get you out of town."

"That makes sense," Manolo agreed, standing in place, next to the bed. "As I said, they'll be looking for him everywhere."

"Hopefully, not here," Antonio presumed.

"Yes," Manolo said, sounding unsure, "hopefully, not here."

Antonio heard Leticia calling his name from the kitchen, and he went directly to her.

She was incensed. "Are you out of your mind?" she spat. "Do you know what would happen if the police find out that you're helping a . . . a Nationalist?"

"What do you want me to do?" Antonio reasoned. "He's my friend, and he's been hurt. I just can't turn him away."

"He's a Nationalist!" Leticia's eyes flashed with anger. "Think of your family. Think of me! We can't afford to be associated with his kind. Think what would happen if this came out. You could be sent to jail for helping him! And then what would happen to me? To the children?"

"Nothing will happen," Antonio soothed. "No one needs to know anything. I'll get the doctor here, and then he'll be gone."

"But where?" Leticia demanded to know. "It's bad enough we're helping him. This is dangerous!"

Antonio reached out to touch her, reassure her. She drew back, still incensed.

"Letty," he said, "Papo is my friend. He needs me. I just can't desert him. I just can't. It's not the Christian thing to do."

"Christian?" Leticia scoffed. "Is it the Christian thing to put your family in danger? To jeopardize all we've worked for? And think of my father and our family and our standing in town. Think of yourself! This is madness." She flicked a thumb toward the bedroom. "You should send him away!"

"I won't send him away," Antonio said resolutely. "He's here, and we'll care for him whether you like it or not. I'm the head of this family, and what I say is law. Do you understand?"

Leticia's nostrils flared. "You're a stupid man. My mother was right: I should've never married you!" She turned abruptly and headed for the other room.

Manolo had been standing quietly to one side, not wanting to intercede in a family argument. "I'm truly sorry I brought you this problem," he mentioned again. "I don't want to get you in trouble with anyone. If there was someone else, I would've . . ."

"Don't worry yourself," Antonio reassured. "You did the right thing. Papo, whatever his beliefs, is still a friend, and we can't abandon him." He laid a hand on Manolo's shoulder. "We'll get him to safety."

124

"Thank you, Toño," Manolo said. "You're a good man." He looked around as if trying to find something but afraid to ask. Finally he said, "Toño, it's been a long day, and I think it's going to be an even longer night. Uh, you wouldn't happen to have something around? Y'know, just to calm my nerves."

Antonio understood immediately. "I know. It has been a long day." He gestured to the living room. "There's some rum in the liquor cabinet. Help yourself."

For the first time that night, Manolo exhibited a wide grin. "Thank you, Toño. You're a true friend."

CHAPTER SEVENTEEN

ORDINARILY, ANTONIO WOULD have contracted Rumaldo García to take him to town in the old carriage. This time was different; he needed quick transport. Octavio's life depended on it. Instead he requisitioned La Playa's sole fire truck and drove it to town himself, though admittedly his driving was a bit rusty since he hadn't driven a vehicle since his time in Napoli, years before. Yet they made it through the tortuous roads to the residence of Dr. Marco Rincón Nievez, who, as of late, had been treating Leticia for some menstrual problems. And the doctor assumed this was a part of it until he got to Antonio's house and saw he would have to treat a wounded and bleeding Nationalist.

Antonio prevailed upon Marco Rincón to do his duty as a citizen and medical man. Wasn't he there to treat all people afflicted by illness, even an independentista? Besides, as Manolo had mentioned, the renowned doctor was a frequent visitor at doña Fela's emporium. Such news would be a blot on the good doctor's impeccable reputation.

The doctor had no choice but to treat Octavio Mendosa, removing the bullet from his leg and patching him up as best he could. He advised that Octavio should rest for the next few days. Time permitting, he would be back to check up periodically on Octavio. To which Antonio revealed that this might be a problem. They needed to get Octavio out of town as quickly as possible. This would be difficult, Dr. Rincón stated; police were everywhere looking for Nationalists, Nationalist sympathizers, and suspected Nationalists.

"We'll get him to safety," Antonio vowed. "And you, Doctor, will come to see him again. I promise."

Lying off eight miles from Ponce was Isla Caja de Muerto, Coffin Island. It was so called because from the Ponce shoreline the island had a mountainous outcropping that, from a distance, looked like a cadaver floating in the ocean. It was mainly an abandoned strip of isle infested with wild goats. It was also a sometime destination for fisherman or Ponce residents who would venture there to trap some wild goat meat or simply to get away from their wives and kids, if only for a day.

Antonio got Federico Mendez, a local fisherman, to row him, Manolo, and Octavio to the island. Federico was a close friend of Octavio's and could be trusted. That wasn't the problem. Octavio would have to remain on the island for five days. Manolo and Federico the fisherman would go out on a daily basis, seemingly going fishing, when in fact they would check in on Octavio, bring him food and water, and change his bandages as needed. Dr. Rincón, in the guise of going fishing in his leisure time, would get to look in on Octavio as well, and supply whatever medication was necessary.

This went on for three weeks while Octavio Mendosa recovered. In the interim it was learned that there was a backlash of indignation, even in the US Congress, as to what was now being called the Ponce Massacre. This was made more poignant by the fact that Octavio's friend Bolivar Marquez, the one he had seen crawl over his body and reach a wall, had written upon that very wall, with his own blood, the words "Long Live the Republic, Down with the Murderers!" In light of all this, the US government had created a commission to investigate the massacre.

For Octavio Mendosa, it made no difference to his condition. He was still holed up under a makeshift canopy in a goat-infested island, sleeping under wet blankets, and dreaming of the day he would have his revenge.

Antonio knew he had to get him out, and soon. He spirited Octavio from the island, in the same rowboat he had used to get him there. Octavio was deposited with some extended family members of Manolo's who had a house in Cabo Rojo, along a remote part of the western seacoast. Antonio made it worth their while, paying them well for the upkeep of his friend.

Octavio remained with the family for three months, slowly recovering from his wound. Then, when Antonio went to visit him, he was told that Octavio had departed. He had packed up and left without saying a word to anyone. Where had he gone? No one knew.

CHAPTER EIGHTEEN

MILAGROS NESTLED CLOSE to him, her arms spread over his body, her head resting on his chest. "I'm glad you're here," she said, almost noiselessly.

He smiled in the quiet of the room. "So am I. It's been a trying time for all of us."

"Especially for you, I'm sure," she noted.

Antonio began stroking her closely cropped hair, cut so short he could almost feel her scalp. "I'm just glad to be here with you."

"As am I," she breathed. "This is your home too, you know."

"It's your house," he said. "I bought it for you."

She lifted her head, and touched his face gently. "I'd like to think it's our house. Our home."

He smiled at her. "It is our home."

Once more she rested her head on his chest. "I'm glad I can offer you rest from out there."

"Yes," he sighed. "Rest from out there." He looked up at the wooden ceiling, then toward the window, with the curtains half-drawn. It was night and very dark outside. A solitary wick lamp gave a semblance of light to a portion of the bed. "Do you like this house?" he asked.

"Yes, I do," she responded. "It's the only house I've lived in except for my mother's house, and . . ." Then she grew quiet.

"Those days are over," he said. "This is your own home now. And I'm here with you."

"I wish you could stay here forever," she said into his chest.

"So do I. But you know I have to . . ."

She raised a hand to his lips, quieting him. "I know. You don't have to explain. It suffices that you're with me now. And you're safe."

"Why wouldn't I be safe?" he asked. "I'm with you here."

"I know. It's just that so much has happened lately. What with the Ponce massacre and all. I worry about you. I don't want you to get hurt."

He angled his head down, looking at his hand caressing her hair. "Why would I get hurt?"

She fingered the small sprout of hair on his chest. "I don't know. It's just that I was concerned. I know you have friends who are involved with the independentistas, and I don't want you to get in trouble."

"I have one friend who belongs to the Nationalist Party," he corrected her. "And he's . . . he's gone. I don't know where."

"Was he involved in the massacre?"

"Yes."

"Was he injured?"

"Yes."

"What happened to him?"

"As I said, I don't know."

She raised her head, looking at him intently. "Toño, you're not involved with these people, are you?"

His eyes bore into hers. "No, I am not."

She responded as if she hadn't heard. "I don't know what I would do if something happened to you. I love you, so it would . . ."

132

"Don't," he shushed, "please. Nothing will happen to me. That I promise. Don't worry yourself about it."

"How can I not worry? I love you."

"I know, I know. And you know how I feel about you. You're very important to me." He ran a hand along her cheek. "Nothing's going to happen. Everything will be alright."

She stared into his face. "You promise?"

He made a slight grimace. "Didn't I just promise that?"

She wagged an admonishing finger. "You better not get hurt."

"I won't," he grinned.

"Or get in trouble."

"I won't."

"Good." She laid her head again on his chest. "I just want my man to be safe."

He smoothed her hair. "I always feel safe when I'm with you."

"I'm glad," she said.

They were quiet for a spell. Milagros could feel the thud of his heart as she rested her head on his chest. "I feel so bad for all those people that got hurt," she said in time.

"You mean, the massacre?" he guessed.

"Yes, that. I heard it was really bad. A lot of people got hurt. A lot of people got killed."

"Yes, I know," he said. "But I'm afraid this is only the beginning."

She raised her head again. "What do you mean?"

"This . . . this massacre has only inflamed the Nationalists. They're mad, and they'll want revenge, and that's bad."

"It's bad," she said thoughtfully, "but I can understand their anger."

"And so can I. It's just that sometimes two wrongs cannot make a right. That's something that Jacobo once told me."

She wrinkled her brow. "Jacobo?"

"The Scholarly Jew," he explained.

She had a vague recollection. "Oh yes, I've heard of him. They say he is very wise."

"He is. And he knows about things. I think he would agree with all of us that it was a tragedy, an injustice, the killing of all those people. But it's not over. It may have just begun." Antonio took a ragged breath. "I have a bad feeling this is only the beginning and there's more to come."

CHAPTER NINETEEN

SWEAT STREAMED DOWN Antonio's face; it dribbled down his back, plastering his shirt to his skin. He halted, doffed off his straw hat and fanned himself with it.

"Come! We must hurry!" exhorted Angel, his guide up the mountain peak.

Antonio expelled a breath, put his hat back on, and continued up the hill. On each side were rows of bramble, foliage, and bush. It's like a jungle up here, he thought. When will it end?

As if reading his mind, Angel said, "It's not far, señor. We're almost to the top."

Antonio lifted his head to look up. All he could see was the morning fog burning off in a radiant, scorching sun. He thought ruefully that whoever said it was cooler up here, they were out of their mind.

He latched onto a tree branch and forced himself forward, step after arduous step. The bushes were as dense up here as they had been down in the valley below. At least he could discern a hidden path of stamped grass where others had gone up this way.

Also, the mosquitoes were fiercer here. They flapped incessantly around his head, and he was so tired, he didn't even wave them away anymore. How much longer?

"We're almost there, señor," Angel said.

Heaving another tattered breath, Antonio forced himself onward.

They finally came upon an outcropping of land, an oasis surrounded and shaded by tree and brush, with a small wooden shack smack in the middle of the forest.

Angel stopped, waved for him to come forward. Antonio reached him, panting. Angel pointed to the base of an old, gnarled tree, and instructed, "Sit down, señor. Your friend will be out shortly."

Antonio noticed they weren't alone in this secluded spot. A young woman, dressed in a blouse and calico skirt, had appeared out of nowhere. She carried in her hand a round leather canteen, which she offered to Antonio.

He mumbled a "thank you," took the canteen, and gulped mouthfuls of precious water. He handed back the canteen, lay his head back against the old tree, and exhaled wearily.

Out of the wooden shack, in the midst of that copse, stepped Octavio, closing behind him a door constructed of hollowed sugar cane poles. The minute he saw him, Antonio knew his friend had changed. He was leaner and somehow seemed more self-assured, but as he came closer, Antonio saw that his eyes had aged. Not his face, but his eyes.

Octavio gave a big grin and rushed up to Antonio. He kneeled by his friend. "You made it," he greeted, thumping Antonio's shoulder.

Antonio smiled back. "I almost died coming up that hill." He took a look around. "Where the hell is this place?"

"It's the central mountain range, the sierra of Cayey," Octavio said. "No one will ever bother looking for us up here."

Antonio surveyed the surroundings. They were on a peak enclosed by tropical forest. "I can see why," he said in understatement.

"It's a good hideaway." Octavio glanced inquiringly at his friend. "Why are you here?"

Antonio closed his eyes a moment, resting his breath. He opened his eyes, focusing on the face inches from his. "As I told your people down in the valley: I wanted to see you. I was worried about you; not only me but all your friends. We hadn't seen you since"—he stopped to take another breath—"since the massacre in Ponce."

Octavio bit his lower lip. "And a massacre it was, for which the yanquis will pay. That I swear."

"Papo," Antonio said, "I came here to warn you, to ask you, to stop this thing. Taking action against the Americans will only make matters worse. Ponce is like a city under siege now. There are police everywhere, not only police but also the National Guard. If you escalate this thing, it will only get worse and a lot of people will suffer."

"You're right about that, my friend," Octavio griped acidly. "It will get worse. That, I promise you. We'll pay blood for blood. We'll continue our fight until don Albizu is free and we're an independent country."

"You can't possibly take on the American government," Antonio pleaded. "It's insane."

"Is it insane to fight for one's freedom?" Octavio grouched. "And if not us, then who?"

"Can't this be done through other means?" Antonio asked.

Octavio looked aside to a nearby outcropping of rock. "If you've come here to convince me otherwise, you've wasted your time."

"I thought we could talk," Antonio offered.

"We are talking," Octavio muttered. "It's just that I'm in the right and you're in the wrong."

Antonio's face twisted up. "I didn't come to argue. I wanted to find out how you are."

"As you can see, I am well."

"I'm glad you're well," Antonio said. "I was afraid something had happened to you."

"Nothing will happen to me," Octavio guaranteed. "But I'm glad you came. It's good to see you."

"Likewise," said Antonio.

They shared a brief silence. Then Octavio asked, "How are my parents?"

"They're well," Antonio said. "They're worried about you. Your mother lights a candle in the cathedral every day and prays for your safe return."

"I miss them." Octavio sat on the ground beside his friend, looking thoughtful. "Tell them that I'm okay and I think of them every day."

"I will do that," Antonio promised. He thought for a moment and then said, "The guys at the ironworks asked about you. They miss you. They say you were the best machinist in Ponce."

Octavio shared a happy memory. "Yeah, I was a good machinist, wasn't I? I miss them too. I really liked that job, and I was good at it. The foundry was a good place to learn a trade." He was deep in recollection. "When I first started working there, I was always put off by that printed inscription in the front gate: 'The Porto Rico Iron Works.' The stupid yanquis couldn't even spell the name right." He made a face. "'Porto Rico Iron Works'—they didn't even bother to correct the spelling of our island, use our proper name. Even so, I enjoyed working there." He jabbed the air with his finger. "You know, I started there when I was seventeen. I was apprenticed to Javier Mechado, probably the best machinist of his day. And I learned quick; even the American bosses noticed." He nodded to himself. "Yes, I miss the place."

"You could still go back there," Antonio encouraged. "I'm sure they would want you back. And your parents would be so relieved, it would—"

Octavio cut him off. "No, I couldn't. You know that. Too much has happened. My course is set. I must do what is right."

"What you're doing could get you killed."

"I don't fear death, Toño. What I fear more is that we'll never have our country, our own destiny. That's what I fear."

"But there has to be another way," Antonio contended.

"No!" Octavio said angrily. "Not after what happened. Not after the massacre. That was definite proof that the time for compromise is over. Now we have to fight for independence and we have to take up arms."

Antonio knew it was a losing argument. He gazed around again and asked, "Is this one of your base camps?"

Octavio gave a dismissive wave of his hand. "Nah. This is just one of our hideouts. The yanquis would never think of looking for us here. They're too busy searching the cities and towns."

"That they are," Antonio said reflectively. "They've searched every nook and cranny of Ponce, looking for Nationalists. Right after the massacre, they rounded up hundreds of suspects, but then they let them go. They had no proof. And the backlash, even in the United States, has been enormous. A lot of people view the massacre as an act of murder, which it was. There was an investigative commission that said as much."

"Yes, but was anyone punished?" Octavio retaliated. "Was anyone convicted of this crime?" And he answered his own question. "No one! From what I hear, no one has been held responsible. Not the police, not the police chief, and not that pig Winship."

"Papo, they're still investigating," Antonio offered in argument. "It takes time for the wheels of justice to—"

"'Wheels of justice'!" Octavio snarled. "There's no justice here. Not for us! We have to take our freedom! Just like the Irish freedom fighters. There's no turning back now."

Antonio gave his friend a look. "So, is this what you want, more bloodshed?"

"We didn't start this fight. They did. The yanquis. It began when they invaded our land, and it will end when we have thrown off the yoke of oppression."

Antonio looked aside, saying nothing.

"What?" Octavio prompted.

"I've heard all this before," Antonio said in a sad voice. "Back in my homeland there were those who sought to change the government, take back what was theirs. It only led to more problems."

"I know nothing about your homeland," Octavio declared. "But I know this: until we have driven out the yanquis, we'll never have the right to call this land our own."

"And what happens after they're gone?"

"We'll be free. We'll have our own nation."

"Free to starve, you mean."

"Free to call ourselves Puerto Ricans!"

"You are Puerto Ricans now."

"We are slaves now," Octavio said with certainty.

Antonio angled his head toward the ground. "I don't know what to say. We see things so differently." The deep brown eyes studied Octavio shrewdly. "But whatever happens, please promise me you'll be careful. I would hate to lose a good friend."

"Nothing will happen to me," Octavio insisted. "I have a mission to accomplish."

Antonio gave a sigh. "I know."

Octavio said earnestly, "You're very tired. You can stay with us this afternoon and rest some. Then Angel will take you down again to the valley." His shoulders lifted and fell. "We don't have much to offer. Some rice and plantains, that's it. But you're welcome to share with us before you go."

"Thank you." Antonio was truly moved. "Just to be here and see you well is thanks enough."

"Papo, can we speak?" It was the young girl in the calico skirt. She had been standing nearby all the time.

Octavio turned to her, nodded, then said to Antonio, "I'll be back."

Octavio and the girl walked to one side of the encampment. Antonio saw that the girl gestured frantically as they spoke, with Octavio sometimes listening, sometimes nodding yes, and sometimes shaking his head no. Antonio could tell it was a heated debate.

Octavio came back, angled his head toward the girl, who stood silently eyeing Antonio. "Carmen, my associate, doesn't trust you. She doesn't trust anyone who isn't one of us. She thinks it was a mistake having you come here. And she could be right. You found our hideout. How can we be sure you won't tell the americanos?"

Antonio opened his mouth to explain, but before he could say anything, Octavio continued, "I told her I trust you as I would my own brother and that you would never betray me. Of that I'm certain."

"Thank you," Antonio said, relieved. "You're correct. I would never, ever betray someone that I consider like family. I came here because I was worried and concerned. I promised your parents I would do all I could to seek you out and make sure you're okay. I would rather die than betray a trust."

"I know," Octavio remarked in a low voice. "I know." He called over his shoulder, "Carmencita, start making some rice for us." He looked fondly at Antonio. "Our friend is staying to share a meal. Afterwards, Angel can take back him down to the valley."

The young woman did not move, nursing a grudging silence. "Carmencita?" Octavio called again.

Finally she moved toward the shack, with Angel, the guide, trailing behind.

CHAPTER TWENTY

WHEN ANTONIO CAME back from his hike in the hills, Leticia suspected that this had been more than an ordinary trip. Yet part of her did not want to know. Instead she complained that food prices, especially rice, had again risen, and they were running short on other household provisions. Antonio did not volunteer any information on where he had been.

His eye did catch an announcement in *El Imparcial,* the daily newspaper, which had been left on the kitchen table. A short caption at the bottom of the first page noted that Governor Blanton Winship had moved the annual celebration of the United States' invasion of Puerto Rico to Ponce instead of the traditional locale of San Juan. The article stated that His Excellency, the governor, had chosen the city of Ponce to demonstrate that his "Law and Order" policy had been successful against the Nationalists.

Antonio felt ice in the pit of his stomach. Octavio's defiant words rang in his memory. This was not good. A parade in the heart of where a recent massacre had occurred? Either the authorities were stupid or insane, or both.

He quickly changed clothes and had Rumaldo hitch up his carriage to take Antonio to the mayoralty office in town. Given his status as one of La Playa's leading entrepreneurs, Antonio didn't have to wait long to see the mayor, Jose Tormos Diego, who greeted Antonio with due deference but was surprised that Antonio, not even a paisano, would have second thoughts about the upcoming celebration.

"Toño, you're not the only one who has qualms about this coming parade," the mayor revealed. "My office has been inundated all day with people who think it's a bad idea. But I didn't expect you to be one of them."

Antonio said, "Sir, I don't care about the Nationalists and their ideology. But you have to admit, having a parade to honor the invasion, here, at this time, is not the best of all ideas. What if the Nationalists use the occasion to create trouble? That wouldn't be good for anyone."

Mayor Tormos was all confidence. "Don't worry, Toño. I've been informed that every precaution will be taken for the parade to go forward without incident. Believe me, the governor and his people are very aware of what's going on. They will do everything possible to prevent any unpleasantness."

To which Antonio warned, "Mr. Mayor, it only takes one hothead with a gun to create 'unpleasantness.'"

On the day of the parade, Antonio forbade anyone in his household to attend, even Elena the housekeeper. When Leticia, who liked venturing to the town whenever possible, objected, Antonio resolutely said no one in his household would attend, to which Leticia accused her husband of being a Nationalist sympathizer, and there was nothing worse than that, given current events.

Antonio appealed to her reason, explaining that, yes, given current events, it wasn't safe to go into town. He had a bad premonition about this celebration, and he just wanted his family to be safe. Leticia made it clear she didn't like this at all, but was gratified that he still cared for his family. She would stay at home this one time, but never again.

And then she asked what he had planned for the day, and where they would go. It'd be nice if they could go to one of the seafood places in Los Meros. She heard they had the best conch meat in all the island.

Antonio replied that he was going to the parade, alone, and would return in the evening.

Leticia was genuinely puzzled. "But I thought you said it'd be dangerous?"

"Yes, I know," he tried to convey. "But I have to be there. I just can't explain why, but I have to be there." He took her hands, pressing tightly. "Just trust me, please."

CHAPTER
TWENTY-ONE

THE PARADE WENT off as planned. In addition, the parade planners were very pleased since a larger-than-expected crowd showed up for the event. Almost every side street bordering the mayoralty office was crammed with onlookers, as detachments of the National Guard along with local school bands, workers groups, veterans groups, and civic associations marched past the reviewing stand where Governor Blanton Winship, with his salt-and-pepper hair and milk-white mustache, stood ramrod straight. He was flanked by other dignitaries, American and islanders. As a show of solidarity, standing alongside the governor were the Speaker of the Puerto Rican House of Representatives, the island's commissioner of agriculture and commissioner of commerce, and other notables from the local government, as well as the Ponce mayor. To most of those gathered on the street, it seemed as if the tragedy of the previous year had been all but forgotten in the spirit of this new celebration.

Antonio Boglione had managed to wriggle his way to the front of the crowd, and directly facing the reviewing stand. At the mayor's insistence he had come dressed in a suit and tie, and he sweated rivulets under a hot sun. His only saving grace was the Panama hat he sported, which Leticia had insisted he wear as a measure of comfort. It didn't help, and he kept dabbing at his face with a handkerchief.

Against all protocol Antonio removed his suit jacket and draped it over his shoulder, hooking it on his bent forefinger. In this fashion, still mopping his sweaty face, he perused the reviewing stand. All the dignitaries seemed in high spirits, or at least they had been instructed to appear as such. The governor, attired in a white tropical suit, white shirt and dark tie, chatted amiably with the mayor, offering this comment and that.

He seemed to be enjoying the celebration; and as a veteran of the Spanish-American War and the Great War, he clapped enthusiastically when the National Guard segment marched in precision for his review.

Antonio idly took in the others on the reviewing stand. Standing directly behind the governor was a man in uniform. Antonio recognized this individual from photos in the local newspapers. He was Lieutenant Colonel Luis Irizzary of the Puerto Rican National Guard. It was fitting he should be here since it was his men who had participated almost with joyous abandon during the previous year's massacre.

In the next row of dignitaries, there was another man in a white navy uniform standing behind the governor. Antonio noted he had pale, sallow skin that, under the hot tropic sun, was developing red blotches. Despite it, he stood erect, with his naval officer's cap and white-gloved hands clasped in front of his body. It was the eyes. He had eyes strangely similar to Leticia's: bluish-gray. Uncannily so.

Antonio's gaze spanned the crowd watching the celebration: typical townspeople, and even some jíbaros from the outlying hills, all dressed sensibly in white shirts or *guajaberas*, and the women in soft cotton dresses. Only a few men wore suits and ties, as Antonio had.

One of the local secondary school bands had just passed the reviewing stand. What made it noteworthy was they had played John Philip Sousa's "The Stars and Stripes Forever," to which the governor and his party of representatives enthusiastically applauded, bobbing their heads in solid approval.

Out of the corner of his eye, Antonio saw it. A young man had made his way to the front of the crowd and bumped Antonio, rushing past him. The young man looked very familiar. Then it dawned on Antonio: "Angel," he uttered in a whisper. The young man seemed so nondescript in a white short-sleeved shirt and brown slacks, with his dark hair parted to one side. But he had gone past Antonio and was rushing closer to the reviewing stand.

There and then, Antonio knew what was about to happen. "NO!" he shrieked, with those around him turning to look at him curiously. Angel Esteban Antongiorgi, the same youth who had guided Antonio to Octavio's lair, hefted a revolver from his front pants pocket and began firing his gun in rapid succession at where the governor was standing.

The crowd scattered, and Angel was left alone as he fired. Antonio saw that, somehow, Angel had missed his target. Colonel Irizzary, the one standing behind the governor, fell. Then two others on the reviewing stand went down. Next, the governor's chauffeur, dressed in a dark jacket and slacks and his black chauffeur's cap, went down.

Blood dripped from the reviewing stand as the assailant fired shot after shot, some bullets poking holes in the wood of the structure.

Uniformed police standing guard just below the reviewing stand quickly drew their weapons and fired volley after volley at the lone gunman. Round after round imploded into the gunman until his chest was pockmarked with gleaming red holes. He fell, along with others who sought safety from the attack.

Instinctively, Antonio dropped his jacket and went for the ground, covering his head with his hands.

CHAPTER
TWENTY-TWO

AMAZINGLY, ORDER WAS soon restored. Throughout the shooting, Governor Winship remained in the reviewing stand, while police fanned out, looking for more assailants.

A total of thirty-six people were wounded in the crossfire, mainly by trigger-happy police who had riddled the assailant with shot after shot. Among the dead was Irizzary, the National Guard colonel. The wounded included the commissioners of agriculture and commerce and the Speaker of the House of Representatives. No American in the governor's retinue was injured.

It was noted that during the crossfire Governor Winship was heard to state, "What damn poor shots they are." It wasn't clear if he was referring to the assailant, who has missed him completely, or the police response.

He knew that all eyes were on him and his administration, and he was very self-conscious of the fact. Therefore, while medical personnel and people in the crowd were attending to the wounded, he remained standing firm and insisted on reading his prepared address.

The celebration continued, and the governor read his speech stating the importance of Puerto Rico's retaining the help and sympathy of the United States, and how important it was that the Puerto Rican people do nothing to cast doubt on the fact that the island, as a whole, was unquestionably and decidedly loyal to the United States government and the American flag.

Rumaldo Garcia had taken Antonio to town in his carriage, which he had parked a few blocks away from the reviewing stand. Unlike Antonio, he was not up in front, rather deciding to remain somewhere in the back where he could periodically check up on his carriage.

He had heard the shots and the screams, and had seen people running from the parade. Like many, he did not know what was going on, just that it had turned to chaos. Nevertheless, he ran to the front, where he found Antonio face down on the ground, his hands covering his head. Rumaldo help him up, dusted off his jacket, and escorted Antonio back to the carriage.

Just before they climbed up into the carriage, Antonio took in the whole scene: the wounded being evacuated; police, with guns drawn, looking for more assassins; the governor on the stand reading his speech as if nothing had happened; and Angel, the young man who had guided him to the base camp, being carried in a brown horse blanket held at each corner by four policemen. His body was a bloody mass—there was no other way to describe it—the bullet holes oozing globules of red.

"Madness," Antonio murmured. "Madness."

CHAPTER
TWENTY-THREE

ONCE AGAIN PONCE and the surrounding area went into lockdown. A curfew was put in place. No one was allowed on the streets after 8 p.m.

A special unit was set up in the mayoralty to investigate the incident, and a list was quickly made up of those individuals "of interest." Eyewitness accounts stated that Antonio Boglione, Ponce entrepreneur, had once been seen attending a Nationalist meeting at La Perla Theatre. His name was added to the list.

As a result, he was summoned for a "meeting" (they didn't call it questioning) at the mayoralty. Antonio didn't know what to expect as the guards closed the iron gates behind him and led him to the outer courtyard with the oval fountain in the center.

He was escorted upstairs and greeted by Mayor Tormos himself, who thanked him for coming at such short notice.

"What's going on?" Antonio asked.

To which the Mayor replied that Antonio was being summoned as a witness to the recent tragic incident, as so many others had been. It was, as the mayor insisted, "standard procedure," and Antonio would return home shortly.

On the second floor of the mayoralty building, Antonio was led into a corner office, where, sitting behind a desk, was the same naval officer he had seen at the parade. Except this time the officer was dressed in khaki, with a dark tie.

The officer dismissed Antonio's escort and, in somewhat-accented Spanish, thanked Antonio for coming and directed him to a chair facing the desk.

The man went behind the desk and identified himself as Lieutenant Clayton Walker, USN. He picked up a pack of cigarettes from the desk and offered one to Antonio, which he declined. Lieutenant Walker sat down facing Antonio, picked up a sheet of paper from the desk, and began reading: "Mr. Antonio Boglione, of Lorenza Bizo in La Playa, is that correct?"

Antonio said yes, then was about to ask why he had been summoned. Lieutenant Walker stopped him with an upraised hand. "This is not an interrogation," he said. "You have been summoned as a witness regarding the recent assassination attempt on General Winship. We're trying to piece together as much information as we can regarding the attempt. You're one of many who have been called to testify." He paused and then said further, "I've been informed by His Honor, the mayor, that you are one of Ponce's most respected citizens. The mayor vouches for your honesty and loyalty. Of that there is no doubt. We just have some questions that, hopefully, may be of use in explaining this incident."

He put down the sheet of paper and asked, "Do you know Mr. Angel Esteban Antongiorgi?"

Antonio tried to remain still in his chair, though inside his guts were churning. "I recognize the name from what was reported in the papers. He's the man who tried to assassinate the governor."

"That's not what I ask," Lieutenant Walker said pointedly. "Do you know him personally?"

"No," Antonio lied.

"Do you know Tomas Lopez de Victoria?"

"No," Antonio answered truthfully. "Who is he?"

"He's the captain of the Ponce branch of the Cadets of the Republic. And he and five others in that organization have been arrested on suspicion of participating in the attack on General Winship."

"This is the first time I've heard his name," Antonio informed. Throughout, the Lieutenant kept an unnerving gaze on Antonio. Those cold blue-gray eyes, so similar to those of his wife. Could there be American blood in her? he thought.

"Are you familiar with one Octavio Mendoza?" Antonio heard him asking.

"Yes," Antonio answered. "He's a friend who works at the ironworks in La Playa."

"Worked at the ironworks in La Playa," the Lieutenant corrected. "He hasn't been seen nor heard from in weeks."

Antonio considered this last bit of information and said nothing. Walker continued, "Are you close with Octavio Mendosa?"

Antonio knew he had to tread carefully. "We were friends. I know his parents," he mentioned casually.

The blue-gray eyes were unerringly on Antonio. "Did he ever mention to you his Nationalist ties?"

"I knew he had an interest in the independence movement. But it was something we didn't talk about too often. It led to arguments."

The blue-gray eyes perked up. "What kind of arguments?"

Antonio cast his eyes down to the desk, then back up to the blue-gray orbs. "I thought his association with the Nationalists was not beneficial to him or his family."

An eyebrow went up above a blue-gray orb. "Really? You don't approve of the Nationalists?"

Again, Antonio thought carefully before he answered. "I'm a businessman. I deal in profit and loss. Politics for me is irrelevant. I'm not interested in anyone's political views. I only seek to work hard and provide for my family."

155

Walker patted the sheet of paper on his desk as if affirming some thought. "Yet for someone who is 'apolitical,' you were seen at a Nationalist rally recently."

"It wasn't a rally," Antonio defended himself. "I was led to believe it was an academic function at La Perla Theatre. I was invited at the behest of Papo, Octavio. I attend various functions at La Perla. It's a cultural Mecca for us playeros. My wife and I go there often."

"But this was not an 'academic' function," Walker cut in. "It was plainly a political meeting for Nationalist sympathizers."

"That's not what I was told," Antonio pressed on. "La Perla has plays, readings, lectures by various learned personalities. I was told, and it was advertised as being just another lecture from someone with a different point of view."

Walker leaned back in his chair, steepled his fingers. "And what did you think of this lecture?"

"I was left cold. I thought it was too farfetched, too . . ." Antonio sought the right word. ". . . too radical."

Walker leaned forward again, hands down on the desk. "In what way?"

"This man who spoke, I can't recall his name . . ."

"Albizu Campos," Walker put in.

"Yes, him. I couldn't understand why he would rail against the American government. We have a worldwide depression, and we eat and live because of the Americans. They provide our food, they provide our safety, and they leave us alone to pursue our affairs. They bring business to the island. Why would you want to stop that?"

"Interesting." Walker leaned his head to one side, studying the man sitting across from him. "And what was Octavio Mendosa's response?"

"He couldn't understand it. He argued for the Nationalist cause. He was really taken by what this guy Albizu had said."

156

"And you were not?"

"As I've told you, sir, my business is making profit, not politics."

Walker absently patted the desk. "Have you seen or spoken to Octavio Mendosa recently?"

Antonio kept his eyes locked with Walker's. "No."

"Has he tried to contact you in any way?"

"No."

Walker's stare did not deviate. "I see."

This was a game, Antonio was thinking, and it was his turn to start asking questions. "Lieutenant, do you think Octavio Mendosa was involved in this assassination attempt?"

"Right now we're investigating every possibility," Walker said formally. "And we are pursuing every lead. An attempt was made on General Winship. This is the first time that's happened. You can understand our concern and our efforts to prevent such happenings in the future." Walker looked aside, collecting his thoughts. He studied Antonio again. "The Nationalists are a cancer in this land. I firmly believe the majority of Puerto Ricans are loyal citizens. But a cancer, even in the body politic, has to be eradicated, cut out. They will bring ruin to this island if they continue their activities. You're right. We provide a measure of prosperity, and law and order. This island is a part of that great enterprise: the American system. And it's to its benefit."

Walker sat back, considering what he had said and its effect on Antonio Boglione.

For his part, Antonio thought it best to play along. "I agree wholeheartedly, Lieutenant. We have too much at stake, and we can achieve much more with the help of the American government. As a businessman, I would be the first to endorse any measure that helps us to advance our living standards. I have been on this island for many years now. We've come a long way, but we still have much to do."

Walker recalled a piece of information: "I'm told you're from Italy."

"Napoli," Antonio said.

"Yes, Napoli." A smiled appeared on Walker's face. "I was there once on shore leave. It was a while back, but I remember how friendly the people were. But I do recall that parts of Naples were a bit backward."

Antonio gave an expressive shrug. "It's like this island. There are parts of it that still need to be improved."

Walker brought the interview to a close. He offered a hand. "Thank you for coming, Mr. Boglione. I appreciate your time and cooperation."

Antonio shook the hand firmly. "Thank you for your time, Lieutenant."

"I hope to see again sometime," Walker offered informally, "in a more pleasant and social circumstance."

"I will be looking forward to that," Antonio said.

Another smile, and Walker sat down once more behind his desk as he watched Antonio depart. He idly picked up the pack of cigarettes, extracted one, and lit a match. He inhaled deeply, still considering what Antonio had or had not revealed.

The door opened and Mayor Tormos entered the room. "So, what did you think?" he asked.

Walker removed a flake of tobacco from his tongue. "He's an interesting person. He's not from here, which is unique. He seems to have done well in this part of the island and—"

The mayor broke in, anxious to get to the relevant part: "Do you think he has Nationalist ties?"

"No, I don't." Holding the cigarette, Walker pensively rubbed his third finger with his thumb. "He is above suspicion in that regard. He made it clear he has no sympathy for the Nationalist movement."

The mayor looked relieved. "I told you so. He's one of our most prominent citizens in La Playa and is held in high regard by almost everybody."

"So I've heard," Walker said laconically. "Supposedly he came here with nothing, and has made a success of himself." Walker thought on it. "I'd be curious to know how he did it."

"He worked long and hard," the mayor offered. "I should think he epitomizes your ideal of American industry and ingenuity."

"Perhaps he does," Walker said. "But that's not the question."

"What is the question?"

"I don't know." And then Walker considered it further. "Regarding Mr. Boglione, I just don't know."

"You said he's above suspicion."

"I would tend to think so," Walker decided. "I just find him interesting, that's all."

"Do you find all your Nationalist suspects interesting?"

"That's something else altogether. That's political. I don't think Mr. Boglione is political at all. He's interested in making money."

"Nothing wrong with that."

"I guess not," Walker agreed.

"Other than Toño Boglione, how is the investigation going?" the mayor wanted to know.

Walker stared at the lit end of his cigarette. "It's coming along, but it's a long process. The governor wants quick results, but this is going to take time."

Mayor Tormos warbled pleasantly, "I should think this would be a feather in your cap, Lieutenant, being picked to head such an important investigation."

Walker didn't seem that impressed. "I was picked for this assignment because I'm the only one on the governor's staff who can speak passable Spanish. Otherwise, it would have gone to somebody else."

"Still, it was you who was picked, and it's a high honor."

159

"It could be a high honor, or a dismal failure if I fail at this investigation. We need to round up Nationalist suspects and we need to do it fast."

"You'll do well," the mayor asserted. "Rounding up the usual suspects is a common occurrence in this place." He looked at his watch. "Lieutenant, you've been at this inquiry since this morning. I'm sure you're tired of speaking to suspects and witnesses. Why don't you join me for lunch here at the mayoralty?" The mayor's cheeks gleamed. "I have some twelve-year old *añejo*. My private stock. I'm sure you would find it most enjoyable."

Walker took another puff on the cigarette. "Sir, to be truthful, I'm a bit tired of rum. That's all they have here. Right now I would sell my soul for some good old Kentucky bourbon."

"Alas, we cannot provide that at the moment," the mayor commiserated. "For the time being, my private stock will have to do." Mayor Tormos spread his hands out. "Besides, as you yourself know, when in Rome ..."

Walker finished for the mayor, "Yes, when in Rome do as the Romans do. Problem is, this isn't Rome, imperial or modern day."

CHAPTER
TWENTY-FOUR

THE TOWN NEEDED something to lift its spirits. Massacres and shootings were not good public relations, inside or outside of the island. During the height of the interviews, or interrogations, depending on how you looked at it, it was decided the mayoralty would have a grand social function, a show of friendship and comity between the local government and its American friends.

Prominent Ponceños were invited to this gala. Lo and behold, Antonio Boglione, who the previous week had been under scrutiny, was one of the invitees.

Leticia was thrilled. Her father would be there, no doubt, and it would be fun to see her social equals outside of the confines of La Playa. Antonio was less enthused. He would go, naturally, but he felt increasingly trapped in a world that no longer made sense. The only time he found peace was in the arms of Milagros in the beachfront house not far from the municipal cemetery. He was spending more and more time there. Amazingly, Leticia didn't seem bothered by his absences. She took it on principal that he was out working on his various businesses. Or maybe she just didn't care.

In the heat of the evening, Antonio once again donned a dark suit and tie appropriate for the occasion. Leticia was thrilled to once again wear one of her formal gowns. She would look ravishing as always, even if her husband didn't seem to notice.

They were driven to the mayoralty house in Rumaldo Garcia's trusty carriage, something on which Leticia insisted. To Leticia's mind they still represented that vestige of Spanish nobility and breeding. Only un-schooled unsophisticates would show up in automobiles.

The function was held downstairs in the main ballroom. For Antonio it brought to mind a comparison between the sterile office upstairs on the second floor, where he had his meeting with Lieutenant Walker. It seemed like a different world down here, a different reality. Men and women of high status in all their finery sipping on rum and champagne offered on serving trays by unobtrusive servers in livery flitting about with smiles pasted to their faces. Did anyone think about the shooting or the massacre? Antonio wondered. It was as if by sheer force of will, or denial, the past few weeks had been erased from everyone's memories.

"You came! How good it is to see you, my dear."

It was don Eduardo, Leticia's father, who beamed as he held his daughter's hands. "How stunning you look. You make me proud."

Leticia showed an appreciative smile. "Thank you, father. It's so good to see you. Toño and I always wonder when you'll come to visit us in our humble home, don't we, Toño?"

"Yes," Antonio echoed diplomatically. "We don't see you often enough, don Eduardo. And the children always ask about their grand-father."

Don Eduardo looked abashed. "You are so right; I wish I could see them every day. You know how much I enjoy their company. Every time I see them it makes me feel young, but"—he gave a weary shrug—"I've been so busy as of late. What with the current crisis . . . You understand how hectic it's been. I really wish . . ."

Midsentence, Leticia patted her father's chest with her embroi-dered fan. "We know you've been very busy, father. That we understand. Your service to Ponce has always been an honor to us. Toño and I always hold you in our hearts, isn't that right, Toño?" Antonio's attention was elsewhere. "Toño?"

He was observing Lieutenant Walker, this time in his formal navy whites, conversing with Mayor Tormos across the ballroom. "Toño?"

He snapped back to present company. "Yes, of course, don Eduardo. You're public service to Ponce is immensurable. I only wish I could be of more assistance."

"But you have," Eduardo Benítez lauded. "You have given me two beautiful grandchildren. What more can a man ask for? And you have put La Playa on the map. You do me proud."

"Thank you, don Eduardo. Coming from you, that's great praise indeed."

"And worthy of its recipient." Just then Eduardo happened to catch a glimpse of the mayor, who was beckoning him with a flutter of the hand. "Ahhh, His Honor wants to speak to us. Come, let us not disappoint him." He proffered a hand in the direction of the mayor and the lieutenant.

"Are you sure he wants to speak to us?" Antonio asked. "Maybe he just wants to speak to you about some important matter."

Eduardo waved away the thought. "No, of course not. He wants to converse with you as well. He knows how much you've done for this town. And he would certainly enjoy conversing with my beautiful daughter."

"Father, you make me blush." Leticia covered a portion of her face with the fan.

"It's the truth," Eduardo maintained. "You're the most beautiful woman here, as Toño would attest."

"Yes, by all means," Antonio said quickly.

Eduardo guided them to the spot where the mayor and Lieutenant Walker dutifully waited.

163

"Eduardo!" Mayor Tormos greeted. His eyes regaled Leticia. "Your daughter is ravishing as always, and it's always good to see you, Toño."

"It's a pleasure to be here." Antonio offered the mayor his hand, all the while keeping his gaze on Lieutenant Walker.

The mayor shook his hand vigorously. He turned to the lieutenant. "You remember Lieutenant Walker, I'm sure."

"How could I forget," Antonio said deadpan.

He shook hands with the lieutenant, who responded, "It's a pleasure to see you again, señor Boglione."

"Please call me Toño." Antonio then introduced his spouse. "This is my wife, Leticia."

Leticia offered her hand. Walker took it and gave a tilt of his head. "A pleasure, señora."

"The pleasure is mine," said Leticia. "My husband has often spoken about you."

"Oh, he has?" Walker said, brows raised.

Leticia kept her smile. "Yes. He said how industrious you are in your investigation." She entwined her husband's arm with her own. "And he wished he could have been of more assistance."

"I am in his debt," the lieutenant said. "He provided a very useful outlook with regard to Ponce and the current events."

"I'm sure." The smile was still on Leticia's face.

"We're here on a special occasion," the mayor announced, rubbing his hands. "We have a chamber quartet all the way from San Juan. They will perform next week at La Perla, but we've convinced them to debut here tonight. I'm told they are superb."

"We've heard about this function you planned," Eduardo Benítez commended. "I, for one, cannot wait to hear them. Leticia, Toño, I saw them perform last year in San Juan. You won't be disappointed."

164

Leticia held that enticing smile again. "It should be a grand evening."

"It's been a long time since I've heard a chamber quartet," Lieutenant Walker put in. "It will be a pleasure."

"Of that I'm sure," the mayor vouched. "Come, let me guide you into the main hall. They're setting up right now. The seats have been reserved."

In an adjoining hall, wicker chairs had been set up in various rows formed in a semicircle. Mayor Tormos and Lieutenant Walker sat in the center of the front row. On either side of them were other notables, mainly uniformed and civilian representatives from both the local and national government. Antonio, Leticia, and don Eduardo sat in the same row, but at one end of the semicircle.

Leticia considered it a great privilege to sit in the front with all the dignitaries. She mentioned such to Antonio, who agreed, though somewhat ambivalently. He found the whole thing boring. Classical music was not his strong suit, and he had to learn fast how to yawn while keeping his mouth closed.

Lieutenant Walker, the mayor, and their group seemed genuinely pleased and captivated by the chamber group, who performed Mozart's String Quartet No. 15 in D minor and other classics.

There was a brief intermission during the evening. Most used this time to head for the latrines in the back of the mayoralty house or else avail themselves of the various chamber pots stored in one room at the rear of the building. There had been frequent talk of having indoor plumbing installed at least in the mayoral house, but it hadn't yet come to pass.

Lieutenant Walker used this opportunity to get some fresh air on the lower veranda adjacent to the main hall. He stepped out into a sultry evening replete with the sounds of the ever-present coquis chirping from the bushes. He extracted a cigarette case from his breast pocket, took out a cigarette, tapped it on the case, and lit it with his American lighter.

He exhaled pleasurably. His thoughts were on the files he had amassed during his investigation, inclusive of the one on Antonio Boglione.

"Lieutenant, are you enjoying the performance?" His reverie was interrupted by a dulcet voice.

He turned to find Leticia Benítez's gaze on him. "What do you think of our humble chamber group?"

"They're not so humble," Walker credited. "The last chamber performance I was privy to was in Charleston. The artists here today are worthy of any such ensemble in the world."

Leticia thought for a moment. "Charleston? That's in the southern United States, right?"

"Charleston's in South Carolina. And, yes, it is the south."

"I've never been there," Leticia mentioned, "but I'm told it's a charming city."

"That it is," Walker said with pride.

"Are you from Charleston?"

"No, señora. I'm from Texas."

Leticia thought again. "Texas?"

"You call it 'Tejas,'" Walker explained.

Leticia flashed recognition. "Oh yes, Tejas. It was once a province of Spain. But long ago."

"Yes, long ago." Walker sucked on his cigarette, blowing smoke to one side.

Leticia pointed to the cigarette case Walker had placed on the veranda. "Can I have one of those?"

Walker wasn't expecting this. Women smoking was frowned upon in Ponce. He recovered quickly. "Oh yes, by all means." He opened the case, offered a cigarette to Leticia, and lit it with his lighter.

Leticia took a long, pleasurable inhale. "How long have you been on our island?" she asked.

"Not long," Walker said. "It's been about a year now. This is shore duty for me."

"Do you enjoy being here?"

"It's interesting," Walker said.

"Your Spanish is very good," Leticia remarked in passing. "Where did you learn it?"

"I hate to contradict you, señora, but my Spanish is not that good. It's passable. I need to work on it."

"I disagree, Lieutenant. You Spanish may not be Castilian, but it's very adequate."

"Thank you." Walker seemed pleased. "I take that as a compliment."

"It wasn't meant as a compliment," Leticia said tersely. "It was meant as fact."

"Still, coming from you, señora, I feel privileged."

"It is I who am privileged," Leticia stated. "I've never conversed with a naval officer before."

"And I've never conversed with someone as lovely as you, señora."

Leticia was taken aback by the remark. No one had ever been so forthright on such short notice. "Well, thank you, Lieutenant." She couldn't help blushing. "I must say, you are direct."

Now it was Walker who was taken aback by the remark. "I'm sorry, señora, if I've offended you."

Leticia disregarded it. "Oh, no offense, Lieutenant. It's refreshing to meet someone so forthright. I wish it was more the common norm."

"Oh, there you are!"

Leticia heard her father's voice coming from inside. She quickly cast the cigarette to the floor and squashed it under her shoe.

Her father was next to them now. "I've been looking for you. The concert is about to resume."

"Blame it on me, don Eduardo," Walker said gallantly. "I find your daughter intellectually stimulating. She obviously takes after her father."

"You are a diplomat, Lieutenant," Eduardo Benítez said, "even when flattering an older man."

"I am sincere in my praise," Walker said, his eyes on Leticia. "You should be proud of your daughter, and your son-in-law as well. I've heard great and positive things about him. You have a worthy family."

"Again, thank you, Lieutenant." Don Benítez held an outstretched arm. "The music awaits."

Leticia took her father's arm and walked with him into the next room, with Lieutenant Walker dutifully following the guests.

CHAPTER TWENTY-FIVE

LIEUTENANT WALKER SAT in his chair in his small, airless office on the top floor of the mayoralty house. He smoked a cigarette, while his hand lay atop a file folder containing the latest remnants of his investigation. The gala downstairs was over, and he was glad. Now he could focus his attention on the real work.

The office door opened, and Mayor Tormos appeared, carrying a small sack. "I imagined you'd be here, Lieutenant," he said. "You're a stickler for work."

"We must complete a mission once it's been given," Walker countered crisply.

"How did you like this evening's affair?" the mayor asked, trying to make small talk.

"It was quite nice," Walker admitted. "I got to hobnob with some of Ponce's most illustrious, inclusive of Mr. and Mrs. Boglione."

"Señora Boglione is quite beautiful, is she not?" the mayor queried.

Walker took a drag on the cigarette, thought about it, and said, "Indeed she is. But right now I'm more interested in señor Boglione."

He patted the file folder on the desk. "I have his file here. He's a fascinating individual. Not a native to Ponce, but still he has managed to build its one movie house, its one eatery, and he was instrumental in forming the fire department in the area where he lives. He owns numerous properties in town and in the outskirts. He has done rather well for himself. Question is: How did he make his money?"

"As I've said before," Mayor Tormos noted, "he worked hard, the way most of us make our money. How he got rich is not the question; it's whether he is a loyal citizen or not. That's the question. And I, for one, do not doubt his loyalty."

Walker stubbed the cigarette on an ashtray on the desk. "I'm not questioning his loyalty. I just find him an interesting person."

"You've made note a few times about how 'interesting' he is." Mayor Tormos looked at Walker sidelong. "And what do you think of his wife?"

"As you said, she's very attractive."

"She's considered one of Ponce's great beauties. It was a shock to us all that she would consent to marry Toño Boglione. After all, he comes from La Playa, not even the town. But he is an up-and-comer." The mayor nodded sagely. "In retrospect, a good union."

"I'm sure." Walker placed his elbows on the desk and rested his chin on his hands. "Señora Boglione is striking."

"Yes, she is," Mayor Tormos readily concurred. "Did you notice her eyes? They're a lot like yours in a way. Some would say she has American blood in her. It makes her distinctive."

"Yes, it does."

The mayor looked placidly at Walker, then held up the sack bag he carried. "But I came here for other reasons, not to discuss Ponce gossip." He extracted a bottle from the bag, showed it to Walker. "I thought you would like this."

The blue-gray eyes twinkled. "I don't believe it!"

"Yes, you do." The mayor handed the bottle to Walker, who cradled it lovingly in one hand. "I. W. Harper, my favorite bourbon." He looked up, surprised. "How did you get this?"

170

Mayor Tormos gave a conspiratorial smile. "This is a present from the Ferrer family. You met señor Ferrer tonight at the gala. They often travel to the United States and bring back items seldom found here. Señor Ferrer was kind enough to offer the bottle as a gift, which I present to you."

"I'm in your debt." Walker admired his gift. "I haven't had good bourbon since I've been here."

"Enjoy it in good health, Lieutenant," Mayor Tormos said. "Heaven knows, these days such pleasures are hard to come by."

CHAPTER
TWENTY-SIX

SHE SCOOPED UP a mound of dirt, placed the seeds in the small pocket of earth, and covered the seeds with more dirt. Next, she tapped down the earth. A shadow crossed her gloved hands, and she looked up.

Antonio was looking down at her with a sense of wonder. "Are you growing a garden or burying a frog?" he asked.

Milagros looked up, smiling. "Growing a garden," she said.

He put out a hand, helping her to her feet. He scanned the mounds of earth in the backyard, with the old mango tree to one side, a tree with a profusion of mangoes that, when in season, would litter the ground. "You never cease to amaze me. When did you decide to start gardening?"

Milagros wiped her forehead with the back of a gloved hand. "I just thought I might as well put this yard to use. So I'm planting some flowers and some vegetables. I hate for this good earth to go to waste."

Antonio bent down and grabbed a handful, rubbing it between his fingers. "It is good earth, isn't it?"

"That's what my mother said when she was last here. It was her idea to start a garden. It's good to give back to the earth, she said."

"She's right." He pointed to the large straw hat she wore. "It's good you have head covering. The sun here is fierce."

She began removing her dirt-stained gloves. "The sun is always fierce in Ponce. My mother said that in the old days they use to call it the Devil's Cauldron."

"I've heard that before," Antonio remembered. "Your mom has it right."

Milagros noted the brown package he cradled in one bent arm. "What's that?"

Antonio looked down at the brown bag. "Oh, it's something I got in town."

"What is it?"

He gave a devious smile. "It's a present."

"A present?"

"Yes. For you."

"What is it? Let me see." She reached out for the package.

He turned, placing his arm with the package behind his back. "Not until we go into the house."

"Toño," she said in a dejected tone, "I want to see my present."

"Let's go inside first," he suggested. "Then I'll show you your present."

"Promise?"

"Yes."

She followed him inside, into the kitchen. "Okay, let's see it!"

"Not yet."

"What do you mean, 'not yet'?"

"We gotta go in the living room first."

She had a dubious look. "Toño, what's going on?"

"You'll see."

She tried grabbing the package away from him. He held it out at arm's length. "You're a devil," she accused.

He laughed. "I know."

She followed into the living room furnished with rattan chairs and tables with plaster figurines of eighteenth-century dandies and ladies in hoop skirts. It had become a passion for her, collecting these figurines.

"You're going to show me now?" she urged.

"Yes." With a regal gesture he opened the paper bag and took out a white vase with ornate oriental flower patterns inscribed on it.

Amazed and awed, she clutched her cheeks. "It's beautiful!"

"I thought you'd like it." He handed the vase to her.

She took it gently in her hands, turning it over to inspect the workmanship. "I love it! Where did you get it?"

"One of my clients owned me a debt," he said. "But the gentleman has fallen on hard times and he has no cash, so instead he paid with this item."

She held the vase admiringly. "It's Chinese! I've seen things like these in movies. It's beautiful!"

"That it is. It's probably the only Chinese vase in La Playa."

"Maybe in all of Ponce." She held out the vase, inspecting it from a different angle.

"Could be," he said. "It's yours now."

She clutched the vase close to her breasts. "Thank you, Toño. It's the most beautiful gift I've ever received."

"It's as beautiful as you," he flattered genuinely. "You deserve it."

"Oh, Toño." She held out a hand, seeking to touch him.

He took her hand, looking at her lovingly.

"You're a good man, Toño," she said.

"Not really. I just happen to love a good woman."

She looked around her living room. "Now, where can we put it?"

"Wherever you want."

She supported her face on one finger, deep in thought. "Hmmm. I don't think it goes with my figurines. Perhaps . . ." She had a flash of inspiration. "I know! We'll put it in our bedroom. It'll be our Chinese vase. Just for us, no one else."

"If that's what you want."

She was emphatic. "That's what I want."

"Whatever you say, my love." He came closer and cupped her face in his hands. "I just want to make you happy."

"I am." She looked around again. "Let's see where we can put this." She led him to the bedroom, and she found the spot: right on the dresser next to the bed. She set down the vase. "Doesn't it look beautiful?"

"Yes, it does."

She stroked his cheek. "Thank you, Toño."

"No," he said, "thank you for making me so happy."

She turned to look out the window in the bedroom, to the trees outside that surrounded the house. "Are you happy?" she asked almost in a forlorn tone.

"Yes, I am."

"I'm glad." She became quiet, and it made him curious. Something wasn't quite right.

"Milagros?"

"Yes."

"Something wrong? You don't like the present?"

"I love the present."

"Then why are you so glum so suddenly?"

Still looking aside, she said, "Toño, I'm pregnant."

He stood still, not moving a limb. "What?"

She raised troubled eyes at him. "I'm pregnant, with your child."

"When . . . when did you find out?"

"I was late, and I thought maybe it was just something else," she began, "but then I went to see Dr. Rincón, and he . . ." She stopped, silent again.

"He verified it," Antonio concluded.

"Yes."

She turned away again, looking out the window. "What are we going to do, Toño?"

He stepped closer and took her in his arms, her face nestling into his chest. She was crying softly. "This is our child," he said. "Nothing can take that away from us. This is our child."

She snuffled into his chest, staining his shirt with her tears. "Toño, I'm sorry."

He stroked her hair, still so short, almost like filaments of hair more than anything else. "This is our child," he repeated. "Nothing can take that away from us."

"But, Toño, your family, your—"

He didn't let her finish. "Don't worry about them. Our concern now is our child, no one else. We have a son. That's the important thing. We have a son."

"It could be a daughter," she said.

"No matter. It's our child."

CHAPTER
TWENTY-SEVEN

IT BEGAN AS a storm out in the Atlantic. Once it moved west from the Cape Verde islands it had become a full-blown hurricane. That's what it became known as: The Great Hurricane. Meteorologists from the US Weather Bureau calculated that a warm front to the east of the storm would push the hurricane due north of Puerto Rico and east of the Bahamas islands. Puerto Rico had always been susceptible to hurricanes, and for the next twenty-four hours the storm traveled 300 miles west by north at the speed of twelve and a half miles per hour.

In the mid-1930s the US Weather Bureau had been reorganized and had set up a local office in San Juan. It was part of a more extensive communication system that provided data, but mainly to the US, with emphasis on the eastern seaboard. For those living in the interior of the island the system was scant, if non-existent.

Those living on the southern coast of the island were more fortunate. The Ponce mayoralty did get a report from San Juan about the incoming hurricane, and a select few were notified. This included don Eduardo Benítez, who was informed of the incoming storm by Lieutenant Walker.

Telephone lines were not yet installed in La Playa, and don Benítez had to travel to Antonio's house in person to inform him of what was coming. The bright morning sun had given way to a cloudy gun-metal sky, with the clouds hanging low like huge sponges waiting to be squeezed.

Don Benítez found his daughter, like everyone in La Playa, apprehensively gazing at the sky. Storms and hurricanes were a natural phenomenon in this area. Most knew the difference between a short rainfall and a massive storm. Added to that, it seldom rained in Ponce. You either had a light shower or a massive downpour. Early on the Ponceños had learned to tell the difference very quickly. Songs had even been written about hurricanes and their impact. This time it was no song; it was fact.

Antonio was up on Lorenza Bizo Street conducting his business with Juan-Carlos Quiles. It was relegated to Elena, the housekeeper, to get someone from Carmelo's cafetín to go inform Antonio that Eduardo Benítez was at his house and needed to speak to him quickly.

Antonio had an inkling of what was to come. Doña Saro early that morning had also inspected the gun-metal sky and told him, "This is not good."

When Antonio asked what was wrong, Doña Saro had replied in two words: "San Ciprian." That had been the massive storm of '32 that had left most of Ponce in desolation. And as she pointed upward, this was the same cruel sky.

When Carmelo's messenger reached him at Juan-Carlos's house, Antonio was ready for what was to come. He left Juan-Carlos and came home to find Leticia ready to place the children in the carriage and head for safer ground in town. For the duration, they would stay at the Benítez home on Victoria Street. The home was not of the flimsy construction of most of the dwellings in La Playa. Leticia, the children, and Elena would be safe there until the storm blew over.

Antonio agreed this was the wiser course and thanked don Benítez for his concern. He, in turn, alluded to the slight breeze coming in from the north, a damp, cool breeze unusual for Ponce. Leticia snuggled the children in blankets and wrapped a shawl around her shoulders. Elena, also wrapped in a shawl, complained about the cold. It was a sure sign that the Ponce weather had changed.

"We must hurry," Eduardo Benítez said to everyone.

Antonio stated that he would stay behind. Now that his family would be safe in town, he felt it was his duty to check on doña Saro and others in La Playa.

When Leticia, miffed, asked why, he said it was simply because that's where his businesses were. He still had to make sure the receipts were counted and his work accomplished. Besides, once he knew doña Saro and Juan-Carlos were alright, he would travel back to town. He did not tell her that he was also concerned about Milagros, who lived on the other side of town.

Leticia told him to be careful and come to her father's house as soon as possible.

Antonio promised he would.

Don Benítez flicked his whip, and the carriage wheeled forward, heading for Padre San German Street, then turned at the cemetery, and into town.

Antonio set about locking up the house. It was in the middle of shutting up the windows that the first rainfall happened. There followed a howling wind, and finally torrents of water began tearing into the structure from the outside. The rain had intensified. The storm was on its way.

CHAPTER
TWENTY-EIGHT

DOÑA SARO REMAINED in the back of her house, tying down the various basins and tubing with sturdy rope. Outside, the rain slammed against the wooden slats. She had closed the windows and nailed them shut from the inside, but the wind seemed intent on tearing the wooden planks apart. It was as if her entire house was inside a vortex of wind and water. It got so bad that one of the planks ripped open and sailed across the room, missing her head by inches. Then water started cascading into the room from the outside. She tried to push back the wooden shutter that had been flung open by the wind, now useless; the rain smacked into her face and eyes. She finally gave up on it and nestled in a corner beside her lead-lined basins and bottles of homemade rum. She flung a blanket over her head and began praying. The sound of the wind roared past her like some insane creature.

Just as quickly, the wind died down. It was now a whoosh rather than a roar. That's when she felt the water pool around her feet. Then the house lurched to one side like a boat about to capsize. This terrified her, and she screamed.

The water was now surfing through her ankles and feet. She threw off the blanket and looked about. The room was filling up with water. It came from beneath the planks in the house, through crevices where the floor met the walls. Her house was drowning beneath her.

She shut her eyes, crossed herself, and prayed harder.

The rain stopped. She could feel droplets from the roof, and it wasn't battering the house anymore. A miracle, she thought, the house had survived the storm. Then she felt it lurching slowly to one side again.

She got up and, walking at an angle since the house was no longer upright, made it to the kitchen, where plates had shattered all over, and then to the living room, also partially filled with water. Part of her veranda was still there, although half of it had been blown away. It looked like a slanting, ripped fence. The stilts that she had installed to keep the house safe from the water were now gnarled pieces of wood floating alongside the flotsam and jetsam of Ponce.

Trying to keep upright on the angled floor, she made it to the upper part of her veranda where a portion of the veranda fence still held. She sat at the edge of the house and waited, the water continually rising. If she was finally going to meet her late husband Ramon, so be it, she thought. She had lived too long anyway.

She wasn't going to meet Ramon again, at least not this day. Floating up the street that had become a river came a small rowboat with two occupants, one manning the oars and the other sitting at the front. The man at the oars rowed strenuously with the current; he wore a yellow raincoat with a hood that partially covered his face. The other occupant was definitely a woman, with a shawl covering her head and upper body.

The rain had left a residue of mist, more like fog, floating above the water. The boat came closer to the slanting veranda. "Toño!"

Straining against the oars, Antonio maneuvered the rowboat close to the edge of the sinking house. He pulled in the oars, scooped up a rope from the bottom of the boat, and tied it to a piece of the partially defunct veranda. He stood up uncertainly, reaching for a piece of veranda wood, and pulled himself up to the floor not yet inundated.

He took Saro by the hand and helped her down into the rowboat. Saro sat on a boat plank, still wrapped in her blanket and facing the woman at the front of the rowboat, whom she recognized immediately. "Milagros?"

184

Milagros removed her shawl and bared her close-cropped head. "It's good to see you again, doña Saro, even under the circumstances."

Saro remained silent for some seconds, taking it all in. Then she asked, "How did you both get here?"

"Toño got us here."

Antonio climbed back down into the rowboat. He sat down and took up the oars again. "You know each other?"

"I've known Milagros and her mother all my life," Saro revealed. "Her mother and I both come from Vieques." She turned to face Antonio. "I guess it's lucky for both of us you came when you did." She fingered the rough-hewn wood where she sat. "Where did you get the boat?"

"It belongs to Juan-Carlos Quiles," Antonio said. "Normally he uses it to travel to Coffin Island." Antonio measured the watery surroundings. "But not today."

"And how is Juan-Carlos? Is he safe?"

"He was smart," Antonio answered. "He left early this morning for his daughter's place in town. He had a premonition this storm was going to be a bad one."

Saro eyed the half-inundated house with the rapidly sinking veranda. "He was smart. This is a bad one. Just as bad as San Ciprian."

"So I've heard." Antonio took hold of the oars, about to row off. "But first I've got to get both of you to safety."

Saro drew a breath, visibly troubled. "Toño, Jacobo lives on the Dead End. It's murderous when that river rises, and this is the worst it's been in a long time." Her gaze turned to the inundated street, sunk in gloom. "We can't leave him there. He may be in a bad way."

"She's right," Milagros affirmed. "He's an elderly man. He may need help."

"We all need help," said Antonio, resting his hands on the oars. "But you're right. I hadn't considered Jacobo and the others who live in the

185

Dead End." He started rowing again, away from the sinking veranda. "We're going there right now."

Like doña Saro, Jacobo was stuck on his veranda, but by choice. Since he lived on the second floor of the house owned by Domingo the carpenter, his second-floor domicile was, up to now, free of flooding. But Domingo's first floor had been inundated, with the water in some areas going up to mid-waist. He had hustled his two adolescent daughters and wife up to Jacobo's second floor. And like Saro's home, some of the stilts had buckled or been washed away so that the house inched downward at an angle. The water was now even with the second-floor veranda.

Jacobo had provided the wife and children with bed sheets and shawls to keep them relatively dry. With his wood stove Jacobo had made hot chocolate for everyone. Then he and Domingo had taken up a vigil on the veranda, waiting for whatever would come next.

From their vantage point on the veranda, Jacobo and Domingo saw the river still rising. Unless something happened soon, it was conceivable that all of the Dead End would be inundated in no time.

Whereas Saro had seen one solitary figure on a rowboat coming toward her, Jacobo and Domingo saw three individuals: two wrapped in a blanket and shawl, and another in yellow raingear.

As the boat came closer, they could discern that it was Antonio manning the oars, with Milagros and Saro sitting up front, guiding him closer to the veranda.

"Toño, you're a welcome sight!" exclaimed Domingo.

"I see that, like Noah, you've circumvented the flood," added Jacobo. He looked down to doña Saro, sitting calmly in the boat. "Glad to see you as well, Saro."

"Same here," Saro said.

He regarded Milagros. "I have seen this lovely young lady in the plaza. Welcome."

186

"It's a pleasure to meet you, don Jacobo."

"The pleasure is all mine, albeit I wish the weather had been more appropriate."

Antonio climbed up over the veranda parapet. "Glad to see you and Domingo are okay," he said. "But we have to get you out fast; the water's rising."

"It's not just us," said Jacobo. "Mingo's family is inside. We have to get them to safety."

Antonio aimed a finger to where both Saro and Milagros waited. "We only have space for two or three more people. This could pose a problem."

"But I have my family inside," Domingo pleaded.

Jacobo offered a solution: "Mingo, you and your family go. I'll stay here and look after the house."

Saro heard that and she called out, "But if the water rises more, what will happen to you?"

"Don't worry about me," Jacobo asserted. "I'll be alright. Just get Mingo and his family to safety."

Antonio wasn't so sure. "Look, even if we get Mingo and his family out, one of us will have to stay here with you, Jacobo. There's room for only three more in the boat."

"I'll stay behind," Domingo volunteered. "You go on."

Antonio and Jacobo exchanged glances. Each knew what the other was thinking, and Antonio spoke up, "Mingo, you can row the boat to higher ground. I'll stay here with Jacobo. We'll keep watch on the house."

"But the river's rising!"

"Don't worry," Jacobo reassured. "Toño and I will be alright. The river's bound to crest soon enough. We'll be safe."

Domingo gulped. "But what if it doesn't?"

187

"Trust me," Jacobo said. "We'll be fine. You take care of your family and the others. We'll see you shortly."

"You swear," Domingo demanded.

"I swear."

Domingo's brown leathery face turned to Antonio. "And you."

"I swear," Antonio echoed.

"Soon as I can I'll come back for you," Domingo told him.

"You just go," Antonio urged. "Get them to higher ground."

Domingo clasped Antonio arm. "Thank you. I will come back."

"I know," Antonio said.

They went inside the house and guided the children and Domingo's wife out to the veranda. Then Domingo climbed down the veranda parapet and into the boat. Antonio helped the family climb over the veranda, while Domingo helped them into the pitching boat. Last was Domingo's wife, Adelaida, who at first refused to leave Jacobo to face the elements alone. Jacobo appealed to her reason, stating someone had to look after the children. They couldn't be left abandoned.

Adelaida acquiesced and went down into the boat. Domingo started rowing them away, but not before Milagros called out, "Don Jacobo, Toño, take care, please!"

"We will." Antonio waved them off.

They watched as Domingo rowed the small, lumbering boat away from the Dead End and up to higher ground and safety.

Once the boat was out of sight, Jacobo took Antonio inside, into his living room. The water now dribbled to foot level. Jacobo blew out his breath disgustedly. "I thought we were over this, but it looks like we're not. I remember the San Ciprian hurricane." He took in the room with one sweep of a hand. "This is just as bad."

"I'm told it comes with the territory up here," Antonio quipped.

Jacobo clapped him on the shoulder. "You know, I have a bottle of brandy that I've been keeping for a special occasion. It seems to me this is as good a time as any to enjoy that brandy." He went over to a small cabinet in a corner of the room, opened it, and brought out an oblong bottle. "This is something that I managed to take with me when I left my homeland. I've been saving it ever since. Come join me." He took out two tumblers from the cabinet, offering Antonio a glass.

Antonio held out the glass while Jacobo pulled the cork top and poured the brandy. "This is Fundador," Jacobo said proudly, "a very popular brand in my homeland. I, myself, prefer Felipe Segundo, but this is all I could get my hands on before . . ." He stopped, as if recalling a bad, stinging memory.

Antonio breached the silence. "Under the circumstances, this is an honor. It's been a long time since I've enjoyed Spanish brandy." He held up the glass. "¡Salud!"

Jacobo poured himself some brandy. "L'chaim!"

Antonio gave him an odd look, not knowing the toast.

"To life!" Jacobo said, taking a good swallow.

They spent the remainder of the day and part of the night drinking brandy in the damp aftermath of the hurricane. Eventually the river crested and the water stopped rising. More boats came floating out throughout Ponce, the only mode of transportation for days to come. By the time the water dissipated, the streets and remaining houses were covered in mud.

CHAPTER TWENTY-NINE

WHILE ANTONIO AND his people struggled with the hurricane, Eduardo Benítez and his daughter fared no better. On the way to town the sky had become an ominous, dark shroud. The wind had increased, and tree branches and palm leaves pelted the coach and horse at a rapid clip.

The horse struggled valiantly against the oncoming wind, and the carriage veered from side to side as the wind buffeted the wooden rig. Eduardo Benítez had to use all his strength to keep hold of the reins. On top of it, the eldest child, Camilo, started squalling in conjunction with the howling blasts. Leticia cooed to him and embraced him closer, but to no avail. All the while, the youngest child, Maria, looked on with a sense of unconcerned wonder.

And he stopped crying. Just like that. The wailing gave way to a disturbing quiet, since suddenly the wind had died down and an eerie calm ensued, almost like the child was taking his cues from the environment around him.

Don Benítez and Leticia traded worried looks. Somehow this new-found calm was just as unsettling as the previous belching wind.

Eduardo Benítez took a gander up at the blackening sky, then looked to each side. The palm trees were now motionless, like statues set in stone. Even the branches and sticks littering their path remained still.

He quickly rummaged behind the back seat of the carriage and whisked out a rumpled horse blanket. "Cover the children!" he ordered.

His tone unsettled Leticia. "What's wrong?"

"Get in the back seat and stay covered with the children."

"Why?"

"Do it. Now!"

Leticia didn't argue. She climbed down into the back seat, holding the blanket. As she began to cover the children and herself, the wind roared again, smacking against the coach. Then she felt the rain on her face, the little droplets making a dull, thudding sound on the fabric of the blanket.

The droplets increased. In seconds they were fistfuls of rain, followed by a seeming wave of water rocking the carriage and its passengers. The wave surged, and it was coming at them from all sides. It seemed the sky had grown massive arms lugging huge bucketfuls of water.

The horse brayed. Don Benítez could not hold on. The beast had become as crazed as the elements. It reared upward, the rain pecking at its eyes and face. It struggled to set itself free from the yoke tied to the coach. Don Benítez whipped at its back, trying to get the horse into line. A massive wall of rain slammed against the coach. The horse lunged forward, the coach overturned, and the horse broke free of its restraints, rushing headlong into the storm, dragging behind the wooden sidings now torn free from the carriage.

The carriage landed on its side, one wheel spinning madly, the other clamped under the weight of the carriage and passengers.

The children screamed. Leticia screamed. Their world was now turned sideways, and everything was at an angle.

When the carriage overturned, Eduardo Benítez was thrown to the ground, falling on his right side. Luckily, the ground had turned to mud, which cushioned his fall, and he didn't sustain any injuries. He scampered up from the mud, hearing the screams of the children and Leticia. He rushed to the upended carriage and pulled Camilo out of the carriage. Next he pulled out Leticia, who held tightly to Maria. A blast of wind

192

knocked Eduardo backward, and he fell on his behind, into the mud. He scrambled up just as quickly, grabbed the soaked blanket, and draped it around Leticia and the children.

He quickly measured his surroundings. A massive, sturdy palm tree was still standing to his right side, a few yards away. There was always the danger the tree could be uprooted by the massive hurricane, yet they could not stay in the mud while the storm raged. Whatever comfort they could find was better than none. So he ushered them to the tree, where they huddled under swaying palm leaves and branches, waiting for some sort of rescue.

The deluge came in spurts. It would thunder out of nowhere and submerge everything around them, churning up the mud and threatening to tear off branches from the palm tree. Just as suddenly it would stop, and there would be relative quiet for some moments. Then the massive clamor would begin again.

It was during one of these quiet intervals that they saw it coming toward them: a black phantom on wheels. They could hear the car engine straining against the wind and rain, the wheels treading on mud. The automobile lurched from side to side, just as their carriage had done, but each time it righted itself and came nearer.

The car stopped in front of the tree. Its headlights illuminated the spectral rain. The driver's side door swung open, and into the mud stepped a figure cloaked in an olive-green poncho. He maneuvered his way through the mud and came closer. When the man pulled back the hood of the poncho they recognized him immediately.

"Lieutenant Walker!" Don Benítez could not contain his surprise and glee. "¡Gracias a Dios! How did you get here?"

Walker hooked a thumb toward the black Ford sedan. "I was able to requisition one of the few cars in the mayoralty."

"I thank our Lord that you came," Eduardo Benítez said gratefully. "I feared we were lost in this hurricane."

Walker was looking at Leticia and the children huddled around her. "How are you doing, señora?"

"I'm fine," said Leticia. "It's the children I'm concerned about."

"They'll be fine once we get you back to town." Walker reached down and took one of the children from Leticia. He cradled Camilo in one arm and with his free hand helped Leticia get to her feet. He walked them to the back seat of the car, guiding Leticia inside; then he handed her the child.

He came back to the tree, where don Benítez was trying to get up while holding onto Maria. Walker took Maria in his arms and helped don Benítez to the car. The child was deposited in the back seat along with her mother and brother. Don Benítez sat in the front, with Walker behind the wheel.

Don Benítez noted the water splattering on the windshield. "This rain comes in spurts. It gets vicious at times. Do you think you can make it back to town?"

Walker grabbed the wheel, looking straight ahead at the storm. "I've been in worse spots with this car. I'm a navy man. I know about water. We'll make it."

"I sincerely hope so," Eduardo Benítez said, sounding doubtful.

Walker looked in the rearview mirror, at the back seat. "Are you okay, señora?"

"We're fine," Leticia said. "And thank you for coming to our aid."

"It was just chance. But I'm glad it was you I found."

"As are we," Leticia said, looking back at the gray-blue eyes in the rearview mirror.

They reached town through fits and starts in the pouring rain. Just as with the carriage, the car swerved from one side of the road to the other. Unlike a frightened horse, the car engine rambled on. Walker expertly maneuvered the steering wheel, going with the direction of each skid, rather than in the opposite direction, so that when the car veered he quickly got it back on course and drove on. Twice they were engulfed in rivers of mud, and Walker and don Benítez had to get out and push the car forward until they were free. Walker had given his poncho to Leticia so that she could cover the children in an added layer of warmth. While outside, his khaki uniform was splattered with mud until its color was a dark brown.

They reached the mayoralty building and settled on the main-floor ballroom where cots were set up for the family. Everyone was treated to hot chocolate while they rode out the storm. Don Benítez went upstairs to the second floor to confer with Mayor Tormos, while Leticia looked after the children downstairs. They were soon asleep on a cot while Leticia, sitting next to them, watched their even and slow breathing as they slept, oblivious to everything around them.

Walker came downstairs, bringing a thermos of hot coffee. He poured some into the thermos cup and handed it to her. "You've had a hard day, señora." He looked out toward one of the glass windows smeared with rainwater. "Hopefully, the worst of the storm has passed."

Leticia took a sip of strong coffee, felt it warm her body. "It's been a hard day for all Ponceños," she said. She eyed him from beyond the rim of the cup. "Please, stop being so formal. My name is Leticia, and thank you for all your help."

"It was just pure dumb luck that I came upon you and your family," Walker confided. "I was heading for the mayor's own house on the outskirts of town. He had asked me to check on it. He had fears that it might be vandalized during the storm. People these days will do anything to get something for free."

"These are hard times." Leticia handed the thermos cup back to Walker. "But I'm glad you found us. I don't know what we would've done under that tree with all the rain and wind coming at us." She viewed her sleeping children, wrapped in blankets on the cot. "I was worried about the children more than anything else. It would've been terrible if..."

"No need to worry now, señora—I mean, Leticia. You and the children are safe. This building is the best place to be during a storm."

Leticia couldn't help but smile. "Is it so difficult to call me by my name?"

Walker grinned in return. "You have to forgive me. I'm not the best with social norms."

"I would disagree," Leticia said. "I've seen you interact with others in the mayoralty. You don't have to worry about social norms."

"Thank you." A short silence ensued. Then Walker said, "Is there anything else I can get you?"

"No, thank you. We're alright now. The children have had hot chocolate and they're asleep."

"What about food?" Walker asked. "Have you or the children eaten anything?"

"Miraculously, I'm not hungry. Food is the farthest thing from my mind right now. I'm still nursing my daughter, and I may need some fresh milk for myself later on."

"That will be no problem. I'll get you anything you need."

"Again, thank you, Lieutenant."

"What about your husband?" Walker asked. "Where is he now?

"He stayed at the house. He was worried about some others in La Playa. I fervently hope he's okay."

"I'm sure he is," Walker offered in assurance. "I've heard amazing things about your husband. I'm sure he'll be fine. He strikes me as a survivor."

"That he is," Leticia said knowingly. "Still, I'll feel better when I know he's alive and well."

"He'll be alright," Walker consoled. "I'm sure of it."

"I hope you're right, Lieutenant," Leticia said in a faraway tone. "I sincerely hope you're right."

Walker capped the thermos closed. "I'll come back later to check up on you and the children. If you need anything, don't hesitate to ask. The mayor's secretary is upstairs. She's at your beck and call."

"You've been very kind to us, Lieutenant," Leticia said. "I'll remember that."

"I am honored to have assisted you in any way."

"It is we who are honored," Leticia said in return.

CHAPTER
THIRTY

LIEUTENANT WALKER ENTERED the ballroom dressed in his white uniform. Leticia never before had noticed how resplendent he looked with his row of ribbons above the left breast pocket. Every head turned as he strode confidently into the room, with its mass of well-attired Ponce elite. Everyone of note was there: Mayor Tormos; her father, don Eduardo; the local police chief; even Juan-Carlos Quiles from La Playa. The only one not present was Antonio, and she wondered why.

Walker ignored everyone in the gathering and made a beeline to where Leticia was standing with a group of other ladies, flouting their best finery. He approached, showing a dazzling smile. "Leticia, how good it is to see you."

"It's my pleasure to see you again, Lieutenant," Leticia replied.

"Please call me Clayton, I insist."

Leticia matched his smile. "Very well, Clayton, if you insist."

"I insist." Walker bowed his head slightly to the others present. "Ladies."

The three women standing with Leticia showed proper radiant reserve, but all seemed taken with the dashing naval officer. Still, it did not go unnoticed how attentive Lieutenant Walker seemed toward Leticia. And she noted it as well, which made her slightly uncomfortable.

"It's a shame you didn't come sooner, Lieutenant," one of Leticia's friends commented. "They just finished playing a marvelous piece. Mozart, I believe."

"I'm sorry to have missed it," Walker responded, looking toward the small stage where the musicians huddled with their instruments. "They're a very good string quartet."

"Indeed they are," Leticia said. "I remember in San Juan—"

Just then a loud, rhythmic sound was heard emanating from the stage. And it wasn't chamber music. It was the loud, quirky rhythm of a *plena*, the music of the jíbaro. Amazingly, everything had been transformed on the stage: The cello had been replaced by the shaped ten-string guitar known as the cuatro; the viola had become an accordion; one of the violins had turned into a hand drum, while the second violin had become the scraped handheld gourd known as a *güiro*.

The music was loud and infectious in its melody and sound. Everyone in the room started clapping to the beat of the music. Some men and women started dancing in the long, twirling movements that epitomized the plena. The mayoral ballroom had suddenly become a dancehall. It was now akin to the barrio of San Antón, where the plena had evolved long ago.

Someone grabbed Leticia's hand and pulled her toward the dance floor. It was Walker, who just as quickly released her hand and began to dance, his hands on his waist and rotating his hips, like a true paisano. Leticia found herself dancing in tandem, following his footsteps and adding a few movements of her own. She had never felt so free, so alive!

She began to rotate about the room, hands over her head, twirling and whirling with the rhythmic chant of the instruments. Walker followed suit, clapping his hands over his head, as alive as she in the tumult of the dance.

That's when the change began. She saw the fingers of Walker's hands elongate like growing twigs, with nails extending from the fingers into

200

sharp yellowed points, and then she saw his face transform. The ears grew upward into fleshy points, his eyes glittered like burning suns, and his nose sprouted into a deformed snout. When his mouth opened it seemed a large, dark void about to engulf the entire room . . .

She screamed and awoke drenched in sweat. The room was totally dark except for the reflection from the moon outside the window. Her breath came in ragged heaves. She wiped her forehead with the back of a hand. Her head slumped into her chest, while her breathing slowed and calmed.

After some moments she looked up toward the window with the semi-light of the moon reflecting on part of the bedspread. She roused herself and looked toward the side of the bed now empty. Antonio had sent word that he would be up late counting receipts with Juan-Carlos. It was no surprise. He spent more time in Lorenza Bizo Street than anywhere else. It was as if the business had consumed everything. Was there more to it? She refused to face it, at this time. Best to play along, as her mother had constantly reminded her; men have their needs.

She sprang her legs over the bed, feet on the floor, and stood up, her nightgown damp with sweat. She left the room and checked in on the children's bedroom. Maria slept in her bed, her breathing slow and sure. The same for Camilo. Elena would be back in the morning, and all would return to normal. As for Toño? He would come when he would come.

In the dark, she made her way to the living room and the liquor cabinet. She took out a bottle of rum, a glass, and poured herself a drink, about a finger's worth. She took one sip and placed the glass back on the cabinet top. It hadn't helped; the desolate feeling was still there.

She sat on a cushioned chair and waited in the dark for Antonio to come home.

CHAPTER THIRTY-ONE

HE PULLED BACK the slide of the automatic pistol and engaged the slide stop catch. He inspected the barrel and chamber of the .45 pistol and, using a toothbrush, began cleaning the weapon. For Walker it was a solitary labor of love in his small, airless office on the second floor of the mayoralty. He seldom had time for himself. At least now he could devote some time to what actually mattered, and he could think, undistracted, while cleaning his pistol.

A surprise when the office door opened and there stood someone he had never expected to see in the middle of the afternoon.

"Leticia, how are you?"

"I'm fine, Clayton." She wore a light summer dress with a blue, feathered hat. In one cotton-gloved hand she clutched a small pocket purse. "Am I disturbing you?" She stared at the pistol in his hand, with the slide pulled back showing the elongated barrel.

"No, of course not." He rested the toothbrush on his desk, then quickly slid open a desk drawer and placed the pistol inside. He slid back his chair and rose. "It's a pleasure to see you." Just as quickly he added, "I've been thinking about you the last few days."

"As have I." She was suddenly quiet, seemingly as uncertain as him.

"You look lovely as always," he said.

"Don't flatter me unless you mean it," she snapped back.

"I do mean it." He stepped from behind the desk, took a step toward her.

She put out a hand, stopping him. "Don't, unless you mean it."

"I don't understand," he said.

"I think you do."

Their eyes locked; he came closer. She reached out and touched his cheek. He pressed his hand over hers, turning his cheek and kissing her palm. She gave a half smile, then removed her hatpin and hat, which she cast aside to the floor.

He pressed her to him, his mouth on hers. It all occurred as in a fog. Seconds later she was half resting on the desk, while his hands anxiously raised the hem of her skirt. Then the skirt was up to her waist, and she helped him pull down her panties, which snagged on both sides of her garter belt straps. They rushed ferociously as he fumbled with his pants zipper and she strove to pull up her skirt.

He was inside her, and she gasped, his face nuzzling her hair, while outside the Ponce mayoralty business continued as usual.

CHAPTER THIRTY-TWO

BARRIO CANAS, LIKE La Playa, was one of the five coastal barrios in Ponce. It bordered a deserted beach area known as El Tuque. Apart from the remnants of a farm that had fallen into disrepair, nothing of note sat on the beach. What was left of the farm was a small wooden shack, which no one bothered to visit. The shack did have a caretaker, named Anibal, who earlier in the year had been contracted by Lieutenant Walker to clean, sweep, and maintain the place. This is where the lieutenant and Leticia would meet for their trysts. It was far enough away from town to ensure there was no fear of discovery, and Anibal had been paid well by Walker to keep his mouth shut.

In this small habitat Anibal had installed a straw mattress that, needless to say, Leticia and Walker put to good use. The era to which Leticia and Walker had been consigned was appropriate to this activity. In the future, by the mid-1960s, the beach would be developed into a complex of gazebos, a restaurant, a beach area, and a swimming pool.

But this was yet to happen, and most Ponceños took the beach for granted. Like native New Yorkers who have never been to the Statue of Liberty, most residents never bothered to visit the beach. Why should they? They were surrounded by water everywhere.

In this relative privacy, Leticia and her lover would meet, strip free of their clothes, romp on the beach and sand, and make love next to the surging waves. Then they would repair to the shack, dress, exchange ardent kisses, and plan when they would next meet. Walker would walk Leticia to the nearby road, which in time would become Highway 2. They would get into his Ford sedan and drive off.

Walker would always drop off Leticia at Monte Rey Street, which at the time was on the outskirts of town. On this day, Jacobo Levy had to visit one of his clients with a new pair of eyeglasses he had just ground to a fine finish. This would be the first of his visits today. The second would be in La Playa.

The house he emerged from directly faced the corner where he saw a black sedan come to a stop. He recognized the naval officer as the driver, and from the passenger side of the front seat came out Leticia Boglione de Benítez. His first reaction was surprise, even more so when Leticia and Walker embraced fervently, engaging in a passionate kiss. Leticia then caressed the lieutenant's face. They were too enthralled with each other to notice that from across the street Jacobo Levy had witnessed everything. Jacobo slunk back behind the wrought-iron gate of the house from which he had just exited, and watched carefully from behind the iron bars of the gate.

Walker got into the car, waved at Leticia, and drove off. Leticia remained in place watching the car until it had rounded the next corner and disappeared. Her lips lifted into a satisfied smile. She clutched her pocket book to her breast, turned, and walked back toward the center of town.

Jacobo gently pushed the gate open again and stepped out into the street. He reached in his back pocket and took out an eyeglass case. Holding it tightly in his hand, he wondered what would come next.

***

Leticia rushed back home, knowing she was late. Hopefully, Antonio, as always, would be absorbed in one of his ventures. More of a surprise when she reached the house on Alfonso XII Street and found Antonio at home in midafternoon. And he wasn't alone.

Jacobo Levy was in the living room, conversing with Antonio, who, sitting on a plush upholstered chair across from Jacobo, was trying on some eyeglasses.

"You're finally here," Antonio heralded. "What do you think of my new spectacles?" He adjusted the eyeglasses, moving them up and down on his nose.

Leticia's attention was on the unexpected guest. "Don Jacobo, it's a pleasure to see you." She swallowed a smile. "To what do we owe this honor?"

Antonio was the first to answer, showing the spectacles. "These are my new eyeglasses. Remember? I had some problems reading the fine print in *El Imparcial,* and you recommended I go see the ophthalmologist in town." He adjusted the spectacles higher on the bridge of his nose. "These are my reading glasses. What do you think?"

Leticia, though caught off guard, managed to say, "They look fine. Uh, yes, they make you look distinguished. I like the horned-rimmed frames."

"It was Jacobo here who ground the lenses. His specialty." Antonio removed the eyeglasses, inspecting them carefully. "Yes, fine workmanship." He motioned with the glasses to Jacobo Levy, who remained quiet while watching Leticia. "Jacobo just brought them in from the eye doctor."

"Thank you for bringing the glasses, don Jacobo," Leticia said cordially. "Toño always says you're the best at your work. I'm sure he'll make good use of the spectacles. At least now he won't have to squint when he reads the morning paper."

Jacobo replied, "It's my pleasure, señora. Reading glasses are very important, as are many other things."

Antonio placed the eyeglasses on his lap and asked his wife, "So, did you get to see doña Sonia, the seamstress? Have you ordered the new dress?"

"Oh yes, I did," Leticia answered quickly. "She says the dress will be ready next week."

Antonio said to Jacobo, "Letty has great taste in clothes. Only Sonia is good enough for her, fashion-wise."

"Yes, I've heard that Sonia Torres is the best seamstress in town," Jacobo said judiciously. "I'm told her sense of style is impeccable." And then directly at Leticia: "I hope the lady was pleased with her service."

"Oh yes, I am" was Leticia's automatic response. "Sonia is making a new lady's suit for me. It's quite beautiful."

Jacobo furrowed his brow. "My, my, to think that now there are suits for ladies. Quite amazing, I must say."

"You're behind the times, Jacobo," Antonio reproved gently. "Ladies' suits are now all the rage. I'm told the whole thing was inspired by this new German actress, Marlene Dietrich. She started wearing one and now every woman wants a suit."

"Yes, I am behind the times," Jacobo admitted, looking directly at Leticia. "There are many things I don't understand. I'm from a different generation, and a lot seems strange these days." He eyes fell to the floor, and there followed a strained silence.

Leticia glanced at Antonio, who shrugged, not knowing what to say. Then she offered, "Don Jacobo, why don't you stay with us for dinner? We seldom see you, and it would be a treat. Don't you agree, Toño?"

Antonio readily complied: "Of course, Jacobo, dine with us, please."

Jacobo forced himself to his feet. "I'm afraid I must go back to town. Dr. Santos has other clients who need spectacles and, unfortunately, I am on call."

"Then we insist you come this weekend and dine with us. Right, Letty?"

"Yes, by all means," Leticia seconded. "You must dine with us this weekend."

"I'll take it under consideration," Jacobo said. He walked over to Leticia, offering his hand. "Señora, as always, it's a pleasure to see you."

"The pleasure is mine," Leticia responded.

"And how are the children?" Jacobo asked Antonio.

"They're well, Jacobo. Elena is with them now. They are growing by the day."

"That is good," Jacobo said, his eyes on Leticia. "Children are our immortality. They see all and they forgive all." He bowed formally. "Señora."

Leticia shook his hand, again glancing at Antonio, who went over and picked up Jacobo's white straw hat, hanging from the armrest on the upholstered chair, and handed it to Jacobo.

Jacobo put on his hat, shook Antonio's hand, and headed for the front door.

When they were alone, Leticia said, "He seemed worried about something. Is he alright?"

"I guess he was concerned that my eyeglasses fit right and were in good order," Antonio ventured.

"Yes, I guess that's it," Leticia noted placidly. She pointed at the eyeglasses. "So, now you can read the paper without squinting."

"Yes, I can. Still, having to wear reading glasses is a sign of aging."

"No, it's not," Leticia dissented. "You're barely thirty. You're still a very young man."

Antonio inclined his head dourly. "Sometimes I feel a hundred years old."

"Is your work that hard these days?" Leticia asked.

"Work and other things," Antonio said. He detoured: "But let's not talk about that. You seem to be spending more time in town these days . . .," and before she could protest, he went on, "And I don't begrudge you that. I know you can't spend all your time here with the children every day. You need to go out. It's understandable. I'm not often here when you need me. I wish I could spend more time with you, but work and all . . ."

"You're a very busy man," she said in a low voice.

Antonio couldn't deny it. "I know." And he sought to make amends. "I promise I'll try to make more time for the family."

"I hope so," Leticia said in that same low voice.

CHAPTER THIRTY-THREE

THEY LAY NAKED on the mattress, reveling in the afterglow of love-making. Walker turned over on his side and reached for the pack of cigarettes on the floor. He picked out one and lit up with his lighter, pleasurably blowing smoke and watching it flow upward into the thatched ceiling.

"I've never been happier," Leticia said, with one arm thrown across her forehead. "I love this place."

He looked down at her. "I love it here too. "It's so peaceful."

"Yes, it is," she breathed, watching reams of sunlight peeking through crevices in the palm leaves of the roof.

After a time, he asked, "What are you thinking about?"

"I'm thinking about your trip to San Juan, and that you'll leave soon."

He took another drag on the cigarette and stubbed it into the ground. "It'll only be for a few days. I won't be gone long."

"A few days will be too long," she said bleakly.

"No, it won't," he denied. "I'll be back in no time."

She removed the arm from her forehead, and turned to look at him. "Will you?"

"Yes," he said and, for emphasis, added, "You know that."

"Do I?" she said almost in a whisper.

"Leticia, I have to do this. I've explained this to you. We finished the investigation and this is the next step. We have four known Nationalists who will stand trial for the attempted assassination of Governor Winship. They will be tried by the federal court in San Juan. As chief investigator for Ponce, I have to testify. It's my duty."

"Why can't they send someone else?"

"There's no one else. I'm the investigator here. I have to go."

"I think you want to go," she accused.

He managed a grunt. "There's no one else. I have to go."

She turned her head to one side, and he noted her displeasure. "Leticia, try to understand. I don't want to go. But this is part of my job, my responsibility." He stroked her cheek. "You know how much I love being with you, if only for a short time. I'll come back as soon as I can. I promise."

"I'm just concerned that you've chosen to drive there rather than take the train," she said, still looking aside. "The train would be safer. The roads in the hills are treacherous. I don't like traveling those roads."

"No one does," he placated. "And who knows, maybe someday you'll have a highway going from Ponce to San Juan. But that's not going to happen anytime soon. The train takes too long, and it only travels once a day. The governor's people want me there immediately. We have to prepare for this trial. Besides, the mayor's office has provided a driver who knows the roads very well. I won't be driving; I'll be sightseeing."

"There's not much to see except winding hills." Leticia's words were guarded. "I don't like it."

"I know," he had to admit. He took a long, lingering look at her arms, her shoulders, her breasts. "I love your body. It's perfection itself."

"I've given birth twice," she complained. "My body is not perfection."

"It is to me," he said.

She reached up and touched his lips. "You say the nicest things."

"I mean it."

She turned and gazed at the open door of the shack, looking out toward the ocean. "I'm going for a swim," she said, suddenly scrambling to her feet, and out she went, running toward the surf. He stood up, grabbing a towel lying at the foot of the mattress, and ran after her.

She waded into the water, her arms dragging behind her, making long lines as she went deeper into the ocean. When the first big wave came, she dove into it, bopping her head up again, laughing joyously.

He watched as she cavorted in the surf, her hair drenched with water, the black triangle of hair between her legs as wet as the rest of her body.

It was then that he realized what he had said was true. She is beautiful, he thought to himself. God help me, I love this woman.

She came back to him, her feet leaving wet imprints in the sand. He went to meet her, holding the large towel and draping it over her shoulders. "You are beautiful," he said.

"Stop saying that!" she objected.

"But it's true."

She wrapped the towel tighter around her body. "Just come back to me. Come back safe."

"I will," he vowed.

On the morning of the journey, Walker put on a laundered and pressed khaki uniform with the requisite dark tie, and packed up his notes in a leather briefcase. He bid Mayor Tormos and his secretary goodbye and climbed into the back seat of the Ford sedan. Usually, he would have sat beside the assigned driver in the front, but in the back seat he could review his files and prepare for his testimony at the trial.

The driver got behind the wheel and took off.

In the central mountain range, the most arduous part of the trip was between the towns of Caguas and Salinas. Here the road inclined upward at an angle that became even more circuitous, with a hedge of trees and foliage bordering the dirt path on one side and a steep edge overlooking a rock embankment on the other side.

It was during one of these hairpin curves, the car hugging the tree wall as much as possible in order to avoid the steep edge, that another car, a Ford coup with two occupants, materialized behind them. If the car had been following them, they were unaware until this moment. The driver's attention had been on the bending road, and Walker's attention had been on his files.

The other car was hugging the tree wall as well. Walker's driver saw in his rearview mirror that the car quickly accelerated and bumped his car. The driver pressed down on the car's horn, which drew Walker's attention away from his files. "What's going on?" he asked.

"I don't know, señor." The driver once more pressed down on the car's horn. The other vehicle bumped into them from behind.

Just as suddenly, another car appeared, this one coming straight at them and also at a fast clip. The driver knew that if he didn't swerve he would crash into the oncoming vehicle.

He pulled the wheel to the right. Then, as the first car passed by him, his intent was to pull back quickly to the left, thereby avoiding going over the side of the road and down into a rocky abyss.

Walker had tossed aside his papers and took hold of the hand strap on the back seat, with his other hand braced on the back of the front seat.

Walker's driver would have righted the car had it not been for the other vehicle coming from behind, which deliberately slammed his vehicle in the rear. The Ford sedan slid sideways on the dirt road. The first car in front bumped into it. The driver desperately tried to bring the vehicle back on course, but its forward momentum was too great, and it went over the edge, with the vehicle diving, front end first, into a rocky outcropping five hundred feet below. When the car landed, it tumbled over and over until slamming into another rock wall on the valley floor.

The car smashed like a jagged accordion against the rock wall, one side crunched into the rock surface and its two top wheels spinning madly, going nowhere.

The two cars left on the road came to a stop. Out of the first car, the Ford coup, Octavio Mendoza and his friend and confidante Carmen got out. They walked to the edge and viewed the carnage below.

Three other occupants got out of the second car. They likewise approached the road's edge.

No one spoke. Finally Carmen said, "It is done."

Octavio didn't respond. He just stood there, silent and pensive. Then he simply walked back to the car, with Carmen following behind.

The three other people present returned to the other car. Both cars turned around and drove away.

CHAPTER
THIRTY-FOUR

LETICIA ENJOYED WRITING long, leisurely letters to her extended family and friends in San Juan. Like her trysts with Walker, it was a measure of escape from her humdrum existence in Ponce. So she put forward her thoughts in fine script with the fountain pen, enjoying the scratch of ink on paper, letting her ideas roam. The children were asleep; the house was drowsy in the night.

Elena interrupted her reverie. "Señora, you father is here."

She put down her fountain pen. "My father? At this time of night?"

"Yes, he has urgent news."

She rose from her chair and left the sanctity of her personal study room to find Antonio and her father waiting for her in the main living room.

"Good evening, father."

"Good evening, Leticia." Eduardo Benítez looked from one to the other. "As I've told Toño, I have news from the mayor's office."

"At this time of night?" Leticia inquired.

Again, don Benítez cast a glance from Antonio to his daughter. "Yes, this news could not wait."

"I hope it's not bad news." Leticia noted that don Benítez carried an envelope in one hand. "Is it bad news?"

"Yes, and no," Eduardo Benítez said. He showed the white envelope. "This is an official notice from Lieutenant Walker and addressed to the authorities in San Juan. In it, the good lieutenant hereby declares that the investigation concerning Toño and his alleged ties to the Nationalists are complete. He vouches that Antonio Boglione is a loyal and upright citizen whose contributions to the community are immeasurable."

Leticia was startled. "I didn't know that Toño was a suspected Nationalist."

"Oh, a lot of people were on the suspect list in view of the attempt on Governor Winship. And a lot of people were arrested, some on the flimsiest of evidence. It's to Toño's credit that Lieutenant Walker has exonerated him completely."

Leticia turned to her husband. "Toño, I never knew that you were a suspect in the assassination attempt. You said you went to the mayor's office to help them in their investigation."

"I went because I was summoned," Antonio said, "and I told them the complete truth as I see it, nothing else."

Don Benítez intervened. "It's a moot point now. Toño is completely exonerated." He lowered his head, the envelope at his side. "I have notified you of what you should know. But I have other news. Bad news. The same Lieutenant Walker who wrote this notice"—he held up the envelope again—"died in a car accident this morning."

"What?" gasped Antonio.

"Yes, he was on an official trip to San Juan, and he decided to go by car, which was tragic. Somehow the driver lost control of the car on one of the roads and it crashed, and there are no survivors."

Leticia stood stunned, immobile. Her breath stopped; it squeezed in her throat. Then her face twisted and she broke out in a long, rending sob that reverberated through the house and the night.

Elena, in her nightgown, came rushing out of the children's room. Eduardo Benítez looked at his daughter with utter shock on his face.

Antonio shared his disbelief, glancing at don Benítez, unable to speak.

Leticia covered her face, wet with tears, and said as she ran into the master bedroom,

"I . . . I . . . Toño, I . . ."

Don Benítez's ramblings were lost inside the shadows of the house. Antonio looked from side to side, like a man lost in a maze, hearing the convulsive moans coming from the bedroom.

Elena rushed into the bedroom to tend to Leticia.

"Toño, I . . ."

Antonio held up a quivering hand. "That's alright. I'll see that she's looked after."

"Yes," Benítez mumbled low. "I'll go, and I'll see you tomorrow."

"Yes." Antonio felt his chest tighten. "Tomorrow."

Eduardo Benítez grabbed his hat from a nearby chair, jammed it on his head, and flew out the front door.

Antonio headed for the bedroom, a mix of feelings welling up in him. Elena was sitting on the bed beside Leticia, who was crying incessantly. Elena was stroking Leticia's back, but nothing could console her.

Antonio didn't say a word. He looked at Elena and flipped a hand toward the door.

Elena quickly headed out of the room, leaving them alone.

Antonio couldn't contain it any longer. He plopped on the bed beside Leticia, grasped her by the shoulders, and forced her to sit upright, looking at him.

"What is going on? What is this?"

She just kept on crying.

"Letty!"

He threw her back on the bed, got to his feet, and paced the room, wringing his hands. "What is going on, Leticia? WHAT IS GOING ON?"

She sat upright. "Nothing's going on!" she blubbered. And in a voice as loud as his, "You wouldn't understand!"

He stared at her, eyes smoldering. "Understand what? That you care so much about this, this American? And why?"

She dropped her voice almost to a whisper. "I don't have to tell you. You know why."

"What the hell are you talking about?"

She didn't answer, just stared at her hands folded on her lap.

A rush of anger swarmed through him. All he saw was red. He came at her again, grasping her by the arms, lifting her to her feet, glaring into her face. "You bitch!" His face contorted with anger. "How could you!" He threw her back on the bed.

She propped herself up, with arms tensed. "And what about you and your whore? The one on the other side of town! And your bastard son! Everyone knows about it, everyone but me! You're no angel, you know!"

"SHUT UP!" he yelled.

Her fierce eyes matched his now. "NO! I won't shut up! At least ..." She sought the right words, the right, cruel words. "Walker showed that he loved me! Yes, the American, he loved me! And he showed it! And I loved him!" Her voice was as raging as his. "You could never understand that! You'll never be the man he was!"

Antonio rushed at her again, hand raised to strike.

"C'mon, hit me!" she dared. "Show what a man you are! What a stupid, simple man you are!"

Mouth clenched, Antonio's upraised hand quavered with rage. It formed into a fist as he resisted every impulse to strike at her, to crater that beautiful face, to blot out every memory of ...

He turned and bolted out of the room.

Leticia crumpled onto the bed, sobbing into her hands.

CHAPTER
THIRTY-FIVE

THEY SAT IN brooding silence in Jacobo's study, Antonio staring glumly at his glass of rum, Jacobo staring at Antonio.

At last Antonio stirred. "I don't know what to do."

Jacobo angled his head to one side. "It's difficult now," he said. "You're both raging, and with good cause."

Antonio gnawed his tensed lips. "She betrayed me!"

"Yes, she did," Jacobo agreed. Idly he swirled the rum in his own glass. "But the question is: Why did she do it?"

"I don't care why she did it!" Antonio's tone was rough. "Enough that I'm a cuckold now. A fool!"

"We're all fools," Jacobo commented. "Some more than others." He placed the rum glass on a small table next to his chair and leaned forward, his hands joined. "Sometimes people do things because they're unhappy with their lot. Or they seek revenge. Or they can't help themselves. We humans are complex. Sometimes we do terrible things that can't be explained. And for some of us, that's how we grow, how we learn."

"You say I should learn from this?" His rough tone was still strong, still festering. "Learn what?"

"I don't know," Jacobo said in all honesty. "You're hurting now. And I would say, so is Leticia. You're both hurting, each in different ways. It will take time for that hurt to pass."

"I don't care about hurt," Antonio said. "I care about . . ." He stopped, going no further.

Jacobo said to him, "You care about your pride, your standing. You rightly feel a sense of anger and shame."

"Me, shame?" Antonio snorted. "She's the one that should feel shame. She's the one that brought this shame on our family."

"I am not assessing blame," Jacobo said. "I'm just trying to understand what you're both going through. Honestly, what you've experienced, I've never experienced. But I've felt the taste of betrayal from those I've trusted. I've felt anger and, yes, shame for not being strong and worthy, and denying certain things." Jacobo gazed at the near dark in the room, where one solitary wick lantern was aglow. "In the end I realized that anger and vengeance were not the solution. We must try to understand each other, understand what makes us do these things that we do. Why we sometimes bring pain to others and sometimes bring joy."

"I could never understand your thinking, Jacobo," Antonio said without reservation. "I could never be so casual about things."

"I'm not being casual," Jacobo defended. "I'm being honest." He leaned back in his chair, observing Antonio as if from a distance. "What're you going to do?"

Antonio squirmed stiffly. "What can I do? I've been betrayed by someone I love. I can't love someone who doesn't love me. That'd be idiotic. This marriage is at an end."

Jacobo wrinkled his brow. "So you're going to file for divorce?"

"Yes."

"Is that wise?"

"What do you mean?"

"You know what I mean," Jacobo said outright. "Next to the Ferrers, the Benítezes are the most prominent family in this town. You're part of that clan now, even if by marriage. I don't think old man Benítez would approve of a divorce in such an upstanding Catholic family."

Antonio curled his lip derisively. "Okay then, I'll get an annulment."

"That won't work either," Jacobo argued.

"What do you mean?"

"Think of what I've said. The Benítezes cherish their standing above all. A breakup in their family structure would be unthinkable. The loss of face would be enormous. They would never agree to a separation, even if both you and Leticia wanted it." Jacobo pressed on: "And you don't know if Leticia would agree to a divorce anyway."

"Why shouldn't she?" Antonio asked, sure of his argument. "We don't love each other anymore."

"Let me tell you something," Jacobo stipulated. "Most marriages are not based upon love in this land. They're based upon need. Whether you like it or not, both Leticia and you need each other. You need the Benítezes' influence behind you if you want to continue doing 'great things' around here. And Leticia needs the social standing that a solid marriage brings."

"This marriage is not solid."

"Not to you. Not to her. But it is to the outside world."

"So we should continue living a lie?"

"You should continue doing what you do and try to work out your problems."

Antonio took a sip of rum, sighed. "Easier said than done."

"I know. Believe me, I know. I've been through it."

Antonio took stock of Jacobo, seeking a new understanding. "You've been through a divorce? A separation?"

"No, not a divorce or separation. In my religion that is basically frowned upon. But I've separated from my homeland, and from those I loved. A lot was taken away from me by others who simply hated the fact that I'm a Jew." His mouth puckered like something tasted bad to him. "There are many kinds of separation, many kinds of pain, in this world."

Antonio's face was hard. "All I know is that when I'm hurt I fight back."

"There are many ways to fight back. You just have to be logical about it. But don't take it to such an extreme that you hurt yourself in the process."

"I don't intend to hurt myself," Antonio said cruelly. "I intend to hurt others who hurt me."

Jacobo was shaking his head. How to make him see? "You will consider what I've said, won't you?"

"I make no promises," Antonio said.

Jacobo expelled a deep, heartfelt breath. "So what are you going to do now?"

"I'm going to the only place I know where I can be happy. I'm going to Milagros's house. It's the only place where I can find peace."

"Oh yes, Milagros," Jacobo recalled. "Under the circumstances, do you think it's wise to go there?"

"Like I said, it's the only place where I can find peace."

"There are many places where one can find peace," Jacobo said in a measured tone. "That's what churches and synagogues are for."

"Right now church would be of no use to me," Antonio said indignantly.

Again Jacobo frowned in thought. "Yes, I understand. I wish I could be of more help."

Antonio rose and placed his drink on the small table next to Jacobo. "You have. It's always good to talk to you. You give me a new perspective on things."

226

"But I haven't convinced you about keeping your ties to the Benítezes, have I?"

"I'll think about it," Antonio said simply.

"You do that," Jacobo said. "You do that."

CHAPTER THIRTY-SIX

HE HEARD THE music the moment he entered Jacobo's study. It came from the gramophone on a small stand in one corner. The voice was mellifluous and glorious.

"Who's that singing?" Antonio immediately wanted to know.

Sitting in his easy chair, Jacobo shifted toward the sound of the gramophone. "It's one of my favorites, Carlos Gardel."

"He has the voice of angel," Antonio admired.

"Yes, he does," Jacobo agreed in a low, hoarse voice. "He brings the tango to life."

"Is he Puerto Rican?"

"No, he's Argentinean," Jacobo informed. "Throughout the Americas, no one can capture their music like he can."

"I can see why." Antonio listened to the melody, relishing the sound and inflection of the song.

Jacobo said, "After the Great Hurricane, the first thing I did after fixing the house was to get a new music box. Luckily, I managed to salvage some old record discs, Gardel among them. In my reflective moments, he brings a measure of joy."

Antonio forced himself away from the song. "But you didn't send for me just to listen to some Argentinean. What's up, Jacobo?"

Jacobo heaved a weary breath. "I was concerned about you."

"No cause for concern. I'm fine."

"Are you?"

"Yes."

Jacobo mouthed his words carefully. "Have you decided what you're going to do regarding . . . ?"

"Yes, I have," Antonio said before Jacobo could finish. "You can rest easy, Jacobo. There'll be no divorce. Leticia won't give me one. She wants to make my life sheer hell. It's her revenge, I guess."

"Maybe it's not revenge. Maybe it's just necessity. She needs you."

"She needs what I can provide materially," Antonio said with some bitterness.

"Material necessities can be just as strong as personal necessities." Jacobo's voice caught, and he coughed into his hand. It went on for some moments.

"Are you alright?"

Jacobo waved away any concern. "Just a temporary condition. I'll be fine."

"You sure?"

"Yes." Jacobo reached across to the small table by his chair. "Here, I have something for you," he rasped. "It may be of use to you."

Antonio came closer and took the small box Jacobo held out to him. "What's this?"

"It's a safety razor," Jacobo explained. "During the Great War one of my clients was issued this when he was in the army. In fact, he was issued two sets, and he gave me one." Jacobo fingered his beard. "Could never figure out why since I don't need it. But I thought you might use it. I'm told that in what they call 'America,' hardly anyone uses a straight barber's razor anymore." He lifted a finger toward the small box in Antonio's hand. "With this type of razor, you won't have to worry about cutting your throat when you shave."

230

"Thank you, Jacobo." Antonio lifted the top of the box and viewed the razor inside. "I don't think anyone in La Playa has one of these."

"Not unless they're a veteran of the war," Jacobo said. "This is an improvement. It's good to move with the times. By the way, there are razor blades included in the box. You've got the whole kit just as they were issued to the doughboys."

"Doughboys?"

"According to my friend, that's what they called the servicemen during the war. I have no idea why."

Antonio took out the safety razor, holding it in his hand, admiring its detail. "I shall put it to good use. Thank you." He replaced the razor back in the box. "And how are you doing?"

"I'm doing fine." Jacobo was looking away to some corner of the room. "Why do you ask?"

"Nothing. Just wondering."

"There's no need to wonder." Jacobo expelled another troubled breath. "I'm fine." He went back to topic. "I'm glad you and Leticia are not parting. Hopefully, in time, you may come together again."

"Not as man and wife," Antonio clarified.

Jacobo asked in a phlegmy voice, "Then why stay together?"

"As you said, we have mutual needs."

"And how does Milagros fit into all this?" Jacobo asked.

"That's none of your business," Antonio said coldly.

"You're right. That's none of my business." A vague sound gurgled in Jacobo's throat. He brought a hand to his mouth and hacked into it.

"You sure you're alright?"

"I'm fine," Jacobo reiterated.

The record disk had come to an end. The needle made a reedy, scratching sound on the vinyl.

231

Antonio watched as Jacobo lifted heavily from his chair, turned, and ambled over with slow steps to the gramophone stand. He lifted the needle, removed the black record disk, and placed it in a record folder. His movements were as slow and measured as his walk.

"If you need anything, I can come back tomorrow," Antonio offered in passing.

"Thank you," Jacobo said in that same hoarse tone. "I don't need anything except some sleep. My body seems to crave more of it these days."

"You're headed for your second childhood," Antonio joked.

Jacobo formed a half smile. "Yes, I'm headed for my second childhood."

Antonio came closer, placed a hand on Jacobo's arm. "Thank you. I'm grateful for our talks."

"As am I," Jacobo said.

Antonio headed for the door, stopped, turned, and announced, "I will come to see you tomorrow, you know."

"There's no need," Jacobo assured him.

"There's always a need for friends to talk." Antonio turned and walked out the door, leaving Jacobo standing alone in his study, among his books and music.

CHAPTER THIRTY-SEVEN

THE SCHOLARLY JEW was dead.

Domingo Madera, the carpenter and Jacobo's landlord, discovered the deceased on an overcast Ponce afternoon. Jacobo was an early riser. Domingo could set his watch by Jacobo's routine. So when he didn't see Jacobo come out from his second-floor habitat and it was already afternoon, Domingo's wife voiced concern. This certainly was unlike Jacobo Levy.

Adelaida prevailed upon her husband to go check on their tenant. Domingo dutifully did so and found Jacobo peacefully asleep. But he wasn't asleep. Mingo couldn't shake him awake. He called his wife; she came upstairs, and the minute she saw Jacobo her face turned ashen.

"He's dead," she murmured.

"How do you know?" her husband asked.

"I know."

To be sure, Domingo went downstairs and quickly returned with a small hand mirror. He placed it directly beneath Jacobo's nose. No imprint of any breath on the glass. The Scholarly Jew had passed on.

The first one notified was Juan-Carlos Quiles, who informed doña Saro, who informed Antonio. He left his home office and rushed to the Dead End.

"What to do about the body?" Domingo asked all who had gathered.

"We bury him," Saro said.

"Yes, but where?"

"We bury him in the cemetery."

Domingo's leathery, beaten face was questioning. "But he's a Jew."

"So?" Saro said.

"We've never buried a Jew in the cemetery."

Juan-Carlos pitched in: "That is correct. We've never had a dead Jew before. I don't know if we can bury him in a Catholic cemetery."

Standing to one side, Antonio was forced to ask, "Why not? A cemetery is for dead people, and Jacobo is dead. What's the problem?"

"He's a Jew," Juan-Carlos mentioned again. "I don't know if we can bury him in the municipal cemetery. In fact, I don't know if Jacobo, were he alive, would want that."

"He's not alive. He's got no say in it."

Juan-Carlos tried to reason: "Toño, all I'm saying is, I don't know if he can be buried in a Christian cemetery. He is—was—a Jew. He's different."

To Antonio it didn't make sense. "How is he different? Our Lord was a Jew. And Jacobo here is now a cadaver. He needs burial."

"Yes. But is it right for him to be buried in our Catholic cemetery?"

"It's not your Catholic cemetery," Antonio pointed out. "It's a municipal cemetery."

"And that's the problem here," Juan-Carlos concluded. "We don't know if the cemetery will allow this."

"This is a fine turn of events," Saro remarked sourly. "Now we can't even bury poor Jacobo."

Jacobo Levy's burial turned into a major headache for all concerned. The caretakers at the cemetery stated they would have to check with the mayoralty office before they could inter the body in La Playa. The mayor's office said they would have to check with the authorities in San Juan. Antonio Boglione asked why; it was a municipal cemetery. What did San Juan have to do with it?

Mayor Tormos replied that this was beyond his jurisdiction. He had no problem with Jacobo Levy being buried in Ponce, but—a big "but"—he was a Jew, and it did make a difference. No Jew had ever been buried on Ponce grounds. That being the case, he could not take action without consulting the government representatives in San Juan. Definitely, their sanction and approval would be needed in such an extraordinary case.

Soon enough word came back from San Juan. Some bureaucrat—whether American or Boricua, that wasn't clear—definitively stated that a Jew could not be interred in a Christian cemetery. The decision was final. No appeal would be countenanced.

"What the hell is wrong with them?" was Antonio's first reaction.

"It's the times we live in," Juan-Carlos offered in explanation. "When the Spaniards first conquered this island they decreed that no Jew could migrate here. They weren't even allowed to live in this island. The laws that applied to Madrid applied to us." He pursed his lips. "Old customs and traditions still plague us. They never die. They haunt us."

"Sometimes old customs and traditions need to be changed," Antonio said caustically.

Something had to be done. Antonio and doña Saro could not accept that the Scholarly Jew be consigned to some potter's field somewhere on the island like some forgotten vagabond.

About half a mile from the cemetery was the beach. Here, along the shoreline, amidst a row of palm trees, was a decrepit and abandoned house. It had been so for the longest time, though the older folk in Ponce remembered that way back, during the time of the Spaniards, an old widow, doña Lourdes, had lived there with her cat, which had a funny name from some old opera. Doña Lourdes had passed on long ago, and the house had fallen into disrepair. Since she had no heirs, her property had reverted back to the municipality. It was here, away from the main cemetery and prying eyes, that Antonio decided Jacobo would be buried.

He went to town and had the Ponce town clerk look up the old deed to the half-acre property that came with the house. Antonio bargained with the town clerk, providing him with a hefty bribe in the process, and he acquired the property for a rock-bottom price.

Antonio then had some locals from Carmelo's cafetín come demolish the house. This was done immediately. And in that small plot, not far from the beach, surrounded by palm trees, Jacobo was buried.

The local priest, Father Ignacio, refused to officiate at the graveside service since Jacobo Levy was a Jew. Antonio was forced to scour for some clergyman to do the service, but found no one.

It was Juan-Carlos Quiles who suggested, "You know what? You don't actually need a clergyman at the graveside. What's wrong with just having Jacobo's friends present? That will be the service. Someone can say a few words, and Jacobo will have the proper burial he deserves, even for a Jew."

So it was. Antonio hired two gravediggers, Domingo Madera fashioned a wooden coffin, and Jacobo's body was driven to the site via a fire truck, which, as honorary fire chief, Antonio had requisitioned.

All of Jacobo's acquaintances assembled at the grave site. It was a large crowd. Almost everyone in La Playa at one time or another had intermingled with the Scholarly Jew. All of the habitués from Carmelo's cafetín were present. Old women and men came; young women with children came. Regulars at the movie house or Antonio's fonda were there. All gathered around the deep pit of the grave that would hold Jacobo Levy.

Antonio said a few words. So did doña Saro, Domingo Madera, and Juan-Carlos. All lauded the Scholarly Jew for his kinship and humanity, though Domingo Madera then and there swore that he and his family would never again attend services at the local church since the priest,

Ignacio, had insulted the memory of Jacobo Levy. To which doña Saro replied that the memory of Jacobo could never be insulted since he had been a good man.

The coffin was lowered by ropes into the grave. The gravediggers shoveled in the dirt, and a gravestone was planted in the ground. Since no one knew where the Scholarly Jew had actually come from or when he was born, the inscription on the gravestone was Jacobo's name followed by one word: "Amigo" (friend).

It was during the service that Rumaldo's carriage appeared, and from it stepped down Leticia, dressed appropriately in black and wearing a small pill-box hat with matching face net.

Everyone was surprised. But the most stunned of all was Antonio, who had not expected Leticia to be present since among the mourners was Milagros Pagan, also dressed in black. Murmurs rippled through the crowd, and someone tittered.

Leticia walked stoically among the mourners, who reverently parted as she approached the graveside. She looked straight ahead, acknowledging no one. She came forward and laid a single white rose on the grave. She crossed herself, turned, and walked back to the carriage.

Like the others, Milagros Pagan watched her throughout, not saying a word, although she also crossed herself and whispered what those nearest to her heard was a simple "Vaya con Dios." Go with God.

Everyone then began drifting away, some silent and reflective, others talking and gesturing among themselves, relishing the new gossip.

The last to depart were Saro and Antonio. Not knowing why, Saro did something she had once seen Jacobo do when they had passed by the municipal cemetery. He had picked up a stone and placed it on one of the graves. Likewise, she now picked up a stone and propped it up against Jacobo's gravestone. Afterward, Antonio took Saro's hand and led her away from the graveside of Jacobo Levy.

BOOK TWO

THE TOWN
(1950–1964)

CHAPTER THIRTY-EIGHT

A BLUE PLYMOUTH was parked on one end of Victoria Street. Inside the vehicle a man and a woman kept a watchful vigil on the storied house, painted white, and imposing on the fabled street.

The man and woman waited patiently. They knew their quarry was a creature of habit. Punctuality was one of his main assets. They were not disappointed when the man they sought appeared on the sidewalk, walking briskly, with chin held forward. His hair had a few flecks of gray in it, but his pencil-thin mustache was still dark. As befitted his status, he wore a white long-sleeved shirt and striped dark-blue tie. His slacks were dark gray, and his shoes, highly shined.

"He looks like a businessman," said the woman, watching from the front seat of the car. "He is," corroborated the man sitting behind the wheel. "I remember when he first came to La Playa. He had nothing. Even then I knew he would do well."

The woman turned to look at her companion. "Do you still want to do this?" she asked.

"Yes," the man said, his eyes straight ahead.

The woman stared at him steadily. "He's not one of us. He doesn't believe in our cause."

"He was and is a friend," said the man, "no matter what his politics."

"I don't like this," she said.

The man smiled at her and replied, "I know." He reached out and squeezed her hand affectionately.

She gripped his hand in hers. "You will be careful?"

"Aren't I always?" he said, still smiling.

"Just don't be too long," she cautioned. "We have to be back for tonight's meeting."

"I know." With that, he stepped out of the car and crossed the street to stop at the front gate of the house. He noted that the house now had a buzzer alongside the wrought-iron gate, one of the few residences in Ponce to do so and a further show of status. He rang the buzzer. A tingling, erratic bell sound was heard from inside.

The front door opened, and out came an older woman with gray hair tied atop her head in a bun. Her walk was slow and deliberate down the front steps of the veranda. When she reached the closed gate, she glanced through it with inquisitive eyes. "Yes?"

"It's me, Elena."

The old woman screwed up her face, trying to focus on the stranger.

"Don't you recognize me, Elena?"

The old woman blinked, looking closer. Then she put a hand to her mouth, surprise reigning over her face. "Papo? Is it you?"

"Yes, Elena," Octavio Mendosa replied. "It's me."

"It is you! How . . . ?"

Octavio grinned at the old woman. "It's good to see you again, Elena." He pointed to the front door. "Is Toño in?"

"Yes, he is. How are you?"

"Can I see him?" Octavio requested.

"Yes, of course!" Elena squealed. "He'll be so glad to see you." She unhooked the latch to the front gate. "Come! He's just arrived from work. What a surprise this is!"

Octavio stepped in from behind the gate and followed Elena to the door. She opened it quickly, calling, "Toño! Toño! You have a guest!"

Antonio was in his bedroom, removing his tie, when he heard the housekeeper. He came out of the room with the tie in his hand. His first reaction was astonishment, then elation! "Papo!" He dropped the tie, and his arms opened wide.

Octavio and Antonio embraced, gripping each other tight. Antonio stepped back, holding his friend's elbows, inspecting Octavio's face. "How are you?"

Octavio grasped Antonio's arms. "I'm well," he said. "It's good to see you, my friend."

"Same here," Antonio acknowledged "I've missed you."

"And I've missed you too."

"You've put on some weight," Antonio said, referring to Octavio's incipient paunch.

Octavio patted his potbelly. "It comes with the joys of family life."

Antonio noted Octavio's wedding band. "You're married! You have a family now?"

"Yes," Octavio admitted gladly. "Just like you and—"

Antonio didn't let him finish. "So who's the lucky woman who became your wife, or should I say the unlucky woman who became your wife?"

"Carmencita," Octavo let know. "I believe you met her once, long ago."

Then it dawned on Antonio. "Oh yes, I remember. The girl with the calico dress up in the hills."

"Yes, up in the hills," Octavio said pensively.

"Congratulations," Antonio offered. "You, a married man."

"And with two kids."

"That is wonderful news," Antonio noted approvingly.

"I got two boys," Octavio revealed. "Miguel and Efrain, both strong young men and devoted to the cause."

"Yes, the cause," Antonio said almost in a murmur. A shared silence hung in the air.

Octavio looked about the room, said finally, "So now this is your house." He looked pleased. "I'm happy for you."

Antonio dropped his arms to his sides. His face changed. "I consider it more Leticia's house. But when don Eduardo passed away she insisted we move back in."

Octavio viewed with approval the plush furniture and decorations on the wall, inclusive of some recently acquired modernist paintings. "It befits your status in the community. I can see why she would want to move back here."

Antonio's voice was neutral. "I would have preferred spending the rest of my days in La Playa. That's where I belong."

"That's where I would have to agree with your wife and disagree with you," said Octavio. "You belong in this house. You've earned it through hard work and sweat. Don't begrudge your good fortune, Toño."

Antonio's face grew long. "Good fortune that keeps me in town." He frowned. "I hardly get to see my friends in La Playa anymore."

"You've outgrown La Playa," Octavio considered. "This is where you belong."

Antonio showed a whimsical expression. "You sound like Leticia Benítez."

"And where is your wife?" Octavio queried. "I would love to see her. Is she as beautiful as always?"

"She's not here, if that's what you're asking," Antonio said in a flat voice. "She spends her time in town among her many committees and projects, hobnobbing with the elite."

"And you don't hobnob with the elite?"

"When have you ever known me to hobnob with the elite?" Antonio answered somewhat accusatorially.

Octavio placed a hand on Antonio's arm. "Same old Toño." He smiled his words. "That's what I like about you, my friend: you've never let success go to your head."

Antonio took a glance around his home. "If you call this success." His tone was gloomy. Then he perked up. "But you're here, and it's great to see you again. Come, let's share a drink!" He took two quick steps to a polished wood stand with handcrafted decanters and matching glasses. "Whiskey?" he asked.

"Whiskey?" Octavio laughed curtly. "I must say, we've come a long way. I remember at one time the only drink available was rum."

Antonio picked out two crystal glasses. "That was way back. Now the stores in town carry every kind of liquor available. If you have the money, you can buy what you want."

"If you have some *añejo*," Octavio decided, "I'll take that."

"Coming right up." Antonio waved toward an upholstered chair. "Sit down. Tell me all about yourself."

"Not much to tell." Octavio removed his straw fedora and sat down. He took the drink Antonio offered and leaned back, holding the glass in one hand and his hat in the other. "Actually, I'm more interested in what's going on in La Playa these days. So much has changed since I've been away."

"Where have you been?"

"Oh, I've been in the States—New York, Baltimore—just traveling around."

"Is this business?"

Octavio stared at his glass of rum. "You could call it that."

"I was in New York last winter with my kids," Antonio referenced offhand. "They loved it, even the cold."

Octavio's brows shot up. "Oh, you visited the city. So, did you sail on the *Marine Tiger* like everybody else?"

"Nah, we flew. Now there are direct flights from San Juan to New York. The *Marine Tiger* is no longer in business."

"Too bad." Octavio rolled the glass in his hands. "That old boat was instrumental in getting the boricuas to the East Coast." He had a dreamy look. "I can understand the allure of a capitalistic society." Suddenly he broke his train of thought. "How did you like New York?"

"I found it too cold, both the weather and the people," Antonio complained. "But Leticia was charmed by it. It was her idea to go. She decided the children should be more 'cosmopolitan' in their outlook." A little grin touched Antonio's mouth. "Actually it was an excuse to go on a shopping spree. But the kids did enjoy the sights. They really took to the city, especially Maria, the youngest."

"And how are your children?" Octavio asked.

A genuine smile appeared on Antonio's face. "They're great. And I'm happy to say they do well in school, particularly Camilo; he's the bookworm. He's twelve now. Maria, she's a year younger and..." Antonio shrugged. "Well, she's more of a free spirit"—he tapped his head—"but smart. She picks up on things quick. Can't put anything past her."

"I'm glad to hear that," Octavio said. "Children are what keep us going." He sipped the drink, swishing the rum in his mouth, enjoying its taste. "Tell me, how are things in La Playa? Has anything changed, or is it still the same old crowd?"

"Most of the old crowd is gone," Antonio told him. "Juan-Carlos has passed on, and so has Carmelo. His cafetín is now run by his daughter. Domingo Madera, the carpenter, died last year. As you know, Jacobo Levy left us years ago. And Manolo finally drank himself to death." Antonio pondered it. "It took him a long time." Then his voice cheered. "But, believe it or not, doña Saro is left. She lives in my old house. I donated it to her when we moved back into this place." Antonio took another dubious look at his spacious surroundings. "She doesn't make bootleg rum anymore. It's too much hard work. She just sits out on the veranda, in her rocking chair, watching the passing scene."

"She must be in her nineties by now," Octavio threw in a guess.

"Yes, she's an old bird, but a tough old bird. I wager she'll be dancing on all our graves."

Octavio held up his glass. "Here's to doña Saro."

Antonio lifted his glass as well. "To doña Saro."

They both drank; then Octavio asked, "And how is that old house on Alfonso XII Street?"

"Beautiful as ever. I still think it's the best house in La Playa."

"But unlike here," Octavio said ruefully, "I bet it still has an outhouse."

"Every house in La Playa has la latrina," Antonio stated. "That hasn't changed."

"So they're still waiting for indoor plumbing down there," Octavio said more as a fact than a question.

"Yes, they are."

"How about electricity? Have they got any electric lights yet?"

"Nope. Almost every house still has the old wick lanterns."

"So when will they get the amenities of civilization?" Octavio asked sharply.

"We don't know," Antonio said. "After the war a lot progressed in Ponce proper. All municipal buildings and most houses have toilets and lights, but as you know, La Playa has always been the forgotten stepchild, the barrio."

"Leave it to the Americans to screw the playeros," grouched Octavio.

"The Americans have nothing to do with it," Antonio contradicted. "It's the crooked government in Ponce. They don't give a fuck about La Playa, or any other barrio outside of town. What money they don't squander, they pocket. There's talk of creating a new housing complex by the Dead End. This will be done through federal funds, so the crooks in the mayoralty won't get their hands on it, thank God. And I believe the ironworks in La Playa has functioning toilets, and, yes, there's one in a Catholic primary school in La Playa. But if you want to take a shit in comfort, you gotta do it in town."

Octavio was shaking his head. "It's criminal that in today's day and age people should live like that. Here we are, 1950, and almost nothing has changed." He looked at Antonio. "I'm surprise you lasted as long as you did in La Playa."

"I would have stayed in La Playa forever," Antonio declared. "I can do without the 'amenities.' I just love the folks down there. They took me in. They're my family. It was Leticia who insisted we move. And she had a good case when it came to our children. Like any parent, I want them to have the best in comfort as well as education."

Octavio listened attentively. "You've come a long way, my friend, and I'm happy for you." He ran a finger along the rim of his glass. "I would have stayed in La Playa too had it not been for . . ." He stopped, his gaze going from his glass back to Antonio. "But I came to tell you something else. As you know, the Maestro is back on the island. After ten years of imprisonment by the yanquis, he was released, and he's been giving speeches, inspiring all true boricuas."

"You're not going to start this all over again, are you?" Antonio scolded.

Octavio continued, ignoring the remark, "The imperialist pigs want to turn Puerto Rico into a 'commonwealth' of the United States'. As don Albizu says, this new status is a colonial farce. Well, we're preparing an armed struggle against this crime."

"This is idiocy!" objected Antonio.

"Whatever you may think," Octavio said levelly, "our plan is still to regain our freedom, to make this nation our own."

"Papo, after all that's happened, you can't be serious."

"Listen," Octavio put up a hand and continued in his strong voice, "I came to you because you're a friend and I need your help. Next week, some of my people will be coming to Ponce. We need a place to stay. It's too risky for us to stay at the Melia Hotel or any other public place in town. We need a nice, quiet place that won't raise suspicion. We can say we're family members visiting relatives in Ponce."

"You want to stay here?" Antonio guessed.

"Yes. Your house is a perfect place. You're not being watched; it's in the center of town. We can conduct our business without raising eyebrows."

"No," Antonio said before Octavio could finish.

Octavio stopped, not believing what he had heard. "No?"

"That's right, no." Antonio's voice was incisive. "I won't have any part of it."

Octavio continued his case: "But you don't know what we have to do in order to—"

Antonio couldn't be swayed. "I said no. I don't want to know what you have planned or are planning. I want no part of it. I refuse to put my family in danger for any cause."

"Even if it means fighting for our country? Gaining our freedom?"

"I told you years ago this is not my country. I come from Napoli. And even if I were native-born, I wouldn't take part in any cockeyed scheme about independence or whatever."

Octavio stared at his friend. "I thought you were one of us. I thought at least you understood what it is to want a free nation. To not be under the thumb of the yanquis, to not be oppressed."

Now it was Antonio who put up a hand. "I have heard it all before, Papo, and I'm not convinced. Besides, my family and I have a good life here. I don't want to put that in jeopardy."

"You would give up your integrity for a 'good life'?"

"I don't believe what you believe," Antonio said deliberately. "We don't live under a dictatorship. I believe the American presence here has been more beneficial than bad. We're not starving, like in Cuba or the rest of the world. We get Social Security, just like in the US. We have a paisano governor now, Luis Muñoz Marin."

"He's a puppet," Octavio derided contemptuously.

"Puppet or not," Antonio kept on, "the island is being rebuilt. We're in the process of industrialization. And, yes, eventually even La Playa will get all the 'amenities,' as you call it. Tourism is booming in San Juan, we—"

Octavio downed the last of his drink and sprang to his feet. Antonio was still spouting the benefits of America rule. He broke in, quoting: "'Those who would give up essential liberty to purchase a little temporary safety deserve neither liberty nor safety.' An American founding father said that. Yes, a yanqui, when they were fighting for their freedom before they took away ours. You should consider those words, Toño. If your heart is so cold and you have no pride in this land, then I pity you."

"I didn't ask for your pity," Antonio growled. "I just ask that you have common sense!"

"The blind can never see," Octavio quoted. He went over to the liquor stand and placed his glass on the table. "I won't bother you again. You can be assured I will—"

The front door popped open. They turned their heads in unison to see Camilo and his sister burst into the room. Both youngsters wore their school uniforms: white shirt, blue pants, and dark tie for the boy; white blouse and blue skirt for the girl. They looked excited, and Maria was the first to speak: "Papi, look what we got . . ." She stopped, seeing the stranger standing in the room, with her father sitting, his hands cradling a glass.

Antonio stood up, introducing his offspring. "Papo, these are my children. The excitable young lady is my daughter, Maria, and the young man is my son, Camilo."

"Papi, I'm sorry, I didn't know you had company."

"That's alright. This is an old friend Papo Mendosa."

Octavio said, "It is I who should be sorry. I have intruded on your father, and he is a very busy man." He gave the siblings an appreciative glance. "I'm very happy to meet his children. It's an honor."

Standing behind his sister, Camilo said in a formal voice, "It is we who are honored, señor Mendosa."

"As you can see," Antonio put in, "it's my son who's the diplomat." And to Maria: "What have you got there?"

Maria held up her hands to show the object. "It's a crystal radio. Camilo built it in class today. It was the class project. Isn't it neat?"

Antonio stepped closer and peered at the small wooden board she held in her hands. To the board was attached what looked like a small, round metal cylinder hooked to another smaller wooden board with three round coils of cooper wire. "What does it do?"

"It's a radio, Papi." She held out a wire connected to one of the coils on the board. "Here, it has a headphone attachment."

Antonio took what looked like a tiny, round felt earphone attached to wire. "Put it in your ear, Papi," Camilo instructed. "If the reception is good, you can hear the radio."

Antonio placed the earpiece next to his ear. "All I can hear is static."

"Wait for the reception; you'll hear something."

"That's right, Papi," Maria chimed in, "wait for the reception."

Antonio lowered his hand, holding the earpiece. "Maybe some other time."

Octavio came forward and said, "Crystal radios have been with us for a while now, but I'm amazed that your school has them as a project. You two youngsters should be proud."

"It all comes with private schooling and tutoring," Antonio confided. He examined the earpiece and wire attachment in his hand. "You won't find this in the Ponce public school system."

"You're fortunate to give your children such a fine education," Octavio said to Antonio.

"They'll go to college, that's for sure," Antonio predicted.

"I am going to be an educator," Maria announced with pride. "A professor."

"Really?" Octavio was impressed.

"Yes, and my brother is going to be a doctor."

Octavio looked at Camilo. "Is that right, young man?"

"I have an interest in medicine," Camilo said.

"That is very good." Octavio flung his gaze from the children to their parent. "We need educated citizens on this island. The more education we have, the more our chances of someday calling this land our own and—"

"This is a very good project," Antonio interrupted, taking the small crystal radio from Maria's hands. "Hopefully, tonight, if reception is good, I can hear the ball game." Then to Octavio: "The Ponce Lions and the Santurce Crabbers play at Paquito Montaner Stadium tonight. It should be a good game."

"I'm sure it will be," Octavio agreed. "Anyway, I must take my leave. Toño, it was good to see you. I hope we can meet again in the future." He looked at Maria and Camilo appraisingly. "And your children should make you proud."

"Thank you, Papo. I hope we can meet again soon."

Octavio put his fedora hat back on. "Again, it was a pleasure," he said to Camilo and Mario.

Elena had appeared and stood unobtrusively to one side. She guided Octavio to the door and the outside gate.

"Who was that, Papi?" Camilo asked.

"Just an old friend," Antonio said in a distant voice. He held up the crystal radio. "Anyway, tell me more about this contraption and how it works so I can explain it to your mother when she gets home."

Outside, Octavio made it back to the blue Plymouth. Carmen opened the driver's side door for him. Her first query was: "What did he say?"

"He won't help us." Octavio gripped the steering wheel tightly, staring ahead.

"I told you so," she reminded pointedly. "He's not one of us. He'll never be a patriot. We'll have to go as planned. We still have other people we can rely on in Ponce." She looked at her husband. "The plan is still on?"

"Yes," Octavio answered, "the plan is still on."

CHAPTER
THIRTY-NINE

RAFAEL CONTINUED FILLING the candy jars with wrappers of hard candy, while his boss, Alejandro, was busy with a telephone conversation at the other end of the counter. Rafael could tell it was a tense exchange, though he could barely hear Alejandro's low, muffled voice, almost conspiratorial in nature. All the while, Alejandro scribbled some notes with a pencil on a piece of paper. Stranger still, it was almost noon and Alexandro had not yet opened the drugstore for business.

He saw Alejandro hang the telephone receiver back on the hook. The older man stood motionless for a moment or so. He looked down at the message he had composed on the paper. His forehead furrowed, he took up the pencil again and scribbled some more. He put down the pencil. "Raffa!" he called.

Rafael stopped what he was doing and dashed to the other end of the counter.

Alejandro folded the piece of paper twice, three times, then handed it to Rafael. He looked intently at the young boy. "I want you to take this to the house across the street," he instructed. "You know the one I mean?"

Rafael swallowed, nodded yes.

"Hand this message to Papo Mendosa, no one else, and do it quick! Don't stop for anything else." Alexandro scanned the boy's face carefully. "Do you understand?"

Another swallowed nod.

"Good. Get going! Go through the back door; it's unlocked."

Rafael stuffed the message in the breast pocket of his khaki school uniform. "And after you deliver the message," Alejandro was saying, "you head for school. Tell the teacher you had an emergency at home—that's why you're late. If he gives you any trouble, tell him to call me. Understand?"

A third swallowed nod.

Alejandro planted a hand on Rafael's shoulder. "Good. Now go!" He watched as the eleven-year-old boy scampered out the back door of the store. In the solitary quiet Alejandro lifted his eyes toward the ceiling. Dios mio, he thought, it has begun.

The house across the street from Alejandro's apothecary was painted a light green. It was nondescript among the many other wooden structures, all painted in light colors and all with the ubiquitous veranda in front. What was notable about this house was that the front door was locked. At the time almost no one locked their front doors in Ponce, especially if there were people inside. As was the case here: in the kitchen in the back, four men sat around a table, anxiously awaiting the knock on the door, which came in due time.

Octavio Mendosa rose from the table and headed across the living room to the front door, while the others watched with guarded expectation. Octavio opened the door to find young Rafael bearing a folded piece of paper. Octavio took the paper, thanked Rafael, and promptly closed the door.

Rafael stood in place for some moments, wondering what was going on. It had started out as a strange day. He stepped back toward the veranda, down the wooden steps, and out into the street, heading back to the drugstore to pick up his schoolbooks.

Inside, Octavio made his way back to the table and handed the message to one of the men. The man, Ramon Pedrosa, nervously smoked a cigarette. He stopped long enough to unfold the paper, gave it a cursory read, and said to the others, "The revolt has begun. Don Albizu has just sent word; so affirms Tomás López, the leader of the Liberation Army. He's in Arecibo right now."

"We can finally move!" cried Octavio.

"Not so fast, my friend." Ramon Pedrosa exhaled smoke impatiently. "As always, there are complications. Don Albizu has learned that the police have gotten word of the planned revolt. How? We don't know. But it's very possible that they will raid your mother's house"—he pointed to another man sitting across the table from him—"and if they do, they will confiscate the weapons stored there. Melitón," he said directly to the other man, "you know what that means. Our whole plan in this part of the island can go up in smoke. It's your family's house, and you as the president of the Ponce section of the Nationalist Party have to make this decision."

The other men leaned forward with their hands clasped across the table. But before he could answer, another question came his way, this one from Octavio: "Melitón, how much weaponry do we have stashed in the house?"

"A lot." Melitón rubbed his chin with the back of his hand. "It's one of our biggest stores of weapons. We have pistols, rifles, bullets, even incendiary bombs. It's crucial to us at this point."

"But our orders were to attack the police station here in Ponce," Octavio pointed out.

"But what about the weapons cache?" Ramon questioned. "We can't afford to let it be confiscated by the police. It's our main weapons arsenal in this part of the island."

"But if we divert from our mission in Ponce now," Octavio fended, "that puts the whole plan in jeopardy."

"Our whole plan is already in jeopardy if we lose that cache of weapons." Ramon flicked his cigarette toward a younger man sitting to his right. "Francisco, what do you think your uncle would want us to do right now? You know his thinking. What would be his advice?"

The younger man took in the whole group at the table with one long look. He said, "I believe my uncle, don Albizu, would want us to safeguard the weapons we have stored in Peñuelas. To him that would be the highest priority, so I believe."

Octavio asked, "Even if it meant postponing our attack in Ponce?"

"Yes," the young man replied.

Shaking his head, Octavio said, "I don't like it."

"We have no choice." Ramon blew smoke toward the ceiling. "The revolt has begun. We got word from don Albizu; we can't stop now. I say we go and defend the weapons we have stored. We need those weapons if this revolt is to continue. There's no other choice." Then he referred again to the other man across the table: "What do you say, Melitón?"

"You're right," Melitón concurred. Then to the others: "We go get those weapons now. Francisco said that's what don Albizu would have wanted, and that's what we do."

Octavio took a breath, his voice dropping to half an octave. "Let me go tell Alejandro, the druggist, what we've decided to do so he can inform the others that the action in Ponce will have to wait." He turned to the younger man. "Francisco, you go tell Carmencita and her people to hold tight. Tell her I'm heading for Peñuelas with the group."

Francisco bid everyone good luck, got up from the table, and left to deliver his message.

Octavio then asked quietly of the man with the cigarette, "Ramon, do you really think this is the best plan?"

Ramon was quiet for a moment, pulling on his cigarette. "We must follow our new strategy. The gears are in motion. We're committed." He took a last puff, ground the cigarette on the table. "Gentlemen, let's do our duty."

The meeting adjourned. Octavio went across the street to the drug-store, while the others set about preparing for the crucible to come and closing up the house. They put their hats on and piled into Octavio's blue Plymouth, parked in front. Octavio returned, got behind the wheel, and drove off for the town of Peñuelas, seven and three-quarter miles away.

CHAPTER FORTY

THEY ARRIVED IN Barrio Macaná, in the town of Peñuelas, around late evening. Everything was normal in the barrio neighborhood: the local cafetín was open, with its regulars enjoying an after-work drink in the only place that had electric lights. All the other surrounding houses showed dim lighting from the wick lanterns indoors.

Octavio parked the car alongside the yellow-painted house at the end of a side street. The three men who got out of the car were greeted by Melitón Muniz's mother, who hadn't expected them. Melitón explained that the revolt had begun and they needed to secure the stored weapons.

Melitón's mother, a stout, sensible woman, took out a wooden coffee grinder and began making coffee for the men. While she was in the kitchen, Octavio asked Melitón Muñiz, "What do we do now?"

"We wait for the others," Melitón answered.

"The others? Who?"

"We have seven more men coming in. And they'll bring word as to what the Maestro wants us to do with the weapons."

"As I understand it," Octavio enumerated, "our mission is to attack police headquarters and federal post offices, burn all Selective Service cards, and then proclaim the Republic of Puerto Rico. The longer we wait here, the more time we lose. Especially, as we believe, the police know about the weapons here. Why wait?"

Ramon Pedrosa joined in and he said, "Papo, we can't move until we get word from don Albizu. He insisted we wait for the other men. We are too few in number right now. We need the others to complete the mission. In the interim, safeguarding these weapons is paramount."

Octavio had reservations. "Right now, Carmencita and her group are waiting in Ponce. We should strike while we have the advantage of surprise."

"We don't move until we get word from don Albizu to do otherwise," Melitón said with finality. He turned to Ramon, who bobbed his head in agreement.

"Let it go on record that I don't agree with this plan," Octavio voiced out loud.

"Noted," Melitón said crisply.

Ramon Pedrosa had another thought: "It might get a bit messy tonight. It's not right we should put your mother in danger. Is there someplace that she might go and stay? And be safe?"

"She has a sister in the barrio," Melitón said, looking somber. "I'll ask her to go there for the night, though she's not gonna like it. This is her home. And she can be stubborn at times."

"It's for her safety," Ramon stressed. "You have enough to do without putting your mother in danger." He then turned to Octavio and said, "Let's check on the weapons stash while we wait for the others."

The seven other men arrived throughout the night. The last to arrive was Guillermo González Ubides, who came with the final orders from Albizu Campos. Guillermo, mustachioed, tall, and imposing even with his horned-rimmed glasses, stated that the Maestro wanted the men to safeguard the weapons cache at all costs. They knew the police were on the way, and the weapons must not fall into the hands of the authorities.

Firearms were distributed. The group hunkered down inside the house and waited.

At around 4 a.m., with the barrio bathed in a creeping silence, Octavio, lying on a coach in the living room and cradling an M1 carbine, was roused from an uneasy sleep. He heard distinct noises coming from outside: car engines coming to a stop, car doors slamming shut. He got up and tiptoed over the other men sprawled asleep on the floor, as Melitón Muniz got up from a wicker chair, eyes red from uneven sleep.

Guillermo González and another man, Arturo Ortiz, had been on watch outside. They rushed into the house. "They're here!" Guillermo announced loudly. Some men were dozing on chairs in the kitchen. They snapped to and rushed into the main living room.

One of the men, José Ramos, inquired anxiously, "What now?"

Melitón held a revolver in his hand, and he brandished it for emphasis. "We safeguard the weapons!"

Guillermo was peering through one of the locked window shutters. "They're surrounding the house!" he cried.

Ramon Pedrosa, who had come in from the kitchen, ordered everyone to take up positions, adding, "You know what we have to do." He then instructed the men to put out all the wick lanterns.

Five police cars beamed their headlights on the house and its veranda. Khaki-clad policemen took up positions behind the cars, some armed with pump-action shotguns. They were augmented by four others armed with riot guns used as tear gas launchers.

Most of the other residents in the surrounding homes, upon being awakened by the noise and seeing the police cars, promptly closed their doors and window shutters. Nobody wanted part of what was coming next.

Three policemen, holding flashlights in one hand and pistols in the other, cautiously approached the Muñiz home.

One of the window shutters was flung open. The policemen nearest to the house aimed his flashlight at the window and saw two silhouettes aiming guns at him. The policeman dropped to the ground and began firing his weapon at the target.

Crouching behind the window, Octavio and Arturo Ortiz returned fire, Octavio plugging away with his carbine and Arturo Ortiz firing with his revolver.

The policemen behind the cars let loose with everything they had. Within minutes the front of the house was riddled with bullets and buckshot. The men inside flattened to the floor or hid behind wooden beams as shot after shot peppered their surroundings.

Except for Arturo Ortiz, who stood up screaming and still firing his weapon, was suddenly out of bullets. A volley of rounds and buckshot slammed into his chest. The impact threw him back onto the floor.

"Arturo!" Octavio scuttled toward his friend, trying to make out the severity of the wounds in the darkened room. Ramon Pedrosa came alongside him, jostling Arturo's shoulder. "Arturo! Arturo!"

Arturo was dead. Enraged, and oblivious to the shots dancing around him, Octavio rushed back to the now-shutterless window and resumed firing from his carbine, aiming for the headlights of the cars. Some found their mark. Automobile headlights instantly went dark. Crouching behind car doors or from inside the vehicles, police tried to maneuver their driver's-seat spotlights to find targets.

Inside the house, the shutters from the second window were flung open. More gunfire cascaded toward the police cars. Guillermo González pulled open the front door and came out onto the veranda. A barrage of bullets met him, with random shots scattering all along the wooden posts. Some found their mark. He staggered back; then he straightened again, all six feet of him, and once more he raised his gun at the police.

They returned another barrage of fire, some rounds shattering his eyeglasses, and he fell back through the door.

José Ramos had been firing his gun from the second window. When he saw Guillermo González get hit, he rushed toward the open door and tried to pull his friend's body back inside the house. As he did so, he was shot in the head, and he fell alongside his friend.

Now the police resorted to their last weapon of choice. They began lobbing tear gas canisters.

Tear gas smoke enveloped the main room. Men coughed and stumbled into furniture and each other in the waning dark. Eyes swelled and watered, lungs filled.

Ramon Pedrosa grabbed a handkerchief from his back pocket and covered his nose. He lurched toward the kitchen.

Octavio saw him and followed, covering his mouth with his forearm and gasping for air. He made it to the kitchen, where the tear gas had not yet completely penetrated. Next to the tin sink was the door that led to the backyard. Through the dimness, he saw Ramon Pedrosa fling open the door and tramp out into the backyard. He was close behind, and they were soon at the rear fence. Ramon rammed part of the fence with his shoulder. It was of flimsy construction, and the wooden slats broke open. Ramon and Octavio elbowed their way through the opening and were soon facing a grassy field behind the house. Then they were running into the grassy patch and beyond, heading for the back road that led away from Barrio Macaná.

CHAPTER
FORTY-ONE

THEY LISTENED INTENTLY to the radio broadcast. The disembodied voice of the announcer on WIAC radio related with prefect intonation how "nationalist disruptions" had occurred in Santurce, Peñuelas, Arecibo, and Jayuya; how police forces were massively responding to these incidents. The government in San Juan had proclaimed martial law, and there were rumors that the National Guard would be called in if these "incidents" mushroomed.

Sitting in a metal folding chair in the backroom of Alejandro's drugstore, Carmen Mendosa intoned, "The revolution has begun. The yanquis cannot deny it now. The day has come at last."

Facing her across the room, also sitting in folding chairs, were Octavio and Ramon Pedrosa. Each listened with growing anticipation, not deviating from the black radio perched on a small wooden stand and blaring the latest bulletin.

Alejandro stood next to the radio, his head cocked low so he could hear better. He said what they were all thinking; "The question is: How will the government respond?"

"We know how they'll respond," Ramon griped bitterly. "We will lose many men, just like we've lost Arturo, Guillo, and José. But that is a price we're willing to pay."

"But what happens now?" Carmen asked. "Why are we waiting? Why don't we begin the attacks in Ponce? My people are ready. It makes no sense to just sit here."

Ramon Pedrosa looked at her soberly. "Carmencita, you and your husband here are my tigers, ready for anything. But as Papo will agree, we can't go forward without the okay from the Maestro. That was agreed to beforehand."

Octavio backed up Ramon. "He's right. After what happened in Peñuelas, we have to proceed with caution. We've lost three men and possibly the weapons cache in Peñuelas. We can't afford any more mistakes."

"What mistakes?" Carmen argued. "It's obvious someone tipped off the police. The same can happen here. To wait is stupid!"

"To go off without instructions is even more stupid," Octavio offered.

Husband and wife stood their ground, staring at each other. Ramon Pedrosa stepped in. "Carmencita, Papo is right. Listen to reason. Ponce is important, but Jayuya and Utuado are more important. They're located in the center of the island. That means they're the most important part of the revolt. It's imperative that we take control of these municipalities first and cut the supply lines to the enemy, which will delay troop reinforcements to the western part of the island. Can't you see that?"

"What I see," Carmen grumbled, "is that the longer we wait, the less our chance of surprise." She scrutinized her husband. "Papo, you yourself said that not long ago."

Octavio looked morose. "Yes, but in view of what happened in Peñuelas, I now believe we should."

The back-room door thrust open, stopping Octavio in midsentence. Rafael, Alejandro's delivery boy, rushed into the room and breathlessly handed a piece of paper to Alejandro. He gave it a peripheral glance, then stepped forward and gave the paper to Ramon Pedrosa, who gave it a quick once-over, then looked up from the message. "Tomás López, leader of the Liberation Army, speaking for don Albizu, says we should immediately transfer what weapons we have to Utuado by way of Adjuntas."

"That settles it," Octavio concluded. "Carmencita, tell the others we move for Utuado. Get whatever vehicles we have and start loading up. Also, instruct them that we'll head for Utuado along different routes out of town to avoid suspicion. But once they get to Adjuntas, head for Utuado, where we'll make our stand."

"Understood," Carmen said grudgingly. She stood, then said as an afterthought, "As soon as we're set and that's done, I'll come back and we'll head for Utuado."

Ramon and Octavio exchanged knowing glances. Ramon was the one to speak up: "Carmencita, we think it wise you stay behind in Ponce. If something happens on the way to Utuado, we don't want to lose all our top people. We need someone to remain behind in case we decide on a Ponce action, and you're the best we've got here."

Carmen gave her husband a questioning look. "Papo?"

"Ramon is right," Octavio said gently. "We need you in Ponce if—"

She stopped him in midsentence: "But what about you?"

"I'll be okay," Octavio assured her. "You just do what needs to be done."

The frown on Carmen's face was visible to all. Ramon stepped in again. "Don't worry, Carmencita. You know that Papo can take care of himself. And I'll see to it that he's alright, I promise."

Octavio lifted from his chair and approached Carmen, enfolding her hands in his. "Don't worry about me. I'll be fine." He smiled into her face. "You just take care of our end in Ponce. That's more important. And make sure that Miguel and Efrain are safe. That's all I ask."

Carmen did not look pleased. "You will be careful?"

"Yes," Octavio promised.

Ramon clambered to his feet, pushing back his chair. "Let's get started, then." He said to the pharmacist, "Alejandro, you stand by for further instructions. And let us know if there's any change."

"Will do." Alejandro patted Rafael on the shoulder. "I've got my trusted associate here." He smiled down at the boy. "He's our eyes and ears in Ponce. We'll keep you informed."

"He's a patriot, just like you, Alejandro. A true boricua."

The boy's chest swelled. Hearing such adult compliments was honey to his ears, though the blaring from the radio had not abated and it spoke of "incidents" and "government response" and martial law, terms he did not yet understand completely, but which left an inexplicable wonderment and a touch of fear.

CHAPTER
FORTY-TWO

AS PLANNED, VARIOUS vehicles were commandeered to transport the weaponry to Utuado, where the decisive battle would be waged.

The cars, some with their trunks loaded with pistols and rifles, others crammed with Nationalists eager for battle, set off in the morning. They left at different times, some leaving from La Playa, others from the town, each heading for their appointed spot in the central Cordillera Mountains.

Octavio, Ramon Pedrosa, and four others, including Francisco, Albizu Campos's nephew, crammed into Octavio's blue Plymouth. Octavio ensconced himself in the driver's seat. He looked at his watch. It was nine-thirty in the morning. With luck they would reach Utuado by noon.

Just as they were driving along the road bordering the beach area of Los Meros, Octavio noticed another car following his. He looked closer into his rearview mirror and noticed distinctly that it was a blue-and-white police car. "We're being followed," he told the others.

Sitting next to him, Ramon Pedrosa looked into the side-view mirror next to the passenger seat. "Step on it," he instructed.

Octavio stepped on the gas. The car rammed forward.

And so did the other car, which likewise increased its speed.

In the back seat, one of the other men asked, "What do we do now?"

Ramon expelled a breath. "I don't know." He thought for a moment. Then: "Papo, slow down."

Holding nervously to the wheel, Octavio asked, "You sure?"

"Yes," said Ramon. "Let's see what they do."

Octavio shifted gears and eased back on the accelerator. The car behind them came closer. He half hoped it would just continue and go past them.

It did not.

The police car drove around and then swerved in front of them, forcing Octavio to come to a stop.

Octavio reached down and pulled on the emergency brake, but kept the engine running.

Two policemen got out of the other car, and they approached slowly, warily.

The men in Octavio's car waited.

The policemen came near, one on the driver's side, the other officer near the front passenger side. Octavio noted that the policeman on his side was older, and he had two stripes on his shirt sleeve. He was the senior man. The man on the other side was younger and seemed more nervous, and he was staring directly at Ramon Pedrosa, with his hand on his holster, gripping the handle of his weapon.

"You're going pretty fast," the older man said to Octavio. "You in a hurry?"

Octavio didn't answer. It was Ramon, from the passenger side, who said, "We have business in Adjuntas. We need to see some family there."

The policeman's eyes narrowed. "Business or family? Which is it?"

"Officer, we're just trying to get to Adjuntas and visit our relatives. Really, we just—"

"They're lying!" This came from the younger policeman on Ramon's side of the car.

"Really, we're just—"

"I say we arrest them all and take them in." The younger policeman's voice was gruff.

The four men in the back seat stirred. Young Francisco squirmed farther back into his seat.

"Get out of the car," the older policeman ordered. He stepped back, placing his hand on his gun holster.

Octavio placed a hand under his shirt.

The policeman's face turned hard. "Get out of the car! Now!"

Octavio whisked out the revolver from under his shirt and shot the policeman point-blank in the chest. Blood splattered on his hand and gun.

Ramon Pedrosa likewise brought out his revolver and shot the younger policeman twice. The cop fell back on the unpaved road, still gripping his own weapon, which he had drawn, but too late.

"Let's go!" Ramon yelled.

Octavio jammed on the accelerator and the car took off, leaving behind two policemen bleeding on the ground.

CHAPTER
FORTY-THREE

SHE PICKED OUT an extra-ripe mango from the tree. It was full and supple, about to fall from the branch and join the mass of other mangoes littering her yard. The sweetness of the mango would provide a good dessert.

She needed something sweet now. She could hear the radio echoing from inside. The last two days had been an unsettling experience for everyone in La Playa. All ears were tuned to the latest development from San Juan, Jayuya, and Utuado, where the announcer stated that now bomber aircraft had been called in to quell the disturbance. Against all odds the independentistas had held the town of Jayuya for two days, and the National Guard had been called in. The Americans did not want the same thing to happen in Utuado.

Even in her garden the radio chatter was incessant. She considered that the whole town listened as if the revolt were a ball game, taking stock inning by inning. A ball game of death.

She heard something else. A car came up and stopped at the front of her house. What now? She put down the fruit basket she carried, wiped her hands on her apron, and went inside, heading for the door. She passed Rafael in the kitchen, where he sat at the table, doing his homework with two books spread out before him.

The radio reverberated in the living room, its volume way up so that Rafael could hear it in the kitchen. "It's too loud!" she carped, hoping

Rafael could hear her. She went and lowered the volume, then stepped up to the door.

"Esteban?" It was one of the local policemen standing at her doorway. He didn't look too happy. "What's wrong?"

"Milagros, I'm sorry," the policeman began, fidgeting with a pocket flap on his khaki shirt. "I hate to disturb you at this time, but we need to talk."

"What's this about?"

Esteban stepped inside the house, looked around nervously. "Where's Rafael?"

"He's in the kitchen doing his homework." A worried look crossed Milagros's face. "What's going on?"

Esteban cast somber eyes her way. "I need to speak to him."

"Why?"

"We have a situation with your son."

"'A situation'? What do you mean?"

Esteban was still looking around, swerving his head from one side to the other. "Can I speak to him?"

Milagros stiffened. "What is going on?" she asked again.

"I need to see him now, please."

Milagros gave him a guarded look. Then she called toward the kitchen, "Raffa, come here now!" And to the policeman, "What's this about?"

Esteban didn't answer; instead he waited for the boy to appear. His eyes shifted from the boy to his mother. "I need to take him in," he said to Milagros.

"What?"

"Milagros, please, I have to."

Milagros wrapped a protective arm around Rafael, whose own face displayed worry and dread. "What do you mean, 'take him in'?"

Esteban asked the boy, "Raffa, where's your bicycle?"

Rafael glanced from his mother to the policeman. He uttered, "In the back."

"His bicycle?" Milagros viewed the policeman with sudden suspicion. "What do you want with his bicycle?"

"Can I see it?"

Rafael moved his head from one adult to the other. He swallowed and answered, "Yes."

Milagros wrinkled her brow. "What has his bicycle got to do with anything?"

Esteban stepped back, stuck his head out the door, and called to another policeman standing beside his vehicle parked outside. "Jorge, check on the bicycle, please."

The second policeman touched his cap with his hand to acknowledge the request, went up to the waist-high front gate, unlatched it, stepped inside the front yard, and went around to the back of the house, seeking the now-important bicycle.

Milagros pressed fingertips to her forehead. "Esteban, what is going on?"

"Where were you this morning?" the policeman inquired of Rafael.

Rafael glanced anxiously at his mother.

"What has that got to do with anything?" Milagros asked, now with a touch of anger.

"Your son works for Alejandro the pharmacist, does he not?"

"Yes, but what has that got to—"

"Was he at the drugstore today?"

"Yes, but—"

"He rides the bicycle to town, does he not?"

"Yes, but—"

"Have you seen the bicycle lately?"

Milagros was at a loss. "What?"

"Have you seen his bicycle lately?" Esteban repeated.

"Yes, um . . . ," Milagros stammered. "I mean, no. What's so important about his bicycle?"

"He has a pennant on the bicycle," Esteban related. "It's a Puerto Rican flag." He paused and his face lengthened. "As you know, it's illegal to display a Puerto Rican flag anywhere on the island, even in one's own home. That is a law that was passed by the Puerto Rican legislature. You son has violated that law by displaying the flag. You know what's been happening all around the island. In this atmosphere it was stupid of your son to display that pennant."

Milagros stared hard at Rafael. "Raffa, is that true? Do you have an island flag on your bicycle?"

Rafael's bowels were churning; he couldn't respond.

"Raffa was seen riding the bike with the flag shown in the back this morning when he went to town." Esteban took a fair-sized breath and continued, "More than one person has complained about it to us." His voice was urgent. "Milagros, people are upset. There's a virtual war going on in Jayuya. The independentistas have even attacked the governor's mansion in San Juan. As we speak, there's a gunfight going on in La Fortaleza, the governor's home. In this environment it was not wise to go around showing the Puerto Rican colors. I have to take him in."

"NO!" Milagros stepped in front of Rafael, shielding her son.

Esteban extended a hand. "Milagros, please."

"NO! You will not take my son!"

"Milagros, I promise, it's only for questioning," Esteban sought to appease. "We know he works for Alejandro, and we think Alejandro is part of the conspiracy."

"What conspiracy?"

"We have long suspected that Alejandro is part of the Nationalist movement," Esteban responded gravely. "But we had no proof until now. We need to know what Raffa saw or heard while working for the druggist. It's all part of—"

"No! You can't have my son!"

"Milagros, I'll see to it no harm comes to him. You have my word."

Milagros shot a hand toward the door. "Get out of my house!"

Esteban turned and called, "Jorge, come inside, please."

The other policeman was soon inside. "Jorge, take the boy, but be gentle."

"NO!"

Jorge tried to sidestep around Milagros so he could get to her son. Milagros barred his way, thumping at his chest with her fists. He tried to block her hands. Esteban stepped forward and enfolded her with his arms, pulling her away, while Jorge grabbed a stunned and frightened Rafael by the arm and led him away from the house. All the while, Milagros continued yelling and screaming at the top of her lungs, while Esteban tried to assure her that he would look after Rafael.

CHAPTER
FORTY-FOUR

"AFTER THREE HOURS of a vicious firefight, Vidal Santiago Diaz, owner of the Salón Boricua barbershop in Santurce and personal barber to Albizu Campos, has been dragged out by police. He is believed to be severely wounded. . . . In other news, the town of Jayuya, in its third day of the revolt, has been attacked by ten United States bomber planes and by land artillery. It is believed the town is still held by Nationalists, although the 296th Regiment of the US National Guard has begun extensive operations to recapture the municipality and . . ."

"Mami, there's someone at the door."

Leticia reached out and lowered the volume on the radio. "What is it?"

"There's someone at the door," Maria repeated.

"Who?"

"I don't know, but she says it's important," Maria answered indifferently.

"Can't you get your father?"

"He's in his study. Remember? He said he doesn't want to be disturbed."

"Yes, of course. He never wants to be disturbed." Leticia grasped the armrests of the chair and got to her feet. Before she left her room, she turned off the radio.

At the front door stood Milagros Pagan. The shock streamed through Leticia's face, though she tried not to show it.

Milagros said in a hushed tone, "I need to see your husband. Please."

"Uh . . . um . . . I . . ." Leticia found it difficult to form her words.

"Please, I beg of you. It's very important. My son has been taken in. I need to speak to Toño."

"'Taken in'? What, what do you mean?"

"Please let me see him," Milagros implored. "I wouldn't have come here unless it was—"

"He's very busy right now."

"I know he's busy!" Milagros almost shouted. She lowered her voice. "Please."

"Wait here a moment." Leticia turned to see Maria standing close, suddenly interested in this new visitor. "Tell your father he has a visitor," Leticia announced. "Tell him it's important."

Mario left for her father's study.

Back at the door, Leticia offered, "Please come in."

Milagros remained in place. "Thank you, but I'll wait here if you don't mind."

"Of course," said Leticia. "Can I offer you anything? Coffee, tea?"

"No, thank you."

A strained silenced spanned between the two women. It was broken when Antonio appeared. "What's so important?" he said in a crabby voice. "You know I don't want to be disturbed when I'm . . ." He stopped. "Milagros?"

Milagros wore a hat, almost like for a formal occasion, and her gloved hands clutched a small pocket purse. "I'm sorry to disturb you, Toño. I would never have come here unless it was necessary."

Antonio's stomach tightened. "What's wrong?"

Her eyes flicked from Leticia and back to Antonio. "Can I speak to you alone?"

Leticia turned to her husband. "Toño, perhaps you should speak in private. I suggest your study." She turned back to Milagros. "If you need anything, please let me know."

"Thank you." Milagros gripped her purse tightly.

Leticia said to her daughter, "Mario, tell Camilo to stop listening to all that stuff on the radio in his room. Tell him to join us in the yard. I'm making some lemonade."

She left with her daughter without saying another word.

In the kitchen she took out lemons from the refrigerator, while Maria scoured the kitchen cabinet for a juicer and some sugar. She took her time preparing the lemonade, placing the ice cubes in a pitcher, while Camilo and his sister carried a tray and glasses to a table in the backyard. All the while she did her best to seem unconcerned, yet she was bothered by what would possess Milagros Pagan to come to her house. It was an unwritten rule that she would never appear at their door.

While she was pouring lemonade for her son and daughter, Antonio came into the yard and asked Leticia to come into the kitchen.

"I must go," he said in a breathless voice. "We have a major problem on our hands, and I must deal with it."

"What is it?" she asked before he could finish.

"Rafael is being held for questioning by the police."

"Questioning by the police? He's a boy!"

"Yes, he's a boy, but he was seen with a Puerto Rican flag on his bicycle. You know the law. We can't display that flag. Anyone caught doing so is considered a Nationalist right then and there."

"Why would he be carrying a boricua flag?" Leticia asked, ashen-faced.

"I don't know." Antonio shook his head glumly. "But Milagros needs my help, and so does Rafael. I'm going to the mayoralty right now to see if I can do something."

"Is he being held in La Playa or Ponce?"

"Milagros tells me he was transferred from La Playa to town. How long they'll hold him, we don't know. But I'm going to see Churumba right now. He owes me a few favors, and maybe I can fix this thing."

Leticia tried keeping her voice calm. "Toño, please be careful. This is a dangerous and difficult time right now. Remember that."

"Oh, I do. Definitely I do."

CHAPTER
FORTY-FIVE

MAYOR ANDRES QUINTANA listened quietly, his hands folded atop his crossed legs. He could understand the anxiety.

Still, when Antonio finished recounting his tale about Rafael, Mayor Quintana chose his words carefully. "Toño, I know how difficult it must be for you right now, and as a father myself I must tell you—"

"Don't patronize me, Churumba!" Antonio snapped. "I need your help; that's all there is to it."

"But, Toño, this is a delicate matter."

"I don't care about any fucking 'delicate matter,'" Antonio raged. "What can you do about it?"

"Toño, this boy is in a difficult situation. We have to—"

"This boy is my son," Antonio interrupted frankly. "Don't talk to me about any 'difficult situation.' I'm sure you've had worse situations in your time."

Mayor Quintana proceeded in a reasonable vein. "We are currently in a crisis. You know that. You know what's going on. The Americans have been spooked by this Nationalist revolt, and anyone showing sympathy for the Nationalists is suspect, no matter who they are."

"He's just a boy!"

"It makes no difference what his age is. He is suspect under the current Gag Law. Displaying an island flag is treasonable under the circumstances. Even at his age he should have known that. We can't make excuses."

Antonio made a scoffing sound. "I'm not asking you to make excuses!"

The mayor's eyebrows arched. "No? Then why are you here?"

Antonio glanced sourly at Andres Quintana. "You know why I'm here. You would do the same in my place!"

"Yes," Mayor Quintana said cordially, "I probably would do the same if it were one of my sons." Then he looked doleful. "But, Toño, think of my position. I have to answer to the powers in San Juan. I can't just quash an ongoing investigation, especially with this Nationalist revolt going on. You're asking too much."

"Am I, Churumba? Is it asking too much to save my son? A mere boy who was given a flag by the pharmacist he worked for in order to help out his mother. What does he know about Nationalists and revolts? He thought it was a gift, so naturally he planted it on his bicycle. How was he to know it was 'treasonous'?"

"How could he not know it was treasonous?" Mayor Quintana gave Antonio an inquiring look. "Because of this episode we've uncovered an active Nationalist cell in Ponce. The druggist was part of it. Did you know that they planned to attack police headquarters and all government offices, including the mayoralty? I, myself, could've been a victim of this thing. Lucky for us we uncovered the plot in time; otherwise we would've been in the same fix as Jayuya and Utuado. A lot of innocent people have died because of these fanatics." The mayor's tone was resolute. "I have no sympathy for them or anyone who supports them."

"Rafael supports no one," Antonio said firmly. "He is a child caught up in circumstances. He happens to work for Alejandro the druggist. How was he to know Alejandro was a Nationalist?"

"How could he not? He worked for the man for months. Why didn't he tell his mother about Alejandro's sympathies?"

"Maybe he didn't know. He was just the guy's delivery boy!"

284

"Whether he was the pharmacist's delivery boy or not is immaterial. He was seen displaying the island colors. Under current law that is enough to indict him."

"Even if he's just eleven years old?"

"Yes, even if he's just eleven years old. Under the Gag Law there is nothing about age or experience. He violated a federal statute." Mayor Quintana spread out his palms. "There's nothing I can do."

Antonio sat in a chair facing the mayor's desk. He leaned forward, twisting the hat he held in his hands. He gnawed his tight lips. Then he sat back in the chair and closed his eyes. He opened his eyes again and studied the mayor for some seconds.

"Churumba," he said at last, "remember when you first ran for office and you didn't win? Everybody said that a jíbaro from La Playa could never be elected town mayor. And I said—"

"Toño," Mayor Quintana cut in impatiently, "let's not rehash ancient history."

"Let me finish!" Antonio snarled. "You're going to hear me whether you want to or not."

Mayor Quintana drew back in his chair. His friend's rage was manifest. And then Antonio dropped his voice so that it was almost a monotone. This disturbed the mayor even more. "Remember that, Churumba?" Antonio let that tidbit sink in. "I said that 'they,' the experts, were wrong. I knew it was time for a paisano from La Playa to run the show. We had always been considered the outsiders. It was time for one of ours to run the mayoralty. I even thought that your nickname, Churumba, would be a plus. Remember when you used to play with a spinning top in front of doña Saro's house, the one I gave her? It was she who started calling you Churumba. Why? Because that's what we call someone who plays with a spinning top all the time. And it worked. You became Churumba to everyone, and that was your catch-call when running for election the second time. 'Vote for Churumba!' was the battle cry. And it got you in office, with my help and finances."

Mayor Quintana was forced to intervene. "Look, Toño, I know all you've done for me, and believe me, I'm grateful, but—"

"I said let me finish." Antonio's neutral tone didn't deviate. "I didn't come here to relive the past or remind you of what has gone before. I know you're in a tough spot. But like me, you're a survivor. Also, you know what's right. To let a young boy suffer because of politics is not right."

"It's not just politics," the mayor responded tersely. "It's the current situation. As I said, we're in crisis. If I were to do what you ask, it would—"

Antonio's gaze turned stony. "Churumba, let me make it clear: I am not asking; I am demanding."

"Demanding what?" the mayor asked irritably.

"I am demanding you do what's right."

Mayor Quintana swallowed hard. "Who do you think you are, coming into my office and demanding some—?"

"You got here with my support," Antonio reminded. "I hope you haven't forgotten that."

Quintana's mouth tightened. "No, I've not forgotten that. But you should know your place. I am now the mayor. I don't take kindly to—"

"Shut up."

Quintana reddened. He clammed up immediately.

"Now listen," Antonio went on in his calm, even voice. "You got here because of me, and now I need your help, and you're going to help me. Why? Because I can undo everything you have. I know things. You're Mayor Quintana, but that's not your real name. That's the name you got from your stepfather, Agosto Quintana. Your real name is Pacheco, as

286

in Felicia Pacheco, more commonly known in the old days as doña Fela, the proud owner of that great red house on the outskirts of La Playa, the most famous brothel in this part of the island. I don't think the town citizens would be too happy to learn of their renowned mayor's past, especially when he worked for Fela getting young girls involved in the trade. Not only that but you pimped for her. That's how you got started."

Quintana showed alarmed. "How dare you!"

Antonio continued, quietly forceful. "It's my business to know things, Andres Pacheco," emphasizing the name, enunciating it so perfectly that it rang out in the quiet of the room. "What I'm asking is what any father would ask to save his son. You of all people should understand that. You owe me this one, Churumba, you owe me." He gave the mayor a dagger of a stare. "I can make things very difficult for you. I don't want to do it, but if I have to, I will. You do whatever you need to do to get my son out of this mess. You call in whatever favors you have to; otherwise . . ."

He let that last word hang.

Mayor Quintana looked stunned. "You wouldn't dare."

Antonio kept his stare even. "You want to take a chance on that? You've known me a long time now, and you know I don't make idle threats."

"What you're asking is—"

"What I'm asking is a favor. Simple. Do this, and I'll never trouble you again. You can continue as the popular jíbaro mayor of the town, playing up your position as defender of the barrio and the man of the people. And you can still continue enjoying your position and your family and your mistress."

A small nerve on the mayor's temple began to throb. Neither said a word. He leaned forward with both hands on his desk and said crisply, "I'll do what I can to—"

"You'll do what you have to," Antonio emphasized.

The mayor blew out his breath. "Alright, as you wish. But let me tell you right now, this squares it between us. I owe you nothing after this. You and I are done, is that clear?"

"It's very clear, Mr. Mayor."

Quintana turned his head to one side, nursing a look of distaste.

And having got what he wanted, Antonio left the mayor's office.

CHAPTER FORTY-SIX

THE HEADLINE IN *El Imparcial* was stark:

US AIR FORCE BOMBS UTUADO

Nationalist Plan Revealed

New Shootings in Mayaguez and Arecibo

Antonio raised his eyes back to Milagros, sitting across from him at the kitchen table. "You should've been aware of what he was doing," Antonio said in an exacting voice. "How could you not see the flag on his bicycle?"

Milagros sat straight, not looking at him, resting her forehand on her hand, which held a crumpled, wet handkerchief. "Please, Toño, don't task me. Not you. I blame myself enough as it is, already."

"But he is your son. Don't you care?"

"He is our son!" she fired back. "And of course I care. How can you say that? This whole thing has got me sick with grief, and I don't want to lose my son."

"You won't lose him," Antonio mollified. "I've taken care of that. But you must watch him carefully from now on. See that he stays . . ." Antonio gestured with his hand, trying to explain.

"Don't you think I look after him? What kind of mother do you think I am?" Her eyes smoldered. "I care more for him than my own life!"

"No one is accusing you of being a bad mother," Antonio said with a measure of feeling. "Just that this episode has made it difficult for you, for me—"

"So that's it," Milagros spoke acidly. "The great benefactor, Antonio Boglione, is worried about his reputation!"

"That's not fair," Antonio refuted. "I don't give a damn about my reputation where Rafael is concerned. You should know that. I've provided for you as best I can. I have not turned my back on Rafael."

"And you haven't acknowledged him as your true son either!"

Antonio moaned. "Milagros, let's not go there again, okay? Let's not dredge up past mistakes."

"So he was a mistake?"

"I never said that," Antonio objected. "He is my son and I love him, as I love you."

"Let's not talk about 'love' now, please."

"Milagros, you're upset, and I can understand why, but you should've been more aware of what was going on at Alejandro's pharmacy."

"How could I have been more aware? He worked there. He was a delivery boy. We needed the money and he wanted to work. It gave him a measure of independence. He's a good boy. This is all just a terrible mistake."

"Mistake or not, that flag business has marked him in this community. These Nationalist actions have caused severe problems on the island. Anyone connected with them, in whatever capacity, is suspect."

"Even an eleven-year-old boy who was trying to earn some spare change?"

"Even an eleven-year-old boy," Antonio said in a dry voice.

Milagros dabbed at her nose with the handkerchief. "Then there's something terribly wrong with this island."

"It's not the island," Antonio explained patiently. "It's the Americans. Churumba said they got spooked by the Nationalist revolt. And he's right. Their reaction is to clamp down, and I would do the same if I was in their shoes."

"Raffa is not a radical," Milagros said with conviction. "He's just a schoolboy who happened to work for one of the Nationalists and—"

Antonio had to jump in. "He's a schoolboy who was seen sporting a Puerto Rican flag, a treasonable offense these days."

"He doesn't know about treason! He's a good boy, caught up in this …" Milagros grappled for words.

"I know he's a good boy," Antonio offered. "That's why I went to see Churumba. There will be no investigation regarding Rafael. Alejandro and his clique will probably go to jail, but Rafael is cleared."

"And I thank you for that," Milagros offered in turn. "I know it was difficult for you."

A small silence fell. Antonio regarded Milagros intently while she stared at the floor. He said, "I would like to speak to Rafael now."

She looked up. "He's in the other room. I'll tell him you want to see him." She began to rise from her chair.

"No, you stay," Antonio requested. "I want you here when I speak to him."

Milagros looked concerned. "You will be gentle. You're not going to blame him, are you?"

"No," Antonio answered. "I'm not going to blame anyone. I just want to speak to my son, and I want you here."

"Alright." Milagros turned and called out, "Raffa! Come here please. Don Antonio wants to speak to you."

Shortly, Rafael appeared inside the kitchen. He was still wearing his public school uniform, and he held his hands tight in front of his body. When he saw Antonio, he lowered his head.

291

"Rafael," Antonio began, "I want to speak to you about what happened. Are you aware of what's been going on in Ponce and other parts of the island?"

Rafael nodded, remaining quiet.

Antonio looked to Milagros before continuing. "You mother was very worried about you, and so was I." He tossed another look from mother to son. "Did you at any time know what was going on in Alejandro's pharmacy? Where you aware of what they were planning?"

Rafael's eyes remained glued to the floor.

"Raffa?" his mother cued.

"Rafael," Antonio asked again, "what was going at the pharmacy?"

"Raffa?"

"I just did deliveries, sir," Rafael said almost in a whisper.

Antonio leaned forward in his chair, eyeing his son. "And what else?"

"Just deliveries, sir," Rafael repeated.

Antonio leaned back, fingering his jaw. "Why were you carrying that flag on your bicycle?"

Rafael stared at the ground. "Don Alejandro gave it to me. He said it was a gift. He said to take it and put it on my bike. I thought it was pretty."

"You thought it was pretty?" Antonio repeated dubiously. "Rafael, in the future, if you receive a gift from anyone, you tell your mother about it. You keep her informed of everything you do, you understand?"

"Yes, sir," Rafael said almost inaudibly.

"And you continue doing well in school. You hear? Your mother says you're a good student. Don't disappoint her." He glanced at Milagros with warmth. "There will be some other boys at school who will say things about what's happened and tease you about it and accuse you of things. You ignore them. You don't to listen to them. You listen to your mother. And if you need to talk, I'm always available. We are very proud of you, and we want to remain that way."

"Yes, sir," Rafael affirmed in his low voice.

Antonio straightened, his face softening. "I'll see you again soon. You make sure your mother is well. That's your responsibility. You're the man of the house here. Do you understand?"

"Yes, sir."

"Good. Now you can go back to your studies or whatever."

"Yes, sir."

When they were again alone in the kitchen, Antonio glanced about and said, "You've done well with this house."

"I know." Milagros fingered her handkerchief.

Antonio sought the right words. "Look, I'll be around tomorrow. If you need anything, let me know. I'll try to make more time." He took in her glum expression. "I do care," he said sincerely. "I do care for our son and for you. You must believe that."

She looked aside. "Yes, I believe that."

"Milagros, this will blow over. You'll see. Rafael is safe, and that's the important thing."

"Yes," she responded simply, her eyes taking in some far corner of the kitchen.

CHAPTER
FORTY-SEVEN

Dispatch from Octavio Mendosa, San Juan, to Griselio Torresola, Bronx, NY:

Griselio:

The Americans think we are through, done. Don Albizu is once more imprisoned. The heroes of Jayuya, Utuado, and La Fortaleza have been killed or captured. Your own sister, in the battle for Jayuya, was unfortunately shot and captured. And your brother Elio has been arrested. They will be honored and remembered, that I promise. Because whatever the imperialist propaganda, we are not through. We have just begun. We believe in the righteousness of our cause. They cannot take that away from us.

As you know, United States law mandates that President Truman take direct charge in all matters concerning the island of Borinquen. And the puppet, Muñoz Marin, is required to consult and kowtow to the whims of the White House. They have clamped down on the news coming out of Puerto Rico. They now claim that our heroic stance is an "incident between Puerto Ricans."

We must prove them wrong! We must show them that this is a war between two countries, one the oppressor and the other fighting for independence. You must go to Washington, to the heart of the oppressor, and make a stand and draw their attention. No one cares about the island or its people. Only don Albizu cares, and those that follow him. Your action will change history. You and Oscar are in a position to do it. You, as a member of the Maestro's bodyguard in Jayuya, know this. Don Albizu has given you command in the United States. This is your moment, our moment, to demonstrate the wisdom of don Albizu and the boricuas who yearn to be free. You are soldiers of the Republic of Puerto Rico, and as soldiers you must do your duty. And if you die in battle, it will be a soldier's death. You will be consecrated along with the many others who have fallen.

As to the plan, you must familiarize yourself with the area. We know that Truman is staying at the Blair House while the White House is being renovated. Blair House stands at 1651 Pennsylvania Avenue, right across the street from the White House. Note that it has a guard booth in front. You must approach the residence from opposite directions and shoot your way inside. Given the security, there is no other way.

You and Oscar Collazo will take a train from New York to Washington, D.C. You will check into the Hotel Harris separately. Then you will go on a sightseeing tour. You will cruise past Lafayette Square and Blair House, and take stock of its entrances and exits, police presence, and Secret Service agents. Memorize everything that you see. Do not take notes. Commit everything to memory and then back at the hotel finalize the plan.

As to the weaponry: The police have standard .38 caliber revolvers, and they only hold six rounds, which have to be loaded one at a time. You own a German Luger and, as I witnessed in Jayuya, are skilled at using a weapon. Oscar is not, and you must instruct him on how to handle a gun and load it. The weapon you will purchase for Oscar is a Walther P-38. I enclose a money order for that purchase. With our contacts, it should not cost more than $35. Both your Luger and the Walther are standard service automatics of the Third Reich. They are the perfect weapons, both in design and effectiveness. They are more efficient and lethal than the guns used by the police. They fire a high-powered 9-millimeter cartridge with steel-jacketed bullets. They can be loaded quickly, and their magazines hold seven rounds. The oppressors' weaponry simply cannot match yours. And you will have sixty-nine rounds of ammunition, more than enough to get the job done.

Our cause and its future are now in your hands. Don Albizu has instructed you to do the mission without hesitation of any kind. I know you will not disappoint us.

¡Viva Puerto Rico libre!

Papo Mendosa

BELFAST NEWS LETTER

November 2, 1950

PRESIDENT TRUMAN SURVIVES ASSASSINATION ATTEMPT

An attempt to assassinate President Truman was made yesterday by two Puerto Rican Nationalists. They tried to shoot their way into Blair House, the President's temporary residence.

Washington—A revolt is at present going on in Puerto Rico.

After a gun dual with the president's guards, one of the men was killed and the other seriously injured. Three guards were wounded, one dying later and one being in critical condition. The president was unhurt.

The British ambassador to Washington, Sir Oliver Franks, called on President Truman last night at Blair House to congratulate him on his escape. Sir Oliver also conveyed a note of congratulations from Anthony Eden, Deputy Leader of the Opposition.

Mr. Truman's secretary, Mr. Ross, gave the following accounts of the president's movements throughout the shooting: The president, he said, was sound asleep, having his usual after-lunch nap, when he was awakened by shots. He had taken off his outer clothes and was resting in an upstairs room with the window open. He rushed to the window and saw the gunman lying on the steps. By this time the shooting had stopped.

Mrs. Truman apparently got a mistaken impression that one of the Secret Servicemen whom she knew very well had been killed, and she was very much upset about it.

Mr. Baughman, head of the US Secret Service, said both gunmen were members of the revolutionary Puerto Rican Nationalist Party.

The dead man was identified as Griselio (or Lorenzo Angelina) Torresola. He was described as "young."

The injured gunman was identified as Oscar Collazo. His age was given as 37.

Mr. Baughman said the two would-be assassins had come to Washington two days ago and were staying in a hotel. He said Collazo had confessed that he and Torresola had come to the capital with the express purpose of shooting President Truman.

CHAPTER FORTY-EIGHT

SHE WAS PACKING her beloved plaster figurines when she heard the front door open. She knew immediately who it was by the sound of the footsteps. She didn't even bother to turn around, but simply continued placing the newspaper-wrapped figurines inside the box.

"You're really going to do this," he said, glancing around at the packed boxes scattered about the room. "And I can't convince you to stay."

She turned to face Antonio and said, "No, you cannot. I've made up my mind." She went over to a side table and picked up a ball of twine and a pair of scissors.

"Milagros, it's not too late to change your mind. Think of your family, your son. Is this the right thing to do?"

She could hear the concern in Antonio's voice. "My mind is set on this. I can't stay here any longer. I'm doing this for myself and my son. After all that's happened, it's the best course."

"You're going to take him away from all he knows, from his friends, his—"

"We have no friends here," she said sternly. "Not anymore. After the revolt and the shootings and everything else, it's as if we've been marked. Raffa can't bear to go to school anymore, and the people in La Playa treat me as if I'm not one of them."

He approached closer and touched her hand. "This will pass, you'll see. It's just a phase we, the island, is going through. "You'll see. Just give it time."

301

"I've given it time, and I've decided I have to go."

Antonio looked torn. "But why to New York of all places? Why not to another part of the island? You have family in Vieques, you could—"

She didn't let him finish. "We can't stay on the island. We need to start anew. Raffa needs a place where he can learn, where he can grow." She looked indignant. "It's not here."

"I think you're making a mistake," he said.

She smiled ruefully. "We're all allowed one mistake in our lifetime. I've done that. Now I need to move on." She went back to the table with the boxes and began pulling out string from the ball of twine. When she had the required amount, she cut the string and began tying up the box.

Antonio watched her work quietly. "Where will you stay?" he said at length.

"I have a cousin in New York, in the barrio. She's willing to put us up in her place until I find a place of my own."

"What about money? Expenses?"

"I'm still young and strong; I'll find work."

"What about Rafael?"

"He'll adapt. Most children do. And it'll be better than staying here."

"I could stop you know," he remarked in a cold tone. "I could insist Rafael stay here."

She turned to look at him. "Stay where? With you? Your family? You know that wouldn't work. It's a pipe dream. He's better off with me, his mother. I can take good care of him."

"Can you?" he challenged. "You're going off to some place you've never been. You don't even know the language. How's that going to help Rafael?" Antonio stared at her, assembling his argument. "If he stays here with me, he'll have a better chance."

"At what?" Milagros stared back. "Here he's the bastard son of don Antonio Boglione. In America he'll be his own man. I'll see to that."

"So nothing I say will change your mind," Antonio said resignedly.

"No," she said once more.

He looked again at the row of boxes stacked about. "What are you going to do with all your stuff?"

"My figurines I'm giving to doña Sara. She loves them as much as I do. Everything else I'm just giving away. Anybody who wants to can come and take what they want."

"That should make a lot of people in La Playa happy," Antonio said sourly. "What about the house?"

"I'm giving it back to you," she informed.

"To me?" He was suddenly taken aback.

"Yes, to you. It's your house after all."

"It's your house!" he barked.

"It was never my house, Toño. It was your gift to me, and I'm giving it back."

Antonio frowned. "I don't want it back."

Milagros showed her little smile again. "Then sell it, give it away, I don't care. It's no longer my concern. You can add it to your many properties in La Playa. One more possession won't matter."

Antonio sounded horrified. "I never considered this house a possession. I considered it our home!"

Milagros decided to be frank. "It may have been our home, but you were seldom in it."

"I always considered this house a refuge from"—Antonio grasped at an explanation— "from all else."

"It would've been nice if you had spent more time with us," Milagros said with a touch of sadness.

"I tried," Antonio justified. "You know that."

"Yes, you did," she admitted dismally. "I just wish you had tried harder."

"Are you going to blame me now as well?"

"No," Milagros said mildly. "I'm not blaming anyone. If anyone's to blame, it's probably me. I'm the one that fell in love with you and had your child." Her black eyes twinkled. "The only good thing to come out of our relationship."

"I'd like to think there was more to it than that," Antonio said with feeling.

Milagros put down the scissors and the twine. "It's all in the past," she mourned quietly. "It's the future I have to look to now, and my son's welfare."

Antonio gave one last try: "I still think you're making a mistake."

"I know," she said.

There was a knock on the front door.

"That must be the boy doña Saro sent to pick up the figurines." She made for the door.

"Can I help?" he offered.

She reached up and tidied her hair. "No, that's okay. I've got everything organized here."

"I'm going to take a look at the mango tree," he decided. "I always liked your backyard."

Milagros gave him a warm look and went to open the door.

Antonio stepped out in the backyard, with Milagros's fine vegetable garden and the old, verdant mango tree. He went up to the tree and touched its bark, inhaling the fresh scent of mango dangling from the branches.

"So you're going to let her go?"

Antonio turned his head to answer Jacobo Levy, standing beside him.

"I have no choice," Antonio responded. "She's made up her mind."

"Yes, I have no doubt," Jacobo Levy said. "Perhaps it's for the best. And perhaps it's not for the best."

Antonio smirked. "Jacobo, you always had a way of making a question out of an answer."

"One of my many failings, I suppose," Jacobo said wearily. "You will provide for her when she's abroad, will you not?"

"If she allows me," Antonio answered. "She's a proud and stubborn woman. She insists on doing it on her own." Antonio was clearly puzzled. "And I don't know why."

"You should know why," Jacobo scolded. "Throughout her existence in this town she's been known as the mistress of the great don Antonio Boglione. She even bore you a son. She has the small house as opposed to your large house where your other, legitimate family resides. Now she wants to relegate that to the past and start anew in another place, another world. You can't deny her that. She wants what we all want, stability."

Antonio rankled. "What stability is there in tearing up your roots and going someplace else where no one knows you or cares?"

"She can make a new life for herself and her son. That's all that matters to her now."

"And what I care doesn't count?" Antonio retorted.

"No, it does not," Jacobo said deliberately, "not at this point. You must learn to accept change, Toño, even when it breaks your heart."

Antonio refused to consider it. "I'll never accept this change."

"Who are you talking to?"

He turned to face Milagros, standing before him. "Are you alright? You were talking to someone."

"I was talking to no one," Antonio denied. "I was just thinking out loud." He motioned toward the house. "Is everything taken care of? Did the kid cart the figurines away?"

"He's taking them to doña Saro on his bike. It may take two or three trips. At least now I know they'll be safe." She looked at him wistfully. "Would you like some refreshment now that you're here?"

He shook his head. "No, I came to say what I had to say. Now I must go." He looked back to the mango tree. "I'll miss that tree." His eyes moved down to the garden and then the backyard fence. "In fact, I'll miss this whole house."

"It's yours," Milagros reminded. "You can come here whenever you want."

"No," he said. "It won't be the same without you and Rafael."

Milagros looked aside. Suddenly, tears were welling up in her eyes. She turned and rushed back into the house.

Antonio took one last look at the tree, trying to visualize where Jacobo Levy had stood moments before.

CHAPTER
FORTY-NINE

LETICIA WATCHED HER husband, sitting across from her in the large living room, wringing his hands, head slumped low. She had never seen him so crestfallen. And she wondered when it had all gone sour. When had their love stopped? When had simple affection ceased? After all these years the shadow of Clayton Walker still hung over them, like some gruesome epitaph. Today would be worse, she was sure. She knew his thinking. When Saro was gone he would feel totally alone, and there was nothing she could do about it. And it seared her guts.

"You can see her now, but remember, she's very weak. We can only try to make her comfortable." It was elderly Dr. Rincón speaking to her husband.

"Thank you, Doctor." Antonio did not raise his head, keeping his gaze on the floor. Still, he said, "I appreciate your being here. I know you're very busy in town, and coming to La Playa must've been an imposition."

"For doña Saro I would go anywhere," Dr. Rincón said outright. "It matters not that she's from La Playa. To us old-timers, here and in town, she's regarded with great warmth."

Antonio glanced up at the doctor. "That's very kind of you to say."

"It's not about kindness," Dr. Rincón declared primly. "It's a fact." He tapped Antonio on the arm. "Now, go see her, but don't be too long. She needs her rest." He went over to a chair and sat down next to Leticia, who sat quiet with her own thoughts.

Antonio hauled himself to his feet and went into Saro's bedroom. There was a stale, aged odor in the room. Saro lay in her bed, wrapped in white sheets up to her shoulders. Her skin was thin and transparent, with the veins protruding on her face and forehead like small, pale filaments.

He sat down in a chair beside the bed and reached out for one of her skeletal hands, holding it tenderly. "Toño, is it you?" The voice was a low husk straining out of her labored breathing.

"Yes, Saro, it's me. How are you doing?"

"I'm dying, fool," she managed to say, a disgusted look showing through her sallow cheeks.

It brought a smile to Antonio. Same old Saro, he thought. "Dr. Rincón says you should rest, conserve your strength."

"Rincón is a quack," the strained voice replied. "I've had so much rest, and I still feel like shit." A small cough caught in her throat, with a wheezing sound coming up from her chest. Her head briefly angled up from the pillow as the coughing came and went.

Antonio leaned closer. "You want some water? Some juice?"

Her head plopped back on the pillow. "No, nothing." Her voice was a whisper. "I wish I could have some of my brew."

"Not now," said Antonio. "When you get better we'll both have some of your famous brew. It'll be something to look forward to."

Slowly her head turned to one side as if she were looking at something beyond the room. "I won't have any with you." She took a breath. "You'll have to drink alone."

"Don't say that, Saro. You know I could never drink alone. It wouldn't be a party without you."

"It's a party I won't be able to attend."

"Don't talk like that," he rebuked gently.

She made a slight grimace. "I'm dying, Toño. You know that and I know that." Her breath caught again, and she gulped some phlegm. "I'll miss you and Milagros." Another slow inhale as her eyes roamed from the far corner and settled on his face. "Is she alright in . . . ," she spoke with great effort.

"She's in New York now," he informed her. "And, yes, she's fine. So's Rafael. He seems to be picking up English very fast. He's made new friends."

"He was always a good, smart boy," she said quietly. "I'm glad for her and him."

"They send you their love."

"I know." She looked aside and was silent for a spell. Then her voice came back. "Toño, you must be good to Leticia. What is past is past." It came out slowly, haltingly. "Children need to know their parents love them and each other. You cannot remain alone. Milagros is gone and you need someone. My fear is that you have no one. A man, a woman cannot exist like that. I want you to be happy."

"I am happy, Saro."

The shriveled face showed displeasure. "No, you're not. Don't lie to me. I've known you since you were a young man . . ." The shrunken voice returned. "You're the son I never had, and I want you to be happy. Promise me you'll . . ." Her voice stuck in her throat and then stopped.

Antonio leaned closer, staring at the grayish face. He watched her for a moment or so and then settled back in the chair.

His eyes snapped open. Had he dozed off? "Saro, SARO?"

Doña Saro's eyes remained wide open, but no longer staring at what had gone before.

He jumped up from the chair. "Doctor, DOCTOR!"

Dr. Rincón rushed into the room. He brushed past Antonio and placed his fingertips to doña Saro's jugular. He looked back at Antonio and shook his head. He extended his hand and closed Saro's eyelids.

Leticia was in the room, her eyes on Antonio. He looked down at doña Saro's corpse, then shuffled out into the kitchen. She heard a rending wail and then uncontrollable sobs. Dr. Rincón snapped his head toward the kitchen. He took a step, but Leticia placed a hand on his arm, holding him back. She shook her head no.

They left Antonio alone, weeping in the kitchen. Dr. Rincón took out a notepad from his waist pocket and with a fountain pen noted the time of death of doña Monserrate Valdez de Montoya.

CHAPTER
FIFTY

FROM THE NOISE in the hallway she knew the party was in full swing. She rang the doorbell two, three times. The chimes were lost in the noise, so she banged on the door with the bottom of her fist. It opened, and a slim black man with an infectious smile greeted her. "You must be Maria!"

She acknowledged his smile. "Yes, I am."

The black man called over his shoulder, "Camilo, your sister's here." He turned back to Maria, still smiling. The noise in the background had not abated. Maria could hear people laughing inside. The man called again, this time louder, "CAMILO! YOUR SIS IS HERE!"

He gestured with an outstretched arm for Maria to enter the apartment. She stepped inside into the tumult. Rock 'n' roll music played from a phonograph. She recognized the tune: the Everly Brother's "Wake Up Little Susie." Some people were dancing, others waving drinks. In one corner several partygoers were watching *I Love Lucy* on a black-and-white television set. In another corner someone had lit up a joint and was passing it around. The acrid smell surprised her. She looked on with eyebrows arched.

"There you are! I didn't think you were gonna make it." It was Camilo, with as infectious a party smile as the black guy. He began helping her take off her coat. "What took you so long?"

"The subways don't run on time on weekends, remember?"

Camilo folded the coat and draped it over his arm. "I always forget. But then, I avoid riding the trains. They're too crowded, and I can't get the stations right."

"If you lived here all the time, you'd get used to them."

He laughed derisively. "I'll never get used to subways. Give me San Juan any day." He put his arms around himself as if fighting off a chill. "Also, it's cold here."

"When are you going back?" she asked.

"Next week," he said. "Can't stay away too long from medical school."

The black man slipped an arm around Camilo's shoulder, tugging him closer. "New York will miss 'im."

"Oh," Camilo suddenly remembered, "you haven't met Armando." He thumbed at the black man. "It's his party."

"Not really," Armando said. "It's Camilo's going-away party since he's heading back to PR."

Camilo took his sister's hand. "Actually, we're both going back to Ponce. She'll fly out a week after I go. So you could say it's her going-away party too."

"More reason to celebrate." Armando's face shined at Maria. "Your brother tells me you're attending Columbia."

"Yes, I am. The teachers college."

Armando gave Camilo a bemused look. "It's good to know someone in the family has brains."

Camilo cocked an eye toward his friend. "Armando here is jealous that I have such a smart sister."

Armando extended his hand. "And it's a pleasure to meet you finally."

"And it's a pleasure to meet you as well." Maria took his hand warmly. "Camilo tells me you're both attending the university in Puerto Rico."

"That's where we met," Camilo said. "Except that he's studying biology."

"That's me, the biologist," Armando chirruped.

Maria looked around, taking in the scene. Now it was Chuck Berry playing on the phonograph. "But . . . you live here?"

"Oh no," Armando explained, "this isn't my place. It belongs to my older brother, who's out on Long Island. I just borrowed it for this party."

"Hopefully, it'll be in one piece when he comes back," Camilo said primly.

"Let's hope so." Armando then asked Maria, "Would you like a drink?"

"Yes, I'd love one."

"We got scotch, rum, gin. What would you like?"

"Rum and Coke would be nice."

"Rum and Coke coming up." Armando left for the kitchen, where the booze was stored.

"Nice guy," Maria observed.

"Yes, he's a good friend," Camilo said. "He comes to New York often. He's got family here."

"So he doesn't live in New York all year round?"

"No, he just comes here during school holidays. His family is from Loíza Aldea, in San Juan."

"I figured as much," Maria surmised. "Though from his English I figured he was raised in New York."

"He was," Camilo affirmed. "But he went back to study at the university." Camilo changed the topic. "Anyway, I didn't invite you to this party to meet him. There's somebody else I want you to meet."

Marias eyes blinked. "Oh?"

"Yes, somebody you might like."

"Are you trying to set me up with someone?" Maria asked suspiciously. "Has Mami been talking to you again? I'm not an old maid, you know."

"No, it's nothing like that," Camilo tried to assure. "I just want you to meet someone you might find . . . interesting. He's not from here. In fact, he's from Texas, and his family did business with Armando's brother and—"

Maria winced. "Texas?"

"Yeah, Texas. You have something against that?"

"No, I just—"

"Here you are." It was Armando with the rum and Coke.

"I was just telling Maria about our new friend."

"Oh yeah, you mean Jubal."

Maria wrinkled her brow. "Jubal?"

"Yeah, Jubal, that's his name," Camilo said crisply.

Maria was still considering it. "What kind of a name is that?"

"Never mind," Camilo said. He turned and waved toward someone. "Hey, Jubal, come over here."

A sandy-haired young man had been conversing with some others at one end of the room. He excused himself and came over.

"This here's Jubal," Camilo introduced. "Jubal, meet my sister, Maria."

The sandy-haired youth held out his hand. "A pleasure, ma'am."

Maria hesitated, then shook hands with him.

"Don't be so formal, Jubal," Armando chided. "Her name's Maria."

"Very well," Jubal said accordingly. "A pleasure, Miss Maria."

314

Armando and Camilo traded looks. Armando gave a nod. "We gotta go and tend to the drinks," Camilo said. "See you guys later."

Maria and the young man were left nursing a slight, uncomfortable silence. She whisked a hand in front of her face. "It's warm in here."

"Yes, it is, ma'am." Jubal glanced around the room. "All these people packed into one tiny place"—a shaking of the head—"It amazes me about New York, how people can live cooped up in one spot."

"I can imagine," Maria said, trying to make conversation. "I gather Texas has open spaces."

"Yes, ma'am, it does," Jubal agreed. "It's a big state with plenny'a room."

"Please stop calling me ma'am. It makes me feel old."

"I'm sorry 'bout that, ma'—I mean, Miss Maria."

"And I'm not Miss Maria. Plain Maria is fine. I'm not a school teacher yet."

Jubal sucked in his lip. "Yet? Y'mean, you studyin' to be one?"

"Yes, I am. I'm attending Teachers College at Columbia."

"That a mighty fine school, I heard, Miss—" He caught himself and offered a conciliatory smile. "Maria."

"How about you, are you attending school?"

"I'm currently on what you call recess. I'm studyin' architecture."

Maria idly rattled the ice cubes in her glass. "Hmmm, an architect. You should be proud."

"Not really," Jubal responded amiably. "It was my family's idea, especially my father's, to study architecture."

"You don't want to study architecture?"

"I don't mind it," Jubal said. "It's okay by me, and it makes sense."

Maria had a sip of her drink. "In what way does it make sense?"

"Well, my family's in construction. We own a business that's all over the place. So studyin' architecture goes with the territory."

"Is your business in Texas?"

"That's the home base," Jubal related. "But as I said, we're all over, even Latin America."

"Do you do business in the Caribbean?"

"We do."

"Is that how you met Camilo and . . ." Maria had a momentary lapse.

"Armando," Jubal put in. "No, I met 'im and Camilo at a mixer they had at CCNY. Somehow we got invited, or maybe we crashed that party. I can't remember," he confided with a laugh. "Since we were the outsiders we started talkin'. Then we found it was a boring shindig and headed for a local bar."

"What's a shindig?" Maria wanted to know.

"Oh." Jubal was momentarily taken aback. "It's like a party or social event."

Maria sipped the rum and Coke while she viewed the room. "And how do you find this shindig?"

"It's awright. At least there's people heah we know."

They fell silent. Maria idly glanced at those gathered about. Jubal stared at his shoes, then sneaked a look at her.

Maria glanced back at him. "Something wrong?"

"Oh, I'm sorry for starin'. Just that I wuz wonderin'—you Puerto Rican?"

Maria registered surprise. "Yes. Why do you ask?"

"I know Armando and Camilo come from the island, but they don't have blue eyes."

Maria smiled wryly. "It's a family trait. The females have blue eyes. Must be the genes, I guess." She regarded what she had said and added,

"My mother has beautiful eyes. The family legend has it that my father fell in love with her the minute he saw those eyes."

"I can see why," Jubal said, showing new regard.

His stare made Maria somewhat self-conscious. Seeking to change the topic, she said, "Jubal—that's a strange name."

"What's strange 'bout it?"

"I don't know. It sounds like an African name."

"African?" Jubal gave a little laugh. "Never been told that befo'."

"I'm sorry. I didn't mean to offend you."

"No offense taken. But I reckon why you might think it's a strange name. Where I come from, it's a well-known name. In fact, during the war of southern rebellion one of the South's famous generals was named Jubal Early. My father named me after him."

Maria was at a loss. "War of southern rebellion?"

"The Civil War," Jubal explained.

"Oh yes," Maria said quickly, "the Civil War."

"You guys doing okay?" It was Camilo back again. "What about the Civil War?"

"Jubal and I were discussing history," Maria filled him in.

"History? That's a strange topic for a party."

"Actually, Mr. Jubal tells me he's studying to be an architect."

Jubal raised an eyebrow. "Mr. Jubal, Miss Maria? It's just plain Jubal where I come from."

"Touché," Maria conceded.

"Well, you guys seem to be doing great," Camilo said genially. "Tell you what: if you guys are hungry, we have some good food there by the table. Good catered stuff. I suggest you help yourselves before it goes."

"Thank you." Jubal turned to Maria. "Would you like to get somethin' to munch on?"

"Yes, I would. Camilo made tostones and they're great."

"'Tostones'?" Jubal blinked in confusion.

"Deep-fried plantains," Maria clarified. "An island delicacy."

Jubal was game. "I'm willin' to try it if you are."

"I love tostones," Maria revealed.

"You guys go and have some snacks. I gotta help Armando in the kitchen." Camilo sauntered away.

At the table, Maria pointed out the green plantains, deep-fried and pressed into oval disks. Jubal picked one up and had a bite. "They taste like chips!"

"You put a little salt on them," Maria instructed. "These days in San Juan they serve them with French dressing."

Jubal smacked his lips, enjoying the taste. "Personally, they taste great just as is. No need for anythin' else."

"Spoken like a true boricua," Maria complemented.

Jubal had a paper plate in one hand and began filling it with tostones.

Maria said, "I need to freshen my drink. Would you like something to drink, Jubal?"

"Yes, I would."

"I'll get it for you. What would you like?"

"Wow, I must say, this is the first time I've been waited on by such a lovely lady. If you insist, I'll have some bourbon on the rocks."

"I don't know about the 'lovely lady' part," Maria remarked. "But I'll come back with your bourbon."

Jubal couldn't help but smile at her.

Maria made for the kitchen, oozing her way among partygoers, with her rum drink as a wedge in front of her. She reached the kitchen, taking in the crowd one more time and pushing the door with her back.

She stopped in her tracks. Standing by the open door, she saw Camilo and Armando in an embrace, kissing each other passionately on the mouth.

She held in a startled gasp, quickly left the kitchen, and rushed back to the snack table and Jubal. She put down her drink and said, "I must leave."

Jubal looked at her in surprise. "Leave? Somethin' wrong?"

"No, nothing's wrong. I just need to go." She looked around, seemingly out of breath. "Where's my coat?"

Jubal shifted nervously. "Did I do somethin' wrong? Did I offend you? If so, I—"

"No, it's not you, Jubal," Maria explained quickly. "Just that I need to go. I, I have something to do."

"I can't convince ya to stay?"

"No." Maria scoured the room, anxious to leave. "I need my coat. Do you know where it is?"

"All the coats are in the bedroom. I'll get it fer you. Which one is it?"

"It's a long blue one with fur trim. You can't miss it."

"I'll get it fer you right now," Jubal offered. He left for the bedroom.

Camilo and Armando had exited from the kitchen and were going around laughing and greeting guests. Maria suddenly thought of her parents and cringed.

Jubal returned with her coat. He helped her put it on. "I hope we can meet again," he said.

"I hope so too, Jubal," she said hastily. "Please tell Camilo that I had someplace else to go and it couldn't wait." She extended her hand. "It was a pleasure."

Jubal held her hand firmly. "The pleasure was mine, Maria. I'll see you to the door."

"That's okay," Maria said. "I can find my way." She patted Jubal on the chest. "You take care." And she weaved her way among the partygoers, reaching the door and leaving the apartment.

And poor Jubal was left wondering what he had done wrong.

CHAPTER
FIFTY-ONE

THE FULL-SCALE wooden model dominated the space inside the cavernous room. Each miniature house, driveway, and garage had been built to scale. The miniature roads crisscrossing the housing complex, about half an inch wide, circled and meandered around the model like smooth, flat arteries. The houses were painted appropriately, some blue, some green, to give the illustration a sense of lifelike urgency. And small plastic pedestrians and cars dotted the avenues here and there in order to bring Villa Cristal to life.

Antonio looked on the replica with a wellspring of hope and satisfaction. His brainchild would now come to fruition provided they could secure the builders.

Standing beside him, Enrique Ramos, the governor's representative, commented, "It's a good beginning, and impressive. This will put Ponce on the map."

"It will provide housing for those who need it the most; that's the important thing," Antonio said with pride.

"That's a given now that we've secured government funding," Ramos clapped Antonio on the back. "You've done well, Mr. Boglione."

Antonio wasn't so sure. "It could all go to hell if we don't get the construction part going."

"And that's what this meeting is all about," Ramos said. "I'm told that Walker Construction is the best there is." He referred to the scale model on the table. "They just finished doing something like this in Saint

Martin. That project was funded by the French government, and they were immensely happy."

"All we need is just two model houses done to specifications," Antonio enumerated. "That shouldn't be difficult. I still can't understand why we couldn't get a local company to do it." His tone grew flat. "Why do we need somebody from the mainland? Why this Walker Construction?"

And Ramos revisited the argument: "As I said before, Mr. Boglione, majority funding from this project came from the American government. We were lucky to get somebody high up in the Kennedy administration who took interest in this project and—"

"Who got paid for it, you mean," Antonio inferred.

"Let's discuss the project, nothing else." The governor's representative sounded indignant. "We got the funding, and it couldn't have gotten off the ground without federal consent and assistance. We went through a lot of hoops to convince the governor to lobby the Americans to get this going. And they insisted that on-site construction be done by a mainland firm, and we got Walker Construction."

"Who I'm told is based in Texas, the home state of the current vice president." Antonio gave a cynical look. "Some coincidence."

"The project is going to be done, Mr. Boglione. I promise you that. It makes no difference who constructs the model houses as long as it's done well."

Antonio said pointedly, "Let's hope these guys are as good as you claim."

Ramos placed a hand on Antonio's shoulder. "Be on your best behavior, Mr. Boglione. We need these people if your dream is to come true; and don't forget, it's going to be very profitable for all concerned."

Just then, a young man with the requisite tie and eyeglasses entered the room. He was one the Ramos's assistants. "He's here," the young aide announced formerly. "He's waiting outside."

"Tell him to come in," Ramos instructed.

The young assistant left the room.

Within minutes a heavy-set man with a military crew cut was in the room. Unlike Antonio and the governor's representative, who wore blue business suits, he came attired in a light cotton sports jacket, loafers and a striped shirt with no tie. Obviously he was not one to stand on custom in a business setting, or so Antonio considered.

Ramos met the beefy outstretched hand with his own. "Welcome, Mr. Walker. It's a pleasure to meet you, sir." He turned to Antonio. "This is Mr. Boglione, the visionary who initiated this project."

"Mah pleasure, señor." The southern drawl was deep, booming.

Antonio took in the man's face. It was ruddy, animated. And then it came to him: the blue-gray eyes. Familiar, yet . . .

The handshake was firm, confident, almost vise-like.

"It's nice to meet you, Mr. Walker. I've been looking forward to this moment."

The man showed an expansive smile. "Mah name is Dennis Walker, but everybody calls me Dixie."

Antonio didn't know how to respond to that one. He said, "I'm told great things about your company."

"We do okay." Walker let go of Antonio's hand long enough to view the scale model on the table. "So this is what we're goin' to build. Marvelous."

Antonio summarized the plan. "You're going to build two model houses first, and if that meets approval by the zoning board, then we'll have a chance to bring Villa Cristal to Ponce."

Dixie Walker bent down to peer at the scale model, taking in every aspect of the proposed project. "Don'tcha worry none 'bout that, Mr. Boglione. We'll get yer houses done. They'll be approved. Ah kin assure ya that."

"Mr. Walker's firm comes highly recommended," Ramos told Antonio. "If he says it can be done, I'm sure it can."

Walker straightened, stood ramrod straight, and asked Antonio, "How much time we got?"

"Sir?"

"I'm sure you all got a deadline. Every one of these jobs got a deadline. That's normal procedure."

Ramos put in quickly, "We haven't discussed a deadline as of yet, but we would assume it will be done in a timely manner."

Walker looked back at the table. "Two model houses—that we kin do in no time. The rest of it—well, it might take a little longer. But so long as you got the financing for it, it can be done."

"Oh, the financing has been approved," Ramos said confidently. "The governor's office is one hundred percent behind the project, and his legal staff has secured all appropriate warrants. The financing is there. It's the construction that must be finished." He glanced at Antonio, then back to Walker. "Mr. Walker, your firm will be charged with beginning construction on the first government-approved housing development in Ponce. And Villa Cristal will be the first step in a massive construction boom in this area. Isn't that right, Mr. Boglione?"

"More than that," Antonio added. "It will bring modern housing to La Playa and—"

"La Playa?" Walker wondered aloud.

Ramos stepped in. "Oh yes, I must explain. This housing complex will be built in the area we call La Playa. You might say it's beachfront property. Eventually, we envision more urbanizations like this being built in the town itself. It was Mr. Boglione who proposed we begin in the La Playa sector."

Dixie studied Antonio for a moment. "Is that so?"

Ramos thought it prudent to add, "Mr. Boglione was once a resident of La Playa, and his vision is to bring it into the twentieth century."

"Ain't it livin' in the twentieth century now?"

Antonio and Ramos both looked at each other.

It was Ramos who responded. "What we mean is that La Playa has never had modern housing of such scope. And if it succeeds here, then this prototype can be applied to the rest of Ponce." He regarded Walker with a cordial look. "So you see, everybody wins."

"That's good to heah. So when do we start?"

"We can finalize the plans tomorrow at my office."

"Unfortunately I have business in San Juan tomorrow," Antonio said hastily. "Perhaps the following day might be best."

Ramos passed Antonio a questioning glance. In the silence that ensued, the hum of the window air conditioner was the only sound. Dixie Walker stepped into the unexpected silence and said, "The following day be okay as long as we git to secure a good contract."

"That goes without saying, Mr. Walker," Ramos finalized, still looking at Antonio. "You will secure a good contract."

"Please call me Dixie. 'Mistuh Walker' makes me sound like an old man, and I ain't that old. In fact, I stopped a bullet with my knee in Normandy. Did I ever tell ya 'bout that? See, that's how I got into construction. I wuz with the Seabees during the invasion and . . ."

CHAPTER
FIFTY-TWO

THE MASSIVE MAHOGANY doors closed behind him. He saw that the room was painted a dull white, almost gray, with peeling plaster on the walls. One large, rectangular table dominated the room, with two chairs at the exact middle.

He sat down on one of the chairs, placed his hat on the table, and waited.

Shortly, Octavio Mendosa came in, dressed in prison garb: field-gray pants and shirt, no belt, and matching cap in his back pocket. Antonio noted that he walked with a slight limp, almost dragging his left leg behind him. And he was leaner; he had lost a lot of weight. He was followed by a heavy-set guard in khaki with a round brown face and fine black hair. The guard had a holster on his hip with a .38 revolver.

Deferentially, Antonio stood up from his chair. The guard made a motion with his hand for Antonio to sit back down.

Octavio sat in the chair across from Antonio, while the guard planted himself at one end of the table.

"It's good to see you, my friend." Antonio extended a hand, about to pat Octavio on his arm.

The guard loudly rasped the table with his knuckles. Antonio looked up, surprised.

"No touching is allowed," Octavio told him. "Not even if my wife were here."

"I see." Antonio withdrew his hand.

"It's good to see you too," Octavio said. "You look well."

"Leticia sends her regards, and so does everyone else in Ponce." Antonio paused, examining his friend. "How are you doing?"

Octavio's lips curled. "As you can see, I am in La Princesa, the premier jail for all us independentistas. The only consolation is that I'm three doors down from the Maestro." Suddenly his face became animated. "Did you know that he shares a cell with Professor Paoli? Isn't it amazing? Our premier poet and Nobel laureate incarcerated with don Albizu. I'm sure this jail hasn't had such intellectual greatness since its founding by the Spaniards over a hundred years ago."

"I heard that Professor Paoli had been jailed," Antonio revealed. "I didn't know that he was an independentista."

"He is. He was secretary-general of our party, and he's a great man, just like the Maestro." Octavio nodded in the affirmative. "It's good that they share a cell. He can assist don Albizu. He needs someone to look after him."

"I heard. He's not in good health, I'm told."

"It's the experiments they're doing on him."

Antonio looked bewildered. "'Experiments'?"

Once more the guard rapped his knuckles on the table.

Octavio looked to him and then back to Antonio. "We're not allowed to speak about that." He frowned. "Just like everything else."

"I see." Antonio placed both hands, palms down, on the table, not knowing how to proceed.

"Why are you here?" Octavio asked him.

Antonio was quiet for a moment before responding. "It's about your mother . . . ," he began.

Octavio finished the sentence: "She's dead, isn't she?"

Antonio swallowed hard. "Yes."

Octavio sank his head into his chest, trying to hide his grief.

"I am so sorry, Papo. It happened so suddenly. She—"

"It wasn't unexpected," Octavio broke in, raising his head. "It was her time, and she lived a long life." His eyes watered, and he ran a finger under his nose "She had a good run, as they say. She was in her eighties. We expected it." He lowered his gaze, deep in recall. "After my father died, it was only a matter of time. They were together so many years. I expected my mother would go soon after."

"If it's any consolation," Antonio reported, "she had a great send-off. Everybody in La Playa was at her funeral. We buried her in the municipal cemetery right next to your father."

Octavio was grateful. "Thank you for telling me. I appreciate it."

Antonio looked at the guard, still impassive in front of the table. He asked Octavio, "And how is your wife, Carmen?"

"She's at the federal women's penitentiary in Alderson, West Virginia," Octavio recounted in a low voice. "She got twenty years to my seventy in prison."

Antonio looked appalled. "How did it happen?"

"How did it happen?" For the first time Octavio showed a grim smile. "Simple: after our operation against the American Congress, my group—our cell, that is—was infiltrated by an FBI informant. That's how it happened."

"Was your group responsible for the attack on Congress?" Antonio queried.

"We were part of it," Octavio said in a matter-of-fact tone. "We assisted in the planning."

"But reports say the attack on Congress was masterminded by a group in New York."

"No matter," Octavio continued in his matter-of-fact way. "This is the twentieth century. We have cells almost everywhere, and we can communicate anywhere. Ours is not just an island movement. We're also very active on the mainland."

"Yes," Antonio cited, "but attacking the US Congress—that was madness."

"Was it?" Octavio questioned. "We struck at the seat of the imperialists' power. We wounded five congressmen, and we would've done more had it not been for unforeseen circumstances."

"But you've turned public opinion against you."

"Have we?" Octavio's eyes shone bright. "We showed how determined we are against all odds. Right now revolutionaries throughout the world, in Asia, in Africa, applaud our action."

"And the American public is repulsed by it," Antonio maintained.

"Someone once said that you have to crack some eggs to make an omelet. We were cracking some eggs over the head of the oppressor."

"And now you're in jail for seventy years," Antonio reminded.

"I would still do it if it cost me a hundred years. No sacrifice is too great for our freedom."

"You're a fool, Papo."

"Am I?" said Octavio genially. "Who's the greater fool? I'm here because of my beliefs. What are your beliefs?"

"I'm fighting to build Ponce, to build my island; that's my belief."

"'My island'?" Octavio was genuinely surprised. "My, how we've changed. But I'm glad. You finally admit you're a boricua, albeit on the wrong side."

Antonio sighed resignedly. "Papo, I didn't come here to argue. I came here to inform you of things and to see how you were."

"And it's appreciated," Octavio said with feeling. "You were and are the only true friend I had in La Playa."

"Don't say that. You have many friends in La Playa."

"Do I? Sometimes I wonder about that. The informant who spied on us came from La Playa. He told the feds where I was, and they came right to my house and raided the place."

"I heard you were shot," Antonio recalled.

"Yeah, right here." Octavio tapped his left leg. "But I survived—that's the important thing—and so did Carmencita."

Antonio looked again to the guard and then asked, "What about your sons, Miguel and Efrain, are they okay?"

Octavio also looked toward the guard and replied, "They're fine, and safe."

"I'm glad," Antonio responded.

"So am I," said Octavio.

CHAPTER
FIFTY-THREE

"ONCE VILLA CRISTAL is complete it'll have three hundred housing units," Antonio stated with enthusiasm. "And the beauty of it is that it'll be rent subsidized for low-income families." He gave a furtive, shrewd look, "And we got lots of those. And they can remain as long as their income status complies with federal regulations." He paused before revealing another benefit: "It'll be the first such urban renewal project in La Playa. There's already a waiting list, can you imagine? Playeros can't wait to get in on this."

Sitting across the table from him, Leticia remarked, "It's a shame that the sugar cane fields bordering La Playa will be cut down to make room for Villa Cristal. Those cane fields have been there since anyone can remember."

"Don't worry about the sugar cane," Antonio said, unruffled. "There'll still be enough sugar cane on the island to make rum. That won't change."

"What about the sugar cane cutters?"

"They'll get subsidized housing."

Leticia wasn't convinced. "If you don't have a job, you can't pay for the housing."

Antonio was unconcerned. "Like I said, it's taken care off. Don't worry about it."

Sitting at the dinner table to the right of his father, Camilo asked, "And how is this going to be paid for?"

Antonio had a ready answer: "The plans for the operating funds come from the US Department of Housing and Urban Development. As for tenant rent subsidies, they in turn will be administered by the Public Housing Administration in San Juan."

Camilo had another question: "How did you get them to agree?"

Before Antonio could answer, Leticia replied for him, "Your father knows a lot of people in the government. He has some influence."

Sitting to the left of her father, Maria put in sarcastically, "And how many did he pay off?"

"Maria!" Leticia gave her daughter a stern, reproving glance.

"It's alright, Leticia," Antonio said, not at all bothered. "We all know how business is done on this island. There's nothing I have to apologize for."

"I wasn't accusing you, Papi," Maria amended quickly. "I know you've worked had to get this thing done, and it will benefit the people in the barrio. I wasn't trying to be critical."

Antonio smiled at his daughter. "I know that." He turned to his son, changing the topic. "Enough of my ramblings. How did you find New York?"

Camilo looked to Maria, as if seeking support, before saying, "It was nice. I really had a good time there."

"You didn't mind the cold?" his father asked.

"No," Camilo said blandly. "I just dressed warm and went wherever I had to go. I got to see all the sights, took in a couple of Broadway plays—"

Antonio raised his brows at Camilo. "You went to see a Broadway play? Which one?"

"*A Raisin in the Sun,*" Camilo disclosed. "A really great work. I really liked it."

"'*A Raisin in the Sun*'?" Antonio looked vague. "Never heard of it. Is it popular?"

"It's very popular," Maria joined in. "I saw it first and recommended it to Camilo. It's a work by a young playwright, Lorraine Hansberry."

"Never heard of her," Antonio said, disinterested. "The only plays I know are by Calderon."

"Believe me, this lady is very good, and she's a Negro."

Antonio scratched his chin. "Hmmm. A Negro writing a play. Interesting. The blacks would love her in Loíza Aldea."

"It's good to expand one's cultural horizons," said Leticia. "I for one am happy that you were able to see a Broadway play."

"New York offers a lot in that respect. There's Broadway, off-Broadway—"

Again, Antonio was baffled. "What's this 'off-Broadway'?"

Maria and Camilo looked at each other, and it was Camilo who answered. "That's the latest thing in New York. There's a lot of what is called 'experimental theatre.' These are shows that are not along the Broadway strip, but in others parts of the city. And some are very good."

Antonio gave a patronizing laugh. "My children, the theatre buffs."

"There's nothing wrong with expanding one's knowledge, Toño," Leticia admonished gently.

"No, I guess not," Antonio said, knowing he couldn't win this one. He resumed with Camilo: "And now you're back to continue your studies."

"Yes, I am back, Papi." Camilo was looking down at the table. "Back to the salt mines."

"'The salt mines'?" Antonio asked, looking at his son questioningly. "I thought you liked medicine."

"I do. That's going to be my life's work. Just that medical school isn't easy. It takes a lot of work."

"Are you having difficulties?" Antonio sounded worried.

"Oh no, it's not that. It's just that I wish I had time for other things. I would like to see more plays, for instance."

Antonio discounted it. "You'll get to see enough theatre once you get your medical degree. Finishing medical school comes first."

"Toño," Leticia lectured her husband, "it can't be all work and no play, even in medical school."

"Just as long as he gets his medical degree," Antonio muttered.

"You don't have to worry about that," Maria said, looking warmly at her brother. "He's at the top his class."

"Good," Antonio nodded approvingly. "That's what I like to hear."

Maria and Camilo exchanged quiet looks. Camilo shrugged, as if saying, That's Papi.

The table went quiet. Leticia raised her glass and said to Maria, "This wine is delicious. Where did you get it?"

"It's a German wine," Maria disclosed. "I discovered it in New York. It's called Liebfraumilch."

Antonio's face screwed up. "Leeb-fra-what?"

"Lieb-frau-milch. Milk of Our Blessed Lady, in German. I brought two bottles back with me. I knew Mami would like it."

Antonio was examining the yellow glints in his wine glass. "You don't find many German wines in Ponce, that's for sure."

"I love it," Leticia said to Maria. "When you return to New York, bring back some more."

"By all means, bring some more," Antonio backed his wife wholeheartedly.

"At least we agree that the wine is good," Camilo said, raising his glass appreciatively.

***

Dinner was done; Elena was in the kitchen washing the dishes, and Leticia and Antonio were in the parlor, trying to find something to talk about besides Antonio's vaunted project.

Camilo had gone into the backyard to catch a smoke. As he puffed on the cigarette Maria came alongside. "It's a beautiful evening," she said.

Smoke puffed out of Camilo's nostrils. "Yes, it is."

In the encroaching dark, Maria could make out the outlines of the backyard table and its round canopy. She said, "Are you going to tell him?"

Camilo blew out cigarette smoke, staring at her. "What?"

"Are you going to tell him?" she repeated.

"Tell him what?"

"About you and Armando."

Camilo had a guarded look. "What about me and Armando?"

Mario looked him straight in the eye. "I know what's going on. I'm not blind."

"What're you talking about?"

"Camilo, I'm not a fool. I've seen how you and he . . ."

Camilo rubbed his forehead, cigarette cupped between his first and index fingers. "Oh boy."

"I'm not making judgments," Maria continued. "I'm just asking: What are you going to do?"

"What do you want me to do?"

"I don't know," Maria said, sounding forlorn. "I wish you could've told me."

"Tell you what?" Camilo said irritably. "That I like boys. That I'm not like ordinary guys, that I . . ."

Maria looked deep into his face, showing a growing concern. "Camilo, I don't care about your personal life, but I do care about you. I don't want you to be hurt. And I don't want my parents to be hurt."

337

Camilo took a last puff and ground the cigarette under his heel. "I don't want them to be hurt either, you know that."

"What I know is that I saw you and Armando at the party."

He had a sudden recollection. "So that was it."

"Yes, that was it. It made me uncomfortable, so you can imagine how our father will feel."

"You talk about feelings. Well, I can't help the way I feel either." Camilo sounded distraught. "Believe me, Maria, I've tried. I've dated girls; I've even had a girlfriend or two, but it's not the same. I don't feel about them the way I feel about Armando. I can't deny my feelings. It would be wrong."

"And it would be wrong not to tell our parents," Maria said with quiet resolve.

"Tell them what? That their son is a homosexual? That he's a *maricon?*"

"I've never said that."

"I know you've never said that, but that's what you think," Camilo accused. "That's what they all think here, in Ponce. So imagine what our father would say. I don't want to embarrass him or myself."

"It's not a question of embarrassment. It's a question of being truthful."

He drew a harsh breath. "If you were in my place, would you tell him?"

"No, I would not," Maria had to concede. She shook her head slowly. "This is a mess."

"No, it's not a mess. I love Armando and he loves me."

Maria took his hand, held it affectionately, and said, "I wish I knew what to say."

CHAPTER FIFTY-FOUR

ANTONIO AND LETICIA watched with interest as Elena, Maria, and Camilo hefted huge steaks onto the outdoor grill. The smell of seared beef and spices blanketed the whole backyard, and smoke billowed from the iron grates on the grill.

"This was a good idea on Mr. Ramos's part to have this barbecue," Leticia said, entranced by the goings-on on the grill. "It's good to cultivate one's business partners."

"I had never heard of this barbecue thing until Ramos brought it up," Antonio remarked somewhat caustically. "We don't do such a thing in Ponce. It's an American custom."

Leticia pondered it. "I have a feeling that eventually all of Ponce will be doing this *barbacoa* thing. It's inevitable. People like to pick up new customs."

"You're right in that respect," Antonio had to agree. "Ramos says this is the going thing in America. Everybody barbecues in that part of the world." He scowled. "Just that I never came across such things as hot dogs. Can you imagine? They named a food after dogs?"

"It's frankfurters they cook, not dogs," Leticia corrected.

"So why do they call them hot dogs?"

Leticia was stumped. "I honestly don't know."

To Antonio it was still a mystery. "Hamburgers or *hamburgesas* I can understand. But hot dogs?"

"It's all part of the American idiom," Leticia noted cryptically.

Antonio had another consideration. "I hope Dixie Walker appreciates this gesture." He flapped a hand at the round cast-iron grill where Elena and the siblings were searing meat. "I went to a lot of trouble to get one of those contraptions in San Juan and searched high and low to get hot dog buns."

"It will be appreciated," Leticia encouraged. "Mr. Ramos stated how important it is to develop a social relationship as well as a business relationship. It's part of the American way of doing things."

Antonio still had doubts. "Back in the old days all we had to do was meet at Carmelo's cafetín for a drink, shake on it, and it was done."

"Those days are gone, Toño," Leticia said firmly. "This is a new order, and things are done differently."

Antonio made a face. "Yeah, I can tell by the charred meat."

"Give it time, Toño," Leticia counseled. "Give it time."

"Let me check out this contraption," Antonio decided. "See if the money I spent on it was worth it." He left Leticia and made it to the grill.

"How's it going?"

Maria was busily brushing hot sauce on a steak. "It's getting there, Papi."

"Is it cooking okay?"

Old Elena dug a long, two-pronged fork into a steak. "It's cooking, Toño. No need to worry. Your guests will love this meal. I've put my own hot sauce on the steaks." She took in a whiff of smoking meat. "Doesn't it smell good?"

"Yes, it does." Antonio took in the array of jars of mustard and relish, with frankfurters and hamburger meat arrayed on a side table. "You have enough food here to feed an army."

"Better to have leftovers than none at all," Elena stated.

"It'll be a great barbecue, Papi," Camilo told his father. "It will remind your guests of home."

"It better," Antonio said bluntly. "Villa Cristal is riding on this."

Maria dipped the brush into a jar of sauce and began brushing more meat. "Don't worry, Papi, it'll go good. Americans love grilled steak, and with Elena's sauce it can't miss."

"I hope you're right," said Antonio, still sounding doubtful.

"Toño," Leticia called, "your guests are here."

They all turned to see Leticia standing beside three men. One was an older middle-aged gent, with three young men standing deferentially behind him. They were all dressed uniformly in jeans, outsized belt buckles, short-sleeved shirts, and pointed-toed boots, and each wore a Stetson hat.

Looking up from the meat on the grill, Elena remarked, "I didn't know we were entertaining cowboys."

"They're from Texas, Elena," Antonio told her. "Let's just make them welcome." He went over to greet his guests.

Camilo and Maria exchanged questioning glances. "This is a surprise," Camilo chuckled richly. "I didn't know we were entertaining Jubal's people."

"Papi said the people were from Walker Construction," Maria observed, watching her father greet the Walker clan. "But I never thought it would be this Walker family."

Antonio, along with Leticia, guided the guests over to the grill stand. "This is my family," Antonio said proudly. "This is my son, Camilo, who's studying to be a doctor, and my daughter, Maria, who's attending Columbia University in New York."

Dixie Walker doffed his hat and offered a handshake to Camilo. "Mah pleasure." Then he did the same with Maria. Both shook hands with Dixie Walker, trying to mask their surprise.

341

Walker, in turn, introduced his sons. "This heah is my older son, Robert E. Lee; and these are his bruthers, Jeb Stuart Walker and Jubal, mah youngest."

"A pleasure," they all said in unison.

Camilo showed a wide smile. "Jubal, it's good to see you again."

Both Walker and Antonio looked at each other. Leticia kept her gaze on her son and daughter.

"It's good to be here," Jubal said to Camilo. He directed his gaze on Maria. "You look well, as always."

"As do you, Jubal," Maria said.

Leticia looked from one to the other, while Walker's two other sons, Robert E. Lee and Jeb Stuart Walker, had the amused looks of nonparticipants as their father asked, "Yuh know each other?"

"Yes, we do," Camilo said. "We met Jubal in New York not too long ago."

"And how did you meet?" It was Antonio, as interested as Dixie Walker.

"We met at a social function," Camilo said. "I believe Jubal was there on vacation."

"You never tol' me you met Mr. Boglione's fam'ly," Walker inquired of his son.

"And you never told me you knew him," Antonio inquired of his offspring.

"We just met briefly," Maria added. "As Camilo said, it was a social function."

Antonio looked back to Walker. "It's a small world, Dixie, isn't it?"

Walker's lips compressed into a thin smile. "Yes, it is."

Leticia broke the impasse that followed by saying, "I hope you enjoy our barbecue, Mr. Walker. We've got all the delights: hot dogs, hamburgers, and grilled steak, which I'm told is a favorite in your state."

"That it is, ma'am," Walker agreed readily. "And all the fixin's heah look great. Thank you fer goin' to all this trouble."

"It's no trouble at all. It's our honor to entertain our guests. I hope you enjoy our 'fixin's.'"

"I'm sure we will, ma'am."

Antonio asked, "Dixie, would you and your sons like something to drink? A beer maybe? Or something stronger?"

"A beer be fine." He glanced at his sons. "Whatcha say, boys?"

"A beer be good," said both Robert E. Lee and Jeb Stuart.

"Jubal?" his father asked.

Jubal was still gazing at Maria. "A beer be nice," he said at last.

"Please make yourselves at home," Leticia said to all. "And help yourselves to whatever you like on the grill. Elena is a great cook. We don't stand on formality in the Boglione house."

"Ah think I'll have a hot dog," Walker decided. Then to his sons: "Boys?"

"Burger fer me," said Robert E. Lee.

"Double that," said Jeb Stuart Walker.

"Elena?" Leticia prompted.

Elena turned to the grill again and began preparing the items.

"I'll help you," Maria offered.

"Let me assist," said Jubal. "Back home, barbecuing is in our blood. And if I recall, we like to grill our hot dog buns alongside the franks."

"You're welcome to help," Maria said to Jubal.

"Thank you. Mah pleasure."

"Beers coming up for everybody." Camilo made it for a cooler nesting on one side of the yard. He picked up a bottle opener and began scooping up beers and handing them around.

Antonio held up his beer bottle in a toast. "To Villa Cristal."

Walker followed suit. "To Villa Cristal."

Leticia remained to one side quietly watching Maria and Jubal help Elena at the grill.

CHAPTER FIFTY-FIVE

THEY MET AT a restaurant in Los Meros, right next to the Ponce surf. Pepe's Restaurant was the name. Like most places at that time it was a ramshackle affair: a boxy wooden frame with a few tables and chairs, with open windows where patrons could view the ocean as they ordered shellfish and seafood.

This was their first formal date, although Maria would have liked to consider it as a meeting between two friends who had yet to know each other. Jubal Walker had other ideas. Since their first encounter at the party in New York, she had been constantly on his mind; and when he saw her again at the impromptu barbecue, he could not believe his good fortune, although she had been rather distant, smiling at his father's jokes, politely listening to stories about construction projects on the mainland and on the islands. If she acknowledged him at all it was to inquire if he wanted another beer or a hamburger. He yearned inside, trying to get her engaged in some polite banter, but her attention, as with the others, was on Dixie Walker, the guest of honor.

The only one who seemed interested in him was her mother, who treated him with a steely reserve, as if taking stock of this young man who was so obviously interested in her daughter. Her side glances unnerved him. It was as if she were trying to decipher who and what he was, and what his connection was to Maria.

So it was refreshing to see her again on neutral ground. Her brother, Camilo, had been the go-between, in that he had informed Jubal that

Maria would like to meet in Los Meros, a family favorite. And Jubal's heart leapt at the chance.

They both sat at one of the tables, desperately trying to make small talk. He, nervous as hell, but trying to be nonchalant, cool, calm, and collected; she, nervous as hell, but trying to be nonchalant, cool, calm, and collected, and both failing miserably, at least at the beginning.

They began by discussing things of mutual interest. Did Jubal know that Camilo's friend Armando Díaz was back on the island? Oh yes, Jubal let know; Camilo had told him. They were both looking forward to seeing Armando again. He was a "cool head," as Jubal put it.

Maria agreed that Armando was a nice guy and then said no more on the topic.

Then, in passing, she mentioned how this place, Pepe's, had been a favorite of her mother's, though Leticia had never actually stated how she had come to know this small eatery. Maria guessed that her parents had frequented the place when they were younger.

The icebreaker came when they got to order from the restaurant menu. Actually, there was no menu. The seafood dishes were posted on a flat chalkboard to one side of the room, noting what was available from the day's catch, with the prices listed in tiny script alongside each dish.

Jubal couldn't read Spanish, so it was up to Maria to recite what was offered from the kitchen and how much it cost.

They ordered two beers, and Maria suggested they get conch sandwiches, Pepe's premier dish.

As they got to know each other, their initial nervousness succumbed to genuine curiosity and then genuine interest. They both discovered they had a lot in common. They liked films, especially the new French wave that, in Maria's estimation, was transforming cinema. They liked rock 'n' roll. But then, who didn't like rock 'n' roll? That was easy: their parents didn't. Dixie Walker considered it "nigger music." Antonio thought it was trashy noise that didn't make any sense. What was all this "tutti frutti, wop bop a loo" whatever? Who could understand such nonsense? Was this music?

They both laughed at that one.

And they discussed their dreams. Jubal wanted to be an architect in the worst way. Not because of his father, but because it would promote his own independence. He would make his own way creating great structures and edifices that would last for all time. And Maria acknowledged that since her earliest memories she had always wanted to be an educator, someone to mold young minds and impart knowledge. She would change the world through her charges in the classroom.

Within an hour it was as if they had known each other all their lives. They spoke forthrightly, with passion, as all young people are want to do when they meet a kindred soul.

Had they had the chance they would have remained all day at Pepe's emporium. But Jubal checked his wristwatch and knew he had to return to the construction site where Villa Cristal was being erected. It was way past his lunch hour. His father and brothers were probably wondering where he was.

Maria said she understood. She was late herself, and naturally her mother would want to know where she had been. "We don't wanna get grounded," Jubal joked.

"We're adults. That doesn't apply to us," Maria responded.

And they shared a laugh.

Outside Pepe's, the panorama of the sea and surf and coconut trees beckoned them once more.

Maria decided: "The hell with it. It's such a beautiful day. Let's take a walk on the beach."

Jubal was hesitant. "Yuh sure?"

Maria was certain. "Los Meros is beautiful. C'mon, let's walk." She entwined her arm in his.

What the hell, Jubal considered. "Yeah. Let's walk."

They strolled arm in arm away from Pepe's shack, heading down toward the beach.

They stopped, coming across something totally unexpected. Down on the beach, not forty yards from their spot on the hill leading toward the sand, they saw it: two figures running about on the sand, dipping their feet in the water, laughing, cavorting like two kids. But they weren't kids. Even from their distance on the incline leading toward the sand, they immediately recognized the two beachcombers, if you could call them that.

Camilo and Armando were completely naked as they ran and tossed salt water at each other. They tousled each other's hair, Camilo's stark white body a contrast to Armando's deep brown. Their arms swinging about, their penises swinging about, totally unaware of anything of anyone else; completely secure in the quiet and silence of the beach that no one ever visited.

Maria hid her shock by turning her back to the beach below.

Jubal, his mouth agape, was momentarily stunned. He didn't know what to say. What could he say?

He looked to Maria, her back still to the beach. He sought to reach out and touch her, but drew back his hand.

There was an agonizing interval of silence where no one said a word.

Finally Maria uttered, "Let's leave."

Jubal found his voice. "Maria, I . . ."

"Let's go," she repeated.

"Maria, I didn't know."

Maria remained motionless, her mouth tight. "Please, let's just go. I don't want to talk." She began walking back toward the road bordering Pepe's Restaurant, and away from the beach.

Jubal followed, as bewildered as she.

CHAPTER FIFTY-SIX

INSIDE THE CONSTRUCTION shack that served as an office, Dixie Walker pored over the blueprints for Villa Cristal. The lines and drafts formed into a jumble. Outside, the noise of cranes lifting and backhoes moving dirt added to the confusion. His mind was elsewhere. He didn't even notice when Jubal entered the office.

"You wanted to see me, Pa?"

His eyes lifted from the blueprints spread out over the large table. "Yeah, I wanned to see ya. Sit down."

Jubal removed his construction hard hat, sat down on the lone chair in the office. He angled his head toward the table. "Everythin' goin' okay with the plans?"

"Yeah, everythin's goin' okay wit' the construction," Walker said somewhat stiffly. "But that ain't the reason I wanna talk to ya." He paused, as if trying to measure his words. "I heah you been seein' a lot of the Boglione girl lately."

Jubal showed surprise. He didn't expect this. His father's whole mission was getting the project done, and this did not involve the project. "That's true," he said at last. "We been seein' each other."

Walker rubbed his jaw, looking back down at the table. "That's what I wanned to talk t' ya about."

Instinctively, Jubal tensed. "What's goin' on?"

Walker again moved his eyes from the table to his son. "Nuthin's goin' on. I'm just kinda concerned, that's all."

"Concerned about what?"

"'Bout you and her."

"What about me and her?"

Walker hesitated, then said, "Well, y'know..."

Jubal could feel the tension inching from his head to his toes. "Know what?"

Walker knew he had to tread carefully. How to explain it? "Well, she's different. Y'know what I mean."

"No, I don't know whatcha mean," Jubal responded with annoyance.

"Well, it's okay if yuh have a coupla laughs with this gal," Walker tried to conveyed, "but yuh shouldn't get serious."

"Why?"

"Because she's different," Walker said again. "She's not one of us. I mean, I have to associate with her father an' all, we business partners, but you shouldn't go prancin' about wit' some..."

Jubal gave an accusatory stare. "With some Puerto Rican?"

"Yeah," Walker admitted, adding, "she's not one of us."

"You said that already. What do you mean, 'she's not one of us'?"

"Just that," Walker said lamely. "She's not American. Why wouldja wanna..."

"Go out with her?" Jubal finalized.

"Yeah, she's okay fer a few laughs, but if it's serious, then that ain't okay."

"Why is it not okay?"

"Because she ain't one of us," Walker repeated with force. "This mixin' of the races ain't popular where we come from. It's—"

Jubal's nostrils flared. "'Mixin' of the races'? She's as light as you. She has blue eyes!"

Walker stuck to his argument. "That don't make no dif'rence. She's not one of us; she's a sp—" He caught himself and finally said, "Rican."

Jubal was on his feet, eyeing his father as if for the first time. "Y're right, she's not one of you." He put his hard hat back on and stomped out of the office.

Walker banged his fist on the table, angered at his fool of a son and, yes, angered at himself for not explaining it right. The boy should know better, he thought. He's a white American; he should know better.

CHAPTER
FIFTY-SEVEN

FACING ISABEL STREET, Camilo sat on the concrete bench in the Plaza Las Delicias, with the candy-colored firehouse behind him. He took a long, slow drag on his cigarette as he waited for Maria to arrive. The candy-colored firehouse had become the main tourist attraction in Ponce, and he wondered how his father, who had been instrumental in getting La Playa its own firehouse, would react to this new development. Not well, most likely.

It was just past noon, with the bustling surge of workers from Comercio and Cristina Streets angling for a plaza bench on their lunch hour, comingling with the tourists just back from a tour of the Ponce market; and the street vendors selling *piraguas*, shaved-ice cups, which they inundated with flavored syrup. He could hear the cries of the hawkers waving lottery lists, trying to entice whomever with the promise of a winning ticket and instant cash for a mere twenty-five cents.

At one time, or so his father had recalled, all of Ponce would have been immersed in the siesta hour and no business would have been done during that time. Everyone would have been home, napping on a bed or couch and digesting a copious lunch.

Those days were long gone.

He glanced at his wristwatch. Maria should be here any minute, he considered. She was seldom late.

True to form, he saw her approach from the other side of the street, rushing past the on-going traffic.

"Sorry I'm late," she said when she reached the plaza bench. "The *publico* driver coming over here was the slowest man on earth, and the traffic didn't help any."

"No need to apologize." He flicked the ashes from the tip of his cigarette. "Noonday traffic in Ponce is shitty these days. It's called progress."

Maria sat down beside him on the bench. "Progress, my ass," she complained. "What Ponce needs is a workable transit system."

"Tell it to our father; he has all the connections."

Maria grimaced. "I don't think he'd understand. He still thinks Ponce should have carriages to transport people."

Camilo raised his cigarette between his first and index fingers to make a point. "Actually, that's not a bad idea. The tourists would love it."

"Why don't you suggest it to him?" Maria recommended.

Camilo waved away the suggestion with his cigarette hand. "You know Papi; he thinks we should be seen and not heard."

"You're right in that regard," Maria concurred.

Camilo crushed the cigarette butt on the park bench and said, "Anyway, I got a message from Jubal. I think he wants to see you again." He dug in his pocket and took out a piece of paper, handing it to Maria. "Here it is."

Maria eagerly took the paper, unfolding it and giving it a quick read. She was all smiles.

"Good news, I hope," Camilo said brightly.

"He wants to meet in Los Meros again, tomorrow." Her face was glowing. "You tell him I'll be there."

"That's me, the cupid messenger," Camilo teased.

Maria frowned. "Camilo."

"I'm sorry," Camilo retracted quickly. "It was a bad joke."

"No," Maria decided, "it was a good joke. And I appreciate your being the go-between, kind of."

"Why don't you tell Papi that you're seeing Jubal?"

Maria thought on it, pursing her lips. "You know how Papi is. Jubal's father is his business partner, and I don't think either of them would approve."

Camilo didn't agree. "Maria, this is 1960; things are changing. You're a grown woman. Jubal is a grown man. I know he's American and all, but if you want to see each other, it's nobody's business but yours and his."

"It's not Papi I'm worried about," Maria confessed. "It's Mami; she doesn't like Jubal."

Camilo looked at her oddly. "Why? Has she told you that?"

"No," Maria said quickly. "It's just that I know her. And for some reason she just doesn't like him. She makes these . . ." Maria searched for a word. ". . . these offhand comments. You know how she is."

"I'm sorry to hear that." Camilo sighed. "Jubal is a nice guy."

"I know," Maria gushed. "And I like him a lot."

Camilo smiled at her. "I know you do."

Maria stared at the ground, suddenly quiet. Camilo said, "Anyway, you guys have fun at Los Meros."

"We will," said Maria.

"Good," Camilo nodded.

Maria stood up from the bench. "Gotta go. See you later."

Camilo looked up at her. "Have a nice time."

Before she left, Maria asked, "What are you gonna do for the rest of the day?"

"I'm meeting Armando," Camilo answered.

Maria asked, "Where?"

Camilo pointed a finger. "Right across the street at Café Belén."

Maria looked to the place across the street, then back at Camilo. "Enjoy yourself. Give Armando my best."

"I will," Camilo said.

"See ya," Maria said with a flip of her fingers.

"See ya," Camilo replied and watched her go back across the street. He leaned back on the stone bench and again took a peek at his wristwatch. It was time to meet Armando.

He headed across Calle Isabel, toward the café. Since it was in the center of town, Café Belén was a cut above the cafetines in the outskirts of Ponce or La Playa. It contained a large space with wide, open doors facing the street and the plaza. That insured that customers could sit down and watch the passing scene in Ponce central. It had white metal tables and chairs, unlike the hard wooden seats or folding chairs in other cafetines, though that's about as far as it went. There was no table service, and one had to go up front to the bar area and cash register, and behind it the kitchen. Behind the register was a roly-poly, short guy with a round face who took the orders.

Camilo ordered a beer, then headed for one of the tables, where he sat down and waited for Armando. It was still early, but the café was filling up with regulars and tourists seeking a good view of Plaza Las Delicias and its candy-colored firehouse.

A young man with black, pomaded hair came into his view. Somehow the youth looked familiar, though he swept past Camilo with nary a glance. The young man, perhaps in his early twenties, carried what looked like a black leather satchel. He went up to the cashier, made an order, and waited, all the while holding his satchel. He got his beer with a glass atop the bottle, went to a nearby table, and sat down.

The young man looked around, as if seeking someone, yet seeing no one. Disregarding the glass, he took a swig from the beer bottle and wiped his lips with the back of his hand. He looked at the satchel and then took another measured glance around. More people were coming into the café.

The young man quickly got up and departed, leaving the bag behind.

Camilo watched him leave. He poured beer into his glass, brought the glass to his lips. Wait a minute, he thought.

He put down his glass and went over to the cashier. "The man left his bag." Camilo pointed to the leather satchel at the next table.

The roly-poly kid looked to the table. "Is that his bag?" he asked Camilo.

"I guess so," Camilo said. "He came in with it. He might come back for it."

"You're right," the cashier said. He came from behind the cash register and headed for the table.

Camilo went back to his seat and lifted his beer glass. He stopped halfway, suddenly looking at the table and the cashier about to retrieve the bag.

Then the explosion came. A loud, crashing bang. Screams and acrid smoke swallowed the air. His eyes seared; his ears ached and throbbed. The force of the blast had lifted him from the chair, and he ended up on the floor. A searing pain coursed through his right leg, and numbness flowed from his right hand up to his shoulder and back.

He realized he was coughing blood.

CHAPTER
FIFTY-EIGHT

THEY WERE GUIDED to the third-floor emergency ward and the room where Camilo was now recovering. In the hallway, a young doctor told them that Camilo had suffered multiple lacerations on his right leg. In retrospect, he had been lucky. The force of the blast could have sheared off his leg below the knee. Magically, the leg was intact, with no major damage to any tendons or veins, but he would be immobile for a while.

However, he had lost the pinky and third finger of his right hand. They had been torn apart during the explosion. When she heard this, Leticia held back a sob, with Antonio, for once, placing a comforting arm around her shoulders.

The doctor stated they could see Camilo, but for a short period. He'd already had a visitor, and they should make their visit brief, given his current condition.

Antonio and Leticia assumed the visitor was Maria, and they were surprised to find Armando sitting beside Camilo on his bed and holding his hand.

Armando snapped his head up when the parents entered the room, and quickly let go of Camilo's left hand. Antonio gave Camilo and his friend a peculiar look, while Leticia rushed forward to Camilo's bedside. She took his head in her hands and kissed him on the cheek and forehead, her tears mingling on his face.

"I'm okay, Mami," he said. "Please don't cry."

"How could this happen?" she uttered.

He gave assurance: "Don't worry. I'm alright."

Antonio approached the bed, still looking questioningly at Armando. Then he asked, "How's your hand?"

Camilo held up his bandaged right hand. "As good as it can be," he said. "I'll be okay."

Leticia turned aside, weeping softly.

"Mami, please don't cry. I'll be fine."

"The doctor has assured he'll recover," Armando said. "He promised there'll be no long-term damage."

Antonio fixed Armando with a stare.

Camilo stepped into the breach. "Oh, I'm sorry; you haven't met. This is Armando Díaz. He's a friend from the university."

Armando extended a hand. "A pleasure to meet you finally. I'm just sorry it's under such circumstances."

Antonio shook Armando's hand formally.

Armando said to Leticia, "And it's a pleasure to meet you, Mrs. Boglione."

Leticia wiped her nose with a handkerchief and brushed a tear from her eye. She managed to say, "The pleasure is mine. Camilo has told me about you and your studies."

Antonio shifted his head from Leticia to Armando, evidently surprised, but he disregarded it for the moment. He tapped Camilo's shoulder affectionately. "We were so worried about you when we heard of this incident."

"It could've been worse." Camilo brandished the bandaged hand. "As it was, I just loss some . . ."

Again, Leticia sobbed, putting her handkerchief to her mouth.

"Oh, Mami, please. I'll be alright."

"But your hand!" Leticia cried.

"It could've been worse. I could've lost my leg. As it is, I'll be out of the hospital in no time."

"Are you sure?" asked Antonio gravely. "The doctor said you had lacerations and—"

"Nothing serious," Camilo interposed. "I'll be out in time for my medical boards."

"That can wait," Antonio said forcibly. "The important thing is for you to get well."

The room door burst open. They all turned to see Maria, who rushed to Camilo's side. "Are you alright? I was just told that you—"

"I'm okay," Camilo interrupted in a tired voice. "I was just telling Mami and Papi not to worry. I'll be fine."

"The doctor said he should be out of the emergency ward by tomorrow," Armando put in. "They'll transfer him to a regular ward, so you see, he's not critical. I'm told there are some people who are in really bad shape."

"The radio said about twenty people were injured, maybe more," Maria informed. Then to all: "How did it happen?"

"We don't know yet," Antonio said. "Every broadcast just states that they're investigating. It could've been an accident, or maybe not."

Leticia was frowning. "An accident? How?" She was cradling Camilo's bandaged hand.

"We don't know," Antonio repeated "There's an on-going investigation."

Maria affectionately chucked Camilo under the chin. "The important thing is that you're okay."

"I am," Camilo pledged. "Please don't worry about me. I have Armando here to make sure I'm okay, and you guys . . ." He stopped, noting the look on his father's face. "I mean, it's good to have family when you need them."

Maria turned to Armando. "It's good to see you again, Armando."

"And it's good to see you too, Maria."

Antonio turned from one to the other. "You two know each other?"

"Yes," Maria said. "Armando's attending the university in San Juan. He's studying biology. That's where we all met."

"Thank you for your concern for my son," Antonio said to Armando. "It's good to know that he has friends at the university that he can count on."

Armando gave Camilo a genial look. "He has many friends at the university, and they're all wishing him well at this moment."

"That's good to hear," Antonio commented.

The room door opened again, and the young doctor entered. He announced briefly, "Mr. Boglione, there's someone here from the mayoralty to see you. They say it's urgent."

Antonio held the doctor's gaze. "Here? From the mayoralty?"

"Yes," the doctor repeated. "He says it's important."

Leticia glanced up at her husband. "Toño?"

"It's probably something to do with Villa Cristal," Antonio assumed. "To some it's a twenty-four-hour job."

"I'll be back as soon as I can," he said to Camilo.

"I'm not going anywhere," Camilo joked feebly.

"That's right," Antonio commanded. "You're staying here for the time being, and you're going to get well. Is that understood?"

Camilo managed to crack a smile. "Yes, Papi."

Outside, in the hospital hallway, Antonio was met by a uniformed member of the National Guard. He knew the man from the two silver eagles pinned on the shoulders of his khaki jacket.

"Colonel Ruiz, what brings you here?"

"We need to talk, señor Boglione," the colonel said directly.

"What's this all about?"

The colonel drew his head toward Camilo's hospital room. "As you know we've had a disturbance. And I'm so sorry that your son was injured. How is he doing, by the way?"

"He'll survive," Antonio confirmed. "He's had some lacerations on his leg, but it's his hand we're worried about. They had to remove two fingers from his right hand due to the explosion."

"Again, I'm sorry to hear that. I will pray that your son recovers."

"But you didn't come here to talk about my son," Antonio guessed. "Why the visit and why here?"

"I'm here because you need to know what's happened. This incident may have ramifications with regard to your project in Villa Cristal."

Antonio's ears perked up. "In what way?"

"A preliminary investigation has led us to believe that the incident in Café Belén was a terrorist plot. A bomb was planted in the café, set to injure as many people as possible."

"How do you know that?" Antonio asked.

Colonel Ruiz reached into one of his pockets and extracted a piece of paper. Gazing at the paper, he said, "Shortly after the bomb exploded, a man called Radio el Mundo declared, 'This is the Armed Forces of Puerto Rican National Liberation. We are responsible for the bombing today. Free Puerto Rico. Free all political prisoners and prisoners of war.'"

The colonel raised his eyes from the paper. "A second call was made to the Associated Press in San Juan and claimed the Armed Forces of Puerto Rico was responsible for the bombing, and more would go off if 'political prisoners were not freed.'"

Antonio looked aside, scowling. "So they're back again."

"They never left," the colonel said. "The last communiqué from this group states that the purpose of the bombing is to protest the US military presence in Puerto Rico and the increased influence of US-based corporations on the island."

Colonel Ruiz replaced the piece of paper in his jacket pocket and continued, "We take these radicals at their word. Today's bombing in Café Belén was not the only planned attack. Another bomb was placed at the offices of Banco de Crédito in Ponce. Lucky for them, an employee of the bank noticed a handbag left on a windowsill. He found a clock-like device and alerted fifty coworkers to flee the office. Police were called in, and the bomb was defused. It was apparently a homemade device that failed to detonate at the appropriate time." The colonel's voice went low. "Sad that the same cannot be said for Café Belen."

The colonel, holding his officer's cap in the crook of his arm, grasped both hands tightly. "And that's why I'm here, señor. The Villa Cristal construction site may be considered a major target in Ponce. As of now we're placing a security detail on the grounds. Everyone going in or out of the work site will be vetted. We're taking no chances where major targets are concerned."

Antonio was rubbing his chin. "Ironic that Villa Cristal, a project genuinely designed to help the people of Ponce, is considered a major target." His tone was mournful.

Colonel Ruiz listened attentively, nodding. "These are the times we live in, señor Boglione. Let me add that Walker Construction has also been apprised of the situation. We are taking every precaution to ensure this act of terror does not happen again."

"And I thank you for that, Colonel," Antonio said. "If that is all, I must go and tend to my son."

"By all means, señor Boglione," vouched the colonel as he watched Antonio go back into the hospital room.

364

CHAPTER
FIFTY-NINE

LETICIA SAT ALONE in her kitchen, cupping a glass of rum in her hands. Everything was coming apart again, she thought. And it could only get worse.

She heard the front door open. Antonio had returned. She looked up at the kitchen ceiling, apprehensive.

Antonio came into the kitchen, placed his hat on the table, and sat down facing her.

"How did it go?" she asked.

"There's a lot to report," he said. "A lot is happening. The mayor's office is up in arms, and so is everyone else connected with this thing."

"What do they say about the bombing?" Leticia wanted to know.

"Officially, there was no bombing."

Leticia shot her husband a startled look. "What do you mean?"

"That's it. There's no bombing . . . officially."

Leticia couldn't believe her ears. "What are you talking about? Café Belén was destroyed. They almost did the same to the Banco de Crédito."

Antonio rubbed the back of his neck with one hand, expelling a breath. "I need a drink." He called over his shoulder at the kitchen door, "Elena, could you get me a whiskey and soda please? I'm in the kitchen."

"Coming up, Toño," they heard.

"You look very tired," Leticia noted.

"It's been a long day." He rubbed his eyes, then folded his hands on the table. "Anyway, the official line is that there was no 'bombing.' This incident has been deemed an accident: a gas pipe that leaked and exploded at the café."

Leticia fumed. "That's ridiculous; we all know what happened. How can they say such a stupid thing?"

"According to the authorities, it's not stupid. It's makes complete sense at this time." Antonio leaned forward, detailing the argument. "The government does not want to create panic, and they don't want to give the Nationalists a victory. Affirming that this was a bombing, not an accident, would give the Nationalists that propaganda victory."

Leticia's face darkened. "So they lie to the people about . . ." She stopped. Elena had come into the kitchen, bringing Antonio's whiskey. Antonio said, "Thank you." Elena looked from one to the other, but knew better than to inquire. She promptly left the kitchen.

Leticia resumed: "How can they deny what has happened?"

"It's not a question of denying what happened. It's a question of protecting the public and not creating a panic."

"But it's bound to come out anyway," Leticia disputed. "Calls were made to the radio station, employees in the bank saw the bomb, and—"

Antonio didn't let her finish. "The calls to the radio station can be explained as crank calls. They get them all the time. As to the employees in the bank, they have been put on notice. Anybody says anything, they lose their job. Everyone involved had been consigned to strict secrecy."

"What about the increased security at Villa Cristal?"

"Simple," Antonio picked up his drink and had a swallow. "Increased security is due to a fear of theft. We're just trying to protect the equipment and materials at the construction site."

Leticia snorted in disapproval. "It's amazing how this government can turn black into white and vice versa."

"They're protecting their interest, that's all."

"By lying to the public," Leticia condemned.

"By keeping us safe," Antonio countered.

Leticia nervously nibbled at her pinky nail. "It's not right. Camilo's in the hospital—not only him, but all those others who were injured—and the government is lying about it."

Antonio thought it best to change topics. "Talking about Camilo, did you know about this friend, Armando?"

"What's there to know?" Leticia shrugged. "Armando is a friend from the university. His best friend, I would think."

Antonio had a questioning stare. "Are they just friends?"

"What do you mean, 'are they just friends'?"

"Just that, Leticia. Don't lie to me." Antonio was deadly serious. "I saw how they . . ." He faltered, finding it difficult to say what he really meant.

Leticia reached out to touch his hand. "Toño, you should be proud that your son has such a good friend who cares for him, who only wants the best for him."

Antonio drew his hand back from her touch.

Leticia looked down, suddenly sad.

"Leticia," Antonio said bluntly, "I will not have my son, or anyone in my family, engage in unnatural behavior."

Leticia did not look pleased. "Toño, your son is in the hospital, recuperating from a terrible injury. We should think of his well-being, not some ridiculous insinuation."

"I'm serious, Leticia," Antonio emphasized. "I won't have it in my house." With that, he put down his drink and left the kitchen.

CHAPTER
SIXTY

NURSING HIS LIGHT rum and tonic, the young man with black, pomaded hair noticed one other patron at the airport bar. He was a beefy man with a red beard. He wore outsized Bermuda shorts and a striped polo shirt. Probably a tourist, the young man figured, or ex-pat enjoying his daiquiri.

He checked his wristwatch; time to make the call. It was pivotal that he adhere to the schedule. He put some bills on the bar counter and made it over to the phone booth at the end of the bar. He got inside, closed the phone booth door, inserted the dime in the slot, and dialed the number.

After two rings, there was an answer. "¿Sí?"

"The package has been sent," the young man said into the phone.

"I've heard they really liked the surprise birthday card." The voice at the other end was low, metallic.

"Yes, they did," the young man said.

"Good. Enjoy your trip."

"Buenas tardes," the young man said.

"Buenas tardes." Click. The line went dead. The young man hung up the telephone, tapping it with a finger.

He picked up the receiver again and dialed the operator. "I'd like to make a collect, long-distance call to New York." He gave the operator the number.

After a moment or so he heard the greeting: "¿Hola?"

"Mami, it's me."

Laughter at the other end. "Raffa, is that you?"

"Yes, Mami, it's me."

"Where are you?"

"I'm at the airport," Raffa said.

"You're at the airport, so you're flying home."

"Yes, today," Raffa confirmed.

"That's great," Milagros Pagan said from New York. "It'll be so good to see you." Then: "Did you have a good time?"

"Yes, Mami, I had a good time."

"Did you get to see my mother in La Playa?"

"Yes, I saw Grandmother in La Playa. She's well, and she misses you."

"I miss her too," Milagros said. "Hopefully, I'll get to see her before too long."

"That would be nice," Raffa concurred.

"Did you get to visit San Juan and Viequez?"

"Yes, I did. It was good to be back. I really miss the place."

"So do I," Milagros said at the other end.

"I'll be home soon," Raffa said with delight. "Actually, I'll be home tonight. We'll have dinner together."

"That will be wonderful, Raffa," she responded with a slight giggle. "By the way, Estelle will be here too. I told her you were coming. She really likes you a lot, you know."

"Yes." Raffa smiled at the thought. "And the feeling is mutual."

"I'm glad to hear that," said Milagros. "She's a fine girl."

He heard the airport PA system announce his flight. "Look, I gotta go. My flight's leaving. See you soon. I love you."

"I love you too, Raffa. And please be careful. Have a good trip."

"I will, Mami. See you later." He hung up the phone a second time, looking at his watch again. The operation had gone well. He would be off of the island before anyone could tie him or his group to the action in Ponce. Yes, it had gone well.

CHAPTER
SIXTY-ONE

DIXIE WALKER WAS trying everything he could to convince the women. "Look," he claimed, "Ah'm ready to do biz'ness, honey. I'm heah, yore heah, so let's come to an agreement. Whatcha say?"

"Fifty dollars," she declared outright.

"Fifty bucks!" Dixie took a jaundiced look around the Melia Hotel lobby. It was late, and they were the only ones present; just them and the overhead fan slowly rotating hot, humid air that did nothing to mitigate the heat.

"Yuh outta yer mind, gurl."

"Fifty dollars is what I charge," the young woman said again without batting an eyelid.

"Fifty bucks! I could get a better deal on the other side of town."

The young hooker's face remained stoic. "So go to the other side of town."

Dixie ploughed again. "Look, honey, we discussin' a biz'ness deal heah. Yuh git what ah mean? All ah want is a good time. Yuh kin supply it. We come to an agreement, and all is well."

The young woman was unmoved. "The agreement is fifty dollars."

"What 'bout the price of a room?" Dixie asked.

"You pay for the room," the woman said decisively. "That is not included."

"Yuh outta your mind, gurl. Forgit 'bout it."

"As you wish." The woman made to go.

Dixie grabbed her arm. "C'mon, Ah'm a vet'run of the war. I fought fer yuh all."

"Fifty dollars." She unhooked her arm from his grasp and headed for the other side of the hotel lobby. Dixie watched her tight-skirted walk, vivacious and alluring.

"Lesbian," he scowled. Next, he turned and headed for the ornate etched-glass door that led into the main dining room. He walked up to the bar at one side of the room and sat on an upholstered stool with arm-rests.

The bartender, a middle-aged mustachioed type with hair parted in the middle, asked cordially, "What will it be, señor?"

Dixie Walker lifted a finger to the brim of his Stetson and inched the hat higher on his head. "Bourbon, I. W. Harper if yuh got it, neat."

The bartended lifted a bottle from the display behind him and poured the drink.

Dixie Walker took a good-sized gulp, looked around again. He put down the glass. "Whut does a man hafta do to git some fun round heah?"

"I see you were talking to the young lady, señor," the bartender noted.

Dixie's mouth twitched. "Yeah. It got me nowhere." He grew silent. Then he inquired, "Yuh wouldn't know some place round heah where a guy could git a few laughs, wouldja?"

"It depends on what kind of fun you are looking for, señor."

"Yuh know whut ah mean. We're both men of the world."

"I see." The bartender nonchalantly picked up a cloth towel and began wiping the bar counter. "Perhaps I can help, señor. If you're looking for company, I know of a place that is highly recommended. It's just at the outskirts of town."

Dixie showed interest. "Y'do?"

"Yes. It's doña Fela's place. I'm told they aim to please."

"Don-yah whose?"

"Doña Felicia. She is well known in these parts. And her ladies are the best."

"O-kay." Dixie was all ears. "Where is this place?"

The bartender put down the towel, rummaged behind the counter, and produced a pad and ballpoint pen. He began writing. "I'll give you the address. All you have to do is go to the main desk, give the concierge this note, and he'll call a car for you. At this time of night you should be there in half an hour or less."

Dixie showed a big grin. "Wall, thank yuh. Ah do 'preciate it." He took the note the bartender offered, and in a gracious gesture, he dug in his pocket and gave the bartender a ten-dollar bill. "Thank yuh agin, suh."

The bartender pocketed the money. "And thank you, señor."

Smiling widely, Dixie made it to the front desk. Just as he reached the concierge, he noticed the young woman from before, coming down the main stairway that led to the lobby. She was not alone. Her arm was strapped to an older man with light, baggy pants and an outsized floral shirt, obviously an American.

The minute she saw Dixie, the young woman turned up her nose, holding tight to her client. They passed by him.

Dixie had a sudden compulsion. He decided to follow. He just had to know where she was going.

The couple stepped out onto the sidewalk, made a left turn, and headed toward the plaza, about a block up. They continued on the sidewalk covered in the shadows of night, with Walker following from a discreet distance. They waited for the streetlight to change and proceeded to the plaza and beyond.

Walker was about twenty feet from the streetlight when he noted in the distinct shadows a pair of men approaching from the other side of the street. He stopped for a closer look.

He immediately recognized one of the men. No doubt about it: it was Antonio Boglione's son. Walker racked his brain. What wuz his name? Camacho? Camillee?

He had hadn't seen the other man before. His skin was dark brown, and he had nappy hair.

The two men crossed the street and stopped at the corner. They looked around furtively, saw that no one was present, and drew each other tightly in a long, arduous kiss. Camilo pressed his hand on the other man's bottom, drawing him closer.

Dixie's jaw dropped. He slinked back into the shadows of the sidewalk.

The men caressed each other's face, gently, lovingly. Then the black man turned and walked away. Camilo likewise turned around and headed for the empty plaza.

Dixie Walker watched them both go their separate ways, a feeling of shock coursing through his bones. Does Mistuh Boglione know whut's goin' on? he wondered.

CHAPTER
SIXTY-TWO

ANTONIO AND LETICIA sat across the table from each other. Neither said a word. Elena came in with a soup bowl and ladle, placed them on the table, checked their faces, picked up on it, and promptly left for her domain in the kitchen.

They heard the front door open. Antonio and Leticia waited in the dining room. Camilo came in first. "Man, it's hot out there, even for Ponce. We saw more than one car overheat in the plaza."

Maria approached alongside him. She mopped her brow with a handkerchief. "I need some cold water. That sun is fierce." She went to the table, whisked up one the glasses filled with ice water, and swallowed its contents.

"I need a beer," Camilo said. "Elena," he called, "can you get me a beer, please?"

They heard Elena's voice from the kitchen, "Coming up, Camilo."

He pulled back a chair and sat down. Maria did the same on the other side of the table.

"So where did you two go today?" Leticia inquired.

Maria and Camilo crossed looks. Maria spoke up: "I was at the Ponce Museum. They're having a retrospective on minimalist art." She looked from one side of the table to the other and continued, "And that's a change from the classical art they usually display."

"Was it interesting?" Leticia asked.

"Oh, very," Maria said, enthused. "It's amazing what they're doing with art on the mainland. They're experimenting all over the place, and Ponce is finally catching up." She cued her brother: "You've seen the show, right?"

"Yes," Camilo said. "It's a fine show. I saw it last week with . . ." He stopped before adding, "a friend." He paused and then said to Leticia, "You'll like the exhibit, Mami."

"I'm sure I would," Leticia said offhand. She studied her son with mild curiosity. "And what did you do today?"

"Oh, I was tutoring a couple of kids from the local university. They're having problems with chemistry, and they thought I might help."

"That's very good of you, Camilo," Leticia said approvingly.

Antonio broke his silence: "Did you enjoy tutoring those kids?"

Camilo glanced at Leticia, then back to his father. The question sounded vaguely accusatory. "Oh sure. They're Armando's cousins, and they really want to get ahead."

"You mean, Armando, your friend?" Antonio gave Camilo a stark look.

This time Camilo glanced to Maria, whose face showed puzzlement.

"How good of a friend is this Armando to you?" The question was pointed.

"What do you mean?" Camilo's tone was flat.

Antonio now had a set face. "Just that. How good a friend is he to you?"

Leticia intervened: "Toño, please."

"I can't ask my son a question?" Antonio scoured the table, as if measuring each member of his family.

Maria asked with concern, "Papi, what's wrong?"

Antonio banged his fist on the table.

"What's wrong?"

Leticia looked down, knitting her brow. Maria gave her father a shocked look. Camilo remained still in his chair. "I'll tell you what's wrong!" Antonio barked, glowering at his son. "It's my son, that's what's wrong." His forefinger stabbed out. "You know what you two have been doing. I've been told. How can you shame me this way?"

"Papi, what're you talking about?"

"You know very well what I'm talking about!"

Again Leticia tried to intercede. "Toño, please!"

His pointed finger turned on Leticia. "How can you stand this? How can you let this happen? Aren't you incensed, angry?"

"Toño, there's nothing to be angry about. We have to . . ."

"'Nothing to be angry about'?" Antonio's face darkened. "How can you say that?" Again the finger jabbed Camilo's way. "He's shamed me! He's shamed us, the family!"

Camilo sought an explanation. "Papi, what—"

"You shut up! I want to hear nothing from you! You've shamed me and the family. Do you know that?"

"Papi, what are you talking about?" This from Maria.

Antonio's eyes were now dim, angry specks aimed Camilo's way. "He knows what I'm talking about! Him and his, his . . . ," Antonio spluttered, seeking the right epithet, "his Negro boyfriend!"

Camilo placed his hands flat on the table. "I don't have to listen to this." He slid back his chair, rising to his feet.

"You will listen to this!" Antonio flailed his arms. "And you will stop doing it! You will stop shaming me, your mother, your sister."

"Papi, Camilo has done nothing wrong," Maria told her father.

Antonio viewed his daughter as if she were out of her mind. "Nothing wrong? Do you know what he's done?"

"I don't care," Maria said flatly. "He's my brother, and he's done nothing wrong."

"You don't care?" Antonio's face twisted up. "Are you as depraved as him? Is that it? Are both my children deviants?"

"Toño, please stop," Leticia implored. "This has gone far enough."

"You're right there, wife! This has gone far enough. I will not have a deviant in my home. I won't permit it!"

Maria asked with a trembling voice, "Papi, who told you these lies?"

"Lies?" Antonio demanded. His acid eyes again turned to Camilo. "Do you deny it? Is it lies?"

"I don't have to answer your accusations," Camilo fought back.

"Then you don't deny it?" Antonio's voice went down an octave. A strained silence followed. "My son is a faggot!" Antonio said caustically.

"Toño!" Leticia cried.

"Papi!" Maria wailed.

Now it was Camilo who jabbed a finger at his father. "I don't have to take this from you or anyone!"

"That's right. You don't!" Antonio took the dinner napkin from his lap and tossed it across the table. "And I don't have to take this from you." He shot an arm toward the dining room door. "Get out of my house, now!"

"Toño!" Leticia was on the verge of tears.

Antonio kept his arm aimed at the door. "You heard me! Get out!"

Camilo looked at his sister, his mother, and his father, still raging.

He turned and dashed out of the dining room.

"Camilo!" Leticia jumped up from her chair, following after her son.

"Let him go," Antonio said bitterly. "He doesn't deserve to live in this house."

Leticia glared at her husband with a measure of disbelief and regret. "You ever consider that it's you who doesn't deserve to be in this house?"

Maria sprang from her chair and rushed after Camilo. She caught up with him as he stomped his way down the front stairs. "Camilo!"

She latched onto his arm. "Camilo, please, don't go."

"I can't stay in this house anymore." Camilo's chest was heaving. "I can't stay with him."

Maria cupped her lips, leaning toward him. "Where will you go?"

"I'll go to Armando's place."

"What will you do?" Maria was clearly anxious. "How will you support yourself? And what about your studies?"

"I'll find a way." Camilo drew himself up. "I have Armando."

Maria gripped her brother's hand. "Please don't go."

"I have to. He threw me out of the house."

"He's angry," Maria tried to justify. "He'll get over it. Just don't go. It would kill Mami if you left."

"She's got you. She'll be fine." Camilo brushed his sister's cheek. "Goodbye, Maria." He turned, rushing out the front gate.

Maria watched him until he turned the corner and was no longer in her sight.

She slumped down on the concrete front steps, sitting with her hands tight, tears forming at the corners of her eyes.

She wiped a finger under her nose, stood up, and went back into the house.

"Maria," she heard Elena call, but she walked on, quiet and determined. She made it to her bedroom, went to the closet, and brought out an old leather suitcase. She began pulling out dresser drawers and stuffing clothes into the suitcase.

Her mother came in the room. "What are you doing?"

381

"I'm leaving," she said.

"What?"

"I'm leaving."

"And going where?" Leticia asked, dismayed.

"I'm moving in with Jubal."

"What?"

"I'm moving in with Jubal Walker. He's asked me to marry him, and that's what I'm going to do."

Leticia gave a startled look. "You're what?"

"You heard me. I'm going to Jubal's place."

"That's . . ." Leticia felt a hopeless rage. "You can't just move in with a man!"

A frown appeared on Maria's face. "Mami, these are different times from yours. People don't point fingers anymore if you live with someone."

"They do in Ponce!" Leticia exclaimed.

Maria was set on her course. "It makes no difference. I love Jubal and he loves me, and I can't live in this house anymore."

"Maria, please, think of what you're doing." Leticia flung out her arms in a hopeless gesture. "You're going to move in with that American!"

"And what wrong's with that? He's a good man."

"He's a Walker!" Leticia accused.

"So? He's a Walker. So what?" Maria was trying to understand her mother, but finding it hard.

Leticia's mouth was pinched white. "You don't know them!"

"What's there to know?" Maria asked. "Jubal is a good man. He's nothing like his father, if that's what you mean."

He's an American, and they're different from us."

"What do you mean, 'they're different from us'?"

"Just that," Leticia answered with a snap. "Never trust a Walker—not the son, not his father."

"You sound as crazy as Papi," Maria said, annoyed.

Leticia clutched Maria's arm. "Please don't go to this young man."

"Mami, I can't stay here, not after what's happened." She untwined her mother's fingers from her arm. "I can't live with you or Papi, not in this house." Her tone softened. "I'll be alright. And I'll be happy with Jubal. You'll see."

"This will kill your father," Leticia lamented.

"Funny," Maria observed. "Camilo said the same thing about you." She heaved a frustrated sigh. "But it won't. You're both survivors. You and Papi will manage. You have all these years without any . . ." Maria stopped.

"Without any love?" Leticia finished Maria's thought. She gave a heartfelt shrug. "Sometimes love is not what it's cracked up to be." Her eyes grew heavy. "There are other things in life."

"Are there?" Maria regarded her mother with great care. "All I know is that you and Papi haven't shared the same bedroom in years. Camilo and I always suspected something was wrong, but we didn't say anything. Still, even as children, we knew something was missing."

Leticia clicked her tongue against the roof of her mouth. "Maria, someday you'll discover that there is more to life than fairy-tale romance. We all have to make compromises. I just hope you and Jubal can weather that storm if and when it comes."

Maria listened with care, and then she said with equal care, "Jubal and I really love each other. Our love will stay strong. That, I assure you."

A tear smeared Leticia's cheek. "I sincerely hope so. For your sake I sincerely do."

CHAPTER
SIXTY-THREE

ANTONIO DOWNED THE drink in one swallow.

"Pepe, I need another!" He was holding up the now-empty paper cup.

Pepe, the owner of the eatery, was behind the counter, with one bent leg resting on a stool, and twirling a toothpick in his mouth. He and another man at the counter had been watching Antonio. He gave the other man a shrewd glance and strode to the table where Antonio sat, morose and contemplative.

"Another." Antonio was still holding up the cup.

Before taking the cup Pepe hesitated. "Don Toño, it's kinda early in the day. Don't you think you've had enough?"

"Get me another, I said!"

Pepe took the cup. "As you wish." He made it back to the counter, picked out a whiskey bottle from beneath the counter, and began refilling the cup, all the while eyeing Antonio getting sloshed at the corner table. He replaced the bottle under the counter and took the drink back to Antonio.

It was midday. Sunlight streamed through the open doors facing the beach at the rear of the eatery. The front door also had been flung wide open, and rays of sunlight spackled the floor, tables, and chairs. They were the only ones in the place.

The rush wouldn't begin until after four o'clock, when the regulars would start trudging in for their conch-and-octopus sandwiches.

Pepe decided to turn on the small radio behind him. Mambo music pounded through the emptiness of the cafetín.

Into the café's mambo music streamed three other people, two men and a woman. They were young, in their twenties.

From across the space, Pepe greeted one of the men: "¿Qué pasa, Jaime? ¿Cómo estás?"

The youth flipped a hand in acknowledgment, while his two friends sat down at one of the tables.

Antonio stared into his drink as the young man went over to the counter and ordered some beers. He brought them back to the table.

Antonio held up his cup again. "Pepe, ¡otra mas!"

The young people glimpsed Antonio's table. It was unusual for Pepe to give individual service to anyone. Their faces registered the same question: Who is this guy?

Shaking his head, Pepe brought Antonio another drink.

The young woman at the table was complaining loudly to one of the men: "I don't want a beer. I didn't come here to drink!"

"Teresa, be cool," one of the young men said.

"Why should I be cool? He's the one that fucked up." The woman speared a finger at one of the men sitting across from her.

"Teresa, watch your mouth," the other man responded. "You're in public."

"I don't give a fuck," Teresa said indignantly. "You're the one that was screwing her behind my back!"

"Teresa, I mean it," the other man warned. "Don't get me mad."

"Whatcha gonna do about it?" Teresa dared. "You gonna hit me? Here? In front of everybody?"

"I don't have to take this shit." The young man pushed back his chair and got to his feet.

"You're a fucker, you know that?" Teresa shot up at him.

The young man took a step toward her. Pepe, who had been watching everything, was already at the table. "¿Qué pasa, Jaime?"

"It's her!" Jaime spat out. "This bitch doesn't know when to stop."

The woman leaped up, ready to lunge at Jaime. The other man restrained her, pulling her back. "Teresa, please behave."

"You tell him to behave," Teresa snapped, her face becoming mottled, "the bastard!"

Pepe put up his palms. "C'mon everybody, calm down."

"You tell her to calm down," the one called Jaime complained. "She's got a mouth on her."

"And you're a son of a bitch," Teresa retaliated.

Pepe edged himself between them. "Teresa, Jaime, this is my place. Now, you two behave. I don't want any problem here."

"You have no problems with me." Jaime gestured contemptuously at the woman. "It's her and her mouth!"

"You fuck!" Teresa was about to lunge at Jaime. Pepe blocked her. "If you don't behave, I'm gonna ask you to leave."

"Gimme another!" Antonio was calling for another shot.

"I mean it," Pepe told them. "Stop this shit now!"

The men and women quieted and sat back down glumly at the table, with mambo music still blasting from the radio.

Pepe came back to Antonio. "Don Toño, you should go. Really, you've had enough. If you want, my friend Marco over there can drive you back. I'm sure doña Leticia is very worried about you."

Antonio straightened, his face setting hard. "Worried about me? No one's worried about me. No one gives a fuck. They don't care." He pressed the cup to Pepe's stomach. "Gimme another!"

With an acute look of distaste, Pepe took the cup and went back to the counter.

The three other customers had stopped their bickering long enough to watch Antonio's antics. Then they went back at it.

"Teresa, I'm warning you: don't start up again."

The woman didn't start up again. She simply stood up and spat in Jaime's face.

"You fuckin' bitch!" Jaime leaped up from the table, wiping the spittle from his face with the back of one hand. He grabbed the woman, pulled her to one side, and pushed her back roughly.

Falling backward, she stumbled into Antonio's table. His drink splattered all over his short-sleeved shirt. He snapped to, as if coming back to reality. "What the fuck?"

The woman regained her balanced and sprang at Jaime. The other man got between them. Jaime pushed him aside and smacked the woman on the face.

The woman touched her jaw. "You motherfucker!"

Jaime came at her, enraged. His friend grappled his arms, pulling him back.

Antonio got to his feet, confronting the woman. "What's wrong with you?" Then he confronted the man: "And you, you crazy too? I'm just trying to have a peaceful drink here. Get the fuck out!"

Jaime, still being restrained by the other man, responded vehemently, "And who do you think you are? You don't own this place. Pepe does."

"I'm Antonio Boglione, and I say get out now!" He jabbed toward one of the open doors.

Jaime asked Pepe, "Who is this fuck?"

"Jaime, calm down," Pepe said. Then to Antonio: "Don Toño, please. Just stay out of this."

"Yeah, you stay out of this, you old fuck." This from the woman.

"That's right, you old fuck, you stay out of this." And this from Jaime.

"Whadd'ya call me?" Antonio demanded of the young man.

"You heard me, you old bastard."

It was then that Antonio fisted his right hand and jammed it into the young man's face. The force of the blow toppled Jaime backward, and he landed atop the other man who had been restraining him.

Just as quick, the younger man jumped to his feet and rammed into Antonio. But the older man, despite being drunk—or maybe because of it—toppled back, but held his ground, quickly striking Jaime again. Jaime deflected the punch and countered with his own strike to Antonio's jaw.

Antonio stumbled back, but again straightened and went at the youth. Pepe tried to intervene, blocking Antonio's way. Antonio roughly pushed him aside.

Antonio didn't see it. The knife came out of the woman's pocket in the flash of an eye. It was a switchblade, and she jammed it into Antonio's back, just to the right of his spine.

Antonio thought someone had punched his back—that's what it felt like. Then the pain. His arm was raised for another punch, but his legs sagged.

And he crumbled to the ground.

Pepe and Marco, his friend at the counter, were quickly kneeling beside him. Marco, who had been watching everything but was too afraid to interfere, now touched Antonio's back and saw his hand smeared with blood.

He gasped, turning to Pepe.

The two men and the woman quickly ran for the open doors, leaving Pepe's Café, with Antonio slumped on the floor, mambo music trumpeting to every corner.

CHAPTER
SIXTY-FOUR

THE VIGIL HAD begun. Leticia, as required, sat in the front row of the funeral parlor, flanked on both sides by Elena and Maria, also dressed in black. In the four rows behind them sat neighbors and friends, all in quiet contemplation or else conversing in hushed tones reserved for such occasions.

They had come from all over Ponce, from La Playa, from the town, and beyond. Even obese and ancient doña Fela had come out of her reclusive retirement to pay her respects to the late honorable don Antonio Boglione.

Also sitting in the front row alongside Maria was Jubal Walker. Maria had insisted he be present, and Leticia was too tired to argue.

From time to time Jubal would take hold of Maria's hand, she would smile at him, and Leticia, eyes straight forward, would pretend not to notice.

The only time Leticia showed any spark in the gloomy environment was when she saw Camilo and Armando enter the parlor and approach the front row.

Leticia offered a hand. Camilo took her hand and kissed it. She stood, and they embraced. Afterward, Camilo embraced Maria and Elena, each in turn.

"I'm glad you came," greeted Leticia. "It means a lot to us." She turned to include Maria sitting beside her.

"Papi would be happy you're here," Maria said.

"Yes," Elena concurred. "Toño would be most happy."

Camilo shifted his head to Armando. "It was Armando who convinced me I should be here. He made a good argument about family obligations."

"Your father would not have considered it an obligation that you're here," Leticia enunciated carefully. "He would have considered it a blessing."

"I know." Camilo looked to Armando as if for affirmation. Armando nodded in the affirmative. He stuck out a hand to Jubal. "It's good to see you again, my friend."

Jubal rose, warmly shaking Armando's hand. He also shook hands with Camilo. "I'm glad you're both here."

They sat back down. Camilo and Armando remained standing. In the ensuing quiet, Camilo said, "If you'll excuse me, I want to spend some moments with Papi."

"Of course," Leticia granted.

They watched as Camilo approached his father's open casket, Antonio's face waxen, and he was all decked out a dark suit and black tie. Maria had pinned a white rose to his lapel to match the white pocket handkerchief of the suit.

Back in the front row, Armando was telling, "When we heard about don Antonio's passing, we were shocked, as I'm sure was everyone. We never expected this. It was the first time I've seen Camilo cry despite what happened before."

Sitting straight in her chair, Leticia said, "Camilo always loved his father in spite of everything, and I know Toño loved him as well." She shook her head sadly. "It's just a crime that he would have to die because of some Nuyoricans at Pepe's Café."

"Mami, it's passed. Let it go." Maria was gingerly holding Leticia's hand. "Papi would want you to be happy, even now."

Leticia lowered her head, trying to hold back the grief. "I know. It's just that it's going to be hard."

Armando said to her, "Señora Boglione, we're here for any support you might need—me, Camilo, Jubal—you're not alone."

Leticia raised her head. "I know, and I thank you all."

A small sound erupted in the room, almost like a gasp. Everyone heard it. It had come from Elena, who was the first to see them: a small, willowy woman with cinnamon skin and close-cropped graying hair, and also dressed in black. She was escorted by a young man with pomade-tinged black hair.

The only one who had seemingly ignored their entrance was Camilo, who had knelt at the footrest on the casket, with hands clasped, head low, as if in prayer.

Milagros Pagan walked forward to the front row, on the arm of her son, Rafael.

Shock flooded Elena's face. Same for Maria. Jubal and Armando both showed wonder and some confusion. They had never seen this woman before.

Leticia stood up deferentially. "I am honored you have come," she said aloud. "Toño would have been happy to know you're here."

"The minute we heard," said Milagros, also referring to her son, "we both decided to come and pay our respects. Whatever may have happened, we consider it proper."

"I understand completely," said señora Leticia Boglione.

Milagros flashed a smile at Elena. "It's good to see you again, Elena."

"It's good to see you too, Milagros." Elena, getting over her shock, embraced Milagros Pagan.

Leticia turned to Maria, saying, "Maria, this is your half brother, Rafael Pagan."

Maria stared at Rafael, stunned. "My half brother?"

"Yes," Leticia confirmed. "And this is her fiancée, Jubal Walker," Leticia said to Milagros.

Handshakes all around, although Maria was looking at her mother rather strangely.

Milagros told her, "Your father was a good man, a great man. He did a lot for the people of Ponce, and he will be remembered."

"Thank you," Maria said. Then gazing at her mother: "There is a lot about him I didn't know."

"Oh, I can tell you many things about him," Milagros offered.

"Thank you, I would like that."

There followed an uneasy quiet. It was broken when Rafael stated he wished to view Antonio.

"By all means," Leticia granted again.

Rafael went over to the casket where Camilo still knelt beside his father.

"I am Rafael," he said.

Camilo looked up, trying to remember where he had seen this young man before. "Do I know you?"

"I'm your half brother," Rafael said.

Camilo eyed the corpse of his father. "I always wondered if the rumors were true."

"They were true." Rafael motioned to the footrest. "Can I join you?"

"I would be honored." Camilo stretched out a hand for Rafael to kneel beside him.

Kneeling side by side with his brother, Camilo asked, "Have we met before?"

"No, I don't think so. I would have remembered." Rafael made the sign of the cross, joined his hands, and lowered his head.

And the two sons of Antonio Boglione prayed at their father's casket.

CHAPTER
SIXTY-FIVE

AS WAS BOUND to happen, Antonio's funeral became a social event in Ponce. His remains were paraded from the funeral parlor in La Playa to the municipal cemetery, not far from the tree line bordering the beach.

Although they resented that he had wanted to be interred in La Playa, not in the more upscale cemetery in town, the notables came to bid one last goodbye to one of Ponce's best. The mayor was there; the fire chief and police chief were there. Even the governor sent a representative from the distant precincts in San Juan.

The procession lining the street to the cemetery was a lively one. The long black hearse was followed by a throng of playeros, some in *guayaberas,* some in t-shirts—only the mayor and his group were in suits. The women dressed modestly but plainly, except for family members, appropriately dressed in black, and in a second sedan following the hearse.

Along the way, gossip was ripe among the playeros; Milagros Pagan had come back. Not only that, her bastard son was there too. Camilo had come with his friend, a Negro named Armando. Snickers accompanied this nugget. What would happen to all of Antonio's holdings now? Who would take over his family's commercial interests? And who was that americano arm in arm with Maria? Poor Toño must be turning over in his grave over that one.

At the graveside officiated Father Javier, with the proper prayers and homily. Father Javier was successor to the beloved Father Ignacio—except, of course, for the Madera family, who still held a grudge against the good Father.

And just as had happened years before (as some old-timers recalled the burial of Jacobo Levy), just moments before the body was laid in the ground, one lone man showed up, a beefy *extranjero* in a Stetson hat. He came forward, bowed, took Leticia's hand, and in a hushed voice uttered some comforting words to the widow.

He then took his place alongside the family, removing his Stetson hat and respectfully holding it in front of his body.

When the burial ceremony ended and the coffin was lowered into the ground, Dixie Walker put his hat back on, passing by his son, Jubal, who stood beside Maria, looking straight ahead and not saying a word to his father.

EPILOGUE

1969

THEY PARKED THE rented car outside the street facing Milagros Pagan's home, now boarded and shuttered.

The neighbors from the adjoining houses saw a woman step out of the car, along with two children, a boy and girl, about eight or nine years old. From the driver's side emerged, presumably, the father, tall and lanky with freckled skin.

Maria took each child by the hand. "We're here," she said to Jubal.

"You still wanna do this?" he asked.

"Yup," she said.

"Mom, is this the house you told me about?" inquired the son. He mirrored his father's looks, with the same sandy-colored hair.

"Yes, this is the place," Maria said.

"Why are we here? This is an old house," complained Maria's daughter, with her mother's dark hair and the same blue-gray eyes. She was the restless one. "When can we go back to town?"

"I wanted to show you this house," Maria tried to explain.

The daughter pouted. "Why?"

"Maggie," Jubal admonished his daughter, "this is a special treat for your mother, and for you as well. You'll see."

The girl folded her arms. "I don't see why we have to come to this old house."

"C'mon, you'll find it interesting," Maria attested. "There may be ghosts in there." She puckered her lips. "Wooooo."

The boy showed interest. "Really? Ghosts?"

Jubal bent at the waist, looking intently at his son. "Yes. And they'll come and take yuh away. That's why we're heah with you."

Now even the daughter was interested. "You say there's ghosts in there, like Casper?"

Maria beamed down at them. "Yes, just like Casper, but friendlier." She winked at Jubal. He smiled back.

"Wow," the girl reconsidered. "Let's see the house."

Jubal took hold of his daughter's hand, and with Maria holding onto their son's hand, they went into the house.

Inside it was dark and musty. The girl wrinkled her nose. "It's smelly in here."

"Jubal, can you open up some shutters, get some air in here?" Maria requested.

"Sure." Jubal motioned to his son. "C'mon, Carl, help your father with the shutters." They began flinging open the shutters. Soon branches of light danced on far corners.

"It was lucky you got the keys to this place," Maria said to Jubal. "I'm told they're selling it next week."

"Somebody's gonna buy this house?" the daughter asked.

"Yes, someone is," Maria said. "A young couple is moving in."

"Do they have kids too?"

"Yes, they have kids too."

The daughter was flapping a hand in front of her face. "They better get this place cleaned up soon."

"They will," Maria assured.

"Why you wanna come here, Mom?" the girl asked.

Maria made a broad gesture with her arm. "It's a place that holds many memories. Your grandfather lived here once." She grew quiet and pensive.

"C'mon, kids, let me show you the backyard," Jubal said. "There's a beautiful mango tree back there."

This sparked the boy's interest anew. "Mango tree? Does it have mangoes?"

"Let's go and see," Jubal took their hands, and off they went to see the backyard.

Maria stepped lightly into the bedroom of the house. There it was, just as Milagros Pagan had told her: a white ceramic vase with Chinese characters on it. She picked it up gently, blowing away the dust that smeared its surface.

She inspected it, turning it over and over. She looked around the room, trying to imagine how it had been before.

"Is that the vase she told you 'bout?"

Jubal was pointing to the vase in her hands.

"Yes, it is." She held it up to a beam of light coming from one of the window shutters. "Beautiful, isn't it?"

"Yeah, it's pretty."

She clutched the vase to her chest, suddenly looking around. "Where are the kids?"

"They're in the backyard," Jubal said. "They're fascinated by the mango tree. Ah think they're tryin' to climb it."

"Is it safe to climb that tree?"

"They'll be okay." Jubal sounded sure. "Even they will have a hard time tryin' to get beyond the first branch." He gestured with his chin. "What's so special 'bout the vase?"

"It was a gift to Milagros from my father," Maria confided. "It was very valuable to her, so she told me."

Jubal watched his wife closely. "You and she have become close, haven't you?"

"Yes, we have grown close these last few years," Maria admitted. "I'm as close to her as my mother, maybe more." Her voice became somber. "When I found out about her and Rafael, I was shocked and, yes, disappointed in my father. Not because of what happened, but because he never told me and Camilo about it, not even after we became adults. I felt betrayed about that. But as I've grown older, and have kids of my own, I realize that we do whatever possible to shield the ones we love." She took a deep breath, probing no further. "So I've forgiven my father, and so has my mother."

"What's there to forgive?" Jubal remarked quietly. "He provided for you, and he provided for Milagros and her son. He did the best he could."

"Yes," Maria said in a small voice. "He did the best he could."

"What're yuh going to do with the vase?" Jubal asked.

"I'm taking it back to Milagros in New York. I promised her I would."

Jubal stepped closer and embraced Maria and the vase. "You're a good woman, yuh know that? I'm a lucky man."

"I'm the lucky one," Maria said to him.

Jubal disengaged from the embrace, an impish look on his face. "Yeah, I would agree. I'm perfect."

"Don't let it go to your head," she scoffed good-naturedly. "I'm still trying to convince my mother about you."

He let out a disparaging laugh. "Yeah, I know. She's a tough lady to convince; stubbornness runs in the family."

"You should talk," Maria chided, "the son of Dixie Walker."

"I know." Jubal placed his hand over Maria's on the vase. "I'm glad we're here. I know this is very important to yuh." Suddenly he remembered: "I think we should get the kids. They've prob'ly been torturin' that mango tree."

With one hand holding the vase, she followed him into the backyard.

Her daughter came running up to her, with her brother right behind. "Look, Mom, I got a mango, and it's ripe. Carl's got one too."

Maria admired the mango her daughter reverently held. "I'm sure it's tasty. We'll take it back to the hotel and have it for dessert. Whaddaya say?"

"Sure," the girl readily agreed.

"I got one too." The boy held up his mango.

"Another beauty. We're gonna eat good tonight."

Jubal was peeking at his wristwatch. "We better think about goin' back. I promised the real estate guy we'd return the keys to 'im by four."

"Can we take more mangoes?" the son asked in a plaintive voice.

"Some other time," Jubal said. He noted his son's forlorn look. "Don't worry. We'll come back. The new people won't move in till a week from now. We'll have plenny of mangoes." He began herding the children back to the car.

Maria stayed in place.

"You comin'?" Jubal asked.

"I'll be with you in a few minutes," she said. "I just want to take one more look around."

"Make it quick." Jubal began shepherding the children to the front door.

Maria turned and went to the mango tree. She leaned her back to the tree and, holding tight to the vase, scanned the backyard.

"I'm glad you came back."

What? She turned to the sound of a voice, deep and resonant.

Jacobo Levy repeated, "I'm glad you have returned."

She inspected the strange face. "Do I know you?"

"No, but I know you," the strange face replied. "I knew your father. He'd be happy to know you're here."

"How do you know my father?"

The strange face thought for a moment. "Let's say we go back a long way."

Then it came to Maria: "My father told us about a man he knew in La Playa. A scholar. Are you him?"

"Some people claimed that I was a scholar, though I was just a humble servant of those around me." The man spoke distinctly, thoughtfully. "I'm glad that you're here. Your father would be proud."

Maria began to recall. "You're, you're not that . . . ? Yes, you're my father's friend, from La Playa. He told me about you. I remember you now."

"And I remember you."

Maria was considering it all, amazed. "My father would tell me and Camilo about how you lived in La Playa and all the books you had, and how you and he would spend hours talking, and how much he learned from you."

"Actually, it was I who learned from him."

Maria looked at the man from beneath drawn brows. "Oh, so you are him."

"It makes no difference who I am," Jacobo Levy said indifferently. "We're all part of the same circle, and sometimes the circle comes around to its beginning."

Maria was now certain. "Yes, you are him!" She looked out on the yard. "Milagros said that you and my father would come here and enjoy mangoes and—"

"Who are you talkin' to?"

Jubal was looking at her strangely.

"You're talkin' to yourself now?" he questioned with humor. "The kids are makin' you as crazy as they're makin' me."

"I wasn't talking to anyone," she said, composed. "I was just remembering things from long ago." She held the vase tighter. "C'mon, let's go."

As they reached the back door, Maria took one last look at the tree, trying to visualize where Jacobo Levy had stood moments before.

They went out into the street, heading back to the car, hand in hand with their children, in the time of the Americans.